MEMOIRS
OF
MONTPARNASSE

BY JOHN GLASSCO

The Deficit Made Flesh
The Journal of Saint-Denys-Garneau (translator)
A Point of Sky
Aubrey Beardsley: Under the Hill (completed text)
The Poetry of French Canada in Translation (editor)
Memoirs of Montparnasse
Selected Poems

Memoirs of
MONTPARNASSE

JOHN GLASSCO

With the original Introduction by Leon Edel

SECOND EDITION

With a Critical Introduction and Notes on the Text
by Michael Gnarowski

TORONTO NEW YORK OXFORD
OXFORD UNIVERSITY PRESS
1995

Oxford University Press, 70 Wynford Drive,
Don Mills, Ontario M3C 1J9

Toronto Oxford New York
Delhi Bombay Calcutta Madras Karachi Petaling Jaya
Singapore Hong Kong Tokyo Nairobi Dar es Salaam
Cape Town Melbourne Auckland

and associated companies in

Berlin Ibadan

Oxford is a trademark of Oxford University Press

Canadian Cataloguing in Publication Data

Glassco, John, 1909-1981
Memoirs of Montparnasse

2nd ed.
Includes bibliographical references.
ISBN 0-19-540977-9

I. Gnarowski, Michael, 1934-   .   II. Title,

PS8513.L388M4 1995   C811'.54   C95-930860-1
PR9199.3.G53M4 1995

Cover photograph: 'People relaxing at Café le Dôme, in Paris,
a popular Montparnasse sidewalk "hangout".'
PL.7147. Courtesy The Bettman Archive.

1 2 3 5 6 7 8

TO

Elma

Contents

ILLUSTRATIONS ARE BETWEEN PAGES 100 AND 101

PREFACE

For this Second Edition of *Memoirs of Montparnasse* some typographical corrections have been made and I have framed the original text, at the beginning, with my Introduction and its Notes, and at the end with the following appendices:

NOTES ON THE TEXT, explicating various references;
PEOPLE I, including brief biographies of the leading characters in the *Memoirs*;
PEOPLE II, containing notes on the writers, painters, and others whose names are mentioned in passing;
PLACES, describing many of the haunts of the characters in the *Memoirs*; and a BIBLIOGRAPHY.

In my Introduction and its Notes I have included numerous quotations from, and references to, contents of the Glassco Papers, which are in Box MG30, D163 (Finding Aid No. 892) in the Manuscript Division of the National Archives of Canada. William Toye, Literary Executor for the Estate of John Glassco, made available to me quotations from the 'Personal Journal 1965-1969'. I am grateful to him for his assistance, and wish to acknowledge his not inconsiderable editorial contribution. Oxford University Press Canada kindly gave permission for the use of the letter to him quoted in the biographical entry on Kiki in PEOPLE I.

I would also like to thank Mr Gregory Browner of the Man Ray Trust; Ms Beth Alvarez, Curator of Literary Manuscripts at the Theodore R. McKeldin Library, University of Maryland; the Beinecke Rare Book and Manuscript Library of Yale University; North York Public Library; the Special Collections Department of Northwestern University Library; Mr Bruce Whiteman of the Rare Book Department, McGill University Libraries; and Ms Anne Goddard and the staff of the Manuscript Division of the National Archives of Canada for their co-operation and help in securing photographs as well as for providing access to manuscripts and related materials. Carleton University, through the Offices of its Vice-President (Academic) and its Dean of Arts, has been unfailingly generous and supportive.

M.G.

FICTION FOR THE SAKE OF ART

AN INTRODUCTION TO THE MAKING OF
MEMOIRS OF MONTPARNASSE
BY MICHAEL GNAROWSKI

When John Glassco (1909-81) took up his pen in middle age to write the extravagant story of his lost youth, he was returning to a long-standing and only partially realized ambition that, thirty-five years earlier, had led him to write a fragment of adolescent autobiography, which was published in an avant-garde Paris journal. Aged nineteen, and encouraged by a new-found friendship with the American writer Robert McALMON and by the interest of Eugene JOLAS, the co-editor of the literary journal *transition*, Glassco experienced the excitement of being part of the literary community of the Left Bank.[1] He had likely heard of Raymond Radiguet,[2] who died at the age of twenty-one, a scant five years before Glassco's arrival in Paris, and one of whose two published novels, *Le Diable dans le corps* (1923), an autobiographical work, had left an aura of wildness and bisexual exploit in Montparnasse. In very much the same spirit the teenaged Glassco announced to an amused artistic community that he was writing his autobiography. Now, in the 1960s— prompted (perhaps even goaded) by the recent appearance of two books of literary reminiscences that had Paris in the 1920s at their core, and fired by return visits to a favourite city—Glassco set to work to recapture 'the Paris I loved & the period when I'd been happy'.

The late 1950s and early 1960s witnessed a great surge of interest in the origins of literary modernism, and the artistic life of Paris as its centre, in the early decades of the century. This interest expressed itself both in the form of general cultural studies of the period and in the more popular format of memoirs and reminiscences. The books that acted most powerfully and immediately on Glassco were by writers of whom he was not particularly fond: Morley CALLAGHAN's *That Summer in Paris* (1963) and Ernest HEMINGWAY's *A Moveable Feast* (1964).[3] These were only two of numerous books about Paris and its bohemia that helped to focus attention on the artistic life of a city that is now seen as absolutely central to our understanding of the beginnings of the modern age in all its splendid unorthodoxy. From Malcolm Cowley's *Exile's Return* (1934; revised 1951), to Sylvia BEACH's personal *Shakespeare and Company* (1959), through Richard Ellmann's magnificently detailed

James Joyce (1959)—the thrust was towards examining Paris in the post-war heyday of the 1920s. The great reputations of JOYCE and Hemingway at mid-century, and a growing fascination with Gertrude STEIN, helped to maintain an ongoing retrospective interest in the expatriate life of that city, mostly as it had been lived by American and English writers and artists. They also opened the way to the publication of new work on the period and to revelations about its sometimes strange people, and led to the reissue of material that had lapsed into obscurity. Central to this process of rediscovery—and destined, in a slightly delayed fashion, to be a great prompter for Glassco—was the undertaking by the well-known American novelist and short-story writer Kay BOYLE (Diana Tree in the *Memoirs*) to rework and publish, with Doubleday, Robert McAlmon's long-forgotten memoir *Being Geniuses Together: An Autobiography* (1938). This new edition came out in 1968 under the title *Being Geniuses Together: 1920-1930*, with Kay Boyle's interpolations.

Interest in the Paris scene of the 1920s and 1930s, of course, had to do with the public personalities and tired celebrants of a waning post-war expatriate scene. The dissipation, frenzy, and recklessness would soon come to an end with the stock-market crash late in 1929, and there would begin a mass exodus of remittance expatriates, many of whom were Americans. As a matter of fact, Glassco's learning that he is cut off from his allowance from home (pages 151-2) is curiously coincidental, both in terms of the simple economic history of the period and in being artistically sympathetic in its parallelism. To further reinforce the sea-change that occurs at this point, Glassco's companion Graeme TAYLOR returns home because of a sick father, at the same time freeing Glassco of the last significant male connection that had been so much a part of the first phase of his life in both Montreal and Paris. At this point the *Memoirs* becomes less interested in the sophistries of food, conversation, good times—and casual homo- and heterosexuality—and begins to acquire emotional significance and a heterosexual dimension. The paradigmatic process of the Anglo youth moving out of the physical set of sexual experience known at a boys' boarding school (not reported in the *Memoirs* but mentioned in his 'Autobiographical Sketch' in the National Archives of Canada), through the possibly homosexual beginning of his long relationship with Graeme, to his widening experience—still homosexual, with Robert McAlmon and others, but also heterosexual—through the soulless visits to brothels, concludes the first phase of Glassco's coming of age.[4]

The second stage, with Graeme gone, opens a new range of feeling and experience to which Glassco's *persona* is subjected. There is a flicker of that new sentiment in the albeit brief and essentially episodic attachment to Daphne Berners (Gwen LE GALLIENNE) that serves to lead us into the trying and lacerating circumstances of the affair with Mrs QUAYLE. From what we can sift out of oblique references, and some fairly direct evidence, this was the first great trial of Glassco's heterosexual life. The term 'fatal woman' he used in this connection was later used in referring to the woman who was to marry Graeme Taylor in 1941, thus intruding into the relationship/companionship that Glassco and Taylor had resumed, first in Baie d'Urfé near Montreal, and then in the Eastern Townships in Quebec. Taylor, who looms as Glassco's near-permanent companion, would leave Glassco twice: the first time in Paris, when Taylor returns to his father's sick-bed, exposing Glassco to the mercies of a powerful and cruelly unsettling liaison with Mrs Quayle; and then in 1957 when Taylor dies, freeing Glassco to marry Elma von Colmar, to whom the *Memoirs* is dedicated. But the great emotional upheaval of his young life is the affair with Mrs Quayle, in his account of which Glassco shows himself both raised in ecstasy and expectation, and cast down by betrayal and abandonment. Mrs Quayle is the experienced, mysterious, and utterly desirable woman who reveals to Glassco a hitherto dormant aspect of his nature and emotions, and whose icon continued to haunt him in his future life.

About the composition of *Memoirs of Montparnasse*, except for the first chapter—based on Glassco's thirteen-page 'Extract from an Autobiography' that appeared in Paris in the Spring 1929 issue of *This Quarter*[5]—the *Memoirs* was not begun in 1928, or written three years later when Glassco languished as a seriously ill if bored tubercular patient in the Royal Victoria Hospital, Montreal, although there is an entry in Glassco's Journal in July 1934 suggesting that, prompted by Graeme Taylor, he attempted to resume work on the *Memoirs*, only to abandon the idea a while later. The idea for the book likely developed sometime around 1960, the result of Glassco's first return visits to Paris in 1958 and 1960.

His five-page 'Autobiographical Sketch'—typed, single spaced, and dated 9 June 1961 at the 'Royal Edward Laurentian Hospital'[6]—concludes with the following paragraphs:

> The rest of my history is to be found in my book 'Memoirs of a Young Man'
> [the second part of the title was changed later, by hand, to 'Montparnasse'] (frankly

imitated from George MOORE's autobiographical books). This book covers only my years in Paris (where Graeme Taylor and I went in the spring of 1928) up to the period when I was completely without resources in the spring of 1929; the rest is yet unwritten. This part of the book will cover: the period when I was working as secretary and gigolo to The Princess of Sarawak (Mrs Gladys Brooke), as a guide to Montmartre nightclubs, and finally as a call-man in Martha Arlington's brothel on the rue Blanche; a succession of affairs with Robert McAlmon, Mrs William Whitney, Lord Alfred DOUGLAS, Kay Boyle, Jean COCTEAU and the Negro poet Claude MCKAY, none of which lasted more than a month; experiences of ecstasy, starvation and melancholia; my meeting with Mrs Marguerite Lippe-Rosskam and first experience of real love; our trip to Spain, where Marguerite took another lover; my suffering, and the final *revanche* of the last three years' life in the form of tuberculosis; my several months' stay in the American Hospital in Paris and eventual repatriation to Canada to undergo thoracoplasty in three stages, and my emergence from two years in hospital completely, and, I believed at the time, permanently changed.

The remainder of my life has been happy, and after a period of quiet again became fantastic and unconventional; but this belongs to the immediate past and too many persons still living are involved for me to give any account of it.

The serious planning for the *Memoirs* took place in the winter of 1963-4; and between the months of February and December 1964 Glassco recreated the key 'moments' of his concupiscent coming of age in Paris. To them he joined elements and occasions taken from the scattered lives of the so-called Lost Generation in an imaginative borrowing, without much regard for provenance, of fact and circumstances. But when *Memoirs of Montparnasse* was published in February 1970—carrying with it the author's claim, in his 'Prefatory Note', that 'I wrote the first three chapters of this book in Paris in 1928 when I was eighteen, and soon after the events recorded. . . . The rest of the book was written in the Royal Victoria Hospital in Montreal during three months of the winter of 1932-3 . . .'—it was so successful, and rang so true, that Malcolm Cowley, himself an erstwhile member of that expatriate community and a distinguished chronicler of the Lost Generation, extolled it in a review in the *New Republic*, and in his *A Second Flowering: Works and Days of the Lost Generation* (1973): 'Life in Montparnasse has been commemorated in a long series of memoirs, at least eighteen by my incomplete count. . . . The liveliest and most candid is *Memoirs of Montparnasse*, by the Canadian John Glassco, a book written when he was twenty-two years old and expected to die on the operating table.'

To some of us who knew Glassco, however, and saw our reclusive friend during the crucial months of the summer of 1964, the actual dates of composition and completion were known. But no great to-do was made six years later, when the *Memoirs* was finally published. The silence continued when some reviewers, and others, wrote of subterfuge and 'high-level literary tactics',[7] or described the book as hovering between 'a true fictional novel and genuine memoir',[8] or when I labelled the *Memoirs* in print as 'prose fiction'.[9] But ten years later we felt uneasy when certain critics and historians of the period, quoting from the *Memoirs*, began to use the book as a reliable and historically accurate source.

It is now clear that in writing about the people he met or heard about while he was living in Paris, Glassco drew upon circumstances and events of their lives that were all known to him at the time, while bringing to these portrayals the enhancing skills of his own inventiveness, mainly revealed in his ability to create believable dialogue—a *tour de force* that is now seen to be more likely the work of a practised craftsman of a certain age than of a nineteen-year-old literary neophyte. In a note to an early plan for the *Memoirs*, then provisionally titled '2 & 20',[10] Glassco recognized the difficulties of writing about the past as though it were the present. But, like his much-admired literary models and predecessors, George Moore and Frank HARRIS, Glassco was not going to be daunted, and whatever incidents life may have been stingy in supplying he would invent and weave into the loose but receptive fabric of his own memories. The *Memoirs*, then, is a composite of some eyewitness events, some artistic *legerdemain* consisting of borrowing and invention, and what is probably the most interesting and significant element: the entirely serious and painful story of Glassco's coming of age, a sobering process of a young man moving from the hedonism of simple appetites to the complexities of a maturing sensibility.

This was centred on his ardent love-affair with Mrs Quayle, meaningfully called Honour—a name that seems to disarm her young lover—who soon superseded the role of Robert McAlmon. Both led the young Glassco in the way of experience—in his and her own fashion—to new areas of self-exploration and self-realization. McAlmon is the coarser and more immediate guide through the shallows of expatriate life as a drinking, roistering, and cynical companion. Mrs Quayle is the 'fatal woman', a notion to which Glassco is drawn in the *Memoirs* (and was drawn afterwards), and that haunts him in the larger precinct of his psyche and his ambivalent involvements with other lovers.[11] In general, what is most surprising about the *Memoirs* is that, in spite of Glassco's diffidence, we are let into a revealing and confident personal history by a strikingly self-possessed imagination. The first draft of the manuscript is a model of the kind of step-by-step plan that a consummate professional would have prepared for his own guidance. And this plan is methodically carried out, with skilful and necessary adjustments. The daily quota of words is recorded; the infelicities expunged; the brightness touched up; and his lifelong weakness for making knowing, offhand, often dismissive allusions to works of literature and to writers, both famous and obscure, given free rein. A self-confessed night-owl, Glassco would begin his 'day' in the late afternoon and, buoyed up by sips of gin, would settle to the task of composing and revising that resulted in the finely wrought and entirely believable work we now have.

Glassco described the process of composition, and the sentiments that underpinned it, in a letter of 4 May 1964, addressed to his friend, the writer Jean Le Moyne:

> All this winter I have been 1) preparing my next book of poems[12] which will be published this fall, 2) writing the 'memoirs of my dead life' (in Flaubert's phrase) in Paris from 1928 to 1930 . . . My memoirs (no title yet) now amount to 75,000 words, with only 20,000 left to write:[13] this is a gay work, full of ebullience and absurdity; while writing it I am really under 20 again, poor, predatory, restless, happy, taking nothing seriously, always hungry and digesting the nuts and bolts of experience like an ostrich. Every night now I enact the first scene of *Faust*. I shed my robes and my false beard, the wrinkles disappear, I have a new head of hair, and I sport for about 1,000 words in the green meadows of a well misspent youth.

On 5 December 1964 Glassco wrote to Michael Gnarowski saying: 'I have been slaving at my MEMOIRS OF MONTPARNASSE, trying to finish it before the reaction set in. I just made it in time, because now it's just 300 pages that I can't read.' Clearly, his memoirs were seen by Glassco as more than a simple opportunity to capitalize on the vogue for stories of the Lost Generation. Rather they are important as a nostalgic (perhaps self-titillating) return to a rebellious, everything-is-possible youth. They are characterized by an escape from a stultifying past into a frenetic hedonism so typical of that milieu, with its drinking, its *dancings*, and its impermanence, to which is added Glassco's own curious admixture of Edwardian sexuality, with its brothels and champagne, its well-to-do impecuniousness, and the occasional inconvenient but endurable onset of social disease. The result is a rare confection. No other participant in that Paris scene—not even the widely travelled, iconoclastic, and hard-drinking Robert McAlmon—could give those experiences quite the flavour of enjoyable decadence that Glassco was able to impart to his carefully crafted recollections, composed in retrospect. How meticulously ordered they were is evidenced in the final manuscript, which is a relatively problem-free document leading clearly and unequivocally to the published work. There are, of course, the expected creative zigs and zags; but essentially the *Memoirs* remains true to the plan laid out by Glassco in the densely hand-written pages of six school scribblers in which he set down his outline and the draft of his text. In an early attempt at obfuscation Glassco wrote in scribbler #1, in red felt pen: 'begun R.V. H. [Royal Victoria Hospital] 1932', to which he later added in red ballpoint: '—Dec. '64'. Scribbler #2—a child's small exercise book measuring 9" by 6½", of French origin, with the word RHODIA and *Provence* on its orange-brown cover (later referred to by Glassco as the 'Rhodia Scribbler')—presents most of Glassco's plan, and provides us with an insight into how he worked. It contains drafts of chapters 4 to 7 and, inside the front cover, a careful tally of what Glassco calls 'wordage'—an uncannily meticulous exercise of adding up exactly what was written, night by night, by page and chapter, with all leading up to a count of 99,500 words.[14]

In the first typed draft we see Glassco toying with variant titles for his work, almost fixing on *Tender Juvenal*, an epithet from *Love's Labour's Lost* that appealed to him—so much so that he wrote out four lines from Shakespeare's play, considering them as a possible epigraph.[15] Here, also, we find that Glassco's friend Graeme Taylor (identified in the published version) is still called 'George', as in the original 'Extract' that appeared in *This Quarter*. The games with names are a continuing signal of the strange, defensive posture that Glassco struck with the personalities in his narrative. He was wary of using real identities because, one suspects, he feared legal action, or the challenge of those who had been there and could dispute his 'facts'. As a general rule of thumb, persons who were known to be dead appeared under their real names, while those who might still be living—or who might be obstreperous, like the notoriously litigious Daniel Mahoney—Glassco endowed with clever and wonderfully evocative names. Thus the American sculptress and lover of Djuna BARNES, Thelma WOOD, appears as Emily Pine, while Barnes, the celebrated author of *The Ladies Almanack* (1928), is Willa Torrance. In the same vein, the fabulously wealthy Peggy GUGGENHEIM and her then husband Laurence VAIL appear as Sally and

Terence Marr; and Sidney Schooner, the man who befriends Glassco and Taylor shortly after their arrival in Paris, and who is described as 'a lover of whores', was Hilaire HILER, a musician and painter of sorts, a *bon vivant*, and very much a man about Paris who lasted on the scene longer than many of the others. However, having taken the prudent step of disguising some of the names in his account, Glassco had second thoughts, and remained unconvinced of the rightness of that decision. In a note to himself dated December 3, 1964, when the first draft of the *Memoirs* was finished, he considered changing other names (in scribbler #3 he changed Morley Callaghan's name to Curley Mulligan) — then wondered 'whether these aliases were really necessary'.

There are numerous points in the text where Glassco's statements are not to be taken at face value, either as reportage of things said or as a description of how people actually were. For example, on page 26 Glassco describes a situation in which he goes to a party at Eugene Jolas's with Graeme Taylor and where, because they do not know anyone, Glassco and Taylor end up talking to one another. He writes: 'So we mounted an attack on the hidden sentimentality of the poetry of E.E. CUMMINGS, stabbing the air with our fingers . . .' The original version in the scribbler reads: '. . . accordingly we initiated a lively debate on the poetry of Ezra Pound, . . .'* The asterisk directs one to the margin where Glassco has snidely noted: '*Someone better!' In like fashion, and a little further into the story, we encounter the figure of MAN RAY, the American avant-gardist who was famous for his strange and brilliant photographs and his art inventions. In the *Memoirs* he is given the name Narwhal and is described as 'tall and thin', whereas in the scribbler Glassco 'remembers' him as 'a very small man'. We are also told, both in the scribbler and in the *Memoirs*, that Narwhal 'wore his hair in a neat bang', something that is easily disproved by Man Ray's characteristic widow's peak, which can be seen in the photograph included here.

Playing with the facts of circumstance or conversation, very much a part of Glassco's method, is at the heart of the borrower's methodology, a skill in which Glassco had long apprenticed himself and had become truly proficient. He had cut his teeth on Aubrey BEARDSLEY's unfinished *Under the Hill*, a work that Glassco completed; it was published in 1959 under the imprint of the Olympia Press. Later he would 'appropriate' a little-known homosexual work entitled *Quaint Stories of Samurais* by the Japanese poet and novelist Ihara Saikaku (1642-93), translated by an expatriate Japanese writer, Ken SATO, and published 'for private distribution' in 1928 by Robert McAlmon at the Imprimerie Darantière of Dijon (now remembered as the sorely tried printer of Joyce's *Ulysses*). Glassco, having cleverly invented the art of the *collagiste*, published in 1970 a revised version of Sato's work as *The Temple of Pederasty*, claiming it to be 'after Ihara Saikaku'. It begins with an Introduction by John Glassco, in which he presents the stories as an 'example of a literary form unknown to the Western world—the erotic *collage* or interpolation of libertine phrases, dialogue and incident in the body of classical texts. The art has long been practised in Japan . . . [calling for] the greatest taste, humour, delicacy and restraint.'[16] Glassco had had some previous experience in the invention of dialogue and its interpolation when he assisted Kay Boyle in ghostwriting, while typing, the memoirs of the Dayang Muda, Princess of Sarawak (Gladys Palmer BROOKE).[17]

When Boyle was working on her own edition of Robert McAlmon's *Being Geniuses Together*, her announced purpose of revising McAlmon's original text and interspersing it with her supplementary chapters was an incentive for Glassco to revisit the manuscript of his own memoirs, which had been rejected by his agent. (A revisionist text of McAlmon's book also had a possible bonus; he hoped that he and Graeme would have a place in it, since McAlmon had excluded them.)[18] In 1965, after Glassco completed the first version of *Memoirs of Montparnasse*, he had high hopes for what he saw as 'the gayest, most amusing, most readable writing the world could ask for [when the manuscript] was returned by my New York Agent as "not likely to be of interest to a publisher"'.

> The force of this rejection was multiplied beyond endurance by the fact that the book was a reflection of myself, my whole youth, the Paris I loved & the period when I'd been happy. I could hardly believe it: for three days I was numbed.

He had been told that the text was 'unpersuasive', and that 'the "exposé" element was unaffecting':

> So much for telling the truth! Then, I did not even dare look at the returned manuscript: it had been termed a lying chronicle, and with my own wretched suggestibility I would soon have believed the term was correct and that people and things did not happen as I know they did. No, not altogether as they did: I have *re-arranged* many events, telescoped still more, & invented much of the

dialogue—but the facts are all true, & the tenor of life in those days, and the behaviour of everybody, faithfully reproduced.[19]

His despondency led to his denouncing the *Memoirs* in his journal as '. . . a piece of cheap, frivolous, backstairs gossip, a false, vulgar, conceited, adolescent, amateurish book.' He consoled himself by thinking that the rejection was all for the best: 'Had it been published I would have been called a liar, a popinjay, a faker, a libeller, an envious failure. I might have lost what little self respect I have. . . . I had a lucky escape.

> And now it is time to state, in this privacy of myself, that one-quarter of this book *was* lies. This is what I have been trying to avoid saying, even to myself. I never met Frank Harris (it was Graeme who did, and told me about it later); Man Ray never discussed Jane Austen with me; Joyce held no conversation with me about *Ulysses* or 'Gob' (he did attack Richardson); Ford's conversation is more than half fabricated . . . Ah, confession is good for the soul. Already, I feel better.[20]

The psychological subtext of his attacking his own book harks back to the horrors of the abuse that he and his brother had suffered at the hands of a tyrannical father obsessed with telling the truth, and who beat his sons for the slightest fib. This 'conditioning' by a sadistic parent not only made Glassco, by his own admission, an 'incorrigible liar', but also left him with a full range of pathological reactions, from the initial compulsion to deceive, to self-denunciation and the masochistic satisfaction gained from discovery and punishment.

So the *Memoirs* languished in neglect until Kay Boyle informed Glassco, in a letter of 25 July 1967, that she was revising McAlmon's book. On 1 August 1967 Glassco told her that he had some old notes of McAlmon's 'ideas on writing, taken down verbatim, just as he spoke them'; at her invitation, he sent them to her with a letter of 8 August. This was a curious revelation, since Glassco does not seem to have kept notes of any of the conversations he had had in Paris with others, and does not even appear to have kept the letters McAlmon wrote to him when they renewed their contact through correspondence during the war years. In this letter Glassco revealed to Boyle that he had been back to Paris in 1958; that he had spent almost a year there in 1960; and that he had been back again in May. In a letter of 22 November, Kay Boyle asked if Glassco could remember any 'fantastic quotes we put in the mouths of the great', referring to the Dayang Muda's memoirs. He replied on 28 November: 'I'm sorry, I can't for the life of me recall

any other imaginary quotes we put into *Relations and Complications.*'
He also wrote (alluding to their time with the Dayang Muda): 'I've
given an account of some of this in my own memoirs of that era which
I finished about 5 years ago but haven't got around to revising.' He
goes on to say: 'We're all in this book, rather glamourized and fiction-
alized; the chronology is a bit juggled, and the dialogue rewritten, but
I think it catches some of the spirit of those years. The only person
who gets a mild ribbing is Morley Callaghan.' Boyle replied on 3 December: 'Why don't you revise your memoirs and let my publisher have
a look at it?' Glassco responded on 21 December: 'I've looked over
my MEMOIRS OF MONTPARNASSE. It's like a bad novel. I might publish it
under a pseudonym, perhaps, some day . . .' But the rehabilitation of
the *Memoirs* was about to begin. In 1968 Glassco basked in the pleasure
of seeing Taylor and himself included in the revised version of *Being
Geniuses Together.* So reassuring was this experience that he set about
the business of making the *Memoirs* ready for publishers. On 9 September 1968 he announced to Boyle the completion of his revision:

> I finished my MEMOIRS OF MONTPARNASSE last month, 100,000 words of my life from
> 1927 to 1931. It has the form of fiction—i.e., with lots of dialogue, speed, re-
> arranged and telescoped action; never a dull moment—and is more a montage
> of those days than literal truth.

After excerpts had been accepted for publication by *The Tamarack
Review,* Glassco sent Boyle those that involved her. In his accompa-
nying letter of 2 December 1968, referring to his fictionalization of
their relationship, he wrote:

> In short, our friendship has been blown up, glamourized, and made intensely sig-
> nificant in the framework of the story itself. (The events of the whole book have
> been re-arranged, telescoped, speeded up and dramatized in the same way.) You
> see, we have long invented dialogues, do things we never did, go places we never
> went, etc. It's really fiction: I was trying to re-create the atmosphere and spirit
> of the Paris of those days as it was for *me.*

To his surprise, Boyle objected—in a letter of 6 February 1969, addressed
to 'dearest Buffy'—to his portrait of her because the dialogue was quite
uncharacteristic. (Here was someone who was only too happy to put
invented dialogue into the mouths of others in her edition of *Being
Geniuses Together,* but was not pleased when her own speech was re-

ported without perfect accuracy. This was a powerful cautionary lesson.) Glassco replied abjectly on 25 February, saying: 'Of course you're right to mind about the dialogue I've given you in the extract . . . It's not the way you speak, and never was. But how could I remember after 40 years?'

> I think the best solution of the whole problem of your appearance in the book is to *dis-identify* you yourself entirely with the character I created so long ago in your image, and, by changing your name, nationality, appearance, profession and background, turn this character into an imaginary *persona* no one could possibly connect with you.

In a mollifying letter of 1 March, Boyle replied that she had *not* been offended but thought the book would benefit if she were made recognizable. Glassco was apparently incapable of portraying her as she was at the time, so he made superficial changes in the description of the character based on Kay Boyle and changed the name to Diana Tree.

In a letter to her of 19 March, Glassco wrote.

> You see, I look on the real value of 'memoirs' as being not so much a record of 'what happened' as a re-creation of the spirit of a period in time. The first approach is so often simply tedious, faded literary gossip, name-dropping, disconnected anecdotes, etc., like 50% of Bob's book . . . The second approach is that of Rousseau, CASANOVA and George Moore. None of them felt tied to historical truth; they were all liars and produced works of art by *invention*. Who cares about their lies now? . . . I don't compare myself to them, naturally, but my book is in their style. And Casanova is the greatest writer of Memoirs the world has ever seen: *this* is the 18th century, and the portrait of a man as well.'

In 1969 six extracts from the unpublished *Memoirs* were published in Issues 49 and 50-1 of *The Tamarack Review*, of which William Toye, Editorial Director of Oxford University Press Canada, was an associate editor. His interest, and that of his colleagues at Oxford, led to an offer of publication of the book. *Memoirs of Montparnasse*—with an Introduction by Glassco's friend, the distinguished biographer Leon Edel—was published in February 1970.[21] Glassco dispatched a copy to Kay Boyle, on the fly-leaf of which he wrote a twenty-five line dedicatory poem. The first two stanzas read:

> *Dear Kay, this loose and lying chronicle*
> *You'll understand, and all its young intention*

To dress the naked facts and brightly tell
A young man's story and what him befell
In love & other sports I will not mention

For you, the finest writer of our age
Who knows what best to exclude, what to invent,
And how the falsehoods of the printed page
Are the true image of our vocal rage —
Will find the inward sense of what he meant . . .
(6/1/70)

The falsehoods of the printed page. While these words to Kay Boyle allude to Glassco's uncomfortable knowledge that his *Memoirs* was a less-than-accurate account, they can be seen today as ironic. Joan Mellen, Kay Boyle's biographer, has stated that Boyle's contribution to her edition of Robert McAlmon's *Being Geniuses Together*, which deals in part with the same period Glassco wrote about, 'is best read as a work of fiction'—it is 'riddled with errors of fact and of omission'. For example, Boyle softened a conflict between Ernest Walsh—her lover in 1926 until he died, and the father of her first child—and Hemingway; and the homosexuality of McAlmon (whom she loved unrequitedly) was not mentioned because she never accepted this fact—and she was determined to rescue him from oblivion and restore his reputation. But Mellen acknowledges Boyle's vivid and deeply felt reconstruction of the decade the book covers, and her flashes of honesty. At the very end of *Geniuses*, Boyle reports that McAlmon, in a letter of 1929 to Bill Bird, wrote that 'Kay, come hell or high water, had to romanticize every situation.' In her very last sentence Boyle writes: 'This may very well be true.'

The complex psychological reasons for Kay Boyle's ignoring, obfuscating—and romanticizing—facts are one subject. Those for John Glassco's imaginative use of them are another—for which the prime reason seems to be that Glassco wanted to create a memoir of his relatively brief time in Paris as a young man that would be artistic, a work of literature: not exact in the rendition of remembered details—he did not consider facts to be sacred—but true to the behaviour and general characteristics of the people he consorted with and to his own emotions, and above all true to the spirit of the time. This goal carried him into reinventing his past to some degree, and supplementing his memories with later, sometimes inaccurate, knowledge. In doing this he produced a work that, alone among all his published and unpublished fiction, is not imprisoned in stylized scenes and formalized dialogue. His emotional attachment to this golden period of his youth freed his imagination to invent convincing dialogue wedded to a smooth narrative that has humour, spontaneity, verisimilitude, and naturalness. Like all good fiction, it engages the reader's imagination. Firmly based in reality and felt experience, it also has autobiographical significance—as a memoir it probably contains as much fact and truth as fiction. This said, it must be remembered that Glassco wrote to Kay Boyle on 2 December 1968: 'It's really fiction. I was trying to re-create the atmosphere and spirit of Paris of those days as it was for *me*. The way George Moore and Casanova did for the worlds of *their* youth.'

In the twenty-five years since *Memoirs of Montparnasse* was published, it has captivated and persuaded a multitude of readers—a few of whom had experienced the period for themselves. As a memoir it has its own validity. As a portrait of this period in Paris (among countless others that have been published), and of some of its writers, artists, and pleasure-seekers, it is essential. It is one of the best.

NOTES ON THE INTRODUCTION

1   In the summer of 1926, after his first year at McGill, Glassco made his first trip to Paris with $500 given to him by his mother. 'I believe she did this mainly to have some peace in the house, as I was on very bad terms with my father who insisted on treating me as if I were a child and wanted me to be in the house at 10 p.m. Although I was only 16 I was in the company of young men of over 20 most of the time, which made such restraint impossible.' Of his first arrival in Paris he wrote: 'I fell in love with Paris at once and for ever, and when I left for home in the fall of 1926 was only thinking of how soon I could return.' 'Autobiographical Sketch', 1961, p. 4.

2   Raymond Radiguet (1903-23) was the author of two precocious but powerful novels, *Le Diable dans le corps* (1923; translated by Kay Boyle as *The Devil in the Flesh*, 1932), an autobiographical novel of adolescent sexuality, and *Le Bal du comte d'Orgel* (1924). Though bisexual, he was a friend and lover of Jean Cocteau.

3   There are two descriptive 'Odds and Ends' notes in the manuscript materials relating to the *Memoirs* that illustrate amply Glassco's visceral dislike of Hemingway and Callaghan. Of the former he writes:

    Hemingway's one-sided smile which drew his moustache up rather nastily under a handsome nose. He should not have worn a moustache but you could tell he wore one to make his moon face look not so moon. But it did not, it did not. As he might have put it himself when writing about someone else.

and immediately after:

> For Callaghan with his moon face & his little moustache he looked very much like Hemingway; he even had the same shrewd politician's eyes, the same querulous voice and lopsided grin.

4   In his 'Autobiographical Sketch' of 1961, describing his first trip to France in 1926, Glassco mentions a wealthy young man on shipboard who prevailed upon him to leave the ship at Glasgow, instead of Le Havre, and accompany him to his family's Hoddom Castle on the Scottish border. Glassco complied, and later went with him to London. He writes: 'I discovered at this time the great attraction I possessed for homosexuals, an attraction I still possess even at the age of 51. I cannot explain this, as I have never had the slightest sexual pleasure with a man in my life (though I have slept with scores): it can no longer be due to the beauty of face or person, both of which have long faded. When I left London for Paris I went alone.'

5   The first chapter of the *Memoirs* uses some of the episodes described in the 'Extract from an Autobiography', and in brief passages the same wording, but the tight and polished text of the *Memoirs* bears little resemblance to the original youthful narrative, which is flat and wordy—though its self-confident tone and vivid descriptions belie the age of the narrator. Glassco later made many editorial changes to his old text, without transforming it, or bringing it close to what we now read.

6   This was Glassco's pseudonymous name for the Royal Victoria Hospital, Montreal. In Issue 23, Spring 1962, *The Tamarack Review* published Glassco's account—under the name Silas N. Gooch—of his recent long incarceration for treatment of his lungs, entitled 'A Season in Limbo'. It bore the subheading 'Diamond Jubilee Hospital, Montreal'.

7   Louis Dudek in his review in the Montreal *Gazette*, 7 February 1970.

8   Jack Kapica in his review in the *McGill Daily Supplement*, 13 November 1970.

9   Michael Gnarowski, *A Concise Bibliography of English-Canadian Literature*, 2nd ed. Toronto: McClelland and Stewart, 1978, p. 46.

10   The title is an allusion to A.E. Housman's poem 'When I Was One-and-Twenty'. Glassco met the English poet (1865-1959)—then in his sixties—in Paris.

11   *The Fatal Woman: Three Tales by John Glassco*, was published by the House of Anansi Press Limited, Toronto, in 1974. The tales were 'The Black Helmet', 'The Fulfilled Destiny of Electra', and 'Lust in Action'.

12   *A Point of Sky* (1964), published by Oxford University Press Canada.

13   There is an irony implicit in this deliberateness of procedure, if only because of Glassco's observation in the *Memoirs* (p. 26) that he does not 'believe anything worthwhile comes from simply sitting down at a desk every day at a certain hour and writing . . .'

14   As this scribbler is of French origin, it is markedly different from the others in the manuscript group and leads one to think that initial drafting of the *Memoirs* might very well have begun during one of Glassco's return visits to Paris.

15   From Shakespeare's *Love's Labour's Lost*, Act I, Sc. II:

> *Moth*: Why tender juvenal? why tender juvenal?
> *Armado*: I spoke it, tender juvenal, as a congruent epitheton appertaining to
> thy young days, which we may nominate tender.

In scribbler #1, another title—'The Youngest Exile: Memoirs of Paris in the Twenties'—was considered.

16   *The Temple of Pederasty*, Hollywood, Calif.: Hanover House, 1970.

17   *Relations and Complications*. See the Bibliography under Brooke.

18   We know from a letter of March 1942 that Glassco had just borrowed *Geniuses* from McAlmon and wrote to him disappointedly: 'I do wish you had found space for Graeme and me in that book, now! It would have helped along my individual legend in Can. lit' (McAlmon Papers, Yale University). Glassco was of course unknown in 1942—the legend would have to wait for the publication of the *Memoirs*.

19   'Personal Journal, 1965-1969', entry of 2 June 1965, page 3.

20   Ibid., page 4.

21   During a prolonged editorial session when William Toye visited Glassco in Montreal in March 1969, Toye—who, like Leon Edel, was oblivious of the real origin of the *Memoirs*—told Glassco that he had merely mentioned the obviously interesting Kiki in passing: he should describe her fully. The next morning Glassco appeared at Toye's hotel room and handed him a handwritten page containing the paragraph that appears on page 18. Toye also suggested the italicization of the retrospective passages that appear throughout the book.

INTRODUCTION

BY LEON EDEL

I remember the John Glassco—he was always Buffy to his friends—
of these memoirs: his smooth blond hair, his cherub cheeks (just beginning acquaintance with the razor), his slender bearing, even in win-
ters when he wore one of those grotesque 1929 raccoon coats. I remember his bright questioning eyes and his assumed air of indifference
as he flicked the ash from his cigarette and whispered an epigram apol-
ogetically. I can still see his willowy silhouette as he sauntered on the
boulevard du Montparnasse with his friend Graeme Taylor; or slouched
world weary—*aetat 18*—in some bar, often the Select.

Later I found him a tanned and flowering Adonis on the pebbled
beaches of Nice. This was in the early spring of 1929, when I was
on my first journey to Italy. I had known Buffy and Graeme in Montreal,
and had seen something of them in Paris. In Nice I called on them
at their Italian *pension*, the one described in these pages. I ended by
staying for a while in the room lately vacated by Robert McAlmon.
In McAlmon's happily-named memoirs, *Being Geniuses Together*, we
find a mention of Buffy, 'then eighteen, and much the oldest, most
ironic and disillusioned of the three of us'. It was true. Buffy must
have imbibed sophistication with his mother's milk. He was composing
his memoirs on a typewriter. Buffy and Graeme had the girl Stanley
in tow, as is recorded here. She had a boyish haircut and strong plump
prairie shoulders. She came from the Canadian West. Buffy was fatherly
about her: he told me he thought she drank more than was good for
her—Stanley, who with the fine broom of her adolescence sweeps
Bach, Beethoven and Brahms under the rug and settles for Scarlatti
and Rameau. It was the golden time of youth, the period Buffy speaks
of when he says 'we remained sunk in greed, sloth and sensuality—
the three most amiable vices in the catalogue.' I was too busy with
my own life to notice this, I must confess, but in the evenings I would
join the three, either drinking *vin rosé* at a café or watching Buffy
whirl Stanley around the floor of some *dancing*. And I still remember
my room in Nice, the feeling of the South, the hot sun, the cool evenings,
the general leafiness, the strong wine, the food heavily saturated with
olive oil, the aesthetic talk—with constant reminders to ourselves not

to be too serious for, *carpe diem*, nothing really mattered. We were all very pleased because we had fled the lingering Victorianism in Canada and found ourselves youthful members of the literary avant-garde.

I thought Buffy's claim to be writing his memoirs one of his little jokes. He looked like a Nijinsky faun, fresh from some sylvan adventure, and what can a faun, leaping from one woodland delight to another, really remember? But a few months later, when I was back in Paris, he sent me the first—and only—instalment, published in *This Quarter*, Ethel Moorhead's short-lived publication. I have a copy still. It was funny, some of it in a collegiate way, but there was sharpness of recall and a surprisingly precocious wit. Even then I didn't believe he would bother to continue. Yet here are the memoirs, after almost forty years, lively and libidinous, surfacing like some shining tropical fish out of the depths, and with all the elegance of their author's youth. Like Boswell, Buffy had kept the notebook of himself. He had seized the fleeting moment; he had thumbed his nose at evanescence. There is a kind of melancholy joy in all he tells us, whether he is pursuing sex or the house where Paganini died. It is all there—the twenty-four-hour days, the burning of candles at both ends, the obsessions and compulsions, the strange divorce from what was going on in the world, the crazy parties, the beautiful fool's paradise from which the depression ultimately awakened us. Newer generations, who cannot know what Montparnasse was like, will discover its essence in this book; it was a strange stream of creativity and pseudo-art meandering in and out of libidinous bars.

I was to see the Dôme, the Select, the cavernous Coupole and the boarded-up Rotonde on the day before the liberation of Paris in 1944. The snipers were still at their work when our vehicle rounded into Montparnasse in the long cavalcade that brought de Gaulle back to the French capital. Across the gay glass fronts of another day, chairs and tables were heaped up in earthquake disorder. Down the way, at the Gare Montparnasse, Nazis in field-green—the dishevelled unhelmeted children of Hitler's 'master-race'—were surrendering in terror or glum despair. It was strange, stranger than all fiction, to encounter at this moment, in the August twilight, scenes of a dead past. For a brief moment the cafés were filled with people: I suddenly remembered Kiki of Montparnasse; in the midst of war, in the thronged street, I could smell chicory and Pernod, the pervasive *tabac* and stale beer.

The Buffy memoirs have the fascination of a long-buried artifact suddenly turned up by a spade. His keen brown eyes above those cherub cheeks saw everything. He listened to the talk; but he also listened to the messages of his senses. And he had the chronicling gift. His book is more humane and 'actual' than Hemingway's *A Moveable Feast*, which the world has read with malaise. But Buffy wasn't beset by the claims of 'reputation'. Montparnasse was (in our current language) a 'swinging' place and he caught the rhythm of its swing. He allowed himself, in his prose, the emotions that his sophistication (and Anglo-Saxon-Canadian reserve) concealed. His memoirs reflect both the charm and the melancholy of adolescence. This is not always the happiest time of life. Youth has to cope with too many discoveries, too many moods. Yet adolescence also has those intensities which we wish we could recover in the long later years. There were, we can now see in this narrative, ruts in Montparnasse as deep as any in that other provincial *Mont*— Montreal. One couldn't escape one's obsessions, and particularly those of Eros. There was also loneliness and emptiness and despair. Buffy acquired the hard wisdom of maturity at a moment when he might still have had the shelter of college life in Montreal. If his book is more modest than most of the Montparnasse memoirs, it is more immediate—possessing almost the effect of 'instant' memory, total recall. The other memoirs (I have read I believe most of them) look back from middle life. Buffy couldn't wait that long. He wasn't sure, when he wrote them, that he would have his middle age.

To read his book is to discover his fine 'visuality'. His vignette of Gertrude Stein is memorable, as are his glimpses of old lecherous Frank Harris and 'Bosie', or the visit to George Moore, or the talk of James Joyce and McAlmon, or the sudden appearance of Madame Daudet, still alive in 1929, and her son Lucien, Proust's friend. Behind his façade of emotional indifference there were strong literary aspirations and a sense of vocation which enabled John Glassco to be the poet he is today. He foresaw our 'confessional' age in this book, and also the age of *Lady Chat*. The amusing episode of the Saràwakian Princess in Kay Boyle's memoirs is here rounded out from Buffy's side. The gilded bondage of sex pervades his narrative. His Saint-Simonian pen records with truth—and all the candour of the Self.

The passage of Buffy and Graeme through Montparnasse was brief; it was satirized at the time in Morley Callaghan's unkind tale, 'Now That April's Here'. I recall a long café session with Callaghan. I found him very young, very robust, very Toronto, and thus foreign to the insouciant hedonism of the young Montrealers. These memoirs help to correct his caricature. Buffy wrote the greater part of them at twenty-two, when other young men are still on the football field. Facing death, he shored up his small hoard of literary and erotic memories; he wrote not only what he remembered of Montparnasse, but his book's subtitle might be 'the reminiscences of a precocious hedonist'. They become, in the circumstances, all the more vivid, for they are touched by a kind of urgent anguish. And they are at the same time—if I might coin a *genre*—a splendid example of the autobiographical picaresque.

Buffy survived. He escaped the fate of Aubrey Beardsley. And in middle age he has rummaged out this old record of himself, as in those charming cartoons of Max Beerbohm's when the Old Self is confronted by the Young Self. The graceful record illuminates many faces gone from this earth. We sit again at the Dôme or the Select. We attend the parties *d'antan*. Was it all an hallucination provoked by an overdose of *omelette aux champignons*? Was it all a dream? Whatever it was, it is a delightful form of nostalgia—and of truth. *Optima dies . . . prima fugit.*

PREFATORY NOTE

I wrote the first three chapters of this book in Paris in 1928 when I was eighteen, and soon after the events recorded; at that time I wanted to compose my own *Confessions of a Young Man* à la George Moore, and felt I simply could not wait, as Moore did, for the onset of middle age. The rest of the book was written in the Royal Victoria Hospital in Montreal during three months of the winter of 1932-3, when I was awaiting a crucial operation, and I used such notes, taken on the spot, as were spared from the holocaust mentioned in the final chapter; by then my intention was altered, and all I desired was to record, and in a sense relive, a period of great happiness. After barely surviving the operation I turned away from my youth altogether. I did not look at the manuscript again for thirty-five years.

I have changed very little of the original. The revision amounts to the occasional improvement of a phrase and, in the case of the first chapter, the excision of some particularly fatuous paragraphs; also, for reasons of discretion I have given several characters fictitious names. Nothing else has been altered or omitted—in spite of a temptation to suppress or at least soften many passages that expose the youthful memoirist in all his flippancy, hedonism and conceit. And after all, why change any of this? This young man is no longer myself: I hardly recognize him, even from his photographs and handwriting, and in my memory he is less like someone I have been than a character in a novel I have read.

J.G.
Foster, Quebec
October 1969

ONE

Winter in Montreal in 1927. Student life at McGill University had depressed me to a point where I could not go on. I was learning nothing; the curriculum was designed at best to equip me as a professor destined to lead others in due course on the same round of lifeless facts. I was only seventeen and had the sense of throwing my time and my youth into a void.

When I told my father I refused to attend college any longer (I was then in my third year) and had decided to write poetry, he said I was a great disappointment to him and my mother, I was ungrateful and lacking in manliness and could go to work; he would allow me to keep on living at home. After a few minutes' thought I decided to leave both home and college at the same time and live with my friend Graeme Taylor.

My real problem was a combination of precocity, impatience, and inability to take in anything more from books. I already existed in a climate of restlessness, scorn, frequent ecstasy and occasional despair. Graeme had however combined a taste for literature with an ambition to make money out of it. For the rest, we were united by comradeship, a despisal of everything represented by the business world, the city of Montreal and the Canadian scene, and a desire to get away. God knows what would have happened to us if we had relaxed our hold on these simple principles.

We took a run-down apartment on Metcalfe Street and found work in the Sun Life Assurance Company of Canada. In our spare time I threw myself into composing surrealist poetry, and he continued planning the great Canadian novel. But it was on a dream of Paris that our ideas were vaguely but powerfully concentrated. This kept us going; without it we could not have faced the daily routine of rising at eight o'clock every morning, bathing in a small gritty bathtub, dressing without any attention to the niceties and stumbling down the icy street to an honest day's work.

Our office pay was barely enough to live on. But the situation was soon improved by two of our college friends, Pratt and Petersham. Hearing we had taken an apartment downtown, one evening they put on their dark tubular overcoats and bowler hats and visited us with a pro-

1

posal to pay ten dollars a month each for the privilege of taking women there one night a week, from nine o'clock till one in the morning.

The extra twenty dollars was a help, and it was no hardship keeping away from the apartment until late on Wednesday and Saturday nights; moreover, it soon turned out that Petersham was not using the place (his night was Wednesday), though he continued to pay. But a few more friends heard of the arrangement and applied for the same facilities. The apartment was warm, quiet, safe, fairly clean and had a private street-entrance. We were soon taking in seventy dollars a month, which covered the rent.

The difficulty was that I now had to compose my poetry in the early hours of the morning, and arrived at the Sun Life only half awake. By ten o'clock I would finish my morning work of posting up the five- and ten-cent weekly premiums for burial insurance paid by Chinese labourers in Hong Kong, and then go and bed down in one of the toilets in the basement, where I made myself a little nest in my ankle-length raccoon coat. After two months I was summoned to the departmental head's office and told to ask for more work as soon as I had finished my allotment, and, if there was none, at least to keep sitting decently at my desk. The prospect was so depressing that I gave my two weeks' notice to the personnel department the same day.

We were thus once more in financial straits, and to make peace with my father I called on him at the family mansion a week later. He suggested I return home, go back to McGill, and by hard work make up the few months I had lost.

Once again I had to refuse. I had had enough of university life. I was more than ever determined to be a poet.

I had known for a long time what a disappointment I was to my parents. My father had always wanted me to take up law: he pictured me in the robes of a judge. My mother, for her part, would have liked me to enter the church: she saw me as a bishop. These images, and all that went with them, now struck me with such renewed horror that I was able to stand my ground, which I began to realize was stronger than I had thought.

'I hear you and your friend Taylor are running something very close to a house of ill-fame on Metcalfe Street,' said my father. 'Colonel Birdlime, of McGill's Department of Extramural Affairs, tells me it's common knowledge. I hear the same thing at the club.'

'Well, we take in a little rent.'

He was silent for a minute, stroking his great cleft chin. 'You're still set on a literary career?'

When I said I was, he offered me an allowance of a hundred dollars a month if I would live more discreetly.

It was more than I had expected. The way to Paris was now open. But it was a harder matter to persuade Graeme to come along. He said he didn't want to sponge on me.

'No, but I've been thinking of your cousin Jane's husband in the Canadian National Railways. He might get us a free ride to Europe on a Merchant Marine freighter. That's as good as three hundred dollars.'

'True.'

For the next two weeks we waited, sitting quietly in grimy downtown offices while the strings were being pulled—slinking from one government building to another, adroitly passed from one civil-service hand to another. At last Graeme received a note: we were to sail in three days' time on the *Canadian Traveller*, a government cargo-boat of 950 tons leaving Saint John, New Brunswick, on the 4th of February and taking us to Antwerp. Graeme was given a free passage and I was to pay a nominal fare of fifty dollars.

Graeme had a supplemental examination for his Bachelor of Arts degree to take at McGill the next day. But our news was so apocalyptic that he went into Scott's on St Catherine Street and bought himself a wide-brimmed black Bohemian hat.

Paris! We made it after all. This is where I'm writing now, only three months after leaving Montreal. It's a spring night in the rue Broca, and there's moonlight on the unfinished abandoned statues in the yard outside this big studio we moved into last week. The smell of some flowering shrub is coming in through the long window, and there's a bird singing somewhere in the walled garden of the Ursuline Convent at the corner of the rue de la Santé. Down here in the Glacière quarter we're not so close to Montparnasse as we were, but it's better than that hot little room in the Hôtel Jules-César around the corner from the Dôme and the Dingo. And so quiet. For the first time I can feel the movement of my thoughts, the pulse of my youth—as you're supposed to at eighteen. I'm lucky to be here, in this city that I love more and more every day. What do I mean to do with my youth, my life? Why, I'm going to enjoy myself.

Here, as Eliot's girl says, you feel free. This is something Paris does to one, God knows how. I mean to write, of course—but not too much. Literature isn't so important as life, and I've made my choice. I've already abandoned surrealism and decided to write my memoirs—not a journal but a record of my life written in chapters, like one of George Moore's books—to impose a narrative form on everything that has happened since we left Montreal last February . . .

It's getting late now, the bird in the convent has stopped singing, and there is a faint rosy-grey tinge in the sky. Soon

Apollo's upward rising fire
Will make each eastern cloud a silvery pyre.

Graeme, in his sky-blue pyjamas, lies humped up in bed, his face stares at me, crushed sideways in the pillow. He is sleepy, and has been waiting for me to turn off the gas and go to bed. As I begin writing again, his voice startles me in the silence.

'I just saw you in a dream—as an old man with whiskers, writing . . . '

We spent our last night in Montreal going from one bar to another and ended up in a night-club called The Venetian Gardens, where I saw Pratt and Petersham. While Graeme was dancing unsteadily with one of the bar-girls they came up and sat with me.

'I hear you're both pushing off for the Continent tomorrow,' said Pratt. 'How does that affect our little agreement?'

'The rent's paid for two weeks. You can have the place all the time now if you like.'

They exchanged a look.

'White of you, old man,' said Pratt.

'We don't wish to take advantage,' said Petersham. 'What's it worth?'

'Say thirty dollars.'

With an almost co-ordinated movement they reached for their wallets.

'As of tomorrow night,' said Petersham.

'White of you, old man,' said Pratt.

For the rest of the night I drank a great deal too much champagne.

Later, in the fusty over-heated apartment, I lay in bed not daring to close my eyes lest things should start whirling around. Graeme was snoring, apparently with no thought for his examination a few hours away, as I left the room and went down the hall to the w.c., where I vomited. Staggering back to the bedroom I heard a violent knocking and kicking on the street door and my name being hallooed nervously from outside.

I opened the door and Bertie Ballard, a fat little lecher who was one of our sub-lessors, rushed in with a woman in a red hat at his heels, bringing a cold blast of wind with him. He was buttoned up in his enormous silver raccoon coat, and his serious circular face, above the upstanding fur collar, resembled a hen sitting on its nest. He began explaining in a whisper why he had called at five o'clock in the morning.

'But it's not even your night.'

'I know. But don't turn me down for God's sake, everywhere else is closed. I've been working on this all last week. We won't be long.'

I opened the door of the bedroom and he bundled the woman in ahead of him. She was hiding her face, but I thought I recognized the cashier from an all night restaurant.

Waking late the next morning I found the apartment beautifully empty. I shaved and dressed with care, hardly able to believe it was my last day in Montreal. Then the landlady arrived.

'I was thinking,' she said in her polite but barbed manner, her eyes shooting around the room, 'I should have something extra for the filthy state you've got this place into. I never had a tenant who did like you and all the other gentlemen does.'

'Yes, yes, Mrs Casey,' I said, wanting to get her out of the room on such a beautiful morning. 'I'll settle everything in full when the time comes.'

I went out. The loveliness of the late morning was dazzling. The snow, the blue air, the creaking underfoot of the hard-packed sidewalk — everything is so hard and gem-like at eleven o'clock in Canada! Three blocks away, I thought, the day was curling its edges around the granite walls of the Sun Life Assurance Company, while inside the men and women were all busy denying their dark gods. It was a solemn thought to consider that only sheer luck had snatched me from among them.

I walked along St Catherine Street on the way to the McGill Union, with groups of shop-girls passing on the early lunch-hour in their little cloche hats, closely wrapped coats and flapping overshoes, and the young men in form-fitting overcoats and bell-bottomed trousers. I waited for

Graeme on the steps of the Union, not wanting to see any of my former classmates and answer questions. Soon I saw him trudging down the campus, and in front, almost hiding him, the immense figure of Sir Arthur Currie, principal of the university, holder of a dozen honorary degrees and ex-war lord of the Canadian Expeditionary Force. What a poor figure Graeme, in his long green frieze overcoat and black hat, cut behind this white-spatted symbol of the army, attired like the editor of *Vanity Fair*!

Graeme didn't yet know whether he had passed his examination. 'It's a toss-up,' he said. 'I'll get the news in Paris. Now we've just got time for a good lunch and to pack and catch the train.'

We had gathered more possessions than we thought. When everything was stowed we found we would need three taxis to take us to the station. Soon the room was filled with taxi-drivers who fought among themselves over who should take the lighter trunks. To the smallest, who was left with my wardrobe trunk to carry out, I gave my new snow-boots which I would need no longer.

I was surprised that Mrs Casey had not darted up from her cellar as soon as the trunks started moving out. For once she was caught napping. She only appeared when everything was loaded, and came out on the icy steps, dancing up and down with rage and trying to shout above the roar of the taxis; silently consigning her to Pratt and Petersham I gave the signal to move off. As there was no room inside the taxis, Graeme and I had to stand on the running-boards of the leading one and so had a fine view of St Catherine Street, all lit up, as our little fleet of cars bumped and skidded over the streetcar tracks on the way to Bonaventure Station.

Almost until the very moment of boarding the train I was sick with a reasonless anxiety. I could still hardly believe in our luck, and all the time the baggage was being checked and our tickets visaed I kept imagining some disaster would still keep us in Canada. Only when we were marching along the echoing wooden station-platform behind the porters, our arms full of canes, rugs and overcoats, under the great wooden roof that covered the lines of tracks and with the engines shooting off soot and steam all around, did I relax and embrace my first clear moment of exaltation as we walked alongside the train bound for the Port of Saint John.

Two

Our seats were in the last car of the train, and every now and then we went out to stand on the rear platform and watch the rails running away behind us.

'It's a single track we're on, you'll notice,' said Graeme.

'A good omen.'

We then went back inside and continued drinking brandy. By the time we reached Saint John the bottle was almost empty.

On the docks we found the *Canadian Traveller*, slightly larger than a tugboat and entirely sheathed in grey tallowy ice.

'I wonder how we get in,' said Graeme, banging on an iron door that was at last opened by a dwarf.

'Are you two gentlemen the supercargo?' he said. 'The captain told me of you. Do you know him?'

'Not yet. When do we sail?'

'When the agent says, and that's likely tomorrow. So you don't know Captain Pethick? He'll be in a hoorhouse at the moment, I'll warrant. But he's a fine seaman, none better. I have been all around the coast of South America with him when we were peddling betel. Come in, gentlemen, and take a look at your quarters.'

The informality of everything, compared with the venal fuss and courtesy of an ocean liner, was refreshing. 'Are you a friend of his?' I asked.

'I'm naught but a f—ing employee. I'm the steward. Shall I get you a cup of tea?'

The tea came in thick ironstone mugs, with separate portions of Eagle Brand condensed milk and lead spoons to stir it with. But we were delighted with our quarters—a fine half-round livingroom with windows on both sides, a large double bedroom and a private bathroom and toilet; there was even a bookshelf in the livingroom, filled with the works of George Henty, Bulwer-Lytton, and Ouida.

Captain Pethick arrived, small, sandy-haired and lipless.

'As ye go through life,' he said, sitting down in the best seat and taking out his pipe, 'ye'll understand the beauty of tobacco.'

I instantly divined him as the worst kind of bore.

The trip across was unspeakably tedious. Within three days I had become completely constipated, the food was terrible, and there was not a drop of liquor on the boat. Every evening Captain Pethick would descend from his bridge and bore us. From him I learned two things, that sailors call themselves 'seamen' and the standard procedure to ward off venereal disease. 'Smear the knob well,' he said, smacking his palm over his fist and massaging it, 'before and after.'

Halfway across the ocean we ran into a hurricane. The livingroom stood on its end, the water in the toilet pitched out on the floor, and the chairs were all roped to the walls. Captain Pethick was divided between disgust that neither Graeme nor I was seasick and an increasing alarm over the seaworthiness of his ship. One night when the waves had risen and kept crashing over the bridge, on three occasions putting out some kind of light on the mast, we noticed a gradual cessation of the pitching, succeeded by a sense of being lifted up from behind and rolled forward. When Captain Pethick came down for his evening's refreshment of conversation he was smiling grimly.

'Ye'll notice a change in our way of going, eh?'

'Much smoother,' said Graeme. 'Has the wind turned round?'

'No, it's we have done that. Just now we are heading for the coast of Brazeel.'

For three days we steamed away from Europe. Captain Pethick was in a mellower mood now, and not quite so tiresome. He spoke often of Joseph Conrad, under whom he had served at one time. 'A dour man he was, and awful high and mighty. I've heard it said he was a queen, but I do not believe it. And say what they will, he was a real seaman. He was no donkey-master, was Captain Korniowski. His best book is that *Nostromo*. He had the right view of the buggerly natives in Costa Rica.'

By the time we had turned back towards Europe I had almost finished my first good surrealist poem, 'Conan's Fig', which records the impressions gained from sitting in a disused attic in spring. Now, less than six months later, when I have definitely abandoned surrealism, I still think it has a certain idiotic grace.

Long before we reached England we had had enough of the *Canadian Traveller*, and though we were booked to Antwerp we decided to get off at Cardiff. After sixteen miserable days at sea we did so, taking an occasion when Captain Pethick was busy in the agent's office to avoid the nuisance of saying goodbye to him.

We spent that night in London. I disliked the city at once. The

8

streets were too crowded, and the people were presumptuous, brutal, ugly and unintelligible.

'We'll see Westminster Abbey and Rotten Row anyway,' Graeme said.

Both were disappointing. Then it began to rain. There seemed nowhere you could get a drink. At Cook's we found we had missed the Dover-Calais boat and decided we might as well spend another night in England rather than cross the channel in the dark. It was then I had the idea of visiting George Moore.

Moore was at this time still my literary god. The sweep of his memories, the magic of his style, the bland persistent assertion of himself, the dazzling effect by which in a single phrase he gives an almost physical impression of a landscape, an emotion, or a woman—these made him for me the first writer of the age.

'He must be almost ninety,' said Graeme doubtfully.

I looked up his address in the directory. There was no telephone, and we decided to call unannounced in Ebury Street that afternoon.

'Maybe he'll ask us in,' said Graeme. 'After all, we are going to Paris, just as he did when he was a young man.'

The sign 'Ebury Street' on the corner of Buckingham Palace Road gave me a thrill of joy and awe. It was like seeing the awning of the Café de la Nouvelle-Athènes. 'We mustn't forget to say we're from Canada right away,' I said. 'Perhaps the remoteness, the idea of disciples coming from the wilderness, will appeal to him.'

But when we arrived at the black brass-knockered door tucked under its little Grecian white-pillared portico, I lost my nerve and hurried Graeme past it. Fifty yards further on we took heart, turned back and rang the bell. A fat, very old rosy-cheeked parlourmaid answered and dropped a curtsey.

'We have come across the ocean to pay our respects to Mr Moore,' said Graeme, 'if he is at home and can spare us a few minutes. Say we are admirers of his, from Canada . . .'

'Please to step in, gentlemen.'

We stood in a miniature vestibule, sweating, for at least five minutes. I was already thinking that if I did not see this man it would spoil my whole life.

'Mr Moore will be 'appy to see you for five minutes, gentlemen,' said the parlourmaid. 'But no more, please. He is just out of the nursing 'ome. This way.'

He was much frailer than I had ever imagined, but there before me were the sloping shoulders, the beautiful drooping moustache, the exquisite chinless face, the heavy-lidded eyes, the tiny feet. He rose, his hands fluttering slightly.

'From Canada,' he said. 'Dear me.'

His hand felt like paper. The bright eyes looked straight into mine, then dropped to my feet.

'Do sit down,' he said, taking Graeme's hand for the same fraction of a second. 'I am not very well, I'm afraid. Did you have a pleasant voyage?'

'No, sir,' I managed to say, trying to smile.

'Ah, *mal de mer*, I suppose. I am subject to it myself.'

His charm was enveloping. All my nervousness disappeared and I told him how I had admired his work so long and of my happiness in being able to speak to the greatest living English writer.

'Greatest? Oh, indeed no. No, no. But thank you. May I ask you on which of my performances you found your most flattering opinion?'

'*The Brook Kerith*,' I said, 'to begin with—and then the autobiographical books, the *Confessions, Hail and Farewell* . . .'

A faint tinge of pink showed in his cheeks. 'Yes, *Kerith* is my best book, I think. But—the *Young Man?*' He looked at us. 'Really, doesn't everyone look on that as dated, *vieux jeu*, nowadays?'

'No, sir,' said Graeme. 'It is a book that will never date, it's a kind of statement of youth for all time, a youth in which we all partake somehow. Only people who are never young could find it dated.'

'Really. You're very kind. And perhaps you're right, too. Yes, you may be right.'

Then he asked us to stay to tea.

During tea he talked of James Joyce. 'An astonishing performer,' he said. 'That's a most interesting book of his.'

After a minute it turned out he was talking not of *Ulysses* but *The Portrait*.

'Oh yes, *Ulysses*,' he said. 'No, I couldn't quite get through it. Rather dull in the middle, I thought. And a little too earnest and iconoclastic for my taste. Too satirical.' His nose wrinkled slightly. 'All that Irish wit and humour—no. But I should have liked to meet Mr Joyce all the same. When I was last in Paris I went to that little shop in the rue Dupuytren and inquired for him, but a very draconian woman there told he never saw anyone. I left a note for him. I don't imagine he got it.'

Before we left he gave us a thin pamphlet in grey wrappers, *Recollections of the Impressionist Painters*, and wrote in it simply, *Yours truly, George Moore*. 'It's all I have to hand at the moment. Thank you so much for coming, and I hope you enjoy your stay in Paris.'

In the vestibule the parlourmaid asked us to sign a visitors' book.

As we went out I said, 'What luck. We'll remember this all our lives.'

'Yes, and he didn't even ask us our names.'

'By the time you're eighty-seven I suppose you don't bother about names. We signed the book anyway.'

'And we've got this little pamphlet too.'

We were almost dancing as we went down Ebury Street. For us he was more than ever the greatest living English writer, greater even than Thomas Hardy.

The next day we crossed the channel and arrived in Paris around six o'clock in the evening. It was dark, damp, and snowing slightly, and I suppose the city did not look its best from the train windows, but I had only to think I was now in the city of Baudelaire, Utrillo and Apollinaire to be swept by a joy so strong it verged on nausea. Coming out of the Gare du Nord, however, and standing on the wet dark street with a little wall of trunks around me and a vision of half-a-dozen brightly lit cafés opposite, I had a much different impression— the warm, prosy, comfortable feeling of having somehow come home.

On the train from Calais we had seen in a newspaper the advertisement of a hotel 'near the Gare du Montparnasse'. We thought this must be in the Montparnasse quarter itself, and the name, the Hôtel de l'Abbé-Grégoire, sounded amusing. But it was off the rue de Rennes and not at all amusing, and we moved next day to the Hôtel Jules-César on the rue du Montparnasse, mainly because it was around the corner from the famous Café du Dôme.

The Jules-César was a charming hotel: it was neither comfortable nor clean nor warm, but you never saw the proprietor, there was always plenty of hot water, and moreover our room, though without windows, had a skylight over the washstand and by standing on the bidet you could look into a medieval courtyard where they made sections for corrugated tin roofs, apparently by hand. The room cost twenty dollars a month and you could have breakfast in bed for fifteen cents.

The first thing we found was that with the franc at four cents we were much richer than in Montreal. Here I must say that I don't think the rate of exchange is always given its proper importance as an element in the charm of Paris: to be able to live well on very little money is the best basis for an appreciation of beauty anywhere, and I think we admired the city all the more because we could now eat and drink almost as much as we liked.

Another cause for congratulation was the telegram Graeme found waiting for him from his brother, with the news that he had passed his examination and was thus a graduate of an institution of learning.

During our first week in Paris we never left Montparnasse at all, simply moving from one café and restaurant to another. It was then early March and the enclosed stove-heated *terrasses* were the best places to sit and pretend to work, for work at this time was for us more a pretence than anything else. I managed however to finish 'Conan's Fig' — the title is of course not only meaningless but has no connection with the poem itself — and also to write the first lines of over a dozen other surrealist poems; while Graeme resumed work on the plan of his novel, which was to be called *The Flying Carpet*. But it was more fun to play at being a writer. Later I found that a great many other young writers felt and behaved the same way. Indeed Paris is a very difficult place for anyone to work unless he is dull and serious.

After a week we began to find it rather tiresome not knowing anyone. Therefore one evening when we were sitting in the Café Select and I heard a large, benevolent-looking grey-haired man at the next table being introduced to a number of people as Adolf Dehn, I decided to speak to him. I had already seen a book of his lithographs and admired them, especially one entitled *Nine Whores* in which the faces and figures were full of the most ecstatic greed, cruelty and joy. By this time I had had enough to drink to make me capable of such boldness, and as he was leaving I ran after him and said, 'Mr Dehn, my friend and I have just arrived in Paris, and we know no one but yourself by sight. We are going to the Dôme, and won't you have a drink with us there?'

He smiled and said he would be delighted, but he thought we should go to the little *tabac* nearby where it was not so crowded. Dear Adolf, I am still grateful for your kindness that night; but for you we might have continued friendless for a long time.

The *tabac*'s terrasse held only six or eight tables, but one of them, right at the front, was vacant, and we all ordered brandy and soda. Soon we were approached by a tall, thin, slow-moving man dressed in black—I learned later it was Leo Stein—who presented Adolf with a photograph of a long-eared spaniel.

'I thought you would be interested in having this, Adolf,' he said, 'because it struck me as being so like your wife.'

'Thank you, Leo. You haven't one of a bulldog resembling your sister, have you?'

'Gertrude and I are not on speaking terms, Adolf.'

'So much the better for both of you.'

The exchange was carried on with the greatest good humour. Leo Stein then raised his hat and passed on. A few minutes later we were joined by a smiling, short, curly-haired man whom Adolf introduced as Hugo Quattrone, a romantic painter and a Christian Socialist from California.

'He is a very fair painter,' said Adolf as Hugo sat down, 'only he lets his emotions run away with him and he is too fond of suffering.'

'Yes, but not my own, gentlemen,' said Quattrone. 'It's the suffering of the other guy that breaks my heart. Look at all those faces,' he said, pointing at the crowd passing slowly in front of us, 'they are tragic masks of pain. The system that produces them's got to be painlessly replaced.'

'How would you go about it?' said Graeme.

'By exerting the power of good will. The English poet Shelley understood this—I mean that all men are brothers and must not think of themselves. In the first place everyone should stop working.'

His ideas were the index to a character that was very pure but a little boring; however, he did not obtrude them.

'And how is your little girl Irma?' asked Adolf. 'Does she like her job in the creamery?'

'She is happier, I guess. Prostitution, gentlemen, is not only immoral, it's a mug's game. You see, I don't idealize it like Dostoevsky did. But the creamery woman doesn't pay very much and Irma gets pretty hungry. And think of all the food in the shop, all the food in Paris, in the whole world!'

'I feel like having a sandwich,' said Adolf as Quattrone left. 'Shall we go to the Dôme counter?'

At the Dôme we all kept on drinking. Adolf was in his most expansive mood and everyone seemed to know him; in half an hour we had met a dozen of the habitués of the quarter—among them an attractive big-nosed Spanish girl with violently hennaed hair and the beautiful name of Caridad de Plumas, who became interested in Graeme.

'You have a corrupted mouth and kind eyes,' she told him, 'and such awkward hands, and you are thin like a pussycat. You and your friend must come to a party with me tomorrow. How old is your friend?'

'Nineteen,' I said, adding an extra year. I had had six or seven brandies and was feeling a little dizzy from the heat and noise of the comptoir.

'Dolfen says you are poet,' she said. 'How many poems have you written?'

'Only one.'

'Good. I don't like artistes of any genre who produce too much. Now speak your poem to me. I am a very good critic, I will tell you truly if it is good or awful.'

I recited the forty lines of 'Conan's Fig' slowly and with great expression.

'It's awful,' she said. 'But it's very beautiful too.'

'Excuse me,' said a grating, boozy voice at my elbow. 'It's good and it's not beautiful at all. Send it to *The Dial*. No, send it to *transition*. Jolas is taking anything these days.'

'You mustn't pay any attention to this man,' said Adolf. 'He is Harold Stearns, and he knows less about poetry than any living man.'

'I am not a living man,' said Stearns.

At that time his name meant nothing to me. His period as editor of *The Dial* had been years before this, and I did not even know he had come to Paris to play the races and apparently drink himself quietly to death on champagne—though he is still alive, and when I saw him last month, was still wearing the same incredibly dirty white shirt and black business suit.

After a while we went across the street to the Sélect. The hundred yards in the cold night air freshened me up. I decided to switch to champagne, as being milder than brandy.

This was the first time I had met Monsieur and Madame Select. Madame had a high colour, shrewd eyes, and a bosom like a shelf; she wore little black fingerless mittens that kept her hands warm without preventing her from counting the francs and centimes. Monsieur Select, who made the Welsh rarebits on a little stove behind the bar, had long melancholy moustaches like Flaubert's. It was a good night in the Select. The company in bars is, I have noticed, either very good or very bad; there seems to be some force of a minor destiny that draws good company to the same place at the same time. Adolf, Caridad, Graeme, and I ended up by listening to Emma Goldman, who had just left Russia in disgust: the government had cynically betrayed all anarchist principles and she was going back to Chicago. She was short, squat, with feet turned outwards like a webfooted bird, and the famous red hair was now streaked with grey; but her eyes were sparkling with shrewdness, pugnacity and fun. I had never met a woman so free from artifice, so intellectually alive. Her appetite for argument was insatiable, and it was hard to conceive of anyone getting the better of her. 'Stratification!' she was crying. 'It's the same old story in Russia, the same thing all over again. Well, they may come to me on their bended knees to go back, but I won't. Ah, when I think of Rosa Luxemburg.'

'A great woman,' said Adolf. 'But a poor speaker. Her attitudes and gestures always reminded me too much of Danton.'

'Impossible,' said Emma Goldman. 'You never met Danton.'

'I'm referring to his statue on the boulevard Saint-Germain.'

'You don't admire it?'

'I do not.'

'Why not?'

'My dear Emma, the thing is just as absurd as Rosa was.'

'In what way, please?'

'Well, it's the study of an angry child. If Danton were dressed as a boy of five it would be a very fine domestic study—a picture of outraged appeal, say to his mother over some injustice, like the theft of a toy by his elder sister. He's even pointing at her in the distance.'

'Exactly. Outraged appeal. Well put. You prove my point.'

Adolf blinked. 'What is your point?'

'That Rosa and Danton—or at any rate the man who did the statue—reached the emotions of the people in the best and most direct way.'

'By assuming the attitudes of angry children?'

'Certainly. This is good oratory. What better?'

I began to understand something of Emma Goldman's skill in impromptu debate. It was like watching a clever tennis-player drawing his opponent out of position.

'But it's still absurd,' said Adolf.

'What's absurd about hitting your audience in the breadbasket?'

'Rabble rousing, you mean.'

'You don't think the rabble should be roused?'

'Not to Danton's kind of violence.'

'You don't believe in the people, eh?'

'Well, not to that extent.'

'I do.'

By this time Graeme and Caridad had come to an understanding. He whispered his good fortune to me and the next minute he was squiring her across the street towards the rue Delambre, his black hat over one ear.

Adolf lived quite far away, in the rue Vercingetorix, but when I insisted on taking him home in a taxi he demurred. 'Are you rich?' he inquired anxiously.

On my assuring him I was quite rich we took a taxi to his place and I returned home in the early light of dawn.

O Paris dawns, you are always beautiful, I think, no matter what the weather, but there was never one more beautiful than on that bitter morning in early March in 1928, with a sky of ashes and the tall houses grey and cold, the streets wet and only a few lights showing in the little cafés where the chauffeurs take their breakfasts and brandy. It was all too soon when I arrived at the Jules-César and staggered up the stairs to our windowless little room, where I vomited in the bidet and fell into bed with a sensation of pure happiness.

THREE

When Graeme turned up at noon the next day his face had a happy, pale and pummelled look: his night had obviously been a success. But the morning was bitterly cold, and we took turns thawing ourselves out in the hotel bath, which cost five francs for a single filling, and I wore my raccoon coat and fur cap to breakfast at the Dôme.

'When will spring come?' I asked Monsieur Cambon the proprietor.

'Soon now. Your costume will shame it into appearing.'

In the afternoon we went to the party at the house of Caridad's friend Rupert Castle, a rich English expatriate and dilettante who had a big ground-floor studio looking on a garden in the rue Notre-Dame-des-Champs. The windows were rimed and opaque with frost, but there was a stove as well as a fireplace, and mugs of hot whisky-and-water with lemon. There I met the great surrealist poet Robert Desnos, looking barely older than myself and wearing a thin shapeless suit and a long grey tasselled muffler wound many times around his neck; he was much uglier than his portraits and, shivering with cold, he looked as if he had been set upon and dragged through the gutter. His mouth was wide and humorous as a frog's, and his large protruding oyster-coloured eyes, behind thick glasses, were full of wit and intelligence. Caridad introduced me to him in French, adding, 'Here is a young Canadian poet who calls himself surrealist and who has written some touching lines about the effect that bats have on him.'

'*Ah, monsieur, vous vous occupez donc de la poésie?*' said Desnos quizzically. He spoke no English, and the fact of my being one of the few people there who spoke French was probably the only reason he bothered with me at all.

I told him that after reading André Breton's collection *Les Champs Magnétiques* when I was sixteen I had become converted to surrealism, and his own *La liberté ou l'amour* had confirmed me in the faith.

'You like Breton?' he said. 'I will introduce you to him. But first you must read his *Nadja*, which has just come out and which is the finest novel of the century. And you must also read Péret, Eluard, Fargue, Vitrac, Soupault, Schwitters, Sternheim, Marcel Noll, and myself, although I am presently being prosecuted for obscenity. And read Tristan Tzara too, for though he is not much good you can learn from his absurd errors and want of taste, and moreover he is hand in glove with the police.' I learned later this last remark was an allusion to a difference he and Breton had had with Tzara, when the latter was supposed to have advised the Paris prefecture that his two fellow-surrealists should be put in jail.

He then spoke of his horror of public buildings. 'You must know of the anger I silently hurl against every church, hospital, court-house, prison—simply for their damnable impersonality! It is a rebellion against the whole apparatus of medicine, religion and law. These things, and the buildings which embody them, are unnecessary, they disfigure not only the face of the earth but the spirit of man; they are acknowledgements of failure, insults to humanity. My friend, what do these buildings symbolize but the impersonal care of the sick and suffering, the salvation of souls by a system, the maintenance of order for a lot of cowards? They are all signposts on a road leading downwards, monuments to the abrogation of all personal responsibility, wretched plasters on the running sores of suffering and loneliness and fear, Stations of a secular Cross built along the shameful retreat of the self into a collective ant-like consciousness. The duties of man in these three specifically human areas are: one, to tend and sympathize with and assume the sufferings of others,' here he spread out his hands as in the gesture of benediction, 'two, to wrestle in solitude with one's own damnation,' he wrung his hands together, 'and three, to redress all wrongs done to one by acts of instant and personal violence,' and he struck his fist softly into his palm. 'These duties alone possess and assert human dignity.'

The celebrated Kiki was also a guest. At that time, as a newcomer to Montparnasse, I was unaware of her status as acknowledged queen of the quarter; but there was no mistaking the magnetism of her personality, the charm of her voice, or the eccentric beauty of her face. Her *maquillage* was a work of art in itself: her eyebrows were completely shaved and replaced by delicate curling lines shaped like the accent on a Spanish 'n', her eyelashes were tipped with at least a teaspoonful of mascara, and her mouth, painted a deep scarlet that emphasized the sly erotic humour of its contours, blazed against the plaster-white of her cheeks on which a single beauty spot was placed, with consummate art, just under one eye. Her face was beautiful from every angle, but I liked it best in full profile, when it had the lineal purity of a stuffed salmon. Her quiet husky voice was dripping harmless obscenities; her gestures were few but expressive. As a fitting penalty for a journalist recently convicted of blackmail, she was suggesting that it would be enough to drop him in a public toilet. '*Et puis — la corde*,' she murmured, bending her knees slightly and pulling downward on an imaginary chain.

There was also a little knot of handsome girls dressed in dark tailored suits and neckties; they wore low-heeled shoes, spoke in deep voices, and shook hands with crushing force. The most beautiful was Daphne Berners, an English girl with enormous grey eyes, a low thrilling voice and a schoolgirlish sense of humour that was quite at variance with her avowed status of *femme damnée*. Her friend Angela Martin was extremely pretty, with stiff frizzy hair and an air of charming and invincible stupidity that was quite genuine; she had been in the chorus of one of Florenz Ziegfeld's revues but something wayward and unpredictable in her nature had saved her from the fate of so many of these girls, and instead of being kept by some serious stockbroker she had become the *chuchotte* of a succession of avid elderly women and was now living with Daphne in what appeared to be a state of perfect bliss. 'I got tired of all those old biddies,' she told me. 'They call you their dream-daughter and want to keep you away from men. They are bitches in the manger. You have to play the little girl with them all the time too—in muslin, curls and a lisp—and they don't even like you to drink. Now Daphne, she is a real pal.'

In her mannish suit and four-in-hand tie, with her candid greyblue eyes, ragged eyebrows and wide mouth free of lipstick, she was fascinating. I was also astonished by her capacity for drink. The only sign of intoxication was the way her lisp became more marked.

Daphne strode over. 'Angela, it's time you had something to eat. Bring your young man along and we'll have a tuck-in at Rosalie's.'

I found Rupert Castle and thanked him for his hospitality. He stared. 'This is very original,' he said. 'No one has ever thanked me for a party before. Of course I appreciate it, but you must not be too bourgeois, you know.'

Rosalie's restaurant was not far away, in the rue Campagne-Première, and was already filling up for dinner. The food was very good and incredibly cheap, and I was surprised by the amount the two girls put away: they worked their way enthusiastically through the entire menu of the *prix fixe* and I found their healthy girlish appetites stimulated my own. We finished off with chocolate mousse served in little earthenware pots covered by a circle of silver paper.

'You get a good feed here,' said Daphne, sitting back and lighting up one of her rank Gauloise cigarettes. 'Let's have coffee at the Dingo, it's too cold to sit outside anywhere.'

This was the first time I had been to the Dingo. We sat at one of the six little tables and had strong black *filtre* in thick sherbet glasses. Angela drank brandy while Daphne talked about sculpture. 'You mean you don't know Zadkine or Brancusi? You must see Brancusi's "Young Girl". It's the most beautiful female bottom in the world. It positively sings.'

All the time she was looking at me with her lovely myopic grey eyes. Suddenly she said, 'Let's go to the Gypsy first, and then have a party at my place.'

The Gypsy Bar was a little foul-smelling boîte on the boulevard Edgar-Quinet, full of hardfaced young lesbians and desperate looking old women whose spotted, sinewy arms rattled with jewelled bracelets. We were hailed by a tableful of the latter, one of whom, rather younger than the rest, was wearing male evening dress and a monocle. They insisted we sit with them. The conversation, incredibly dull, was carried on with a superfluity of cant words and indecent euphemisms.

'Are you shocked, little bird?' the woman with the monocle asked me, raising her artificially thickened eyebrows.

'Indeed I am.'

'Your health, little mouse! What will you drink? But not beer, it's so *bloody English.*'

I was then obliged to drink a *diabolo*, a sickening mixture of port and grenadine that I had thought was drunk by nobody except prostitutes, and to dance with the monocled lady. She took the lead and I found it rather awkward to begin with. But she was a fine dancer and I soon found myself being waltzed around very pleasantly. There were a few other couples, each arranged in a similar reverse disposition, but most of the other dancers were women, with the male types leading.

A new arrival suddenly evoked screams of joy. A curvaceous squat man in black, with blue shaven jowls covered with violet talcum-powder and eyes loaded with mascara, he held his hands in front of him like a dancing dog.

'Dan! Dan!' everyone shouted.

This was the famous Dr Maloney, the most-quoted homosexual in Paris, a man who combined the professions of pathic, abortionist, professional boxer and quasi-confessor to literary women. He waddled forward and a place at our table was made for him at once.

'I have just had a marvellous experience,' he murmured to the old woman in the purple velvet hat who was our hostess. 'Such a divine piece of rough trade, my dear, with wooden shoes, velveteen trousers *and* a gorgeous three days' beard. Not until our encounter—if you will pardon the expression—was over did I learn he was a genuine gravedigger! I was furious. If I had only known . . .' He snapped his fingers with extraordinary force, and two waiters came running. 'Champagne, champagne, to celebrate the victory of vice over the grave!'

Dr Maloney then treated us to an astonishing harangue revolving around unmentionable subjects and indescribable practices.

Angela, with her big moronic eyes fixed on him, was laughing compulsively. Daphne seized her arm. 'Come on,' she said to me over her shoulder, 'we're going home.'

'Bitch!' said the old woman in the purple hat. 'Boy-lover, cradle-snatcher, peep-hole woman, *flagellante manquée* . . .'

'Have a good time,' said the lady with the monocle.

'While there is yet time,' roared Dr Maloney. 'But in the hour of your utmost abandon, think of me, Dr God Almighty Maloney, the ir-repressible backwoodsman, the original Irish tenor!'

In the cold air outside the Gypsy we found a taxi and Daphne gave the driver the address: 147 rue Broca, just below the Ursuline Convent. When we got there the street was lit by a single dim street-lamp shining on the long pale plastered wall in which was set a small rusty gate surmounted by an ornamental iron arch. With both of us supporting Angela, Daphne unlocked the door and clashed it behind us. I saw vague groups of statuary in stone and plaster in what appeared to be an over-grown garden, and then we were in a great first-floor studio with the moon shining through the skylight.

'Put a few more *boulets* on the stove,' Daphne told me.

The gaslight gave a beautiful illumination to the big studio, which I now saw for the first time, with its bare white plastered walls and a skylight that seemed to rise and disappear into the sky itself. The rural silence outside made it hard to realize we were in the middle of Paris. Angela had dropped on a chair, and I sat down at a battered table and smoked a cigarette while Daphne made coffee. The big iron stove began to glow softly from inside. Angela sleepily called for music on the gramophone.

I found the machine beside the bed and a stack of records. After cranking it up I put on the top record. It turned out to be Gluck's *Echo and Narcissus*, and we listened to the stately strains in the near-darkness.

Echo and Narcissus scraped to an end. I put on the next record from the stack and sat beside Angela.

'*Pagan Love Song!*' she cried. She threw her arms around me as a sugary baritone began singing against a background of mucilaginous guitars,

> *Come with me, while moonlight*
> *Sleeps among the palms . . .*

Our amours, which were rather outré, were accompanied by an astonishing variety of music, from the happy melodies of Offenbach to the nasal breathy voice of Rudy Vallee and the silver snarling trumpets of Purcell. We all fell asleep soon after midnight, with the stove glowing softly and the slanted moonlight silvering the high wall of the garden outside.

I hardly noticed my hangover the next morning. The two girls began eating and drinking as soon as they woke up: buttered tartines, anchovy paste, tea and apricot jam. I said goodbye a little before noon, wanting to explore the neighbourhood by myself.

The quarter was quiet, almost rustic, and in the rue de la Glacière I met a man with a flock of goats, playing a little pipe to announce he was selling ewe's milk from the udder. The sun had come out by then, and it shone on the narrow white winding street, with its noonday workmen in blue blouses and paper caps and squat housewives in black with fringed shawls and shopping baskets and pewter pipkins. I bought a French pastry full of yellow custard and sat on a low stone wall eating it. Paris, I thought, was an even better city than it was in the books.

I found my way back to Montparnasse by way of the Santé prison and the Lion de Belfort, walking down the tree-lined boulevard Denfert-Rochereau as far as the Closerie des Lilas, having missed the direct way by the boulevard Raspail. The streets were dipped in warm sunshine now: it was the first day of spring.

FOUR

DECEMBER 1932
ROYAL VICTORIA HOSPITAL
MONTREAL

I am taking up this book again four whole years later, only anxious to preserve its continuity. Here I am, in an advanced state of tuberculosis, waiting for the final operation that will mean either life or death: since I refuse to entertain any view of the latter, but also since I know my survival is mainly a matter of luck, I would like to continue my record of those years — the years in which I really lived — before the onset of death or the inevitable dullness of a mature outlook: this is to be the book of my youth, my golden age. I have a pen, six blank oilcloth-covered scribblers, perfect mental clarity, freedom from pain, and there's a whole month before me. And so I resume.

I took Robert Desnos's advice and for the next week studied all the surrealist work I could get hold of, finding most of it in a little bookshop on the rue Jacques-Callot off the rue de Seine. From this study I emerged with my whole purpose altered. I was not only dismayed by the scope and brilliance that the surrealist writers showed and that I could not hope to equal but was also struck, in a contrary way, by a certain sameness and monotony of treatment and even of syntax in their work, above all by the reiteration of the heavy mallet-like grammatical constructions of Ducasse — a positive trade mark of the surrealist style — where an endless number of out-of-the-way objects were placed in apposition to adjectives and verbs to which they had no relation but that of surprise.

'I think I'll go back to prose,' I told Graeme, 'and drop surrealism.'

'Most of it's pretty fake, isn't it? Automatic writing, indeed. It smells of the lamp though. But what are you going to do with all those first lines of surrealist poems? They're too good to destroy. Let me see them.' An hour later he had turned them into a Shakespearean sonnet.

'What'll we call it?' he said.

'Something catchy but intellectual.'

'"The Ides of March"?'

'Too literary.'

'"Little by Little"?'

'Trite.'

'"The Great Bed of Ware"?'

'Better, but not good enough.'

'I've got it. "Nobody's Fool".'

'Just the thing.'

That evening I began the first chapter of this book, and when anyone asked me what I was doing in Paris I was now able to say I was writing my Memoirs. The reactions ranged from sympathy to good-natured derision. Adolf Dehn was enthusiastic. 'I'll do a portrait of you for it,' he said.

After this burst of creativity I did nothing for a whole month. It

23

was now spring, and much pleasanter to go to Montparnasse every day or wander about the city. I was more and more enslaved by the beauty of Paris. Merely to ride downtown in an open taxi, over the smooth streets paved with tarred wooden blocks, was a great pleasure. Almost every morning we would take a dash through the Place de la Concorde, thrilling to the absence of traffic regulations and the wild blowing of horns, and then find our way on foot back to Montparnasse for breakfast at the Dôme or the Select.

I was so perfectly happy that writing did not interest me at all.

Soon Graeme and I simply spent the warm sunny days of spring wandering about the odd and archaic parts of Paris—the rue Mouffetard, the Place de la Contrescarpe, the rue des Tanneries, the Halle aux Vins, the rue de la Gaîté, the Alésia district and the little network of streets around the Place St Michel—the rue Galande, the Passage des Hirondelles, the rue de la Huchette, and the churches of Saint-Séverin and Saint-Julien-le-Pauvre. The Grands Boulevards, Montmartre, Passy, and the Champs-Elysées we agreed to regard as out of bounds, and we absolutely refused to enter the Louvre. Once, having made a mistake in the mazes of the subway, we surfaced at the Invalides and were so appalled by the sight of Napoleon's tomb that we fled back down the steps.

It has always been the Paris of André Breton and Léon-Paul Fargue that I have loved; and, greatly impressed by the eclectic double-tongued construction of Arthur Symons' translation of *Les Fleurs du mal*, I wrote a sonnet to Paris in the same hybrid manner, which was later published, together with 'Nobody's Fool', in *Bilge*, a bright irrational little magazine edited by Arthur Loewenstein.

Very soon we were habitués of the Falstaff Bar on the rue du Montparnasse, only a few doors down from the Jules-César. It seemed on the whole better than the Dôme, which was often too noisy, than the Dingo and the Strix, which were too full of alcoholics and Scandinavians respectively, than the College Inn, which though run by Jed Kiley and having a genuine Red Indian barman was too favourite a meeting-place for Americans who really belonged in Harry's New York Bar. Though all these places were amusing and comfortable the Falstaff gained a special charm from the contrast between its rather stuffy oak panelling and padded seats and the haphazard way it was run by the bartender Jimmy Charters, an ex-prizefighter, and the waiter Joe Hildesheim, who came from Brooklyn and was known as Joe the Bum. The Falstaff was owned jointly by two Belgian gentlemen who also shared a mistress, a very plump handsome grey-eyed woman called Madame Mitaine. The three of them sat quietly in the ingle of the fireplace every evening and did not interfere in any way, being content to count the cash when the bar closed at two o'clock in the morning. Madame Mitaine would then enter the figures in a little red notebook. Jimmy and Joe ran the place on the principle that about every tenth drink should be on the house, so that regular clients, and still more the casual visitors, were constantly being surprised by a whispered intimation that there was nothing to pay.

I saw Daphne and Angela occasionally and found them as good company as ever. Graeme's affair with Caridad continued on a friendly but sporadic basis. They were both such casual people, however, that it had not much dramatic nourishment; also, she had no money at all and would take none from him and was obliged to sleep quite often with serious unsympathetic men in order to pay the rent on her little apartment, which was in a lovely courtyard full of trees and birds, just off the rue Delambre.

At this time Graeme interrupted his planning of *The Flying Carpet* long enough to write a short story about a French-Canadian farmer whose wife left him: it was set in the village of Baie d'Urfé outside Montreal but I can remember nothing else—except that the characters used to play three-handed whist on a table they set up at the roadside under the street-lamp in order to save electricity. It was called 'Deaf Mute' and he sent it to Eugene Jolas who at once accepted it for *transition* and asked Graeme to meet him at the Café Lipp.

Graeme could hardly believe it: this was the first story he had ever published, outside of some *juvenilia* in the *McGill Fortnightly Review*, and the fact that it was to appear in *transition*, along with the latest instalment of James Joyce's *Work in Progress*, which was then coming out piecemeal, was overwhelming. Moreover both of us had always thought *transition* the best review in the world and had eagerly read what few copies found their way to Montreal. We had wondered at the grace and daring of the European surrealist work, at the astonishing rhythms and texture of Joyce's new work, and at the crusading spirit that impelled Jolas to publish a manifesto, signed by almost all his contributors, supporting Charlie Chaplin's natural right to engage in the odd sexual techniques that were at that time being alleged by his wife as one of her grounds for divorce; in fact we liked everything in *transition* but the work of Gertrude Stein, which seemed to me (as indeed it still does) pretentious and intolerably arch. Here we had first read Aragon, Fargue, Ribemont-Dessaignes, Eluard, Soupault, Drieu La Rochelle and a dozen others, all enthusiastically translated by either Jolas or his wife; here we had first seen reproductions of Miró, Arp, Klee, Ernst, Labisse, Tanguy, and de Chirico, painters then almost unknown in North America and absolutely so in Canada; here we had learned of the bowdlerized pirating of *Ulysses* by Samuel Roth and laughed at Elliot Paul's burlesque of Hemingway. Now Graeme, at the age of twenty-one, was to appear in the same gallery.

While he was gone I started on the second chapter of these memoirs but could not get past the first few lines and soon gave up. I still believed rather too much in the necessity of being 'in the right mood' to write and didn't understand that the mood can be induced with a little effort; which is not to say I believe anything worthwhile comes from simply sitting down at a desk every day at a certain hour and writing—as Shaw and Bennett claim it does.

When I met Graeme at the Falstaff in the evening he told me of Jolas and his wife. 'He is short, dark, shiny-faced and full of verve,' he said, 'and she is six feet tall, rather plain, very sensitive and full of a charming and indiscriminate enthusiasm for all forms of modern art. He wanted to know all about the present condition of literature in Canada and who were our best authors, so I mentioned Raymond Knister, Arthur Smith, Frank Scott, and Leo Kennedy. We are both invited to a party in the suburbs tomorrow night. James Joyce may be there. We'd better take a bath.'

It was so complicated reaching the party by subway, train, and taxi that we arrived almost an hour late, and as there was no one we knew, we saw we would have to talk to each other to begin with. So we mounted an attack on the hidden sentimentality of the poetry of E. E. Cummings, stabbing the air with our forefingers and capping each other's quotations, and so gathered a small anglophone audience who at last joined in the discussion. Among them was the famous British novelist Diana Tree who had just severed her connection with the editorial staff of the magazine *Hemisphere* and had come to Paris with the baby boy who was one of its visible fruits. She was tall, blonde, beautiful, and carelessly dressed, with a large nose, a humorous mouth, and blue-grey eyes that were always moving. I had never cared greatly for her work but felt an immediate liking for her that seemed to be returned. Taking me by the arm she introduced me to a very slender man with a great tiered pompadour who turned out to be the surrealist poet Georges Pol, author of *Circoncision du Coeur*; he was suffering from such a rash of acne that he seemed almost speechless from diffidence and discomfort. I learned later that he was her current cavalier.

'Who is your greatest Canadian poet?' he asked politely.

'Do you mean in French or English?'

'Why, do you have both?' He seemed delighted. 'But of course, you have the *département* of Québec. Well then, who is the greatest poet of Québec?'

'In the last twenty-five years you have a choice between Morin, the Canadian Gautier, and Choquette, the Canadian Hugo, and Nelligan, the Canadian Verlaine.'

'Then there is no Québec poet in himself?'

'None that I know of.'

'What about your English Canadian poets?'

'We have Lampman, the Canadian Keats, and Carman, the Canadian Swinburne. We also have Smith, who is sometimes hailed as the Canadian Yeats but whom I prefer to all of them.'

'May I ask if you yourself are already the Canadian avatar of someone else, and if so of whom?'

'So far I have not donned any mantle at all, but it was not easy. This is probably why I embraced surrealism.'

'I can understand, it was a way out.'

I soon learned from Diana Tree that Joyce was not coming to the party. 'Perhaps,' she said, 'Jolas may have intimated he was, but the fact is that Joyce goes nowhere. Nora does not allow him.'

'You know him?'

'As well as I know anyone else,' she said guardedly.

I was aware of Robert Desnos at my elbow.

'How goes the life of literature?' he asked. 'But let me take you to André Breton. He is in good form tonight.'

Breton, who was holding forth to a small group of disciples, was stout, handsome, and had an even more imposing pompadour. He was talking, with extraordinary force and rapidity, of crime.

'Peguy has assured us,' he was saying, 'that the sinner is at the very heart of Christianity. He is probably right, though that is of no importance. What is really important is that the criminal is at the very heart of the law. It's obvious: the law could not exist without the criminal.

But the debt is so seldom acknowledged. This enormous, majestic and complicated apparatus of law—its pretentious, portentous buildings; its army of policemen, detectives, bailiffs, turnkeys; the panoply of its actioning, with its robes, bibs, coats of arms, maces, fancy linen, and so forth; the fortunes and honours accruing to its practitioners; the fund of learning, effort and ambition it expends and sets in motion—all this would disappear in a flash but for the poor wretch on whom it all depends, the criminal, the poor stupid crook, the shifty-eyed devil in the dock. Make no mistake, the criminal is the prime benefactor of the law. To borrow a phrase from the science of economics, the criminal is one of the most important *consumers* in our society: he consumes law. And he goes unrecognized and unthanked.'

'He gets no more recognition or gratitude,' said a short man who had compensated for his baldness by a pair of long sideburns, and who I learned later was Léon-Paul Fargue, 'than the sick man does from the doctor. Ah, when I think of the good doctor as we know him nowadays, with his large income, his honoured place in our society, his godship in the hospital, his ghastly cottage in the country, and how all this depends on a wretch not unlike your criminal, André—on the poor, terrified, pain-racked creature in the public ward. Where would the doctor be without him? He would have to find other work.'

'Yes,' said Breton, arranging his hair, 'I envisage a millennium in which lawyers will be reduced to the condition of village secretaries, and doctors to being dispensers of euthanasia and abortion.'

I found these ideas very entertaining in their Gallic way.

Maria Jolas approached me and asked if I would like to be presented to Narwhal, the famous photographer and surrealist painter.

I found Narwhal much more sympathetic than the literary surrealists. Tall and thin, with large horn-rimmed glasses and a talon-shaped nose like an owl's, he walked pigeon-toed, was dressed in black, wore his hair in a neat bang, and was speaking with great wit in a quiet nasal voice that retained a strong Brooklyn accent.

'So this man from the U.S. Internal Revenue,' he was saying, 'he wants to know how much dough I made in the past year. "I don't know, I don't keep records, I'm an ahtist," I said.—"How much do you get for taking a person's picture?"—"It depends. Sometimes I get a lot of dough. The amount varies: sometimes nothing, sometimes I pay the subject myself."—"Well, how much does it average?"—"I told you, I don't keep records. If I did I wouldn't have time to take pictures."

—"You mean you don't have a bank-account—a big-name photographer like you are? You don't keep your money in your pocket, do you?"— "Yes, that's just where I do keep it. Not in a bank, good God no. What would I do walking in and out of a *bank*?"—"Well," he says, "as a citizen of the United States, you got to pay income tax."— "That's what the law says, I know."—"Look, mister," he says, "you're making us a lot of work."—"Sure," I said, "but you're making a regular salary out of it. What's more, you're a man that understands figures, you can *count*, while I'm an ahtist. So you go ahead and have your office figure out how much I might owe you, and then we'll see. After all, if you nailed Al Capone I guess I shouldn't give you too much trouble." So he went away.'

'How did you come out?' I asked.

He peered at me solemnly. 'I don't know, the matter is still pending. They write me letters now and then.'

After a while he said thoughtfully, 'The experience was quite fruitful. It made a lot of things plain to me. I devised a sculpture on the subject, treating it abstractly—not exactly a sculpture, not an *objet trouvé*. No, I suppose you might call it more of an artifact—two squares of black wood fastened together by a piece of old automobile chain. A very powerful thing, it turned out, with overtones of satire.'

'What did you call it?'

'*N is for Nothing.*'

He then told me of his idea of doing an imaginary portrait of the Marquis de Sade. 'You know,' he said, 'there was no portrait of that gentleman ever made, so I'll have a free hand. I'm going to represent him as being real big and fat, as indeed he became towards the end of his days in the Charenton lunatic asylum, and make the face all out of blocks of prison stone, with the courtyard of the Bastille in the background and two or three desolate little figures staggering around inside the walls. Sade is perhaps the most interesting writer in France since Marceline Desbordes-Valmore. We'll be hearing a lot about him very soon. He's the forerunner of all the *Freivögeln*.'

'Not a hypocrite, certainly. But his ideas do not seem well organized.'

'They were at the mercy of his temperament. Of what philosopher or moralist can't you say the same thing? Their masks are simply better adjusted than his, their rational and metaphysical apparatus is a little neater.'

Since then I have re-read all Sade's books and agree with Narwhal's view of him. It was certainly not the view of a simple 'artist', much less a photographer, and testified to a vision that was immediate, direct, naïve in the best sense, and quite unswayed by tradition or prejudice.

'Would you like to meet Ford Madox Ford?' he asked. 'I understand you write, and he is a well-known English man of letters.'

Ford inclined graciously towards us from what seemed to be a height of about seven feet. His reputation, his high wheezing voice, and his walrus moustache were frightening until one saw his small twinkling eyes, which were full of kindness and curiosity.

'You write poetry, my young friend,' he said. 'I wonder if you would mind my asking whether your poems are sad or joyous?'

'Mostly joyous, I'm afraid.'

'Admirable. I was talking to Willie Yeats the other day,' he said, 'about the communication of joy in poetry. Why should it, we were both wondering, be so much more difficult—and therefore so much more seldom attempted—than the communication of sorrow? It is not so in prose. Dickens is at home in either joy or sorrow. Meredith excels in the former, as do the naturalists like White, Jefferies, Buckland and Waterton. But why is there so little joy in poetry?'

'There must be some in Shakespeare,' said Narwhal.

'Yes, but only in the songs, my dear fellow. He knew that joy is something instantaneous, it cannot be held for more than a moment. One does not sift and handle the shining grains, one lets them pour out with a single gesture.' His hand moved like a sower's. 'But Willie and I were asking ourselves what was the most joyous *modern* poem in English. And do you know, we couldn't think. What is your opinion, my young friend? Come now, tell me.' He placed his fingers together like a schoolmaster. 'A joyous English poem.'

'Shelley's "Skylark"? Hopkins' "Pied Beauty"? Of course they're not exactly modern.'

'Good try, good try! But no.' He shook his head. 'No, there's something febrile, almost hysterical, in those two. They just won't do. No,' he repeated with enormous satisfaction, 'there isn't one. All modern poetic effusions of joy are definitely unbalanced. Very well. Now, if poetry expresses the reality of existence—as I believe, along with Willie Yeats, it does, and as I hope you will too, my young friend—it follows that the experience of joy is in the nature of a fever, of hysteria, and not a well-founded natural human experience or condition. Therefore we can say: joy itself is hysteria, a drunkenness, an unnatural state.'

'Would you say that was why the French poet Baudelaire said, "Man, be always drunken"?' asked Narwhal.

'Undoubtedly. You've hit it. The poet, you see—who is essential, veritable man, as we know—is more at home in sorrow. And a further and irrefragable proof of this can be found in that dreadful hymn, "Jerusalem, my happy home", which is sung by thousands of my benighted countrymen on Sundays.'

His logic was overpowering. Driving home later with Georges Pol, Diana Tree, and Graeme, I felt, moreover, that if neither he nor Yeats had been able to think of a joyous modern poem in English there could not be one, and I was further confirmed in my decision to stick to prose.

FIVE

It was April, and to my artistic uncertainty was added the sensuous disturbance of the season. Life in the Jules-César was now much better; the radiators seemed to lose their inadequacy and one could breathe; baths were no longer an ordeal. The sidewalk tables of the Dôme and the Coupole multiplied and spread along the boulevard du Montparnasse, where the few spiky trees were budding in their little iron cages.

In the midst of it all came a letter from my father asking about the progress of my literary career. I answered saying I was studying the novels of Peacock, in whom I claimed to have found the model and exemplar of English prose and whose name I used as a kind of character reference, feeling sure it would strike the right note when repeated to the head of the English department at McGill, in whose judgement on literary matters my father placed the greatest confidence. I knew there was no use mentioning surrealism or *transition*. In using Peacock in this way, however, I was not deceiving anyone, as he had always seemed to me one of the finest English novelists of all time, and the possessor of a style superior even to Henry James'. The only deception as far as my father was concerned lay in the fact that this author was not, as I implied, a new discovery of mine; but I wished to give the impression of breaking new ground.

Here I must admit that I was always, though mainly in self-defence, a great practitioner of deceit. My father's ferocious attachment to truth, and his insistence from my childhood on my speaking it at all times and in spite of the direst consequences, had made me an accomplished liar at an early age; the constant need for lying had in fact sharpened my invention and contributed enormously to my enjoyment of the highest forms of poetry.

Nothing could rouse us from the delicious lethargy of the Parisian spring. Graeme had stopped planning *The Flying Carpet* and I had ceased to write altogether. Our days, like those of Eliot's hippopotamus, were passed in sleep, while the nights were spent at one or other of the small *dancings* in the Latin Quarter in company with Daphne, Yvonne, Caridad, or Adolf Dehn, by whom Graeme and I had been introduced to places like Les Noctambules in the rue Champollion, where one could sit in a comfortable cellar all night long over excellent gin fizzes, listening or dancing to the music of accordions before staggering out into the smoky violet dawns.

On one of these nights Adolf made a fine pencil-drawing of me, half caricature and half likeness. 'I rather missed your self-conscious poetic expression,' he said, 'but the hand, the necktie and the cigarette are first-rate. I think I got the shoulders too.'

'*Merde!*' said a voluptuous black-haired girl whom we had asked to sit with us and whom Adolf had long had his eye on. 'What a fine drawing! Now do one of me, *monsieur le pasteur.*' Adolf's grey hair and fatherly smile had earned him this name with the girls of Les Noctambules.

While she posed with her bust thrown back and her head on one side he rapidly drew one of the cruellest caricatures I had ever seen. She took a single look at it, spat on the floor, and left.

'I knew I couldn't make her,' he explained.

I had received word from Eugene Jolas that 'Conan's Fig' had been accepted for publication, but the date of its appearance was still uncertain. I saw Diana Tree from time to time; and one evening in the Falstaff she called to me from where she was sitting with a small party of middle-aged women in a dark corner.

'I would like you to meet Willa Torrance,' she said when I went to their table. 'Willa, here is a moderately intelligent young man. He comes from Montreal, in Canada.'

'Why?' she said, repeating Dr Johnson's *mot* with a forced sneer.

The famous novelist was dressed in a badly fitting sleazy purple dress and a shapeless Napoleonic hat, with gloves and a long chatelaine; but the costume only heightened her air of distinction. Her eyes, protruding and heavy-lidded, were extremely beautiful, though she lacked any repose of manner.

'Sit down,' said Diana, and introduced me to the rest of the party whose names escaped me except that of a tall, beautiful, dazed-looking girl called Emily Pine, who had the largest pair of feet I had ever seen. I heard later that Emily Pine was a fatal woman, at least as far as Willa Torrance was concerned, and was also a kind of female *bourreau des coeurs*.

'This boy has read so much,' said Diana carelessly, 'and his judgements are original though not to be relied on. I don't think he likes my own work, and I wonder what he thinks of yours.'

I had read two of her novels and found them emotional to the point of hysteria, but I complimented her on her latest effort. She lowered her eyes: 'Thank you.'

The conversation then languished and I felt more than ever out of place among these women, whose faded asexuality was marked by the kind of fiercely possessive passion that is generally and more properly expended on cats and dogs. I believed that my feeling was shared, though dimly and through a miasma of laziness and unformulated discontent, by Emily Pine.

There is nothing, I have found, more dangerous to young people than middle-aged women who have renounced all pretension to coquetry, for the sheer force of their desires is channelled into a cannibalistic selfishness, an appetite that has engrossed all the resources of their charm, brains, and conscious appeal as human beings. True, many elderly men also deploy the same forces *vis-à-vis* the young of both sexes; but there is with them, I think, a less ruthless, mindless determination, and their efforts are generally tempered by a certain sense of decency and measure, of regard for those juniors whom they consider as desirable objects rather than as victims or trophies.

I admired Willa Torrance; but I was made diffident by the sense of a disparity between her interests and my own.

I lapsed into silence. I had often been troubled by the feeling of not belonging in any age-group at all. As a boy whose tastes far outran his years, I was never at home among my contemporaries; on the other hand a certain enthusiasm, even a foolish ebullience of spirit—a kind of irreverence and thoughtless feeling for the superficially absurd—made me quite unfit for serious conversation with adult persons for whom life was necessarily a grave business. The truth was, my limitations were great. I did not have the experience of either poverty, thwarted ambition, or unrequited love.

The women were passing around the page-proofs of a book that was later to cause a small sensation in literary and lesbian circles. I remember being taken by the style, at once sprightly and spinsterish. I have never seen a copy since, but I like to think the book held much of the charming spirit of that year 1928, with its playfulness, its refreshing candour, and its refusal to bow the knee in any house where shallow thoughts are delivered in deep voices. This, it is true, was the time when I regarded Wycherley as the finest English comic dramatist, the superior of Congreve, Sheridan or Wilde, and when I loved the poetry of Rochester this side idolatry.

Emily Pine's lovely brooding face, with its expression of settled discontent, assumed a look of growing disgust as the sheets were passed around. I found her, therefore, the only member of the group with whom I was in sympathy and concentrated my attention on the problem of seducing her.

This, I saw, would be extremely difficult. She was entirely without humour, and one had moreover to pick one's words with the greatest care, as they were all taken literally; on the other hand she looked on any compliment as being by its very nature impertinent and, what was worse, insincere. Yet this almost cretinesque mentality, combined with undeniable charms of the statuesque order and a certain air of heedlessness and helplessness, had a great appeal.

The first problem was to separate her from her tedious companions without attracting too much attention to myself. Accordingly I excused myself from the table, and, calling Joe the Bum aside, asked him to page Miss Pine and tell her she was wanted on the telephone in the back room. When she arrived there I apologized for my stratagem and suggested we meet later in the little *tabac* around the corner. Her reaction was not encouraging.

'Are you sane?' she asked, looking me up and down.

'Certainly. I was bored with everyone out there except you.'

'What a silly trick to play.'

'How else did you expect we were to speak to each other privately? You're being watched liked a vestal virgin.'

'Ha, ha, ha.'

Hearing her deep bray for the first time, I was almost ready to call off my project. She turned to leave but I stopped her, saying, 'At least let me go back a few minutes before you do, so nobody will know.'

She followed me back to the table a good five minutes later, to be met by the anxious inquisition of Willa Torrance, which she dealt with in the simplest manner by refusing to answer a word. She had a great talent for silence, and this, I think, was what made her so fascinating. But the other women were exchanging knowing looks and Willa Torrance was frowning with distress over the mysterious telephone message. I had a moment's remorse, but when I received a sharp look of complicity from Emily my intentions revived. As if the increasing atmosphere of strain that had fallen over the table offered an excuse, I took my leave quietly.

I had not been long in the *tabac* before Emily walked in, sat down beside me, and ordered a Pernod.

'How did you get away?' I said.

'I walked out.'

'Good for you. The company was rather dull.'

'Everything is dull.'

'Not everything. What about the rue de la Gaîté? Would you like to go there?'

She swallowed the rest of her Pernod in a single awesome gulp, paid for it and stood up. 'Let's go.'

We set off up the rue du Montparnasse, crossed the place Edgar Quinet and went up the rue de la Gaîté, which was as lively as usual. Without appearing to, Emily Pine's enormous feet covered the ground with surprising speed, and her way of dealing with the crowd on the sidewalk was to plough straight ahead; when she struck or jostled a passerby she merely staggered, shook her splendid shoulders, regained her balance and moved forward, as if following the impulse of some powerful inner direction. Such determination, however aimless, was impressive. This young woman, I thought, would not be easily stopped or diverted. All at once she halted abruptly and gave me a dazzling smile.

'How about having a drink?' she said, pointing to a workingmen's bar.

We stood at the counter where she quickly drank half another Pernod. Then, looking around at the other customers in their aprons and

35

blouses, she said, 'I like it here. And I like you too. You have a *gamin* quality.'

I understood that in making this idiotic remark she was merely repeating, like a child, something that had once been said to herself and that she had resented.

'Thanks. You know, you remind me of a leopard.'

'Why?' she asked, her eyes lighting up for the first time.

'Because you are independent, luxurious, and quiet.'

Her response to this opening gambit was surprising. Her lids came down over her eyes, then all at once she gripped my hand and ground the knuckles viciously together; her strength was remarkable and I felt such pain that I impulsively raised my heel and drove it back against her shin. Showing her teeth, she dropped my hand and began to laugh. 'Did I hurt you?'

'Not enough to matter.'

We left the bar and walked on up the rue de la Gaîté. I was still wondering just how I was going to seduce her when she stopped suddenly outside the brightly lit Bobino Theatre where 'Papa Becquelin and his Performing Cats' were advertised. 'I'd like to see this,' she said. 'It's my treat.'

The only seats left were in a stage box, which we had all to ourselves. Papa Becquelin had not yet come on and a fat man in a dress-suit was introducing *Jo-jo, le sportif Peau-rouge, dans le célèbre jeu des Iroquois.* Jo-jo, in full regalia of feathers, fringe, and beads, his forehead shortened by a bristling black wig, then displayed his skill and endurance in the celebrated Iroquois game that consisted in balancing iron cannon-balls on his head, tossing them fifteen feet in the air, and letting them land with a shattering thud on the back of his neck. The man was obviously a mental defective.

'I'm getting out of here,' I said. 'I'll be back for the animal act.'

'Quitter.'

I had meant to return in a few minutes, after Jo-jo's act was over, but in the lobby I saw some blown-up photographs of Papa Becquelin— in one of which he was spinning a miniature ferris-wheel to which were fastened half-a-dozen terrified cats dressed in straw hats, trousers and skirt—and decided it was not for me. I went across the street to another bistro and ordered a brandy and water. I had decided to drop the idea of seducing Emily Pine: it was too much trouble.

Then I saw her coming out of the theatre and gazing up and down the street. She looked disturbed, and seeing the tears streaming down her cheeks I called to her. She came to the counter beside me and at once ordered a Pernod. I led her to a table at the back of the room.

'God, those poor pussycats,' she sobbed quietly.

'Don't cry. I'll tell you a story. Once upon a time there were three little princesses —'

'Balls,' she said suddenly and stopped crying. 'You're just treating me like a kid. And I bet I'm older than you are. Let's go to the Petite Chaumière.'

I knew this place in Montmartre only by hearsay, as a high-priced stamping-ground for pathics and female impersonators. But on her saying she knew the *patronne* and we could drink there for nothing I agreed.

'I left my car somewhere near the Sphinx,' she said.

We went back towards the Montparnasse station and found the car parked outside the imposing Egyptianesque building which housed that extremely high-priced brothel. She drove the little red dangerous-looking Bugatti, from which the muffler had been removed, magnificently but like a madwoman. Perhaps we were not going more than forty miles an hour, but the closeness to the ground and the earsplitting noise gave the impression of travelling twice as fast.

The doorman at the Petite Chaumière was a foretaste of the delights of the place. A small wizened man plastered with powder and rouge and wearing a kilt, he helped us out of the little car with giggles and gestures, crying, '*O la belle Emilie, que tu me rends heureuse! Il est si longtemps que tu ne viens. Attends, attends, que j'dirai à Madame Maillot!*' He skipped in ahead of us and came out followed by a huge woman wearing a black lace dress and smoking a cigar, who folded Emily in her arms. We went in and sat at the bar where Madame Maillot stood us some inferior champagne. I looked about the murky pink-lit room and saw a number of men dancing around who were made up and dressed like women, though not very convincingly. I was struck by the bad taste they all showed in their addiction to masses of feathers, beads and costume jewellery; their wigs also were not of the best quality. The waitresses I found much more attractive, for they were bare to the waist; but on looking closely I saw they were also men wearing artificial breasts apparently made of rubber.

'Would you like to dance?' Madame Maillot asked, pushing a blond *travesti* at me.

I found him a first-class partner but was distracted from the pleasure of dancing by his putting his tongue in my ear; after a while I increased the speed of my turns and ended by almost spinning him off his feet.

'God, you've made a hit,' said Emily when he followed me back to the bar. 'Let's give him some of our champagne.'

'Not on my account, Emily.'

I was becoming quite drunk and all my passion for her had returned. I asked her to dance.

'Oh really,' she said, 'I don't dance at all well.'

'Come,' I said, taking her in my arms and leading her to a quiet corner of the floor, 'you must give me this pleasure. Can't you see I'd rather dance with you than with any of these creatures?'

She was a very bad dancer but the thrill of holding this beautiful big body made up for everything. I confined myself to marking time and avoiding her large feet, which was not difficult since the awkward movements of her hips telegraphed their position with perfect accuracy. I began caressing the back of her neck softly and was delighted to see her eyes close.

'You really do care for me, don't you?' she murmured.

'Yes, of course. In fact, I'd like to go to bed with you. Sorry, I hope I'm not frightening you.'

'Frighten me?' she bridled. 'No one frightens Emily Pine.'

'Ask Madame Maillot to let us have a room then. I dare you.'

Without a word she marched off the dance floor and whispered to Madame. In five minutes we were in a hot, dark, airless little nest on the next floor up, all horsehair, mirrors, red plush, and tassels. Emily, staggering slightly, put her arms around my neck. I kissed her, very carefully, on the cheeks. When I came to her a few minutes later she had taken off her clothes and was lying on the bed with her eyes tightly closed. I had never seen a more beautiful body; to find it was quite frigid was a great disappointment.

'Now let's have another drink,' she said.

'No, we'd better go. I think there are peep-holes in the wall over there.'

'Who cares? We gave them their money's worth. You go ahead, I'm staying right here. I'm tired.' Suddenly she began to snore.

I got dressed, went down and spoke to Madame Maillot.

'She's not sleeping here,' she said, puffing angrily at her cigar. 'You take her home in the little car. Right away.'

'I don't even know where she lives.'

'Some hotel around St Sulpice. I'll wake her up and find out.'

'Is there any of that champagne left?'

'No, your blond boy friend finished it.'

'Will you give me a glass on the house? I'm broke.'

She made a hideous face. 'Just one,' she said, signalling to the barman before going upstairs.

She came down carrying Emily with a kind of fireman's lift. I took the other side and we manhandled her into the Bugatti.

'She says it's the Hôtel Récamier on the Place St Sulpice. Drive carefully, now.'

Having no driver's licence, I drove back to the Left Bank at a nice easy pace and had the luck not to see a single policeman. It was just before dawn when I got to the hotel, and after waking the night clerk and a *valet de chambre* I handed Emily over to them, still snoring and insensible. For a minute I thought of driving the Bugatti back to the Jules-César, but decided not to crowd my luck and went back on foot. It had not been an entirely satisfactory night.

Six

Spring was laving the city in warmth and pale gold.

'I have sad news for you two gentlemen,' said the proprietor of the Hôtel Jules-César. 'I must raise the price of your room. This cuts me to the heart, for I understand you are men of letters and I am a great admirer of literature in any language. From now on your room will cost you an extra ten francs a day—to cover my increased expenses.'

'But surely,' said Graeme, 'your expenses will not be so high now, with no heating?'

'Put it in a new way, then. We are all caught up in the inexorable law of supply and demand. It is the month of May, you see, and the Americans are coming.'

Making a survey of hotel prices in the neighbourhood, we found they had all been raised for the same reason. This was discouraging. We saw ourselves forced to spend much less on food or drink, and perhaps on both. That evening we met Daphne Berners at the Dôme. She was looking as handsome as ever in the tailored suit and fedora hat.

'Angela and I are going tomorrow to live with an old hake in Marly,' she said. 'She wants me to paint her portrait—in renaissance costume. I can stretch the job out for two or three months because we both love the green grass and the birds, not to mention all the good country food and the nice fresh milk and cheese. Do you want to sublet our studio?'

We agreed immediately and moved our trunks there the next day.

The place looked even better by daylight. The little strip of garden facing the row of studios now turned out to be filled with friezes and sculptures discarded by former tenants who had either left them in payment of rent or found them too heavy to move. They were of many styles and periods. There was a portrait-bust of a man in a frock-coat with his palm supporting his chin in a fine, melting, bourgeois-romantic attitude; a bas-relief of the Three Graces in which, contrary to custom, they were all seen from behind; and an astonishing sculpture representing a pair of standing Eskimos locked in the act of coitus, like a double peanut, and giving a powerful impression of unity. Opposite the studio was a ramshackle booth housing three stand-up toilets.

The studio itself combined beauty and inconvenience. There was no electricity, only a cold-water wash-basin, and the roof leaked badly though fortunately not on the beds. But it was about 40 feet by 60, 20 feet high at least, with a full skylight and a whole north wall made up of waist-high windows. To us, who had been cooped up in the windowless little room in the Jules-César all winter, it brought a message of physical freedom. For furniture there was a big battered desk with a leather top, a round table to eat at, four comfortable swaybacked chairs, some tattered tapestry curtains flanking the alcove, and two double beds stuffed with straw. There were a few unfinished portraits still in canvas stretchers on the roughly plastered walls—all of them, Daphne told us, by Lady Duff Twysden, who later figured as the insufferable heroine of *The Sun Also Rises*. The only complication, it turned out when we signed the inventory, was that everything in the studio belonged to different people—most of the furniture to Janet Flanner, the hangings to Dr Maloney, and the beds to a man called Boomhower, whom we never met; the only things Daphne owned were the collection of half-broken dishes, the pots and pans, the gramophone, and a great adjustable cheval-glass. We never knew who owned the lease, and merely paid the rent to the concierge, an old woman called Madame Hernie who lived across the street and spent all her time illuminating the entries in a folio-sized album devoted to the records of her family funerals.

This place was to be our home on and off for the next year and a half. It was here that I tried seriously to write for the first time, here I brought my two or three girls, and here I met the woman with whom I at last fell in love and whom, however miserable the outcome of that love, I shall always remember in this setting as she undressed one night in a luminous haze of gaslight and moonbeams before we threw ourselves in ecstasy on one of Mr Boomhower's straw-stuffed beds. It was the theatre of my youth.

The rue Broca was a good deal farther from Montparnasse than the Jules-César, but the studio was cheaper and more comfortable than the hotel-room, and the exercise of walking a mile to the quarter every evening did us both good. We had already had quite enough of the Right Bank and had long since given up the luxury of taxis. We now explored the working quarter to the east, the network of streets running off in all directions from the rue de la Glacière, the home of unusual occupations and trades: of the producers of catskin waistcoats, fake antiques, glass eyes, woodworking machinery, and martinets for punishing children. We learned the elements of cookery, bought a shopping-basket, and came home weighed down with wine and cheese. Waking at eleven o'clock we had a view of sunstruck steeples, chimney-pots, and the greenery of the neighbouring Ursuline Convent, and every day on our way to Montparnasse we passed the handsome medieval walls of the city madhouse and the Santé prison. Graeme had resumed planning *The Flying Carpet* and I was writing the third chapter of this book when I received another letter from my father.

'You have now been almost two months in Paris,' he wrote, 'and after further consideration of your project of a literary career I must once more express my disapproval. As you well know, I altogether disapprove of literature as a futile and unmanly pursuit and one that cannot but lead to poverty and unhappiness. I accordingly advise you that your allowance from now on will be halved.'

This was a blow. However, fifty dollars a month was enough for us to get along on for a while, and the rent was paid for three months.

'Perhaps,' said Graeme, 'one of us should get some kind of work. I'll go to the *Chicago Tribune* and see if they need a proofreader.'

But they did not. In the evening we decided to go to the counter of the Dôme and drink until things looked rosier.

Diana Tree was there. She had by now severed her connection with her surrealist lover and was living alone. She was talking of Raymond Duncan, a walking absurdity who dressed in an ancient handwoven Greek costume and wore his hair in long braids reaching to his waist, adding, on ceremonial occasions, a fillet of bay-leaves.

'He's really not a bad kind of person,' she said. 'He has a heart of gold and some of his designs for weaving are very chaste. Damn it all, he is sincere.'

'Rats,' said a small, handsome, carelessly dressed man standing beside her. 'He's an exhibitionist with nothing to show. He's trying to prove he's something besides being Isadora's brother, and he's not. His milieu is the bourgeoisie. Yah!'

'Have you met Robert McAlmon?' said Diana. 'Bob, these are the boys from Montreal.'

He looked at us with humorous contempt. 'Have a drink,' he said. 'Di has been telling me about you. You're Canadians. I was in the Canadian army for a while during the war but I deserted.'

I had heard of him only as a minor legend, as a man saddled with the nickname of 'Robber McAlimony', which he had gained by marrying a wealthy woman and then living alone and magnificently on an allowance from her multimillionaire father. I was at once impressed by his charm, loneliness and bitterness, touched by his vanity and refreshed by his rudeness; even at this first meeting he was impressive through a total absence of attitude or artifice. I had not yet read anything he had written.

After a few more drinks he proposed going to the bar of the Coupole. 'I've a charge account there,' he said. 'Paying for drinks is depressing. Come on, kids!'

At the Coupole we switched from vermouth to brandy. McAlmon's own capacity for alcohol was astounding: within the next half-hour he drank half a dozen double whiskies with no apparent effect. His conversation, consisting of disjointed expletives and explosions of scorn, was fascinating in its anarchy. He admired no writing of any kind, either ancient or modern; all government was a farce; all people were fools or snobs. He spoke of his friends with utter contempt, insulted Diana and laughed at Graeme and me—but all with such an absence of conviction that one could not take him seriously. He was obviously enjoying himself. I soon became hungry—for Graeme and I, following our new plan of saving money, had gone without lunch.

'We'll have dinner here,' Bob said, and at once ordered a *canard pressé* and two bottles of Moselle.

The duck arrived half an hour later and there was barely enough for three. Diana, however, had made a point of ordering three double ice-cream sodas from the American soda-fountain to finish off with. 'The boys,' she said, 'have good appetites. That duck, McAlmon, is just a snob dish. You always order it. Will you tell me for God's sake why?'

He threw back his head. 'It makes no demands on me. It has an elegant quality and I can face eating it and seeing other people eating it. Now let's all have another drink.'

'Not for me,' she said. 'I have to get back to my love-child in St Cloud, bless his black little heart.' She turned to me as she went out: 'Good night, don't drink too much, and watch out for the Great White Father.'

McAlmon now turned his wit against Graeme and me. I had already noticed his small thin mouth and piercing stare, but it was clear he was far from being the kind of invert whose predilection shapes his whole personality.

'What did Diana say to you?' he said, drawing his chair up.

'Not to drink too much.'

'Rats, what you two need is a good drunk.' He pushed between us, putting his arms around our shoulders 'Come out of yourselves. Be extrovert. You especially,' he pinched my ear. 'Forget all this turd about the literary life for a while. It doesn't suit you at all.'

I nodded. He was rich, famous and extremely amusing, and moreover I liked him enormously.

It soon appeared that his chosen role was to be the fatherly or avuncular, and I began to hope he was more vain of being seen with young men than actually covetous of their favours. This hope was dispelled by a burly, moonfaced man, dressed in baggy tweeds and with his necktie clewed by a gold pin, who came noisily into the bar and greeted our table with a loud, 'Well, Bob, up to your old tricks again?'

McAlmon's sallow face turned pink. 'If it isn't Ernest, the fabulous phony! How are the bulls?'

'And how is North America McAlmon, the unfinished Poem?' He leaned over and pummelled McAlmon in the ribs, grinning and blowing beery breath over the table. 'Room for me here, boys?'

43

'It's only Hemingway,' said Bob loudly to both of us. 'Pay no attention and he may go away.'

Hemingway gave a lopsided grin and moved into a seat at the next table. He was better looking than his pictures, but his eyes were curiously small, shrewd and reticent, like a politician's, and he had a moustache that was plainly designed to counteract the fleshy roundness of his jowls, though it did not. I found him almost as unattractive as his short stories—those studies in tight-lipped emotionalism and volcanic sentimentality that, with their absurd plots and dialogue, give me the effect of a gutless Prometheus who has tied himself up with string.

'See anything of Sylvia these days?' he asked diffidently.

'The Beach? Rats, no! We had a row last year. I don't like old women anyway.'

'No one could accuse you of that, Bob.'

'Leave my friends out of this.'

'Me? You brought them in. Anyway, go to hell.' Hemingway got up and moved heavily to the bar.

'Watch,' said Bob. 'Pretty soon he'll be twisting wrists with some guy at the bar. Trying to establish contact. Ah ha ha ha! and he never will. Just a poor bugger from the sticks. But believe me, he's going places, he's got a natural talent for the public eye, has that boy. He's the original Limelight Kid, just you watch him for a few months. Wherever the limelight is, you'll find Ernest with his big lovable boyish grin, making hay. Balls. We'd better go to the rue de Lappe. I crave genuine depravity.'

He herded us outside and into an open taxi. The night was like velvet, the spring sky full of stars, the air soft and humid and full of the exciting smell of city dust laid by sprinklers. My stomach, at last assimilating the mixture of vermouth, brandy, duck, wine and ice-cream soda, was soon settled by the motion of the wheels. We went down the boulevard Raspail, along St Germain, crossed the Pont Sully to reach the Bastille, and then slid into a mysterious, sinister street lit here and there by the lights of little *dancings*. We stopped outside the Bal des Chiffoniers.

"Now watch out, boys,' said Bob in a conspiratorial tone. 'Don't get high-hat with anyone. If they want to dance with you, go ahead. But don't let them steer you into the can or you'll get raped.'

I liked the Bal des Chiffoniers. Unlike the Petite Chaumière it was brilliantly lit and the atmosphere was genuine. These pale weedy youths

44

in shabby tight-fitting suits, sporting so many rings and bracelets, these heavy men with the muscles of coal-heavers, rouged, powdered and lip-sticked, these quiet white-haired elders with quivering hands and heads and the unwinking stare of the obsessed—all conveyed the message of an indomitable vitality, a quenchless psychic urge. Never had I felt the force of human desire projected with such vigour as by these single-minded devotees of the male; and I felt at the same time that this very desire, barely tolerated and so often persecuted by society, had already made its tragic marrïage of convenience with the forces of a stupid criminality simply because both were equally proscribed and hunted down. These profound thoughts were interrupted by Bob calling for champagne.

Even before it arrived Graeme had been seized upon as dance partner by an odd creature in a silver-laced black velvet doublet and shoulder-length ringlets, who spoke in a strange archaic French because, as he said, he was reproducing the graces, at once virile and baroque, of the age of Louis XIII. For my own part I was soon being waltzed around the floor by a coal-black Negro of ferocious appearance who never ut-tered a word but danced so well that I even began to enjoy myself. The vertigo of the French waltz, whoever one's partner, is always su-perior to that induced by alcohol.

When the band stopped the Negro led me back silently to our table, where Bob was sitting and drinking a magnum of *mousseux*. He was about to leave when Bob told him to sit down.

'I'll bet you're an American,' he said in English. 'Come on. Aren't you?'

The Negro grinned shyly. 'Sure I am, you guessed it. Name of Jack Relief, but trying to pass for a foreigner. I thank you kindly and I *will* join you for a few minutes, being solitary here. My, but don't your friend here dance good! A petal, a feather, a regular pussycat on his foot-sies. Can I offer you all a genuine Cuban cigarillo?' He presented a silver case. Bob did not smoke, but Graeme and I took the thin brown cigarettes and lit them. The aroma was delicious but the smoke was curiously perfumed.

'This is a nice place,' I said. 'Do you come here often?'

'Sure, I admire the atmosphere. It has colour. I'm a great lover of colour in any form. The colour of this place is, to speak right out of my imagination, a kind of yellow-green.'

'No,' said Bob. 'It's mauve, a turd-brown mauve.'

'Perhaps you are speaking, sir, in a popular or accepted way of verbiage. When I identified it as yellow-green I was employing the subjective spectrum of Mallarmé or possibly Rimbaud. In that acception, I would beg to differ, though such impressions are always differential and a matter of dispute.'

'I see you're literary,' said Bob. 'Who is your favourite author?'

'Shakespeare,' said Jack Relief without hesitation. 'And after him Thomas Hardy.'

'Hardy? No, no. Too grim, too rustic. He goes around blowing out the candles of the human spirit.'

'Perhaps he is too Protestant, a Jansenist,' said Relief. 'But what breezes blow through his books! Reading Hardy, I feel the wind of Egdon Heath blowing against my poor cheeks. It is the breath of fate, which is also the breath of freedom. We are all involved in that wind.'

I suddenly realized I was nauseated. The room seemed to be whirling and dipping in its blaze of lights. The Negro's cigarette must have been fortified. I managed to get to the door. Graeme followed me, wearing a worried look. I was aware of Bob paying for the *mousseux* and hurrying out to join us.

'He should have some coffee,' he said, pushing me out of the Bal des Chiffoniers and leading the way to a corner café. We stood at the zinc counter and drank boiling coffee laced with chicory. I began to feel better at once.

'You made a hit with the dinge,' Bob was saying.

'I'm sorry I broke the party up. You never managed to dance. And we didn't even finish the champagne.'

'Don't let that worry you. Come on, Graeme. A whisky, you and me. I'll bet we're both Presbyterians. My old man was a minister.'

'So is mine,' said Graeme. 'He never had a church though, he went out on horseback converting the Indians in the Yukon.'

'Rats! They were all converted long ago.'

'No, not from paganism. He was converting them from Catholicism.'

'How did he make out?'

'I think he re-baptized about a hundred. But of course they all went back to Rome eventually.'

'You should tell Ernest about that, Graeme. He's a Catholic and an Indian lover. Christ, I bet he'd make a story out of it. Another of his constipated stories. To hell with literature. Let's go to Bricktop's. How about you, sweetie-pie?'

46

'I'm fine,' I said. 'Let's go to Bricktop's. Where is it?'

'It's a long, long way, but the night is young.' Holding on to the bar with both hands, he began to dance his feet. 'A long, long way to the Place Pigalle, where the pimps are playing, the whores are swaying, the fairies saying, "Won't you dance with me, prance with me, be my pal on the Place Pigalle?"' He kicked his legs in a wild splay-footed shuffle. 'Come on, where's a cab?'

We found another open taxi at the Bastille and drove along the wide bright boulevards—Beaumarchais, Magenta and Rochechouart—until we arrived in the blaze of lights of the spider-web of tourist traps, clip-joints and dives around the Place Pigalle. I had never been here before, and though the way the lights staggered up and down the steep hill was attractive I found the atmosphere of the whole district depressing, with the pimps slouching at every corner, the touts outside the boîtes yelling at the passing groups of soldiers and tourists, and every now and then a passing busload of middle-aged American women peeping out from the sectioned windows. We stood at the counter of the Café Pigalle and had some brandy while Bob snuffed the air like a hound.

'God, what a wonderful smell this quarter has!' he said. 'Just like a county fair back home. It's got a special quality too, so phony you can hardly believe it. The triumph of the fake, the old come-on, the swindle—it's marvellous, it's just like life.'

After being skilfully short-changed for our drinks we went down the hill, fighting off the whores who came flapping out of the darkness at us like birds, until we reached a leather-covered door studded with brass nails and with a small round *vasistdas* at eye-level.

'Why, Mistah Bob!' cried a big Negro in a scarlet-and-gold uniform who threw open the door at once. 'Come in, Mistah Bob! And how you feelin'? Bricktop baby! Come! Here's the big spendin' man himself.'

A small, plump, glowing Negress with a bush of dyed red hair ran up and embraced Bob, twittering, 'Bob honey, so *good* to see you! Just so *good*. You and you young friends want to sit at the bar, huh? Hey you, Houston, get off that stool and give some room to the clients, you hear me? Get behind that bar where you belong!'

A small grinning black man in a white jacket slipped under the bar and came up on the other side.

'First round is on the house, Houston,' said Bricktop. 'Anything the boys desire, except the champagne.'

We had three of Houston's specials. This was a long drink of such potency that the first sip seemed to blow the top of my head off.

Bob, already restive in familiar surroundings, began eyeing the people at the tables with his usual air of challenge and hostility. Bricktop slid up beside Graeme and whispered to him, 'You make Bob behave till I'm done singing, eh baby? I can tell he primed for mischief. I got some very prominent people here tonight, real big folks from show business, and I don't want Bob to insult them right off.'

'Right,' said Graeme. He was always impressive in any situation calling for firmness and quick thinking, and I admired his way of distracting Bob, who already seemed prepared to launch from his stool and accost a party in ball-gowns and tail-coats, among whom I recognized Beatrice Lillie.

'Listen, McAlmon,' he said, 'just why do you run down every book written in the last thirty years? I agree with you about Hemingway, he's not even a serious writer, but what about Fitzgerald? Now isn't *Gatsby* a good book, perhaps a great book?'

'Great? *Great?* Jesus, what is all that snob-crap compared to *War and Peace?*'

'*War and Peace?* A movie by De Mille. A blown-up mural full of characters from a comic strip. An epic for morons.'

Bob gave his lipless smile. 'You know, Graeme, you're right eloquent. You may even have something there. I thought you were just another Presbyterian from the sticks, but I'm changing my mind as of now. Anyway, the only people I don't like are bankers. Are you with me there, Graeme?'

'All the way. My brother's a banker. Ssh . . .'

Bricktop had begun to sing. Her voice, small but beautifully true, tracing a vague pattern between song and speech, fitting itself to the sprung rhythms of a piano played by an old and dilapidated Negro, seemed to compose all by itself a sentiment at once nostalgic and fleeting, anonymous and personal, inside the song itself; her voice followed rather than obeyed the music, wreathing an audible arabesque around her; the melody, something banal by Berlin or Porter, was transformed and carried into a region where the heard became the overheard and the message one of enchanting sweetness and intimacy.

The polite ripple of applause seemed to infuriate Bob. 'Christ, you'd think it was some leached-out phony like Alice Faye singing,' he said. 'These bastards don't know what it's all about. Balls, balls!' he suddenly yelled. 'Ladies and gentlemen, did you know you were dead? I'm speaking to *you*—yes, you collection of pukes and poops right over there. Just listen for a moment. I'm part of the show here. You're getting my act for nothing.'

Someone began to laugh. This put Bob in a good humour. He stood up and bowed with extraordinary grace. 'You, my friends, have the luck to be listening to an old-fashioned sot I speak to you out of my sub-conscious. Some of you seem to be English: I hate the English. Some of you look like Americans: I hate you too. And if there are any Canadians among you, let me say that I hate all Canadians, only not quite so much as Yanks and Limeys.'

'Hear, hear!' said Beatrice Lillie. 'The maple leap forever.'

'Down with the maple leaf!' cried Bob in a sudden fury. 'Bugger the American eagle! This is the age of the rat and the weed, get that through your thick skulls! You're being pushed out, boys, and I'm glad to see it. You're nice and decorative, sure, you've got a nice way of brushing your hair, but you've got to go. It's in the stars. The writing is on the outhouse wall—'

'Now Bob,' said Bricktop, sliding up to him. 'Please Bob, you keep this clean. Come dance with me, honey, and we give all these people time to study out what you just said. Baby, that was a real message! Walter—music now, please. *Shlo*, huh?'

She pulled him onto the dance floor as the old Negro played the opening bars of *Chloë*. Bob, holding Bricktop at arm's length in country style, flapped his feet awkwardly; the alcohol seemed to be at last affecting his balance. But when the music stopped he jumped back nimbly onto his stool, drained his glass and called for a whisky. Bricktop signed to Houston.

Bob downed half the fresh drink and stood up again. 'I'm going to sing! This is an aria from my Chinese opera.' He raised his arms, opened his mouth wide and began a hideous, wordless, toneless scream-ing. The effect was both absurd and painful; a dead silence fell over the room. Reeling against his stool, his head raised to the ceiling like a dog, yowling, he suddenly seemed to be no longer a drunken nuisance but a man who had gone mad; he was, I thought, actually either out of his mind or trying to become so. Suddenly he turned white, staggered, looked around wildly, and fell back into the arms of the big dinner-coated Negro who had appeared at the bar.

'Gentlemen, you give me a hand with Mistah Bob, huh?' said the bouncer jovially.

'The taxi's outside,' said Bricktop. 'Boys, we just done give him a little quietener. Nothing to hurt. He be all right in a half an hour. You give him my love when he wakes up.'

Bob was carefully carried out and lifted into the taxi.

'Where'll we go now?' I asked Graeme.

'We might get something to eat at the Coupole.'

Bob was still unconscious when we reached the Coupole. Lifting him out we saw a two-man bicycle patrol coming along the street. These police, whose job is to survey the city's night life, are the oldest and most brutal of their kind, a different breed from the smirking, bowing, multilingual traffic police on the Right Bank. Remembering that neither Graeme nor I had identity cards, I felt my stomach turning over.

'Ho, ho, what's this?' said the first policeman, stopping his bicycle.

'It's our friend,' said Graeme quickly in English, gesturing. 'An American, he's a drunk, *eever. Americain, eever.*'

'Oh ho! A drunken American, eh?' He got off his bicycle, stepped up to Bob whom we were holding up, slapped his cheeks, felt his pulse, and fingered his clothes. 'It's an American, all right. They're all Americans. This is not our affair. Good night, gentlemen.'

'My God,' I said. 'Suppose we'd answered in French.'

'I thought you were going to. That settles it, we're going down to the Prefecture tomorrow and get identity cards. Now let's get Mistah Bob into the bar.'

He was remarkably light and it was no trouble getting him through the double doors and onto one of the banquettes. I was arranging his hands over his chest when Gaston came running.

'What have you done to him? Good God, he is not dead? He owes me three thousand francs!'

Bob began snoring loudly.

'Thanks be to heaven,' said Gaston. 'What would you like to drink?'

'Two orders of scrambled eggs and two large white coffees.'

When the food came Bob was still snoring, but his sleep was broken by the occasional groan or curse; the Mickey Finn was wearing off. His eyes, cavernous under the ragged eyebrows, began to open and close, his mouth to twitch. I put my hand on his forehead and found it covered with cold sweat.

'Let's try to get some brandy into him,' said Graeme. 'It can't do any harm.'

'He's been drinking whisky for the last six hours, perhaps he shouldn't change.'

He was already trying to sit up when Graeme put a glass of neat whisky under his long Barrymore nose. The reaction was immediate: his hand came up and knocked it to the floor.

'Poison!' he yelled. 'No more poison! Give me some mother's milk.'

Supported by Graeme's arm around his shoulder he drank deeply from our jug of hot milk, shook his head like a dog, and then began to weep quietly.

'Come on, Bob,' I said. 'We'll take you home.'

'I have no home. No home.'

'Well then, where are you staying?'

'I wouldn't have a home if you paid me. Where's my sister?'

'Look, haven't you got a hotel or something?'

'I'm an exile.' The tears were streaming down his cheeks.

They began turning out the lights in the bar.

'We'd better take him back to the studio,' said Graeme. 'If we leave him here they'll just put him out in the street.'

'Come on, Bob,' I said. 'Let's all go to our place.'

'No, no,' he muttered. 'Take me to the Fitzroy Tavern—Fitzroy Square, just around the corner.'

But he made no resistance when we supported him into a taxi. On the way to the rue Broca he seemed to fall asleep again and we carried him through the garden and into the studio. The first cold light of dawn was coming through the windows as we laid him on my bed, took off his shoes, jacket and tie and covered him with a blanket. Waking uncomfortably a few hours later, however, I found he had made his way between Graeme and me and I began to wonder if he had been quite as helpless as he appeared to be in the Coupole bar.

SEVEN

'Don't be dumb,' Bob said when we told him we were going to get identity cards. 'Your passports will show you've been here two months. That means they'll either fine you a couple of thousand francs or deport you: perhaps both. I know those bastards. There's only one way of fixing this. You've got to leave France for a week or so, get your passports stamped again when you come back, and then get your cards.'

'We can't leave France just now,' said Graeme.

'Why not? Why don't you go to Belgium or Luxembourg? They're only a few hours away.'

'The reason is,' I said, 'we haven't got the money.'

'Rats. We'll all go to Luxembourg. I'll pay the fares. I need to get away from here for a while anyway. I've got to revise a book. You could work on that book of yours too; it may not be so lousy as it sounds.'

We took the afternoon train to Luxembourg, each of us with a single bag. The spring landscape passed by, with the fields already green and the woods a pale olive. At Longwy it started to rain; but it was a relief to see our passports being stamped at the border by the Luxembourg customs officer, a grumpy old woman in a blue-skirted uniform and chauffeur's hat. Bob asked for a receipt for his typewriter.

'How do I know it's yours?' said the old woman. 'How do I know you haven't stolen it? Show me the sales receipt.'

'Listen, madam,' said Bob, suddenly becoming very dignified, 'I am a distinguished American man of letters, and if you make any more remarks of that kind I'll report you to my friend Monsieur Pincengrain in the Customs Department, who will fix your clock. Just make out a receipt so I won't have to pay duty on this machine when I come back, and no more crap about it.'

'What a nuisance you Americans are,' she grumbled. 'Why don't all you foreigners stay at home? You would be much happier, believe me.'

'Who is your friend Pincengrain?' Graeme asked when she had left.

'There's no such person. My God, you Presbyterians are dumb.'

We reached Luxembourg late at night. The city looked unutterably desolate, with its wide straight dark empty streets and enormous buildings without a light showing from top to bottom.

'We're going to the lower town,' said Bob. 'It's supposed to be better than this. If it's not, we go right back to Paris.'

The taxi took us across the great stone bridge and things began to look brighter. We arrived in a small central square, one whole side of which was nothing but brilliantly lit cafés. The taxi-fare came to fifteen cents, and the driver bowed to the ground when Bob tipped him five cents more.

'I think we're going to like it here,' said Graeme.

There were small string orchestras playing softly everywhere. Gorgeously uniformed officers were sitting before coloured ices. Solid men in black, with great beards or moustaches, were drinking swollen mugs of brown beer. Around the square little flocks of pretty girls were walking hand in hand, swishing their long home-made skirts and talking to each other with self-conscious animation, while in the opposite direction marched young men in black velveteen trousers cut very wide at the cuff, large floppy black hats, and short jackets covered with silver chains, pins, and emblems.

It was like being transported into an eighteenth-century Europe, a country out of time and space, something to which I related my impression of Sterne and Casanova—those marvellous travellers who give one the feeling of having discovered a new life in every city they reached, who refreshed themselves in the fountains of romance and desire at every stopping-place, and for whom entering a strange town was like putting on a new skin in which to enjoy the divine restlessness of youth.

We sat down on the *terrasse* of the biggest café and ordered brown beer, which was served with a plate of sugared buns as a bonus.

'This isn't a bad place,' said Bob, looking around. 'Of course it's damned bourgeois.'

Around us the conversation was going on either in the softest German or in a dialect that we found out later was the Luxembourger *platt*, a language that sounded like the passage of water over stones.

When we asked the grey-haired waiter to recommend a hotel he told us we had better take rooms over a good restaurant, and then, turning to a benevolent-looking man with a neat white beard sitting at the next table, he introduced him as Monsieur Beffort, a merchant and one of the city aldermen. After some polite conversation Monsieur Beffort decided the right place for us was Chez Nicolas, just around the corner in the Liebfraustrasse. 'Moreover,' he added, 'Monsieur Nicolas is my first wife's second cousin, and he not only makes his own

53

sausages but also gets his wine from his own little vineyard, and both are delicious. Please present this card.'

Thanking him, we went around to Chez Nicolas. On the way we discovered from his card that Monsieur Beffort's business was in ladies' underwear and stockings, and he was the country's largest importer of ostrich-feathers and an accredited *Fournisseur de la Cour*.

Chez Nicolas was a small, handsome eighteenth-century house, one of whose ground-floor rooms had been turned into a small restaurant. Nicolas himself was a stout man with his hair cut *en brosse*, wearing a frock-coat and a pair of wicker cuffs.

The two first-floor rooms for rent were large and alarmingly sump-tuous, with great bow-windows heavily curtained in velours and big four-poster canopied beds so high they had little sets of steps to climb into them by; all the other furniture—tables, washstands, desks, and chests-of-drawers—were of mahogany, highly waxed and topped with streaky white marble. The only drawback to these magnificent rooms seemed to be the location of the single bathroom, which was at the very back of the house and on the ground floor. Monsieur Nicolas, however, pointed out a little curtained alcove in each room, which held a massive mahogany *chaise percée* with a porcelain bucket.

The price of each room was a dollar a day.

'And the meals, how much will they cost?'

'But the meals are included, of course.'

We unpacked immediately.

Sleeping that night was a curious experience, as both mattresses and bedcovers were made of feathers, so that one sank a foot deep into the one and was nearly suffocated by the other.

For breakfast next morning we had fried eggs, small sausages, new bread, jam tarts, and coffee in oversized cups, all in profusion. Bob went back to bed.

Graeme and I walked around the city, which was charming. It is said to resemble Jerusalem, and used to be considered the most im-pregnable fortress in Europe after Gibraltar. But we were mainly struck by the fact that no one seemed to do any work: the cafés were already again full of the same portly men drinking beer and reading newspapers, and as we passed they all looked up, bowed and said good morning, except a beautifully tailored officer with an elaborate white moustache and a great deal of gold braid, who drew himself up and gave a dis-tinguished half-salute.

After admiring the fortifications, which in places are over 200 feet high, the stone bridge, which is the longest single-span structure of its kind in Europe, the view of Les Trois Glans, three mountain-tops so called from their resemblance to the shape of the human penis— which is indeed remarkable—we found ourselves down by the River Else in a semi-rural region of winding roads and small stone cottages. The sun was now quite hot and we sat down on a jetty, took off our shoes, and dabbled our feet in the water; there was a row of big old willows along the bank, the birds were singing, and we watched a king-fisher for a while.

'If we lived here,' said Graeme thoughtfully, 'we could forget all about money for a while. Do you know what American cigarettes cost here? Fifteen cents a package. There doesn't seem to be any duty on anything. I wonder what they run the country on.'

'It must be self-supporting. You notice there are almost no luxuries like radios or automobiles. Still, how can there be so much money when nobody seems to do any work?'

An elderly priest in a cassock and shovel hat came along the road, and seeing us he stopped and greeted us in German.

'I'm sorry, Father,' I said, 'we only speak French, but won't you sit down and help us with a problem about your country?'

'Certainly,' he said in very good French. 'I should be delighted.'

He then explained the internal economy of the country, saying it depended mainly on the rich iron mines in the east but that there were also distilleries, breweries and tanneries.

'But why is everything so cheap?'

'Oh, quite simple, sir. We import very little, our good Grand Duchess Charlotte is wealthy in her own right and doesn't cost us anything, there are no large landowners or concentrations of capital, and almost no external debt. But most important of all, we have no army.'

'But I thought I noticed a few officers in the café last night,' I said.

He smiled. 'The gentlemen you noticed have military costumes and titles, to be sure, but they are either court chamberlains or members of the Grand Ducal Band. By the way, the band plays every Wednesday and Saturday in the square, and the dress-uniforms are magnificent. You must be sure not to miss them. To return to the reasons for our prosperity, I may remind you that we were not involved in the late dreadful war, but on the contrary were able to sell a good deal of iron and steel to both sides. But I must be getting along. Good day, gentlemen.'

We got back to Chez Nicolas in time for lunch but found Bob was still sleeping. We had soup, trout, veal cutlets, fried potatoes, creamed cauliflower, pancakes, and a large pitcher of dry white wine. I thought of how Daphne and Angela would have enjoyed it.

We took coffee on the square, where the portly men were now drinking liqueurs.

Life seemed very pleasant to me and I began to feel that if I could only get rid of my itch for writing I might be quite happy. What, after all, was the use of tormenting oneself by putting words on paper, endlessly arranging and rearranging them, and then, having at last accepted their inherent failure to say more than one-quarter of what they were meant to, of typing out fair copies and hawking the work around to one editor after another until they were printed and perhaps read, if at all, by a few dozen people all busy doing the same thing? One might end up like Bob McAlmon, screaming with frustration in a nightclub.

'Good afternoon,' said Monsieur Beffort, suddenly appearing beside us. 'I trust you are comfortable with my relative Monsieur Nicolas and he is giving you enough to eat? Well now, having discovered that you are all three men of letters, I have taken the liberty, as one of the committee charged with arranging the festivities in honour of our national poet Lenz, of inviting you to the banquet celebrating the centenary of his birth, which is tomorrow. You will find the cards of invitation at your residence. Perhaps you have not heard of our great poet. Because he wrote all his poems in Letzeburgesch, our own Luxembourger *platt*, he is not widely read outside our own country. Some of the speeches will be, perforce, in our official language, which is French, but the pièce de résistance will be the recitation of fifty cantos of Lenz's epic poem, in the original *platt* of course, by his own granddaughter, Madame Lenz-Bessermann, who is not only a *platt* poetess in her own right but an accomplished elocutionist. I may add that a five-course meal will be served, accompanied by all the suitable wines of our country.'

Surprised and touched, we thanked Monsieur Beffort and accepted his invitation on the spot.

'Your acceptance makes me very happy,' he said. 'The banquet will be held in the open air before the statue of Lenz, in the Lenzplatz.'

When we told Bob the news he professed to be unimpressed but was clearly as pleased as we were.

'Rats,' he said. 'This is just one of those civic shindies. Who in hell is Lenz anyway?'

'I wonder how they knew we were men of letters,' I said.

'I gave our professions when I signed the register for us all here. I wonder if there's a barber anywhere. We all need a haircut, you especially.'

'Not me. I've seen the haircuts they give here. Anyway I'm a man of letters now, I don't need one.'

'That reminds me, let me see this autobiography you're writing. At any rate it can't be as bad as those surrealist poems.'

I gave him the first two chapters of this book, inwardly resolving to pay no attention to his opinion of them. Then Graeme and I went out to look for the statue of Lenz.

It was in a little tree-bordered square at the end of the lower town. The poet was represented at full length in a frockcoat, a Byronic collar, and beautifully tapered trousers breaking over his boots; he was holding a flowing scroll in his left hand, his gaze was fixed on the sky, his lips were parted, and with the fingers of his right hand he seemed to be plucking something out of the air over his head. There were already a number of scrubbed tables set out in the square.

Bob came up while we were looking at the statue. 'For Christ's sake,' he said. 'Is this the guy? We all need a drink badly.'

We went back to the Grosplatz, where the heavy men had now switched from beer and buns to aperitifs and anchovies. Many of them were sitting in front of elaborate ice-filled glass tanks with little spigots extending over their glasses. When I learned these were filters for absinthe I at once ordered one and was served an aperitif glass a quarter full of pale green liquid over which was fitted a flanged and perforated spoon holding a large domino of sugar. A tank of ice was then brought and the glass placed under one of the spigots. I had now only to turn a little tap to let the iced water drip slowly over the sugar until the glass was full.

The clean sharp taste was so far superior to the sickly liquorice flavour of legal French Pernod that I understood the still-rankling fury of the French at having that miserable drink substituted for the real thing in the interest of public morality. The effect also was as gentle and insidious as a drug: in five minutes the world was bathed in a fine emotional haze unlike anything resulting from other forms of alcohol. *La sorcière glauque*, I thought, savouring the ninetyish phrase with real understanding for the first time.

For dinner at Nicolas's there was soup, smelts, roast pork, browned potatoes, fresh cabbage, dishes of sour cream, a large cheese, and a pitcher of rosé.

Next morning I heard the clatter of Bob's typewriter and envied the almost uninterrupted sound of the keys. It must be a wonderful thing, I thought, to be able to write so fast. I remembered he had mentioned having already written nine books, with three more in preparation; and then, moved by the spirit of emulation and thinking also of the honours soon to be heaped on the shade of Lenz, I started writing the third chapter of this book. But after about two hundred words I wondered if I was not too close to the events I was relating. Telling myself I had better wait a month and let them settle into a proper perspective, I closed my scribbler with a sense of relief and went for a walk. As usual, I thought, there was plenty of time.

Halfway across the great stone bridge I was so struck by the beauty of the view that I sat down on the low wall and gave myself up to contemplation. A similarly extensive view of life was what I still lacked. I was still distracted and engrossed by detail, I could see every hair and pimple on a human face, without seeing the face itself. I had, moreover, no experience of anything but ecstasy. I had never known despair or anguish, which I looked on as literary expressions. I had not endured hunger, frustration, illness, or chastity; these were the afflictions of others. I had nothing on my conscience and had never wept except from loneliness, fright, or boredom. How then was I qualified to write? Could I go on treating life as an amusing spectacle, a kind of joke? The only serious emotions I had were connected with my sense of the hideously fleeting passage of my own happiness, of the mortal beauty of everything I saw, of the inexorable progression of my own body to decay and death; but the conclusions to be drawn from these seemed neither original nor profound. I was at last faced with the fact that the only thing bothering me was not having enough money and that all I desired in the literary way was not to be a bore.

This was the time, I believe, when grace should have descended on me, penetrating me with the spirit of some kind of universal love, some nobility of purpose, some feeling for my fellow man, or at least bringing me its characteristic message of hope. But I was not, to use the theological word, receptive. *The great obstacle to the influx of grace was my own perfect happiness, and it is well known that God takes no thought for the happy, any more than He does for birds or puppies, perhaps realizing they have no need of Him and mercifully letting them alone. I also thank Him for the same infinite mercy, now when I am making these observations in a hospital; for I have not yet been taught anything but the pointlessness of suffering and feel no deepening of my spiritual apprehensions. All I can do is record the thoughts of a young man as he sat on the bridge of Luxembourg on a warm summer day.*

I got up and walked across the bridge into the new town, which had all the usual pretentious buildings—the offices of the steel cartel, the workers' unions, and other depressing embodiments of group effort. I turned around and went back.

Returning to the lower town I thought about my favourite English poet Wordsworth, the greatest purveyor of neat emotion in the language. It was difficult to enter the consciousness of this cold, reserved man who so mysteriously combined the poet and the prig; but what troubled me now was the recollection that he had stopped writing good poetry after 1798, when he was still under thirty. At that rate, I thought, I had little more than ten years of creativity left and I had barely started. This reflection put me in a sombre frame of mind for the rest of the day and I was only rescued from utter despondency around evening by the sight of a hairy basset-dog harnessed to a small cart full of milk-cans waiting outside a shop. This dog, looking at everything and ceaselessly wagging his tail, deliriously happy in the sphere to which Providence had obviously called him, delighted me. 'Just to be happy,' he seemed to say, 'is enough for me. I don't know or care what I am doing, I only draw my cart because it belongs to my master who is God, and the pleasure of serving him fills me with such a quality of social joy that I simply keep wagging my tail.'

Dear dog of Luxembourg, where are you now? My prayers, for what they are worth, are given to you tonight.

EIGHT

'If I were you,' Bob told me when I got back, 'I'd throw out all that deliquescent, automatistic crap of surrealist poetry and go on with this book of memoirs. It's genuine, it's a human document. Only try not to be so goddamn arch.'

I said I would.

'I'll send the first chapter to *This Quarter*,' he said. 'Ethel Moorhead will like it, she gets a kick out of the antics of children. Now get to work and finish the book. If you can keep up this quality I'll publish the whole thing myself.'

I knew by now that he had published Hemingway's first book, something of Gertrude Stein's, a novel by Marsden Hartley, and poetry by William Carlos Williams, as well as all his own work, and I was filled with joy and fright. He had said to keep up the quality of the writing and I didn't know if I could.

As it turned out I never got past the first page of the fourth chapter because I became so deeply involved in living that I had no time to write. Only now, when I have the leisure, the brightness of my memories, and the unutterable boredom of hospital life to drive me back to writing, have I resumed this chronicle of my dead youth. My dead youth, yes. I am twenty-one now, and have put aside the pleasant foolish things that amuse a young man, such as fornication, clothes and night life. I am now more serious and my chief concern is not to die if I can help it . . .

The festivities in honour of Lenz were to begin at noon, and having dressed ourselves neatly we reached the Lenzplatz in good time. The crowd was already large and mainly made up of the same portly men in black whom we had seen sitting in the cafés on the square, plus the court chamberlains in their military uniforms and a sprinkling of distinguished-looking men in white ties and turn-down collars of the same vintage as those worn by Lenz himself; they were already drinking at the long tables with that air of restrained jollity which was the mark of the true Luxembourger. There was not a woman in sight. Monsieur Beffort, wearing a frock-coat, a number of medals and the cross of an order around his neck, was running to and fro, summoning and dispatching waiters and carrying on conversations with a half-dozen people at once. When he saw us he led the way to a table where we were introduced to a group of foreign-looking men who were speaking a variety of languages, and showed us where we were to sit. I found myself beside an elegant young man who explained that he was the French cultural attaché, and when I identified myself as a poet from Canada he at once asked me if I was familiar with the work of Lenz. Knowing nothing about it, I thought I would find out as much as I could without showing my ignorance.

'Not at first hand,' I said. 'I understand it is very fine, though of course it is an epic.'

'So they say. Not precisely my own favourite genre, but of course it has its points. The difficulty of epic poetry these days, I should say, is to find a subject, and that Lenz should have done so little less than fifty years ago is immensely to his credit.'

Understanding from this that he knew as little about Lenz as I did, I changed the subject to French poetry and asked him what he thought of the surrealists.

He shot me a cautious look. 'I have heard of them of course, but I have no opinion. Officially I read nothing but Claudel.'

'A great man, certainly. But a little heavy, a little Hugolian, I find.'

'I admit,' he said with another quick look around, 'to a weakness for Monsieur Cocteau. A great deal of wit there, I think.'

'Yes, but so little else.'

'Of course he has no *ideas*, sir. But some very happy turns of phrase. Perhaps you know his 'Batterie', in which the poet, lying unclothed on the beach, invokes the tanning power of the sun in a number of couplets of dazzling ingenuity.

>'Le nègre, dont brille les dents
>Est noir dehors, rose dedans.
>
>'Moi je suis noir dedans et rose
>Dehors, fais la metamorphose.'[1]

---

1 The Negro with his flashing grin
Is black without, pink within.

I am black within, pink without:
Sun, turn me inside out.

I had never read these rhymes, which struck me as extremely witty, and recalled one of my favourite couplets from Marvell's poem on the slaughtered fawn that had fed on roses and slept among lilies.

Had he lived longer, he would have been
Lilies without, roses within.

But as I realized that these lines, though more beautiful than Cocteau's, could not compare with the latter in smartness, especially in translation where the delicate arrangement of accents would be lost, I did not quote them.

The band began to play. As the priest had said, it was a very fine band, composed entirely of wind and percussion instruments, and it discoursed music suitable to the occasion, mainly polkas and marches. The conversation at once became more subdued and the waiters began serving trays loaded with hors d'oeuvres of smoked fish, sausages, potatoes in vinegar, sauerkraut, hardboiled eggs and pickled beets, while other waiters filled our glasses with a good brand of hock. Graeme was listening with attention to a square-faced man in a blue suit sitting opposite, who was speaking in English and who turned out to be from the Danish consulate. He was talking about *Hamlet*.

'From a certain sense the play is ridiculous,' he said. 'Hamlet is one of our worst historical figures, all Denmark is ashamed of him. A drunkard, a pagan, a liar, a seducer, a common murderer, and disgusting in his personal habits. This is all in Saxo Grammaticus. The true hero of that time was the good King Claudius, a graceful and instructed man of state, I assure you, whose death led to a nasty invasion of Jutland by our Norwegian neighbours. Fortunately they did not stay long. No, we are not proud of that revolting clown Hamlet, whose notion of humour consisted in imitating the sound of a rooster. It is not as if his crimes and buffooneries had even the excuse of youth, for he was fifty years old when he embarked on his abominable career of dissimulation, treachery and murder. Your English Shakespeare was sadly mistaken.'

'Shakespeare,' protested Graeme, 'was never tied to historical accuracy. If you reduce everything to the facts of history, what were Romeo and Juliet but a pair of juvenile delinquents? Today they would be put in a reformatory, in your country as well as mine.'

The Dane blew out his cheeks. 'You are changing the point. I was arguing that there is nothing truly Danish in the character of Shakespeare's Hamlet. We Danes are a forthright, friendly, athletic people. We are much prouder of the great Lord Nelson, also a Dane.'

The waiters were now serving the fish course, a pie made of smelts and spinach, and conversation was suspended.

The Frenchman beside me was making appreciative noises over his food. 'Tell me,' he said after a while, 'what are your best Canadian dishes? So far I have only tasted maple sugar.'

'You have been unfortunate,' I said. 'We have a salmon from the Gaspé coast, which when lightly boiled and served with egg-sauce and marinated cucumbers is even superior to the Scotch; we have magnificent oysters and lobsters; we have also two delicious vegetables that for some reason you do not cultivate in Europe, sweet corn and green asparagus. We have also very fine beef.'

'You no longer eat the buffalo?'

'They have almost all disappeared.'

'What a pity. I suppose the Indians have killed them all. By the way, I am most interested in the Indians of your northland, those savages who still incarnate, I have been told, the wild independence of your great country. They are, I understand, dignified, reticent, subtle and brave. I think of them often, with their bows and arrows, their free and migratory life as hunters and fishers. Is it not true that the great American novelist Fenimore has plumbed the Indian soul to its depths?'

As I had always found Cooper unreadable I had no satisfactory reply. But I was struck by this fresh instance of the fascination that the Indians held for the modern European, and by the persistence of their romantic image in the mind of a man who would have laughed heartily at a similar conception of the Paris *apache*.

The pie was followed by a roast of veal with browned potatoes, the veal by chicken croquettes, and these by thin sugared pancakes filled with blackberry jam, while the hock was succeeded by a rosé and then by a local champagne. After this the speeches began, but as they were all in *platt* I could make out nothing but the constant reiteration of the name of Lenz. Speaker followed speaker; the applause rang out at almost military intervals and the sun beat down on the bald or white-thatched orators who kept rising from the head table, one after the other.

'Could you tell me what they are saying?' I asked the French attaché, thinking he would be likely to know something of the native language of the country to which he had been sent.

'I have not the slightest idea,' he said. 'We shall find out all about it in the newspapers.'

I had noticed Bob was becoming restive and had even begun to worry whether he might not give some kind of demonstration, when at last the name of Madame Lenz-Bessermann was announced and amidst a roar of applause a tall gaunt woman advanced to a small reading-desk immediately below the poet's statue.

The granddaughter of Lenz wore a trailing black gown cut on medieval lines, with long hanging sleeves, and a Napoleonic hat surprisingly like that worn by Willa Torrance; her large composed face was covered with so much rice-powder that it looked like a death-mask. Her voice, enormously powerful, seemed to come directly from her diaphragm; after a few brief remarks she launched straight into her recitation.

The effect to begin with was pleasant. Whatever the sense or meaning of the lines she was declaiming, their music was undeniable; the rhymes, apparently disposed in some arrangement like *terza rima*, chimed out like recurrent bells; the rises and falls of the speaker's voice were beautifully managed, and she accompanied her performance with eloquent but modest gestures, raising a white-gloved hand in the more impassioned passages and letting it fall in a graceful arc to mark the end of the period.

After a while, however, I began to be conscious of a certain lack of variety in the performance. By carefully attending to the rhymes, I discovered that Lenz's poem was written in some kind of regular Spenserian stanzas, and each stanza was being given an absolutely identical treatment. Whether it was the fault of the speaker or the poet, I began to receive the impression of a man with an inexhaustible ability to repeat himself. At any rate the inflexions of his granddaughter followed an unfailing pattern: first a low, thrilling opening, a gradual progression in intensity and volume, a ringing climax followed by a short pregnant pause, and then a gradual but swift descent to a hushed close; this pattern was illustrated by the same beautiful gestures of the white-gloved hand. I kept wondering what Lenz had had to say that required such persistence of utterance. Was he telling a story, relating a dialogue, invoking a spirit? It was impossible to tell. The superbly practised voice kept on and on, like a gramophone record that has gotten stuck; the white-gloved hand rose and fell. Everyone seemed entranced: there was a mindless ecstasy on all the faces, flushed with food and wine and sunlight. Madame Lenz-

Bessermann seemed as if she would never stop. But when she did it was in the same way as a horse: suddenly, definitively, inalterably.

The applause beat around her like a storm; everyone stood up, and as she made her way from the reading-desk, clasping her white-gloved hands to her breast, the band struck up a solemn air that everyone joined in singing. I heard later it was a hymn, also written by her grandfather, in which the elements of religion and patriotism were fused in splendid generalizations.

'I'm going for a walk,' said Bob as the crowd began to disperse. He strode off, his chin out-thrust, his torso bent slightly forward in an attitude that was to become familiar in the months to come. He was feeling the bitterness and frustration that any public adulation of someone else, whether living or dead, always aroused in him.

For the rest of the week he spent six hours a day at his typewriter—wearing a woman's hairnet, a whim of his, while working. I also applied myself to my book, but not with such persistence, while Graeme wrote an amusing short story called 'Dr Breakey Opposes Union', in which a Presbyterian clergyman allows his shrewish wife to fall to her death from a defective balcony: it was published next year by Edward Titus. The book Bob was writing or revising was, I think, called *Being Geniuses Together*, which I did not read until about six months later, when I found it exactly like all his others.

All three of us had already exhausted the resources of Luxembourg and were becoming bored.

With me boredom takes on the darkest hues and quickly develops into the deepest depression, plunging me in a mood where the past seems entirely wasted and the future without any promise. It was therefore a great relief to hear Bob announce he had finished *Being Geniuses Together* and was ready to return to Paris. We left the country in a pouring rain.

It had been a pleasant outing, and our finances, thanks to Bob, were now in such a condition that we could look forward to at least two weeks of freedom from worry about how we were to live.

In fact we were feeling so well that we quite forgot the original reason for the trip. We never acquired our *cartes d'identité*, and after that we never needed them.

NINE

Back in Paris we were faced with the delicate question whether Bob was going to live with us in the studio. We were all good friends by now but there was a feeling we would be a little crowded in one room. However, it turned out that old Monsieur Rouvely, the cabinet-maker next door, wanted to sublet his work-room as long as there would be no woman living in it.

'I am only too happy to let you have my premises,' he told Bob. 'But mind, no permanent woman! Women are such extremely dirty types: always cooking. I've no objection to tarts, I am broadminded. But if you mean to install a regular mistress here the deal is off.'

The work-room was full of benches, band-saws, woodworking machinery, and unfinished chairs and sofas, and had the fine astringent smell of sawdust and carpenter's glue. Bob rented a straw-stuffed bed from Madame Hernie, unpacked his single bag and his manuscripts, and settled in.

'This will be a great place to work,' he said. 'It reminds me of Thoreau. This is the atelier of a craftsman, who works with his hands, not the hangout of some goddamn artistic dilettante. It's the real thing, it's ascetic, it's genuine.' Soon his typewriter was clacking away every morning.

He gave me two of his published books, *A Companion Volume* and *Village*. I found it hard to say what I thought of them. I would have liked to admire them but it was impossible. They were obviously literal transcripts of things set down simply because they had happened and were vividly recollected. There was neither invention nor subterfuge; when the recollections stopped, so did the story, and one had the impression of a shutter being pulled down over the writer's memory as if in an act of self-defence against a dénouement either unformulated or too painful to remember. The only unifying feature they possessed was a central figure who was manifestly Bob himself: this man, variously named Fletcher Files, Harold Fletcher, Harold Files, and Files Fletcher, was a mysterious and exasperating character. He was the centre of everything; everyone asked his advice, his intercession, his opinion, and his absolution. He talked interminably, but to no effect or purpose for his ideas were not only negative and confused but expressed with such petulant incoherence they could hardly be taken seriously. There were occasional flashes of observation and understanding, even moments of grace; but the style and syntax revealed the genuine illiterate. I was soon to discover that Bob had in fact read absolutely nothing for over twenty years; he formed his critical opinions of books from reviews and personal contacts and his blanket condemnation of almost everything was mainly due to laziness and pique.

But although unable to write books, he had a genius for titles. Just then he was working on two great panoramic novels, *The Politics of Existence* and *The Portrait of a Generation*. However, the contents of these books were so like each other that he was constantly switching whole chapters from one book to the other and was even unsure whether he should exchange the titles themselves. When he asked me about this final change I was able to say it could make no difference — an opinion that delighted him.

In the meantime Graeme was once more planning *The Flying Carpet* and had resumed his affair with Caridad. For my part I was engaged on the project of seducing Diana Tree; she was the most intelligent woman I had ever known, and though we disagreed on all points of literature we laughed at the same things in life. My admiration of her was, however, confused rather than complemented by desire, and since she was still changing her lovers with bewildering rapidity I found myself simply waiting my turn.

As a youth of barely eighteen I was finding my passions a great problem. This is the age when one has an inexhaustible interest in sex and it seems the most important thing in life. Now, in the full heat of the Parisian summer, I was simmering. It was impossible to work on my memoirs and I spent a good deal of time pursuing casual loves in Montparnasse, where the expense and effort involved, while I did not begrudge them, were quite incommensurate with the results. My great mistake, I see now, was an unreasonable prejudice against prostitutes: at that time I looked on them as hardly women at all. But I was soon to be introduced to the most agreeable aspect of prostitution, and to taste the delights of that heaven-inspired convenience, that port and paradise of young men, the licensed Parisian brothel.

Nearby, on the rue de la Glacière, lived the gigantic American painter Sidney Schooner. He had so far given little indication of his real genius, which had been dissipated in playing the trombone professionally, designing theatrical posters, and writing a book on the history of costume; for none of these activities, which required more patience than he possessed, was he truly qualified. His great talent was for society, and for the serious painting towards which he was then, in company with Pascin, Kisling, and Picabia, only groping his way. He was above all a lover of whores.

We had already met at the Dôme and were soon visiting each other. His studio was furnished with a profusion of black settees and chairs, Chinese screens, and wall-paintings; his bed, tented like the abode of a pasha, was the first I had seen fitted with sheets of black crêpe-de-chine. 'It makes a good background for a fat, white-skinned woman,' he explained, 'and the roughness also tickles the skin very nicely. I'm not a sensualist but I like décor.'

I admired his painting but thought he was too consciously imitating the Douanier Rousseau. I also noticed in one corner of every picture a small baby-carriage. 'It's a curious compulsion I have,' he explained. 'I simply can't keep that baby-carriage out. God knows I try hard enough. I go through agonies, tell myself it's crazy, it destroys the composition, it will get me typed: it's no use. I'm literally forced to put the damn thing in somewhere.' He had been psychoanalysed, but it had done no good.

His regular mistress was a large, fat, wise-looking middle-aged Frenchwoman who worked as a pastrycook on the Right Bank. She had no interest in art and did not seem particularly fond of him; but, as he said, she was easily available and had always a wonderful smell of freshly-baked pie-crust. He was also, however, a great frequenter of brothels, and one evening when Bob was working on *The Politics of Existence* he suggested we accompany him to a place that he praised highly.

'It's very quiet, not at all chichi or expensive,' he said. 'Licensed and inspected, of course. It's even historical: Edward VII used to go there incog., or so they say — anyway there's an oil-painting of him over the bar. First we'll have dinner down by the Porte Saint-Denis. I know a restaurant there that serves the finest snails in the city.'

Graeme had won 100 francs that afternoon throwing dice at the Dingo, so we agreed at once.

The restaurant was very dark, with mouldering tapestries on the walls, gas chandeliers, and tarnished mirrors; it was half filled with elderly, respectable, mottle-faced men, all bent over their plates, many of them wearing infants' bibs to protect their shirts from the juices and sauces. Schooner ordered four dozen snails for us, to be followed by three broiled lobsters and a bottle of Chablis.

I had never tasted such snails; fat, tender and of marvellous flavour, they were swimming in a sauce of browned butter, parsley and garlic. Schooner ate more than half of them, and when the lobster came I was able to enjoy it too as it deserved.

Paris, Schooner told us, was full of restaurants like this, though they took a little finding. 'The one thing to watch out for in a restaurant,' he said, 'is a head-waiter or a maître d'hôtel; as soon as you see one, turn round and walk out. Also, beware of chafing-dishes.'

'But how can you tell a good restaurant?' said Graeme.

'I've found that three good signs are a small menu, darned table-cloths, and an old dog on the premises. Mostly, however, you go by instinct.'

'How about the proprietor being dressed in a blue apron?' I asked.

'Why, that quaint garment is an indication the food may be good, or it may not, but the bill will certainly be far too high and probably added up wrong. No, the proprietor of a good restaurant wears shirt-sleeves in summer and a woollen coat-sweater in winter. Also, oddly enough, the food is always better when he is thin, bald and depressed-looking. You may think all this fantastic, but I assure you I have compiled all these features of a good restaurant by using the same process Lombroso did in arriving at his rules for the physiognomy of a criminal. Lombroso, of course, was a scientist. But the painter's eye, like the writer's, records all these things subconsciously.'

We had coffee at a small café facing the Porte Saint-Denis. It was now almost eleven o'clock, and the July night was soft and perfumed; the sky had still the lingering traces of the violet light of evening; crowds of shopgirls in their long dresses and clerks in little bowler hats and tight jackets were strolling slowly along; up over Montmartre Bébé Cadum displayed her infantile, indecent grin. We had St James rum with our coffee and smoked the last of our American cigarettes. At last we rose to go to the brothel, for Schooner said this was the best time—when the girls were wide awake and still fresh and before the drunks arrived.

'The place opens at six o'clock and closes sharp at four in the morning,' he said. 'By the way, have you got enough money?'

We had almost seven dollars left. 'More than enough,' said Schooner. 'This is no de luxe trap.'

It was clear, as soon as we entered the tall narrow-fronted building at 15 rue St Apolline over which a pink light shone modestly, that the place was no stuffy abode of wealth and tedium. A narrow dark corridor led directly into a large red-lighted and red-papered room filled with low tables and plush-covered benches like those of the first-class Canadian railway-carriages of my childhood; drinks were being served to mixed couples by an elderly waiter in the usual black alpaca waistcoat and floor-length white apron, and it took a few moments to realize that all the women were young and completely nude. At the door was a raised cash-desk presided over by a neat little old sharp-featured lady in black silk, with steel-rimmed spectacles and grey hair drawn back in a tidy bun; at the far end of the room, under a large and smiling portrait of Edward VII, behind a long table covered with glasses of beer, lounged a dozen other naked beauties smoking and chatting. The informality was enchanting. We sat down at a corner table and ordered a bottle of iced *mousseux*. The old lady nodded politely to Schooner, gave Graeme and me a single penetrating glance, and raised a finger to the table of the beauties. At the sign they all rose, ran forward, and fell before our table in a torrent of flesh, wriggling their haunches, shaking their breasts, chattering obscenities, and sticking out their tongues.

'Take your pick,' said Schooner. 'We have to buy three of them a drink anyway. Any girl we don't want will take her drink back to the big table by herself.' He studied them with a jovial but judicious air. 'I rather like the big Norman girl in the middle,' he said, crooking a finger at a splendid blonde with breasts like cantaloupes, who gave a cry of triumph and at once squeezed in beside him.

I had already made my choice: a jolly-looking little brunette with bobbed hair who had shaved in every strategic place and wore a rhinestone choker. She sat down and clasped my hand tightly. Graeme was undecided, and I believe his final choice was determined less by personal preference than by compassion: it was a beautiful but modest-looking mulattress who stood in the background, protruding a pair of superb pear-shaped breasts, with her hands clasped behind her head and eyes raised soulfully to the ceiling.

The girls ordered whatever harmless mixture they were supposed to drink: deep pink in colour, it was served in tall glasses and graced with a spoon.

'This stuff,' confided my brunette, 'is only *limonade* and grenadine. But what can you do? Now I, I like to flush my kidneys with something that has some heart in it. Darling, when Madame Hibou isn't looking sprinkle me a little *mousseux* in my glass for the love of God.'

This was not too easy. Madame Hibou seemed to have a dozen pairs of eyes in her head. However, when a solemn-looking client in rusty black rose from a bench and was led to the cash desk by one of the girls, her attention was taken up by the business of making out a chit for the room and entering the transaction in a ledger. I took the opportunity of filling my friend's half-empty glass with the pink *mousseux*, which she drank off immediately.

The conversation was refreshing though far from intellectual. After a while it became little more than a boasting-contest between the Norman girl and the brunette as they vaunted their abilities in bed: it seemed there was nothing they could not do. Graeme's mulattress, who had recently arrived from Senegal and could speak no more than a few words of French, merely bared her magnificent teeth from time to time and rolled her eyes. 'She is just a child of nature,' said my brunette, 'but she has a heart of gold.'

'Well, I'm for bed,' said Schooner as we finished the bottle of wine. 'For your information the rooms cost fifteen francs and the girls twenty-five each, unless you're staying the night, when it's double—but that's only for businessmen from out of town who want to save on a hotel bill.' At the cash-desk we all paid for our rooms in advance; the girls were to be paid afterwards. Having received our chits from Madame Hibou, all six of us mounted the stairs, arm in arm, and were shown to three adjoining rooms by an elderly chambermaid with a hare-lip who took the chits and then suggested that if we wanted the doors unlocked between our rooms she would do so for an additional fifteen francs. 'It will make for more variety,' she said, 'without any sacrifice of discretion.'

This seemed like a good idea. We paid the extra money and saw the rooms transformed into a suite.

'Mind now,' said the chambermaid, 'you must be out of here in an hour from now when your tickets expire. And Arlette, my girl,' she warned Schooner's companion, 'be sure you behave yourself. No unseemly noise! Good evening, gentlemen.'

We were soon engaged in the business of the evening. To me, this first experience of a French prostitute was a revelation. I had, quite simply, never enjoyed myself so much in my life, and I soon understood the source of Jeanne du Barry's attraction for Louis xv and how well it was comprised in her own terse formula, '*Je l'ai traité en simple putain.*' After a short rest Graeme switched to Arlette and Schooner to the brunette, while I took the mulattress. When it came to my turn with Arlette, however, I was in no condition to continue, and while Graeme and Schooner were running their third course she perched on the bidet and entertained me with the story of her life on the farm in Normandy, 'where I hope to retire some day,' she said, 'and raise a big family and look after some nice geese. But for all this I need money, you know, so won't you give me a little tip? Then I won't tell your friends how *tired* you were.'

Having paid this piece of blackmail to the extent of five francs, for which she kissed me affectionately, I then brushed my hair and got dressed just as there was a loud rap on the hall door accompanied by the chambermaid's voice hissing through her hare-lip: '*C'est l'heure, messieurs. S'il vous plaît!*'

Graeme and Schooner appeared a minute later and the six of us descended the stairs, once again arm in arm. Having settled our modest score with Madame Hibou, we all exchanged compliments with the girls, bade them good night, and sallied out into the velvety Paris night. The Saint-Denis quarter had never looked so beautiful and rosy, with the brilliantly lit cafés and shops and the constant passage of the streetwalkers in their light summer gowns. The sculptured archaic gate itself, standing like a grand portal from nowhere to nowhere, a kind of exquisitely unnecessary obstruction to the traffic, seemed to rise into the sky like a symbol of France. How happy and peaceful I felt!

Schooner was looking at his watch. 'We've just time to catch the Métro back to the quarter,' he said. 'How about a Welsh rarebit at the Select?'

We reached Montparnasse soon after one o'clock and were enjoying those specialities of the house when Diana Tree suddenly descended from a taxi and swept up to the *terrasse*, draped in a dramatic midnight-blue cape.

'Darlings,' she cried, 'I have wonderful news. Schooner, buy me a drink: whisky and water will do . . .'

Over her whisky she became eloquent. Her fourth or fifth novel had just appeared with great éclat in London, and she had just received an advance royalty of £100. 'Enough to live on for a year!' she cried. 'Oh, I could sing for joy. What is it one of Goethe's young men exclaims? "This kiss for the universe!"' She threw her arms in the air and blew a kiss into the sky. 'Well, what have you boys been doing?'

'We have just eaten four dozen snails, among other things,' said Schooner.

'And now you're eating Welsh rarebits. The inner man, by heaven.' She gripped my knee with compelling force underneath the table and her gaze became melting. She had never looked so beautiful, nor had I ever admired her more: the lovely grey-blue eyes were swimming in ecstasy. 'Take me to the toilet,' she murmured in my ear. 'I spent my last sou on the taxi.'

I accompanied her down the steep narrow staircase; on the little landing she put her arms around my neck 'Darling, let's spend the night together, shall we?' she whispered. 'I am so happy.'

'But where can we go? We have to consider Bob and Graeme —

and—well, the truth is, I'm not feeling very well—It must have been the snails—'

She wheeled around in her cape and without a word disappeared into the ladies' room. I put twenty-five centimes on the plate, nodded to the *lavabos* lady, and went back upstairs. The genius of Puritanism, with all its forefixed concatenation of misdeeds and punishments, had served me out properly.

We all went back to the rue Broca together in a taxi, dropping Diana and the indomitable Schooner at his studio. Momentarily saddened, I recovered my spirits somewhat with the help of a bottle of wine and fell asleep thinking of the brunette with the rhinestone choker.

Ten

Today we're meeting the white hope of North American literature,'
said Bob next morning. 'His name is Callaghan, and he's just come
to town with a pisspot full of money from a book called *Strange Fugitive*.
Have you read it?'

'No,' said Graeme. 'But I know his stories in *The New Yorker*. Very
fine and sophisticated. Just like Hemingway's, only plaintive and more
moral.'

'Well, Fitzgerald says he's good, so he's probably lousy. Anyway he
has a lot of dough, so we might get a dinner out of him. He's Canadian
too. What do you think he's like?'

'Well,' said Graeme, 'I see him as tall, thin, blond, cynical, in a pin-
striped suit. It's the way he writes anyway.'

'Rats,' said Bob, 'that doesn't scare me. I know these sophisticated
New Yorker types. They're just a bunch of *arrivistes*.'

However, he shaved carefully, running the razor up to his eyes, shined
his shoes with his socks, and put on a new polka-dot bow tie before
going to meet Callaghan at the hotel-room he was still keeping on the
rue de Vaugirard.

'Join us in the Coupole Bar around four,' he said. 'I'll have him
softened up by then. *Sophisticated*, what the hell! I've handled John
Barrymore in my day. But look, for God's sake, both of you get your
hair cut.'

Graeme and I went to a barber shop and then idled around the
quarter until four o'clock. We looked into the Coupole, the Dôme, the
Select, and the Rotonde without seeing Bob; by five o'clock we had
also done the Dingo, the College Inn, and the Falstaff, still without
success. Coming from the Falstaff we saw Bob sitting with a couple
at the little *tabac* on the corner. He hailed us and we sat down.

Morley Callaghan was short, dark, and roly-poly, and wore a striped
shirt without a collar; with his moon face and little moustache he looked
very like Hemingway; he had even the same shrewd little politician's
eyes, the same lopsided grin and ingratiating voice. His wife was also
short and thickset, and wore a coral dress and a string of beads. Both
of them were so friendly and unpretentious that I liked them at once.
It was like meeting people from a small town. We apologized for not
finding them sooner, saying we had looked in the Coupole.

'I didn't like that Coupole, it's too much of a clip-joint,' said Callaghan. 'The drinks here are just as good, and a lot cheaper. Eh, Loretto?'

'Yes, about fifteen per cent less, Morley. And you have just the same view here. My, this is a lovely city, but the French are right after you for all they can get. You find that, Mr Taylor?'

'Yes,' said Graeme. 'You get used to it.'

'Like hell we will,' said Morley. 'Right now we're looking for an apartment. The hotel we're at charges like the dickens.' Suddenly changing the subject, he asked, 'Say, how do you get to meet James Joyce? McAlmon, you know him, I'm told.'

'You're damn right I do,' said Bob. 'But what do you want to do in Paris, go around like a literary rubberneck meeting great men? I'm a great man too, for God's sake. And here I am. Ask me your questions. I'll even give you my autograph.'

'You're a good writer,' said Morley, all his strength of character appearing, 'but you're not Joyce—not yet. What the hell,' he went on, 'this guy Joyce is great. *Ulysses* is the greatest novel of the century. I wouldn't compare myself to him. Why should you?'

'Oh,' said Bob, 'now you're getting modest. Well, you can't fool me. You think you're one hell of a writer, why don't you admit it? Why do you give me all this crap about Joyce? You're more important to yourself. If you think so much of Joyce, why don't you write like him instead of your constipated idol Hemingway? Lean, crisp, constipated, dead-pan prose. The fake naïve.'

'Now, McAlmon, let's go into this properly. First thing, I don't write like Joyce for the simple reason that I can't, it's not my line. But I can admire him, can't I?'

'No, you can't. You can't admire Joyce and write like Hemingway. If you do, you're a whore.'

Morley reddened. 'You're a funny guy. I don't know if you're talking seriously, but let me tell you I write as well as I can, and though you may not like my stuff . . .'

'I've never read your stuff. I don't read *The New Yorker*.'

'Well then what in heck are you talking about? Perhaps you haven't read Joyce either.'

'Right! I haven't read Joyce or Hemingway. I don't have to, I know them—and I know you too, Morley, and I like you. Especially when you get mad. I know you're a good writer. The test of a good writer is when he gets mad.'

'Are you boys all through arguing?' said Loretto. 'Shall we all go and have supper somewhere?'

'Sure, but none of these clip-joints. McAlmon, where's a good cheap restaurant? Fitzgerald told me you know Paris inside out.'

'My generation doesn't eat supper,' said Bob. 'I'm having another drink. Waiter, five whiskies and water!'

The conversation continued in the same way. Bob was unreasonable and outrageously rude; Morley remained patient and serious. At last things became boring and I let my attention wander.

A little old man in rags came by, holding up a sheaf of pink papers. 'Guide des poules de Paris!' he cried in a shrill quavering voice. 'All the girls in Paris, only ten francs! The names, the addresses!' He broke into a tittering sing-song, smacking his lips. 'Ah, les jolies pou-poules, fi-filles de joie de Paris! Achetez, achetez le Guide Rose! Toutes les jolies petites pou-poules de Paris! Dix francs, dix francs!'

Two Americans sitting nearby began to laugh. The little man pounced on them, fluttering his pink sheets.

'All the girls in Paris for only ten francs,' one of them said. 'It's a bargain.' He held out a blue ten-franc bill, the little man seized it, peeled off one of the pink sheets and ran away. The two men bent over the Guide Rose for several minutes. 'Say, this is the real thing. Listen: "Pierrette gives aesthetic massage." "Chez Suzy, everything a man wants." "Visit Mademoiselle Floggi, in her Negro hut: specialities—"'

'Boy, where do these girls hang out?'

'Here are all the phone numbers—'

'Man, these are just numbers—they don't give the exchange . . .'

They both studied the sheet carefully, then one of them pointed to the foot of it in disgust. 'No wonder there's no exchange! Look, this goddamn thing was printed in 1910.'

'Well for Christ's sake. The little bastard!'

Loretto Callaghan was shaking her head at me. 'Now isn't that just like the French,' she said. 'Always cheating!'

'Well, there goes your sophisticated New Yorker type,' said Bob when Morley and Loretto had left in search of a cheap restaurant.

'They're both very nice,' said Graeme. 'He's got brains and determination and a devoted wife. He'll go far.'

'Rats, he's just a dumb cluck, an urban hick, a sentimental Catholic. All he's got is a little-boy quality.'

'I'll bet he works like a dog,' I said. 'I wish I could.'

'Don't you ever work like he does, kid! Hard work never got anyone anywhere. A real writer just keeps on putting the words down! He gets the emotion *straight*, the scene, the quality of life—the way I do. Nuts to all that literary business.'

I thought of the inchoate maunderings of *The Politics of Existence* and said nothing. I was thinking that if Bob would only condescend to work, his books would be very fine. I see now, of course, that if he had done so they would be still worse than they were.

'All this literary talk is boring,' said Graeme. 'It's almost as bad as the chatter of poets—they're all so earnest, smelling trends, clawing or kissing each other—'

'Keep your skirts clean,' said Bob. 'That's all a writer has to do.— Hello, Caridad, sit down and have a drink.'

'Yes, I will. Graeme, my dear pussycat, you look very serious. You all do! You must stop it at once. And you must all come to a nice party tonight with me—a real party of poets and painters and writers.'

'Not me,' said Bob. 'I know those lousy parties.'

'Oh but this is a very distinguished party—and very, very wealthy. Our hostess will be the great American lady-writer, Miss Gertrude Stein.'

'That old ham! You three go there and lap up the literary vomit. Not me.'

'Let us have dinner first anyway,' said Caridad. 'You will have to pay for mine because I haven't any money. But please, Bob, let us not have one of those awful ducks at the Coupôle. We'll go to a nice cheap place like Salto's where I can eat a lot of spaghetti.'

We went around the corner to Salto's, just above the Falstaff, famous for the size of its portions and its coarse red wine. Here the food was good; there was always a *minestrone* that was a meal in itself and a wonderful *gâteau maison* made of some kind of yellow cake filled with raisins and drenched with marsala. Caridad ate her way through a plate of anchovies, a bowl of *minestrone*, a mound of spaghetti, an *osso buco*, and the *gâteau*, chattering all the time; Bob toyed with a veal cutlet; Graeme and I had a fine spicy rabbit stew made with green peppers, celery and lima beans. We went to the Dôme for coffee.

'Now,' said Caridad, pouring a ten-cent rum into her coffee, 'we shall go soon to Miss Gertrude Stein's and absorb an international culture. Her parties are very well behaved and there are always plenty of rich men—which I find very agreeable. A girl must live. Bob, you must show yourself there—you, celebrated man of letters, publisher, man of the world. It will also make my own entrance so much more impressive—with three cavaliers. Come, it is only a few streets away —'

'Rats, I know the place. I've been to her parties. Never again. Gertrude paid me to publish her lousy five-pound book and we've never been the same since. She thinks I held back some of the proceeds. No, you three run along.'

Although neither Graeme nor I cared for Gertrude Stein's work, we really wanted to see the great woman. I was thinking too of how I would write my father about meeting her, and that (once he had checked her credentials with the English Department at McGill) he might just raise my allowance. The business of living on fifty dollars a month was becoming almost impossible: we were always short of money, we were never able to eat or drink enough, and while Bob was often generous it was apparent his own resources were running low and he would soon have to make another requisition on his father-in-law. As foreigners we could take no regular work, and while Graeme's skill with the poker dice seldom failed, it often took him over an hour to win 100 francs and obliged him to endure as well the conversation of the dreariest types of American barfly; the worst of it was that he had to spend almost a quarter of his winnings drinking with them during his operations.

Accordingly we set off with Caridad down the boulevard Raspail in the plum-blue light of the June evening, arrived at the rue de Fleurus, and were greeted at the door by a deciduous female who seemed startled by the sight of Caridad.

'Miss Toklas!' Caridad cried affectionately. 'It is so long since we have not met. I am Caridad de Plumas, you will remember, and these are my two young Canadian squires to whom I wish to give the privilege of meeting you and your famous friend. We were coming with Mr Robert McAlmon, but he is unavoidably detained.'

As she delivered this speech she floated irresistibly forward, Miss Toklas retreated, and we found ourselves in a big room already filled with soberly dressed and soft-spoken people.

The atmosphere was almost ecclesiastical and I was glad to be wearing my best dark suit, which I had put on to meet Morley Callaghan. I had begun to suspect that Caridad had not been invited to the party and all of us were in fact crashing the gate. But Caridad, whether invited or not, was in a few minutes a shining centre of the party: her charm coruscated, her big teeth flashed, her dyed hair caught the subdued light. She paid no further attention to Graeme or myself, and I understood that she was as usual looking for rich men.

The room was large and sombrely furnished, but the walls held, crushed together, a magnificent collection of paintings—Braques, Matisses, Picassos, and Picabias. I only recovered from their cumulative effect to fall under that of their owner, who was presiding like a Buddha at the far end of the room.

Gertrude Stein projected a remarkable power, possibly due to the atmosphere of adulation that surrounded her. A rhomboidal woman dressed in a floor-length gown apparently made of some kind of burlap, she gave the impression of absolute irrefragability; her ankles, almost concealed by the hieratic folds of her dress, were like the pillars of a temple: it was impossible to conceive of her lying down. Her fine close-cropped head was in the style of the late Roman Empire, but unfortunately it merged into broad peasant shoulders without the aesthetic assistance of a neck; her eyes were large and much too piercing. I had a peculiar sense of mingled attraction and repulsion towards her. She awakened in me a feeling of instinctive hostility coupled with a grudging veneration, as if she were a pagan idol in whom I was unable to believe.

Her eyes took me in, dismissed me as someone she did not know, and returned to her own little circle. With a feeling of discomfort I decided to find Graeme and disappear: this party, I knew, was not for me. But just then Narwhal came up and began talking so amusingly that I could not drag myself away.

'I have been reading the works of Jane Austen for the first time,' he said in his quiet nasal voice, 'and I'm looking for someone to share my enthusiasm. Now these are very good novels in my opinion. You wouldn't believe it but here—among all these writers, people who are presumably literary artists—I can't find anyone who has read her books with any real attention. In fact most of them don't seem to like her work at all. But I find this dislike is founded on a false impression that she was a respectable woman.'

'Jane Austen?'

'I don't mean to say she was loose in her behaviour, or not a veuhjin.

79

I'm sure she was a veuhjin. I mean she was aristocratic, not bourgeoise, she was no creep, she didn't really give a darn about all those conventions of chaystity and decorum.'

'Well, her heroines did.'

'Oh sure, they *seem* to, they've got to, or else there'd be no story. But Austen didn't herself. Who is the heroine, the Ur-heroine of *Sense and Sensibility*? It's Marianne, not Elinor. Of *Pride and Prejudice*? It's the girl that runs off with the military man. What's wrong with *Emma*? Emma.'

'You mean Willoughby and Wickham are her real heroes?'

'No, they're just stooges, see? But they represent the dark life-principle of action and virility that Austen really admired, like Marianne and Lydia stand for the life force of female letting-go. And when Anne Elliott falls for Captain Wentworth—you'll notice he's the third W of the lot—it's the same thing, only this time he's tamed. It's a new conception of Austen's talent which I formed yesterday, and which was suggested to me by the fact that Prince Lucifer is the real hero of *Paradise Lost*, as all the savants declare.'

This idea of Jane Austen as a kind of early D.H. Lawrence was new. Never had the value of her books been so confirmed as by this extraordinary interpretation of them: it was a real tribute.

'Do you happen to know if there were any portraits of Austen made?' he asked.

'A water colour by a cousin, I think.'

'Good! I guess it's lousy then,' he said with satisfaction. 'Because I've been thinking of doing an imaginary portrait of her too. I see her in a wood, in a long white dress. She's looking at a mushroom. But all around her are these thick young trees growing straight up—some are black with little white collars and stand for ministers of the church and some are blue and stand for officers in the Royal English Navy. I'm also thinking of putting some miniature people, kind of elves dressed like witches and so forth, in the background—but I'm not sure.'

'It sounds good.'

'The focus of the whole thing will be the mushroom,' he said. 'It represents the almost overnight flowering of her genius—also its circumscribed quality, its suggestion of being both sheltered *and* a shelter— see?—and its e-conomy of structure.'

'An edible mushroom?'

'You've got it. That will be the whole mystery of the portrait. The viewer won't know and she won't know either. We will all partake of Jane Austen's doubt, faced with the appalling mystery of sex.'

We must have been talking with an animation unusual for one of Gertrude Stein's parties, for several of the guests had already gathered around us.

'You are talking of Jane Austen and sex, gentlemen?' said a tweedy Englishman with a long ginger moustache. 'The subjects are mutually exclusive. That dried-up lady snob lived behind lace curtains all her life. She's of no more importance than a chromo. Isn't that so, Gertrude?'

I was suddenly aware that our hostess had advanced and was looking at me with her piercing eyes.

'Do I know you?' she said. 'No. I suppose you are just one of those silly young men who admire Jane Austen.'

Narwhal had quietly disappeared and I was faced by Miss Stein, the tweedy man and Miss Toklas. Already uncomfortable at being an uninvited guest, I found the calculated insolence of her tone intolerable and lost my temper.

'Yes, I am,' I said. 'And I suppose you are just one of those silly old women who don't.'

The fat Buddha-like face did not move. Miss Stein merely turned, like a gun revolving on its turret, and moved imperturbably away.

The tweedy man did not follow her. Leaning towards me, his moustache bristling, he said quietly, 'If you don't leave here this moment, I will take great pleasure in throwing you out, bodily.'

'If you really want,' I said, 'I'll wait outside in the street for three minutes, when I'll be glad to pull your nose.'

I then made my exit, and after standing for exactly three minutes on the sidewalk (by which time I was delighted to find he did not appear), I took my way back to the Dôme. Graeme joined me there fifteen minutes later.

'That's the last party we go to without being invited,' he said.

ELEVEN

We saw a good deal of Morley and Loretto during the next few weeks and liked them even more. As soon as they had moved from the Hotel New York into a cheap apartment they were much more relaxed. He told me a curious story about their landlady.

'My French isn't so good, but as far as I can make out her husband sings in the Metropolitan Opera in New York,' said Morley. 'But she has this lover who comes in at two o'clock every morning. A little guy in a uniform like a postman's.'

'These Frenchwomen,' said Loretto, 'they certainly make time.'

Morley was now working on another novel, and his example drove me back to this book with such urgency that I managed to finish the third chapter by the end of June. I did not have the courage to show my work-in-progress to him, thinking of the superlative technique and polish of his own stories.

Morley did not work on Saturday nights, and on one of these he suggested we see a little Parisian night life. I at once proposed the brothel at 25 rue St Apolline, but he was more interested in Montmartre. My knowledge of that quarter was still confined to the smart cabarets around the Place Pigalle, such as Bricktop's, Le Grand Duc, and La Boîte Blanche. I told him how expensive they were.

'Not all of them,' he said. 'There's this Le Palermo run by a guy called Joe Zelli. I hear they've got a good floor show, and if you sit at the bar it doesn't cost too much.'

'All right. But not in the *salle*. I think it's the kind of place where they have telephones at the tables so you can speak to any girl you fancy, and that means a hefty cover charge.'

'We'll sit at the bar. It's on me.'

We took the last Métro to Pigalle and walked along the boulevard de Clichy. The ambiance was better than I thought: the boulevard still had its trees, the lights danced on the leaves, and the whores were out in full strength. The girls in Montmartre are the most aggressive in Paris, and as this was a Saturday night in the height of the tourist season they were on their mettle.

'Say,' said Morley after he had been accosted and man-handled for the fourth or fifth time, 'what goes on here? Do we look as rich as all that?'

'It's just our clothes. They think we're Americans.'

'If I'd known, I'd have worn an old sweater and sneakers.'

'They'd still know the cut of your trousers. No, if you want to get by here you have to wear two-dollar French pants without cuffs, a knitted shirt and a pair of fancy pointed shoes. Also you're not supposed to pay any attention to the scenery and horse along as if you owned the whole street. And don't look at the girls. Look over their heads.'

'But then you miss everything. Heck, I want to enjoy myself!'

We went down the rue Blanche (a street I was to know all too well within a year) to the corner where Le Palermo displayed its big electric sign. Morley studied the photographs of barebreasted women posted up outside, squared his boxer's shoulders, and led the way in. By luck we found two empty places at the bar where, by craning our necks, we had an oblique view of the chorus performing on the dance floor; the noise was so deafening that at first we could not exchange a word. Morley ordered a beer and I a brandy and water.

The girls in the chorus were young and beautiful and their costumes elaborate, but unfortunately none of them was able to dance. Moreover they all seemed dead tired, doubtless because they had to put on a five-minute show every fifteen minutes. I watched this ton of listless flesh, these fixed smiles, these snowy pink-tipped contours, with a feeling of sadness. This place was after all only a mutual concourse of wolves, in which the appetites of desire, glamour and money were opposed and never met, where each was expensively dangled before the other and where the only real gainer was Joe Zelli himself—though even this was doubtful, since he was rumoured to be going bankrupt.

Morley also was pensive. In an interval of comparative quiet he pointed to a sign above the bar that read CONSOMMATIONS, 40 FRANCS. 'What's a *consommation?*' he asked. 'Does that mean —intercourse?'

'No, it's just a drink.'

He shook his head pityingly. 'Think of the dopes who'll pay forty francs for a drink. *Consommation!* What's it made of?'

The resumed noise of the band temporarily spared him the news. But when he realized we each had one in front of us he took it very well.

'We can sit here all night on these two drinks, of course,' I said.

'Well then, why not? We'll have to take a taxi home anyway.'

'True. And it's not a bad place. The little dark girl in the chorus, the one on the end there, has some good points.'

83

'I'd like another beer, but not at any forty francs. I wish I'd brought along something on the hip.'

'If you want some brandy, I've got a flask. But be careful. Here, pour a shot in your beer.'

He did so with unobtrusive skill. 'Boy, this is just like the King Eddy in Toronto! You've got to drink hootch out of a teacup there.' He tested his drink with satisfaction. 'Beer and brandy—that's not a bad *consommation* at all. I'm beginning to like this place.'

His pleasure was infectious. I freshened my own drink and we sat back on our stools and watched the chorus. By now our ears had become used to the noise, and conversation was possible.

'I like you and Graeme,' he said. 'So does Loretto. But say, what's biting your friend McAlmon? I can't make him out.'

'He's always that way.'

'I admire his work—in a way. "Miss Knight" is a nice piece of writing. No one has gotten that type of fairy down on paper before. In fact McAlmon's pretty good when he's writing about fairies. How do you account for that?'

I tried to give the appearance of someone forming a considered judgement. 'He just has a natural sympathy for everything eccentric.'

'Yes,' he said thoughtfully. 'I'd say you're right. He likes people who are pretty far out in left field, that's clear enough. But he makes no judgements, he's too uncommitted. Don't you think a writer should commit himself, some time anyway?'

'Like Dos Passos?'

'Hell no, that's just propaganda. Dos Passos will be the forgotten man of American letters in ten years. It's a shame too, because he's got a scope and a sweep, he knows the States up and down and inside out, he gives you the facts and the sounds and smells and talk of the whole damn country—but how come you can't remember any of his people or even what they did, their problems, their attitude?'

'Perhaps because he's so committed. Or perhaps he doesn't know anything about people. He just reduces them to stupid appetites, to organisms looking for sex or money or jobs. Like Zola, in a way.'

'Sure, Zola was over-committed, if you like.'

'And he's got a better collection of facts and sounds and smells.'

He laughed. 'Say, I'm getting a pretty fine collection myself right now. Look at those girls!'

The chorus had come out dressed as birds, with beaked and eared

84

headdresses, trousers ruched like feathers and long pink-tipped mittens which they flapped wearily up and down.

'You were talking about commitment,' I said. 'I can think of no good writer who's committed to anything today. Except Dreiser.'

'*Dreiser*? What in hell is he committed to except telling a damn good success story?'

'I think he's committed to dishonesty in everything except art—to crimes, to stealing and lying and swindling and falsehood in general. He's tapped the American dream.'

'He's got a godawful style.'

'Sure, almost as bad as McAlmon's. Because he just can't be bothered to write well, he hasn't the time, he's too busy drawing the picture and making the story move.'

'When you say he's committed to stealing and swindling and lying aren't you just thinking of those Cowperwood books? What about *Sister Carrie*?'

'She's just as bad. And everyone in the *American Tragedy*. Have you ever met such a crowd of liars anywhere in fiction? Especially the heroines. And they lie so casually, so naturally. That's what makes Dreiser great: he's anarchic, amoral, immature, antediluvian.'

I suddenly realized I was talking like a character in a Huxley novel. This problem of commitment was Morley's, not mine. I had no commitments except, in a vague way, to remain uncommitted. I had no wife, no job, no ambition, no bank account, no use for large sums of money, no appetite for prestige, and no temptation to acquire any of them. I had at that time, I think, already unconsciously assessed them all as so many pairs of weighted diver's shoes—of no use to anyone who wanted to remain on the surface of life. If they had been wings I would have assumed them gladly; but now, *vis-à-vis* the deadly earnestness of Morley Callaghan, a man only ten years older than myself, I had once again the salutary sense of the abyss that yawns for everyone who has embraced the literary profession—everyone from Molière to George Gissing: literature, like every other form of gainful employment, was just another trap.

'Yeah,' said Morley. 'I guess so. But he's committed just the same. I think he's a Communist now. Oh God, here come the girls again.'

This time they were dressed as rabbits.

We watched them for a while, then simultaneously decided we had had enough of Le Palermo. We found a taxi outside and drove to Morley's apartment, splitting the fare. As it was a fine night I decided to walk the half-mile to the rue Broca when he suddenly gripped my arm.

'Look, there's our landlady's boy friend,' he whispered delightedly, drawing me into the shadows.

A small man in a baggy blue uniform was pushing the concierge's bell. As he turned, the insignia on the motorman's cap showed the intertwined initials of the Métro. 'Ah, the Metropolitan,' I thought. We watched discreetly until he had gone in.

'Here's some news for you,' said Bob the next morning, showing me a letter on yellow paper. 'Ethel Moorhead's taking the first chapter of your book for the next issue of *This Quarter*. And here's your cheque— 525 francs.'

I was unable to speak.

'Now I want to see the second chapter properly typed out,' he went on, 'and if it's not too lousy I'll send it to Ezra for *The Exile*. He does pretty much what I tell him, so get to work right off if you want fame and fortune, goo-goo eyes.'

'525 francs!'

'Ezra won't pay you that much, so don't get any big ideas.'

'I didn't expect anything at all.'

'I told Ethel you were broke.'

I decided to blow the money on a party in the studio. As it happened to be Bastille Day as well, there was double occasion to celebrate. While Graeme and Bob went out to contact people by telephone and *pneumatique*, I took a taxi to the Place Vendôme to cash the cheque at the Bank of Montreal; this was not really necessary, but as I had still no identity card I thought I had better go where I was known. Also, I hadn't taken a taxi by myself for over a month.

I picked up an open taxi outside the Santé prison, where it had just dropped a party of melancholy visitors. I remember how the leatherette seat burned hotly through my best check trousers and how the city swam in a haze of heat and happiness. The driver too was one of the best, and as he raced down the boulevards, blowing his horn like a berserk elephant, I had an experience of absolute ecstasy.

Such moments do not come often at any time of life, and since I have been in this hospital they have naturally not come at all. Here, my pleasures are confined to eating an occasional orange or a meal that is not entirely tasteless, reading a letter or newspaper and trying rather listlessly to divine the contours of the nurses beneath their bibs starched to the stiffness of pasteboard. I am not unhappy, merely profoundly bored, and occasionally apprehensive over the outcome of my next operation— which, I have gathered, there is a pretty good chance of my surviving. I am even proud of being regarded as a model patient; there's also a certain negative pleasure in looking out at the sunny, snowy landscape locked in sub-zero air, and reflecting that I am nice and warm here and not yet dead . . .

After cashing Ethel Moorhead's cheque I took the bus back to the Lion de Belfort, standing on the back platform and enjoying the snap-the-whip effect as it swung dizzily around the corners. It took very little to make me happy in those days.

Back at the studio preparations for the party were well advanced. Everyone was coming; there were about thirty bottles of liquor and wine, a tub of ice and a carton of glasses hired from the corner café. Caridad had brought two ship's lanterns to supplement our gas-mantle and was already sweeping the dust into the corners. Schooner had en-gaged a man with a hand-organ to play in the alcove. 'He'll come for ten francs and his wine,' he said. 'His machine is very old, very weak, and it has only four tunes, which is all the better. It will give a fine background effect—festal but not intrusive. By the way, I asked Arlette and the little brunette to come if they can get away from No. 25. Arlette's a lot of fun at a party. She generally ends up taking off her clothes.'

We all had a late dinner at a little restaurant in the rue de la Glacière; by the time we got back at ten o'clock the guests had begun to arrive.

The party gathered a cumulative momentum, for everyone brought two or three friends, and the studio was soon crowded.

The hand-organ had been a brilliant idea of Schooner's. The four tunes turned out to be by Offenbach and never grew stale or tiresome. The machine itself attracted much attention; extremely heavy and mounted on little wheels, it slowly disgorged long rolls of punched paper tapes into a bucket at the side, and the elderly operator, while turning the crank with one hand, rolled them up with the other and fed them back deftly into the receiving end. 'It used to roll the tapes up by itself,' he complained. 'But that part of it is broken and there is no one in Paris who knows how to repair it—which is ridiculous! It was only made in 1886.' The tapes, which were probably of the same vintage, were almost worn out, so that only three notes in four emerged—giving a peculiarly bacchanalian effect without destroying the rhythm. Some of the guests were dancing.

'Darling,' cried Diana Tree, 'this is a marvellous party! And congratulations on your literary début.' She threw her arms around me, and we embraced beside the kitchen sink.

Arlette arrived, accompanied by the brunette with the rhinestone choker. They were both elaborately turned out in long flowered skirts and wore the little Empress Eugénie hats that were then fashionable. Graeme served them glasses of neat brandy and they were soon chattering away with the unattached men.

I had been trying not to drink too much myself, but soon found this impossible. The music, the unequivocal caress Diana had given me at the sink, and the gaiety of everyone else—all combined to give every drink the effect of two.

'Mrs Quayle,' said Bob, 'this is the young man I've been telling you about.'

I shook hands with a small, expensively dressed woman with hooded eyes and a musky perfume.

'You have a beautiful stoodio here,' she said in a deep velvety Bostonian voice. 'Is it where you bring your mistresses?'

'I would, Mrs Quayle, if I had any.'

Her eyes unhooded for an instant, then she turned to Bob. 'We must find him a nice little mistress, Mr McAlmon, don't you think?'

'You've made a hit,' Bob said as Mrs Quayle moved away. 'Come and have a drink.'

'If I do, I'll be sick. I think I want some air.'

As I was going out I saw the tweedy man with the ginger moustache. He glared at me.

'Well,' he said, 'it's you again, damn it. You do manage to get around, don't you?'

'Please. I still feel badly about being so rude to Miss Stein the other night. Do you think I should write her a note of apology?'

'No. You only made a boor of yourself. All I can advise you is not to insult your hosts of this evening—if you were invited here at all. See?'

I moved on outside to enjoy the night air, still deliriously happy about my forthcoming appearance in *This Quarter*. I sat down on the cool stone of the statue of the two fornicating Eskimos and looked into the starry sky. Unlike Pascal, I had never been frightened by the vastness of these infinite spaces any more than by what I could see in a microscope. I was even then a convinced disciple of Bishop Berkeley — the only philosopher, to my mind, who has grasped the real truth of the appearances of things and the proper role of man in the universe. And now, slightly drunk, I fully appreciated his system. *Esse est percipi*, I thought; and I amused myself by closing my eyes, thus annihilating the visible universe, and then recreating it by opening them again. The solipsism of the problem of consciousness was so appealing that I began to examine the fact of consciousness itself. Was it confined to man? No: animals and plants also had it. Did reality then disappear when they closed their eyes or folded their leaves? Could the elementary consciousness of a flower also annihilate the universe as soon as it slept or died? And did not even stones have a kind of consciousness, or at least a reaction to the force of gravity that served them as such? A phrase of Schopenhauer occurred to me: 'if a falling stone were endowed with consciousness, it would believe it was falling because it wanted to; and it would be right.' At this point I decided that it wanted to fall simply because it wanted, also, to be at rest and thus to annihilate the universe of phenomena. This moment, in fact, marked the birth of the philosophical system I was later to elaborate in an essay I called 'The Duality of Will'.

'*Tu as l'air triste*,' said the brunette with the rhinestone choker, pinching my ear playfully. '*Où est-ce qu'on va pour pisser?*'

I led her to the row of toilets, warning her not to pull the chain unless she wanted to be soaked to the ankles.

'My God, but this is primitive,' she said as I left her trying to hasp the crazy door.

When I got back to the studio Arlette had taken off her clothes and was dancing with the tweedy man. The party seemed to be getting better and better and people were still arriving.

'How is the liquor holding out?' I asked Graeme.

'We're down to the last three bottles of brandy. The wine is all gone. I think the organ-grinder has had almost a quarter of it.'

'What are we going to do? We can't buy any more liquor at this time of night.'

'Don't worry,' said Bob. 'We're all invited to Mrs Quayle's somewhere on the Champs-Elysées. We'll just mosey off quietly in a few minutes.'

This seemed a fine solution. Soon the three of us, along with

Schooner, Diana Tree and Caridad, were all stuffed into Mrs Quayle's big touring-car and rolling past the prison towards the river.

The whole city was seething with celebration. Everywhere people were dancing in the streets, and many of the women, like Arlette, had taken off their clothes; the effect was medieval. Mrs Quayle's chauffeur drove slowly through the crowds at St Germain-des-Prés, down the rue Bonaparte, and across the river.

'What a good idea it was to capture the Bastille in July,' murmured Diana, who was sitting on my lap, 'rather than in December . . .'

'They were probably thinking ahead,' said Schooner, who was opposite us on one of the jump seats: 'They're a practical people.'

Allowing my hand to wander, I encountered one of his own ahead of me.

'Darling,' Diana whispered into my ear. We exchanged a long kiss.

The chauffeur stopped the car at the Rond-point of the Champs-Elysées. 'We can't get through the crowd,' said Mrs Quayle. 'We have to walk up the avenoo to my place; it's not far.' But as we got out she saw three or four horse-drawn carriages waiting at the corner and suggested we drive there. The others crowded into two of the carriages, and Diana and I took the third. This was a much better way of travelling, and in any case the crowd would not let anything through but a horse; moreover, I now had Diana all to myself.

'Oh, this is heavenly,' she said.

Our driver was turning left off the avenue to follow the other carriages, but she stopped him. 'Keep on, keep on!' she cried, like Léon Dupuis in *Madame Bovary*. 'Go right around the Arc de Triomphe and then come back!'

As we returned down the avenue a parade came out from the rue de Presbourg. About a hundred students, led by a makeshift band of drums and tin trumpets, were pulling a float bearing a gigantic movable phallus; worked by ropes, its head was slowly rising and falling. The crowd shrieked with joy as it moved slowly into the glare and crawled down the avenue. We fell in behind this symbol of the Third Republic. Reaching the Café Tortoni, our carriage turned off at the rue Galilée and soon stopped outside Mrs Quayle's apartment building. We looked into each other's eyes with rapture: we had become lovers.

TWELVE

The affair with Diana did not last long. We could agree on nothing. She admired Tolstoy, Rebecca West, Virginia Woolf, Cocteau, Hemingway, Dos Passos, Mauriac, W.C. Williams and Ezra Pound, none of whom I could stand. I admired Turgenev, Forster, Firbank, Breton, Dreiser, Proust, Eliot, Ransom and Robert Frost, all of whom she despised. Both of us liked Joyce and disliked D.H. Lawrence, but for altogether different reasons. To crown everything, I thought her own work was hollow and mannered, and she thought mine was silly.

We did not even enjoy the same movies. We almost fought over Eisenstein's *Ivan the Terrible*.

'Darling, it's the most marvellous modern thing I ever saw,' she said as we came out of the little Cinéma des Agriculteurs.

'It isn't modern, it's just crass. Worse than De Mille.'

'Don't be idiotic. The direction was superb. It has a tremendous scope and grandeur.'

'It's addressed to twelve-year-olds. Like a play in the parish hall, down to the false beards.'

'You missed the whole point.'

'No, it kept hitting me over the head till I was dizzy.'

'It has a magnificent visual line.'

'It's a piece of monolithic vulgarity.'

We also went to a few concerts on free tickets. We heard Cortot at the Salle Pleyel.

'Isn't it beautiful?' I said after the Chopin *Études*.

'Darling, it's simply vile. This soft, romantic slush—do you really like it? And that nasty effeminate man with his greasy hair and white face. He's making mistakes all the time too.'

'But he has the right pace, the lyrical bursts and pauses.'

'There's too much moonlight in his bloody garden.'

'You just don't like Chopin.'

'No, give me something clean and sharp, like Stravinsky or Honnegger.'

One day we had free tickets to a concert by Edgar Varèse, with the composer conducting.

'You'll loathe it,' said Diana. 'His music is real, new, vivid, significant, alive.'

The little concert hall was not far from the Folies-Bergère. It was surprisingly comfortable for the avant-garde, with cushions on the seats. The first few items on the program were very appealing—an atonic wailing on massed steel strings. The music seemed to belong in space, like the movement of planets in the ether. There was a good claque, and Varèse himself had a fine presence and personality; as the concert went on, however, the percussion section began to assume greater prominence. I had always been alarmed by heavy volumes of sound, and Varèse's music was growing steadily louder. I watched the preparations for the final item with misgiving, as the drums and cymbals were heavily reinforced and an immense hollow wooden box and three sets of mallets were brought in, along with a fire-whistle. The piece itself did not last very long, but towards the end the noise gradually became deafening. The finale was extraordinarily powerful: the drums were all beaten at once, three men attacked the wooden box, the cymbals clashed continuously, an electric bell began to ring and the fire-whistle was turned on full strength, while Varèse himself, sweating, his crinkly hair standing straight up, urged the players on. For the last fifty bars I had unobtrusively put my fingers in my ears, hoping no one would notice. When the concert was over the audience almost matched the performance in the volume of applause—cheering, howling, stamping their feet.

As we went out Diana looked at me with disgust. 'I saw you! You deliberately missed the whole beauty of the finale. With that last marvellous crescendo he actually achieved the effect of silence.'

There was also the difficulty over money. Her cheque for her novel had all gone towards maintaining her baby boy. We had no settled place to make love; she kept moving from one friend's place to another, each with a narrower and more sagging bed. The affair was doomed.

We had never been really in love, and were able to draw stakes in a friendly way one night in the Select.

'It's no use,' said Diana. 'We're even beginning to bore each other.'

'You could never bore me,' I said. 'I think we just don't respect each other's minds. You think I'm a nitwit, for example—a kind of bright insect.'

'I do. And you think I'm a false face attached to an attitude.'

'You're quite right. Your wit deceived me. You're the most amusing woman I've ever known. But think how awful it would be if we'd really fallen in love. All the tears, fights, swearing, breaking dishes, partings at midnight—me tramping the streets in a rage —'

'And me sobbing into a wet pillow. Isn't this much better?'

'It is a far, far better thing we do.'

'You know,' she said, 'I could never stand that sophomoric, superior attitude you have. Your book is awful too.'

'Maybe it is. But yours isn't much good either. The only difference is, you're *trying* harder.'

'You bastard. That book came out of my entrails. And I got five hundred dollars for it. All you got was about twenty.'

'For one chapter, yes. But there are going to be twenty-five chapters, which would make us equal.'

'You mean you're going to write twenty-five times as much of that bilge as you have already? Good God, darling, can you really keep it up?'

'Certainly.'

'And who do you think's going to publish it?'

'Bob said he might.'

'By God, I think he's crazy enough about you to do it.'

'It's fun when we're not serious, isn't it?'

'I'm not going to be serious about any man again, ever.'

'I don't expect I'll ever find a girl who's as much fun as you've been. You don't think we could keep on?'

'Darling, no! A thousand times no. It's been marvellous, but as you say we don't respect each other's minds. You know what I've been thinking is the best part of our affair? It's the fact we never lived together, and you don't have to reclaim your toothbrush and shaving stuff. It's so neat, so *uncluttered*. I think it's the nicest *affaire* I've ever had.'

The city was becoming unbearably hot. The studio, with its great skylight and windows, was almost impossible to live in during the daytime. M. Rouvely's work-room was no better. Worse than this, Montparnasse was now so overrun by tourists it was hard to find a place to sit down. It was clearly time to get out.

'Let's go somewhere where it's out of season,' said Bob. 'What about the Riviera? Starting with Marseilles.'

We packed and caught the afternoon train next day, travelling third class. The seats were made of wood and the heat was fearful. We had brought no food with us, and since third-class passengers weren't allowed in the dining-car we had to rely on the cheap red wine and sinewy sandwiches sold at the stations by the widows of war veterans. The lack of food did not seem to bother Bob; he never ate anything anyway.

By the time we reached Avignon my stomach seemed to be sticking to my backbone. There was a ten-minute stop, and without saying anything to us Graeme got down and ran off down the platform.

'Where's he gone?' said Bob, opening his eyes.

'I don't know. Looking for something to eat, I hope.'

'Don't worry, we'll have lunch in Marseilles. Shrimps, lobsters, whatever you want. It's only ten hours away.'

Graeme came panting into the compartment just as the train began to move and produced a few chocolate bars and a bag of unshelled peanuts. 'I had a time getting this stuff. But it'll keep us going.'

Bob brought out a bottle of whisky and we passed it from hand to hand until we all fell into a drunken sleep on the wooden benches. When I woke it was to a vision of paradise: through the window was the Mediterranean, even bluer than in the postcards. And there were the square sun-baked houses, the red earth, the grey-green vegetation, the palm trees. My throat was as dry as ashes, I was coated with a mixture of soot and sweat and aching all over; but the sight of that tideless inland ocean, mother of gods and men, nurse of poetry, changeless grandiose fact of the ancient world, made me dizzy with joy. The moment was permanent, unforgettable, Keatsian.

'What are you bawling about?' said Bob, opening his eyes. 'Your conscience troubling you?'

He looked out the window and sat up suddenly. 'Holy Moses, we've gone right past Marseilles! This is the line to Nice. What time is it?'

None of us had a watch. I went into the next compartment and asked the time: it was two o'clock.

'The important thing,' said Bob, 'is to stay on this train till we get to Nice. Look, boys, shall we go to Nice or back to Marseilles?'

'Nice,' said Graeme, 'since we're on the way there now. I don't like the idea of going back anywhere, it's bad luck.'

'Nice, then,' said Bob. 'It's closer to Monte Carlo and Ethel anyway. If the conductor comes through, we just pretend we're asleep.'

'How far does the train go?' I asked.

'Right into Italy,' said Graeme. 'Bordighera, I think.'

'Why don't we go to Italy?'

'Don't be stupid,' said Bob. 'Our tickets are only good to Marseilles. Some bastard at the border will start asking a lot of questions and the first thing you know we'll land up in jail. No, we'll get off at Nice if we can make it. Jesus, here's the conductor now!'

We all curled up on the benches until he had passed.

'Is there any whisky left?' asked Graeme. 'I've still got half a bottle of this chemical wine, but I don't trust it today.'

We were just coming into a small station. He pulled down the window. 'Excuse me, sir,' he said to an unshaven ragged man on the platform, holding out the wine bottle. 'Could you use this, my friend?'

The man seized the bottle, bowed, smiled, smelled it, then handed it back with a florid gesture. 'Thank you, sir. I am deeply touched, deeply obliged, but I must think of my health.' Raising his ragged cap, he moved away.

This was my first experience of the real Provençal courtesy. The curious poetic singsong of his speech was also new. Here was a man dressed like a tramp with the manners of a grandee.

Bob laughed. 'Now have a real drink,' he said. Rummaging in his bag, he produced another full bottle of whisky.

We arrived at Nice a few hours later in an alcoholic haze, quietly slipped off the train with our luggage, and piled into a taxi.

'Promenade des Anglais,' Bob told the driver. 'And then go east. We're looking for a *pension*.'

'An excellent idea,' said the driver. 'And the further east you go, the cheaper and better they are.'

We drove down the Avenue Victor-Hugo till we reached the sea and then turned right. I loved the city immediately, with its wide streets, ornate buildings and Edwardian air. I had never seen so many fat men or so many beautiful women; every fourth person was leading a dog.

We passed the Ruhl, the Savoy, the Negresco—hotels like white wedding-cakes. The stony beach was dotted with bathers, there were the white sails of the little boats, the clouds of seagulls, the palm-trees, and embracing it all the beautiful curve of the Bay of Angels.

After the big hotels came the wealthy villas with their hedges of laurel and acacia—all of them square, flat-topped, with round-topped Moorish windows and encrusted with ornaments. Then came the long, low houses, all with gardens—more modest but still incredibly spacious—with their signs: Pension Miramar, Pension Beaurepas, Pension Suisse, Pension Mon Rêve.

'Pension Mon Rêve sounds good,' said Bob. 'Stop here, driver. No, boys, don't you come in. I can smell a good *pension* better by myself.'

He came back in five minutes. 'No good.'

Pension des Anglais, Pension du Grand Bleu, Pension Anita, Pension

Jeff, Pension Le Hôme. Bob got out, went in, came out shaking his head.

Pension Poggi, Pension Russe, Pension Dora Melrose.

'I think Dora Melrose has the right sound,' he said.

It certainly looked well—a long two-storey house of peeling stucco, set far back from the road with a big dusty garden surrounded by a low stone wall.

'This is it,' said Bob when he came back. '125 francs a day for the three of us. With wine. Wait till you see the rooms. Holy Moses, it's a dream.'

We unloaded our bags and carried them in. The proprietress, a tall, stout woman in black, came forward with a harried smile.

'Madame Melrose,' said Bob. 'These are the two others. Like me they are clean, quiet and honest. We already love your place.'

'You are indeed welcome. But excuse me, I am not Dora Melrose. She died in 1880. I am called Madame Gyp. There is a whitebait pie for dinner tonight, and all the cooking here is done with butter; not oil, mind you, *butter*.'

We went upstairs and into three large bright rooms forming a suite that occupied the whole top storey facing the sea. There was even a private toilet.

'Didn't I tell you?' said Bob. 'It's a palace. I can pick them. I don't even have to see the rooms.'

Thinking of Schooner's recipe for a good restaurant, I asked him how he could do this.

'Simple. The *patronne* must look worried: it means she's human. There's no porter: it means no chichi. And the stairs were scrubbed.'

'Then the name Dora Melrose didn't mean anything?'

'Of course it did. It showed the force of tradition.'

'After all,' said Graeme, 'she could hardly call the place the Pension Gyp.'

'You're wrong,' said Bob. 'If she did it would be only another good sign, showing she didn't know U.S. slang. Now we've just got time for a swim.'

'We haven't got bathing suits,' I said.

'Rats, we'll buy them tomorrow. Just now we go in in our underwear.'

Ten minutes later we were out on the empty beach. The first dip in the ocean was like a baptism: all the grime and sweat and alcohol seemed to wash away in the embrace of the Mediterranean. We frolicked like dolphins—Graeme and I in shorts and Bob in his B.V.D.'s—and then stretched out on the ancient waveworn shingle to let the sinking sun dry and warm us. Hot, crowded Paris, the abominable trip, the sandwiches, peanuts, chocolate, wine and whisky were a thousand miles away. The sun on our skins was a kind of blessing: we had escaped and were happy.

I lay with my hand on my arm, looking out at the Bay of Angels. The little sailboats had all disappeared, the seagulls had gone to roost somewhere, only a few scattered walkers paced the broad promenade; the sky was turning from cerulean to indigo. This was happiness, I thought, licking the salt from my hand. Happiness was still the rule of my existence, a thing to be grasped and enjoyed by right; and hunger and sensuality too. All at once my desire became centred on the image of a woman—calm, warm, voluptuous, and willing—and then by an association of pleasure that was absurd but impossible to resist, on the mysterious prospect of a whitebait pie, something I had never tasted.

THIRTEEN

In two weeks we were all as brown and plump as partridges. The days were passed in swimming, sunbathing and eating. The heat was dry and intense, the ocean always an ecstasy, the food delicious.

O blinding, sunbaked days, O beautiful blue water, will I ever enjoy you again? Lobsters broiled in butter, portugaise oysters, tender little octopuses in black sauce, how your memory haunts me in this abode of corned-beef hash and Jell-O!

We were all working, each on his book. Bob, wearing his hairnet almost constantly, was pouring out reams of a book of which he would tell us only the title, *Promiscuous Boy*; Graeme was still planning *The Flying Carpet*, whose heroine weighed 250 pounds; and I was trying to write the third chapter of this book and feeling handicapped by the recentness of the events. I could not see Daphne and Angela in any kind of perspective and was reduced to stating just what had happened.

Bob had stopped drinking altogether and was becoming still more handsome; his little paunch had disappeared, the whites of his eyes lost their yellow tinge, and he had stopped talking in his sleep.

Our quarters, we found, belonged on a long lease to an elderly Dutchman who had forbidden Madame Gyp to let anyone use them. But he was not due to return till October, so we had the whole long Mediterranean summer ahead of us. On top of all this, Bob had extracted a large sum of money from his mother-in-law. Everything was going well.

'Money,' he said, 'is not so important as Fitzgerald thinks, but you have to have some. Not too much, though. You'll notice this when we have lunch with Sally and Terence Marr tomorrow. They're at the Ruhl, of course. Wonderful people, and they'd be perfectly happy if only she didn't have so goddamn much money.'

'How much does she have?' asked Graeme.

'Twenty, thirty million, how do I know? I bet she doesn't know herself.'

We walked down to the Ruhl next day. It was not the biggest or most ornate hotel in Nice, and not as pretentious as the Negresco, but as soon as we were inside, the aplomb of the doorman revealed everything: this was the abode of quiet millionaires.

Sally and Terence Marr were in a big, high-ceilinged, untidy suite facing the sea. Nothing Bob had told me of Terence could have done justice to his charm. He was not only the best-looking man I had ever seen, but he seemed quite unaware of it; it was not only the perfection of his manners but the natural warmth that radiated from him like sunlight. I especially envied him his nose, curved like a seagull's: less authoritative than T.S. Eliot's and less inquisitive than Casanova's, it was somehow better than either. His eyes were bright blue, his accent curiously Irish.

'What will you have to dhrink?' he said to me at once. 'We've sherry, brandy and Scotch.'

Sally Marr was no less attractive. The shape of her head was in the best Egyptian style, her black eyes sparkled with life. Her breathless nasal voice was irresistible.

Bob had begun drinking whisky, tossing off glass after glass.

'Dora Melrhose,' said Terence thoughtfully. 'The name of your pension has the breath of an old English hedgerow. Tell me, does she wear a veil and mittens?'

'Rats, she died before any of us were born. When are we going to have lunch?'

'Shall we have it here?' said Terence. 'I'll ring.'

'No,' said Sally. 'This room's a mess and the waiter's such a nasty-looking little man. We'll have it in the grill.'

We went down to the grill, where Terence ordered an enormous meal of oysters, langoustines with mayonnaise, sweetbreads and green peas, parsley potatoes, a pineapple tart, and a magnum of champagne.

'We're looking for a villa to rent this winter,' said Sally. 'Where in hell should we go? We don't care for Monte Carlo, Beaulieu is stuffy, and Cap Ferrat is all up-and-down cliffs. We'd like a nice beach.'

'What's wrong with Antibes?' said Bob. 'Mary Reynolds and Marcel Duchamp are there. So is Aleister Crowley, in case you want a Black Mass. There's a nice beach, too.'

'We saw it yesterday,' said Terence. 'Tons of flesh. Bodies laid out like after a battle.'

'Such a lot of *fat* men,' said Sally. 'And their girls.'

'All the world and his misthress,' said Terence. 'Sally, what's wrong with Nice itself? We'll have lots of good company, what with Bob and his friends. Why not take a suite right here?'

'No, I want my own garden and servants. This is a nice place, but no privacy. How about Eze?'

'That's all up-and-down too.'

The conversation was becoming boring. I understood what Bob had said about people having too much money.

'All right,' said Terence when we had finished lunch. 'Let's look at Eze. I'll get the car.'

'For God's sake come along with us,' said Sally when he had gone. 'You're not too busy, any of you? Terence just drives *past* places, he never wants to stop.'

'He's been driving past places all his life,' said Bob. 'So have I. We're footloose, that's all, we don't like putting down roots.'

'Just a pair of bums, you mean. Now you,' she turned to Graeme, 'you're not a bum, you have a nice domestic look. I bet you appreciate a home.'

'As long as it's not my own,' he said. 'I mean, I like other people's homes.'

'I see. A parasite. Somebody else makes the home and you move in. What about you?' she turned to me.

'I ran away from home last winter and so far I'm not sorry. I don't want another one right away.'

She gave me a long penetrating look. 'Just now, young man, you think you've got the world by the tail. But do you know what you're going to be thirty years from now? *A nasty old man.*'

The power of her black eyes was for a moment frightening; her words were like a judge's sentence. Then she laughed her curious dry, nasal laugh. 'Don't worry, it's a long way off. I'll be a witch myself by then.'

'Perhaps we could look each other up.'

'It's a date. 1959.'

As we got up to go the waiter presented the bill with a discreet murmur. Would Madame sign?

Terence was waiting beside the car, talking in Provençal to the *chasseur.* Terence, I was to learn, had the gift of tongues as well as the ability to charm all kinds of functionaries—barmen, porters, waiters, taxi-drivers, cashiers and chambermaids.

The car was a stunning open Hispano-Suiza, with a body of natural wood, like a yacht, yards of aluminum hood, and a metal heraldic bird swooping above the radiator. It was a thing of surpassing beauty, and Bob, Graeme and I sank into the rich leather cushions of the back seat with a luxurious sensation. For me, however, the trip was a nightmare. Terence drove like a madman. There was no question of his skill as a driver, but I found his habit of passing other cars at blind corners and the tops of hills so disturbing that I began to wish I could get out. Graeme and Bob, who had never driven a car themselves, were enjoying the scenery; and at last, reflecting that we are all in the hands of God, I did the same.

We reached Eze in a matter of minutes. Sally had a list of properties to rent and I admired her rapid evaluation of each from the outside.

'Slow down here,' she told Terence every now and then. 'Villa Juanita, yes. No, it's lousy. Go on . . . Villa Mancini: no, too small . . . Villa Bella Vista: I wouldn't be found dead in a place with a name like that . . . Villa Montrésor: just a roadside dump . . . Château des Arbalêtriers. Stop! This isn't too bad.'

Terence skidded to a stop beside a pair of ten-foot-high stone gate-posts surmounted by snarling gardant lions holding shields in front of them.

I. John Glassco in 1928. *National Archives of Canada, PA* 188476.

II. Graeme Taylor, John Glassco, and Robert McAlmon on the beach at Nice. *National Archives of Canada, PA 188182.*

III. Graeme Taylor, John Glassco, and Sibley Dreis (Stanley Dahl), Nice. *National Archives of Canada, PA 188181.*

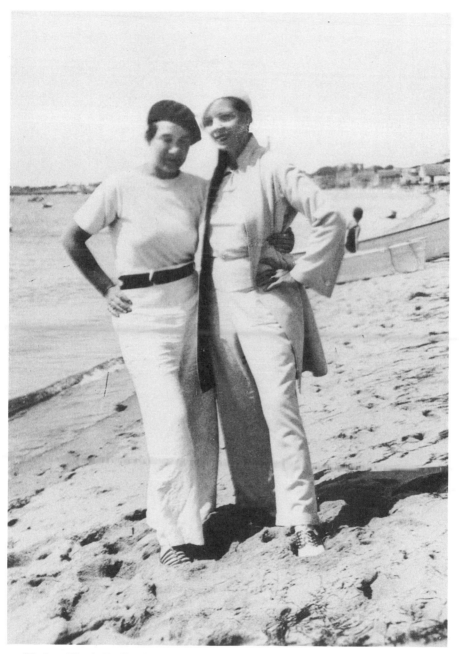

IV. Thelma Wood (Emily Pine) and Djuna Barnes (Willa Torrance), *c.* 1930. *McKeldin Library, University of Maryland.*

v. John Glassco by Adolph Dehn, Paris, 1928. *National Archives of Canada*, C107027.

VI. Man Ray (Narwahl) and Robert Desnos, 1928. *Copyright 1995 Man Ray Trust—ADAGP-ARS.*

VII. The Surrealists, 1930 (*left to right*): Tristan Tzara, Paul Éluard, André Breton, Jean Arp, Salvador Dalí, Yves Tanguy, Max Ernst, René Crevel, Man Ray. *Copyright 1995 Man Ray Trust—ADAGP-ARS.*

VIII. Kiki by Man Ray. *Copyright 1995 Man Ray Trust—ADAGP-ARS.*

IX. The poster advertising the Gala at which Kiki was proclaimed 'Queen of Montparnasse'.

x. Kay Boyle (Diana Tree) by Man Ray, *c.* 1926. *Copyright 1995 Man Ray Trust —
ADAGP-ARS.*

XI. Margaret Whitney, who was probably the model for Mrs Quayle.
National Archives of Canada, PA 188183.

XII. The Dingo in 1925. Standing at the entrance are the American owner Louis Wilson and his Dutch wife Yopi. *Courtesy of Hugh Ford.*

XIII. Jimmie Charters (*left*) and Paris *Tribune* reporter Leigh Hoffman (*far right*), *c.* 1928. *Courtesy of Hugh Ford.*

XIV. The Dôme in the mid-twenties. La Coupole is almost out of sight down the Boulevard du Montparnasse. *Courtesy of Hugh Ford.*

XV. The Hôtel Jules César, now the refurbished Hôtel Unic at 56 rue du Montparnasse, almost directly across the street from the Falstaff. *Michael Gnarowski.*

XVI. 147 rue Broca today (now the rue Léon Maurice Nordmann), with the metal gate at the far right opening into the *impasse*. *Michael Gnarowski*.

XVII. The *impasse*, or dead-end laneway, at 147 rue Broca, with artists' studios. *Michael Gnarowski*.

XVIII. The Falstaff, on the rue du Montparnasse, today. *Michael Gnarowski.*

XIX. The rue Daguerre district today, with some artists' studio buildings still surviving in their original state. *Michael Gnarowski.*

This Quarter

Nº 4   Spring 1929

Edited by Ethel Moorhead

■

ADDRESS:-
ETHEL MOORHEAD
5 Descente de Larvotto,
Monte-Carlo, Monaco.

Price : — 2 dollars.

Extract from an Autobiography

by JOHN GLASSCO

In the winter of 1928, George Graham and I were living in an apartment on Metcalfe Street in Montreal. We were working in the Sun Life Assurance Company of Canada, and we have many times since then agreed that that month and a half was the most wretched period of our lives. To get up at eight o'clock of a Canadian winter morning, to bathe insufficiently in a small bathtub which neither of us ever had the courage to clean, to dress without any attention to an individual appearance, and to stumble down the street with our cheekbones nipped by the frosty wind, all these things might have been endured more easily had there not been the prospect of the long day's work before us.

the employment of he Company for
the time, seemed to justify my doing
pidity and pettiness of McGill Univers-
eatly, and my father and mother could
y I was unable to ignore it all and mere-
ks.   One episode in my dealings with
f McGill comes to my mind, when an
om I was taking a course of writing,
a short story of mine with the words :
nly the work of a night ".   I did not
idered himself any the less because he
activities of an even shorter duration,
give me a fuller appreciation of the
owed me that his understanding of it
me and sex of the principal character.
my father that I refused to go to
(I was then seventeen yerads old, and
ear), and would he. allow me to write,
a great disappointment to him and to
I was ungrateful and lacking in man-
ould go to work : I would be allowed
e.   Thus it was that at this period of
my family that I decided to leave the

— 198 —

This Quarter

Number FOUR.

TABLE OF CONTENTS

XX. (*left*) Three pages from the issue of *This Quarter* in which the 'Extracts' by Graeme Taylor and John Glassco appeared—along with contributions by Ernest Walsh, Joseph Vogel, Robert McAlmon, Edward Dahlberg, Emmanuel Carnevali, and Archibald Craig.

XXI. (*above*) James Joyce and Sylvia Beach, 1920, in front of the first Shakespeare and Company bookstore on the rue Dupuytren. *Reproduced with the permission of the Poetry/Rare Books Collection, University Libraries, State University of New York at Buffalo.*

XXII. The cover of the *Guide Rose*, and an advertisement for the Sphinx, both featuring enticements to the sexual attractions of Paris.

'Do you really want to go in?' he asked. 'It looks dreadful to me. It must be owned by a Ghreek.'

'Yes, go in. It might be amusing. And they're asking peanuts.'

We careered around a number of stately curves and came out in front of a tremendous imitation castle complete with battlements, machicolations and towers with slits for the crossbowmen.

'It's marvellous,' said Sally, clasping her hands. 'Unbelievably absurd. There's everything but a drawbridge. Let's take it.'

'We'd better look inside first.'

'No, dear. I can tell what it's like inside. Stamped-leather chairs, refectory tables, whitewash, tapestry and bad pictures. It's just what I want—big and impersonal.'

'We'll go and see the agent tomorrow.'

'We'll see him right now. Back to Nice we go.'

But going through Cimiez she suddenly said as we lurched around a bend, 'There's Frank Harris's place. I'd almost forgotten the old boy. Stop and we'll see if he's in.'

Terence drew up outside a small ugly house with a weathered slate sign lettered VILLA EDOUARD VII. 'Perhaps he's taking a nap,' he said hopefully.

But to me the prospect of seeing the most celebrated English scoundrel of the last fifty years was exciting. I had read nothing of his except a few short stories and the first four volumes of *My Life and Loves*; but I thought the latter was the best mixture of adventure, documentation and sheer nastiness ever written. It was as vivid as a newsreel, as informative as a police report. The pictures of New York, the Far West, equatorial Africa and fin-de-siècle London were wonderfully alive: one saw and felt a vanished Broadway, plains covered with cattle and cowboys, jungles and native villages, and a great shining city of hansom-cabs, political intrigue and plushy champagne-suppers, as if one were walking through them oneself in the company of a superb raconteur and inspired liar. The book had such life it already breathed immortality.

I told Sally I thought he was better than Rousseau.

'He'll like that,' she said.

She got out and pulled a bell-rope hanging from a cement pillar, producing a hideous distant clang from inside. We waited for a few minutes and at last a shifty-looking butler in a red-striped vest came to the gate and looked at Sally suspiciously.

101

'Monsieur Arriss is not at home,' he said. 'Who shall I say called?'

'Of course he's at home,' said Sally. 'Tell him it's Mrs Sally Marr, and be quick about it. Frank's worried about duns,' she said as the butler went away. 'And the police too, I think. They're all after him for that funny book.'

'You should have let him know ahead,' said Terence.

'And give him time to cook up some fancy scheme for getting money out of me? Not on your life.'

The butler came back smiling. 'Monsieur Arriss will be delighted to receive Mrs Marr and her company. Please enter.'

'Bob,' said Sally, turning around, 'aren't you coming?'

'Balls,' he said from the car. 'I'm not interested in that old Victorian poop.'

We were shown into a long cool room with English-style furniture. A little grey-faced, grey-haired man strode forward, bowed jerkily from the waist and held out a large palm to Sally. He didn't look like Frank Harris at all.

Where were the wig-like hair, the glaring eyes, the duck-like snout and comic moustache of the portraits? This man was extremely good-looking. His light-brown eyes were especially fine; his mouth was wide, roguish, and now that the prodigious moustache had been trimmed to a decent size, it looked sensitive and even surprisingly weak. But what surprised me most were the handsome straight thick grey eyebrows which now softened his whole face. They were certainly not the thin threatening lines of the portraits and photographs, and as they were clearly not false ones I suddenly realized that in the days of his grandeur he must have, in order to make his small eyes more prominent and compelling, deliberately plucked and shaped them into those hypnotic Mephistophelean angles that Rothenstein and Beerbohm had reproduced.

The only thing unchanged was his costume—a black, high-lapelled Edwardian jacket, light waistcoat, enormous striped cravat barred with an ornamental clip, and the famous stiff winged collar, at least three inches high, which was obviously and successfully designed to conceal a reedy and over-long neck. His hands were extraordinarily strong and ugly, his ears like cabbage-leaves.

'Me dear Sally, Terence,' he said briskly. But the famous booming voice, which had at one time been able to dominate dinner-parties of forty people, as well as the entire lounge of the Café Royal, had become little more than a vibrant wheeze. 'Sit down. Join me in a vermouth, all of you. François, glasses—ice—lemon!'

He shot a swift look at Graeme and me that was frightening in its intensity. He had the ability of looking straight through one, and his extremely short stature—even with the well-made lifts in his boot-heels—seemed somehow to make him more impressive: he had the actor's gift of projecting his personality with such force that one felt annihilated. It was easy to see how he had been able to knock editors, cabinet members, millionaires and women over like ninepins.

All his attention was focused on Sally, and he became amusing as he spoke of his difficulties with the police.

'The beggars are still after me for me old *L. and L*s. Hard to believe in a country like France, ain't it?'

'I thought they backed down last year,' said Terence.

'Overtly, yes. Covertly, no. A damn surreptitious lot they are. That book has nearly been the death of me. Times I almost wish I'd never written it.'

'Don't say that, Frank,' said Sally. 'Someone was just telling me it's better than Rousseau.'

'Who? Not Shaw anyway, I'll be bound. Rousseau, eh? He got into a peck of trouble with his book too, poor beggar. But nothing like I have. By the way, G.B.S. is over at Antibes right now, he's coming to call. I'm expecting him any time. He's just written another bad play, I understand. Well, none of us can keep it up forever.'

He suddenly looked tired and old, but he was not a man to court sympathy. When he flagged it was obviously only to withdraw into himself, to some inner source of energy; he could receive no strength from others.

As we left he shook hands with us all in a cordial manner. At the last minute he drew Sally aside, and Terence, Graeme and I went back to the car.

'How was the old whoremaster?' asked Bob.

'Very well for three score and ten,' said Terence. 'But he's almost lost his voice.'

'It's about time.'

Sally came out and got in the car; she looked thoughtful.

'He didn't try to rhape you?' said Terence.

'No, it was just a touch.'

'How much did he want?' said Bob.

103

'A hundred pounds.'

'Poor old fellow,' said Terence. 'I hope you let him have it.'

'I said I'd let him know.'

We roared back to the Ruhl. 'I'm going to the agent about the castle now. Meet us in the Perroquet tonight at ten,' Sally said to Bob. 'All of you. I feel like dancing.'

'The Perroquet? That dump?'

'We'll call for you in the car,' said Terence. 'At the Dora Melrhose. Around ten.'

'Do you know where it is?'

'Terence can find it,' said Sally. 'Terence can find anything.'

The Perroquet was patronized by all the wealthy scum of the Riviera. Why Sally had chosen it I could not make out. The decoration was tasteless, the prices exorbitant, the staff of criminal appearance, the orchestra beneath contempt; but it was crowded to bursting. Terence had reserved the best table in the room, and there was a magnum of bad champagne waiting in an icebucket.

Our entrance caused a minor sensation. Sally was wearing a tiara and a white dinner-dress covered with sequins, and Terence a suit of pale apple-green Egyptian linen. Bob, Graeme and I in our dark clothes provided a good background for them.

I found myself sitting opposite Sally.

'Did you arrange about the castle?' I asked.

'No. As soon as they heard who I was the owner jumped the rent. Sickening. Well, it was probably impossible to heat anyway.'

We got up to dance. The band was playing a jerky *paso doble* and the floor was so crowded it was difficult to move.

After a half-hour in the Perroquet we left and went to the Cicogne, then to the Cacatoès, then to the Flamingo: that was the year (as Scott Fitzgerald would have said) when they were calling the cabarets after birds. All these places were identical. The crowds were heavy, the music bad, the heat withering, the champagne spurious. But Sally became steadily gayer. Her eyes shone, her laughter came in little cascades, she danced continually. Terence was obviously bored but did not say so; Graeme and Bob simply drank heavily; and I began to get a headache. As we came out of the Toucan at one o'clock, Bob announced he was going to walk home.

'No, no,' said Sally. 'You can't go home yet, Bob!'

'Who says I can't?'

'In the first place you can't even walk straight.'

'Then I'll walk around in a circle.'

'Let's all walk around in a circle,' said Terence. 'At any rate we'll get some air.'

We walked, rather unsteadily, through a public garden that was all palm-trees and rhododendrons. The air was heavy with scent, the sky full of stars. A short thickset man in black approached us. 'Good evening, lady and gentlemen,' he said in French in a rich Provençal baritone, taking off his hat and sweeping it low. 'Would you care for a little amusement? Some good movies? Blue, very blue. The show will commence in a few minutes. Just around the corner, in our beautiful old town.'

'Splendid,' said Terence. 'Sally, we haven't seen a good bad movie for a long time. Come on.'

'If it's not too boring.'

'No,' said the man. 'Very bizarre, very coquette. Made in Berlin.'

'How much?' she said.

'Very cheap. One hundred francs each.'

'A hundred francs! Listen, we'll pay two hundred for the five of us. Take it or leave it.'

'Three hundred francs, madame. These movies cost a lot of money to buy. They are really charming. The cast of characters does everything. There are some trained animals too.'

'Two hundred. If the show is any good we'll give you fifty more.'

'Agreed, madame! Please come this way.'

We followed him back across a square. In a few minutes we were in the old town, walking through the narrow winding streets and between high buildings like the sets in *Dr Caligari*.

'How in hell do we find our way back?' said Bob. 'I'm lost already.'

'Don't worry,' said Sally. 'Terence will know.'

The thickset man turned off down a small black passage and opened a heavy wooden door. 'Here we are,' he said. 'Two hundred francs, I beg you.'

Terence gave him two bills and we went into a small pitchdark theatre where the lighted screen was a blank white. The place seemed to be almost full.

'Begin, begin!' a man in the audience growled as we sat down. 'This is an outrage! We do not come here to sit in the dark.'

Everyone else began calling for action; there were almost as many women as men. At last a gramophone began playing a Strauss waltz and the title of the first film was flashed on the screen in German, French and English: *Der Zeitvertreib Rajahs, Les Délassements du Rajah, The Rajah's Recreations*.

It started in rather slowly, with the turbaned and jewelled Rajah lying among cushions talking with a fat Negro eunuch and eating some sweetmeats proffered him by a small boy wearing nothing but a woman's wig; the candies, it turned out, were of an aphrodisiac nature, and the Rajah, at last throwing off a coverlet, sat up and displayed himself in all his valliance. The eunuch smote his hands together and two rather elderly women in loose trousers and boleros ran in and prostrated themselves before the Rajah, who smiled and stroked his handlebar moustache. After a while the eunuch removed their trousers and the Rajah caressed them in a regal and absentminded way while the boy did a little dance. Nobody seemed to be enjoying himself but the Rajah.

'What an arhtist,' whispered Terence. 'But it's not fair, he's carrying the whole scene.'

'I wish to God they'd play something else besides those damn Viennese waltzes,' said Sally. 'Haven't they got *Song of India* or *Dardanella* or something?'

The eunuch had clapped his hands again and two more heavily built women, both nude, ran in and placed themselves before the Rajah, where they began gesturing, rolling their eyes and shaking their breasts. There were close-ups of these gestures, interspersed with views of the Rajah's *tout ensemble* and grinning face. The camera then switched to the eunuch, who parted his robe and, shrugging sadly, showed how indifferent he was to it all. At last the Rajah rose, seized one of the women, and threw her on the couch while the gramophone went into *The Gipsy Baron*. Towards the end his turban fell off, but by this time the camera was switching from one close-up to another with such speed that the whole performance became almost surrealistic before the screen went black, the projector whirred and the word FINIS appeared for an instant.

'Bravo!' cried the audience. '*Formidable! Rigolo! Bis, bis!*'

I looked past Sally and Terence and saw that Bob had fallen asleep.

'Is this an intermission?' said Sally. 'I'd rather like a drink.'

'Here, my love,' said Terence, handing her a flask. 'Obviously there's no bar here. Quite a good turnout,' he said, looking around at the audience who were now faintly visible in the light coming from the luminous white screen. *The Gipsy Baron* was still scraping away on the gramophone. Most of the women, I noticed, were wearing masks.

'This is a neglected art-form, don't you think?' Terence said to me. 'Every time I see one of these films I have the ambition to produce something really good. I could write a better scenario than what we've just seen, to begin with.'

'But where are you going to get the actors?' said Sally.

'I suppose one would have to comb the underworhld. One thing, though, I'd get an option on the Rajah. He's a real trouper.'

'I've had enough,' said Sally suddenly. 'We all need a drink too. Give the man his fifty francs, will you, Terence?'

We came out into the velvety Mediterranean night and Terence led the way back to the square where we had left the car. Graeme was supporting Bob, who was still half asleep.

'I don't think I want a drink after all,' said Sally. 'We'll take the boys home and call it a day.' Her eyes were glowing as she got into the car and moved close to Terence.

FOURTEEN

I now found myself thinking constantly of women. I recalled Daphne and Angela, Emily Pine, Diana Tree and the girl with the rhinestone choker. I considered Mrs Quayle and Sally Marr. I even dreamed of *The Rajah's Recreations*. Moreover, I had noticed a plump, black-eyed girl who often walked alone on the Promenade past our *pension*. She wore white trousers that were extremely tight: I had never seen such magnificent contours. She seemed always lost in thought. Was she merely shy? When we passed she kept her eyes fixed straight before her or looked the other way.

She must be either a Scandinavian, a Turk, or a Jewess—and, as such, unassailable, I thought—and I decided to leave her in peace.

But her image would not do as much for me. I found myself dreaming now of those contours in their prison of white duck. I asked myself angrily: if she doesn't care to be approached, can't she at least wear a skirt?

Bob and Graeme had also noticed her.

'She's almost too young for any of us,' said Graeme thoughtfully, 'and, I'm afraid, much too innocent.'

'Rats,' said Bob, 'don't let that puppy-fat fool you. She's been around.'

'How can you tell?' I asked.

'From her quality, her air, the way she looks at you. But you'd better forget that little tart. She's trouble, I'm warning you. Better stick to your meemoirs. Have you got anything I can send to Ezra yet? The second chapter won't do, it's too long and scrappy, and nobody's interested in that old fart George Moore.'

I typed out Chapter 3 in the evening, the one about Daphne and Angela. He read it through with his lipless grin. 'This is the stuff,' he said, 'it has the real juvenile quality. Ezra will take this. We'll show it to Ethel Moorhead tomorrow too. It will give her a laugh, bless her old heart.'

The bus ride to Monte Carlo along the Grande Corniche, with its plunging view of red rocks washed by white breakers and the crenellated bays lapped by the blue ocean, was enchanting, even better than Dufy. But the town itself was disappointing: it was too full of elderly English and gave an impression of heavy meals, eczema, and too much money.

Ethel Moorhead's house on the Descente de Larvotto was the dreamhouse of an English spinster. Inside it was furnished like a Sussex cottage, with chintz, brass and family portraits—except for two entire walls of bookcases full of avant-garde books. Her desk, facing a fine view of the sea, was piled with manuscripts, drawings and galley proofs, and bore a typewriter that must have been made around 1910.

She herself was tall, lean and angular, and was dressed in an ankle-length skirt and shirtwaist; her lustreless brown hair framed her face in an ugly amorphous bob, and her cheeks, lightly dusted with white face-powder, still kept their girlish contours. She was incredibly shy and immeasurably shrewd. She blushed constantly, yet maintained a soldierly and uncompromising air. I remembered Bob saying her father had been the military governor of Mauritius.

Small glasses of sweet vermouth were served and we sat and talked. She was as little like the indomitable editor of *This Quarter* as one could imagine. It was hard to believe that this diffident, maidenly woman, who spoke so little and listened with such attention, had made literary history as the first publisher of almost every first-rate writer in the past five years; that she had discovered Hemingway, Kay Boyle, and

108

Paul Bowles, defended Joyce and denounced Pound. She had also, it was true, published some of the worst rubbish I had ever read. But after meeting her I wondered whether she had not done so simply to give her magazine its inimitable blend of absurdity and brilliance: there was a mysterious feline humour in her eyes.

This Quarter, as I knew from Bob, was not, like *The Dial, Poetry*, or *transition*, the creation of a wealthy individual. Ethel Moorhead had very modest means and gave a great deal in private and anonymous charity—mainly to writers.

It did not matter whether they were good or only promising writers, it was enough for her if they were sick, starving, or discouraged; in fact she felt an even greater sympathy and compassion for bad writers. If literature ever has any collective voice in presenting candidates for canonization, I would propose Ethel Moorhead as its natural nominee— even at the risk of affronting her severely agnostic shade. Her goodness was so apparent it seemed to shine around her.

Bob gave her the third chapter of my book. To my embarrassment she began reading it on the spot with incredible speed, turning over the pages every fifteen or twenty seconds, her smile broadening.

'It's jolly good,' she said. 'Congratulations, young man. You've skirted vulgarity with great cleverness. Robert, did you say you were going to send this to the man Poond?'

'Unless you want it for your summer number.'

'There will be no summer number. I am discontinuing my magazine.'

'Hey, you can't do that,' said Bob. 'What's going to happen to English literature?'

'It will manage. I think Mr Titus may take over my magazine. But if he does not, there's always the man Poond, with his *Exile*, to keep things moving.'

'Rats, he doesn't know how to edit a magazine. Are you serious?'

'Yes. You see, Robert, I have always thought it a good policy to stop anything just before it seems necessary to stop. It applies to gambling, exercise and eating—so why not to editing?'

It was clear her mind was made up. I did not know then that she was still grief-stricken over the death of the poet Ernest Walsh, and the idea of carrying on a work in which he had been so closely associated was unspeakably painful to her. She told me some weeks later that the very words 'This Quarter', with their recollections of his presence, moved her to tears.

'If this is the last number,' said Bob thoughtfully, 'I'll send you an extract from my new book, *The Politics of Existence.*'

'Robert, I am grateful.' The curious feline humour shone in her eyes for an instant. 'Even though it is like all your other recent work, I promise to print it.'

'What else have you got?'

'Some young men. Dahlberg, Joseph Vogel, Paul Bowles, Archie Craig, and of course more of Carnevali's *Journal.*'

'Oh God. That poor bum. How is he, by the way?'

'I don't think he is long for this world. He sends you his love and gratitude from the nursing home in Bassano.'

'Ethel,' said Bob, 'you can't turn your magazine into a home for waifs and strays. Carnevali's no good, all he has is that mendicant, Mediterranean quality. He thinks he's a troubadour, but he's just an organ-grinder and the monkey too. Oh all right, his *Journal* has a few bright spots, I grant you, but most of the time he's just so damned busy being sorry for himself.'

'You think he has no reason to be, Robert?'

'Of course he has,' he said roughly. 'He knows he's going to die pretty soon. Have you got any whisky?'

'Why yes, Robert, I always keep some Johnnie Walker.'

I only learned much later that Bob had been helping her support Carnevali, who was in an advanced encephalitic condition, for the past two years. There were facets of Bob's character that he kept carefully concealed.

He had reduced the level in the square bottle by almost a quarter before it was time for dinner.

'Let me take you all to Villefranche for dinner,' said Ethel Moorhead. 'It's much nicer there.' She turned to me with a twinkle. 'And there is said to be a colony of inverted young women there too, I believe.'

We took a taxi to Villefranche and walked down the shallow steps of the street to the little harbour. The evening was already cool and the stars were just coming out. The three or four cafés threw their lighted reflections on the water, accordion music was coming from somewhere overhead; farther out, in the bay itself, the triangle of lights on an American battleship sketched the outline of a gigantic sailboat. Ethel Moorhead had reserved the best table at the Auberge des Palmiers, looking directly out over the water; she had also ordered oysters, bouillabaisse with rice and three bottles of chilled Moselle.

'I know your favourite wine, Robert,' she said. 'And as you told me your young friends enjoy these little octopuses, I ordered plenty of them mixed in with our fish stew. But no more whisky.'

The oysters were so fresh they quivered when touched with the fork, the rolled and buttered wafers of brown bread were light and nutty, the bouillabaisse was like a glowing eclogue.

The conversation was neither profound nor frivolous. Ethel Moorhead managed it so adeptly one was not even conscious of her doing so. We all talked about ourselves in turn—always an irresistible subject—and over our dessert of a small open apple tart she herself spoke of her experiences in the suffragette movement, when as a girl she had been among those who chained themselves to the iron railings outside the House of Commons.

'Then,' she said, 'they put us all in jail for about a week. There was even some public agitation to have us birched! And such common, brutal women the wardresses were! They would have loved to do it, I'm sure.' She paused, blushing slightly. 'But Miss Pankhurst never lost heart. "Girls," she said, "if they should inflict this indignity on you, remember it is only another chance for you to show your loyalty to the cause of woman's suffrage." Ah, she was a heroine, a saint and a true English gentlewoman. And I don't use those terms lightly.'

A yellow moon was now shining on the sea and there was a faint sound of mandolins from nearby. Ethel Moorhead sighed as she looked out into the night. 'I have had many friends,' she said, 'but none better than Miss Pankhurst and her little band of girls back in those days. It was a privilege to serve with them. And we conquered, after all, didn't we? Yes, we beat that man Winston Churchill!' She paused, savouring her triumph rather sadly for a moment. 'But come, let's all go to the Casino for a half-hour or so. I understand neither of you young men has yet been there, and you mustn't miss the experience.'

'It's a dump,' said Bob. 'But perhaps these kids will get a kick out of it.'

We climbed the steps of the street to the highway. I would rather have stayed where we were and enjoyed the quiet dream-like beauty of Villefranche than go into a gambling saloon; but I sensed it was our hostess herself who really wanted to stake a few hundred francs, according to what Bob had told us was her nightly habit. It was not therefore a great disappointment to find, when we arrived at the doors of the Casino, that I was refused entrance.

'Madame Moorhead,' said the smiling dinner-coated man behind the desk. 'I am sorry—but we have our little rules.'

'My dear Monsieur Locatelli,' she said, 'he is young naturally, but I can vouch for the ripeness of his intelligence and judgement. Years are not to be counted by the calendar.'

'Alas, the Casino knows no other way. Everything here is mathematical, as you know. If the gentleman would, however, let me glance at his passport . . .'

'There is no need,' I said. 'I am only eighteen.'

'How I envy you!' exclaimed Locatelli, raising his eyes ecstatically to the ceiling. 'A golden age indeed. Come now, Madame, put yourself in my place. You understand my position as a functionary.'

'This is absurd,' said Ethel Moorhead, drawing herself up. 'Very well, then none of us shall go in.'

'But I don't care for gambling at all,' I said. 'I'd much rather sit outside and wait for you. I've never been at the Café de Paris over there and I'd like to sit and soak up the atmosphere. But I wish you'd put fifty francs on the sixth transversal for me and we'll split the gain or loss.'

Her eyes lit up. I could see she was now doubly anxious to get to the tables. 'The sixth transversal, you say?'

'Sixteen to eighteen.'

'The golden age,' murmured Monsieur Locatelli, taking her entrance money.

They all went in and I strolled over to the Café de Paris, telling myself that Graeme, with his fine novelist's eye, would be able to describe the decoration of the Casino just as well as if I'd been there myself. Then I saw the girl of the white trousers sitting at a table all by herself.

I bowed to her and sat down at the next table. I noticed she was nursing a bock and ordered one myself. The situation seemed to call for a certain boldness and I said in French, 'We are both quite far from home, mademoiselle, aren't we?'

She tossed her head irritably. *'Je ne parle pas français.'*

Her accent, with its flat mouthed vowels, was unmistakably North American.

'Excuse me,' I said in English, 'I was saying we were some way from home. I didn't realize it was more than 3,000 miles.'

She looked startled, then a timid smile broke over her face.

'I've been trying to speak to you for the past two weeks,' I went on. 'I'd like to be friends with you.'

She said nothing. I looked at her deep black eyes, the plump curve of her cheek, the small blue-white teeth, the sulky preRaphaelite mouth. Before I could continue, however, her whole personality almost visibly altered: she was suddenly someone else—younger, more defenceless.

'I'm in a bad temper tonight. I'm sorry.'

'Let's have another *bock*. And would you like a cigarette?'

'Please.'

'Here we are in Monte Carlo, the haunt of vice and sophistication, the world of E. Phillips Oppenheim. Let's pretend we're two old Riviera hands. Beer, cigarettes, the Café de Paris, a summer night—'

'Sure. Damn the expense. Give the canary another seed.'

'No wisecracks. We don't have to do that—with the Mediterranean sky, these lights and the moon. Think, at this moment we could be creating memories to last us for the rest of our lives. Or if you want to, look at the famous Casino: isn't it like a yellow Easter egg tied up with plaster ribbons?'

Her voice broke suddenly. 'I came all the way here from Nice and they wouldn't let me in. The little bastard at the door said I was too young.'

'He told me the same thing.'

'No! Then we're in the same boat.'

'Tell me your name.'

'I'm Stanley Dahl. A Canadian. From Winnipeg.'

'I'm Canadian, too. From Montreal.'

'I thought you were a Scandinavian—so tall and so fair.'

We sat in a rapturous silence looking at the moon. Behind us the string orchestra was playing something by Kreisler. I had the feeling of having picked up a stray kitten which I already loved and could not bear to part with.

'Here's your party,' she said. 'Go back to your table now.'

'Come and meet them.'

Ethel Moorhead and Stanley liked each other at once. Their mutual attraction must have been due to a common shyness and sincerity, for there was nothing else to unite them. Ethel was also in high good humour from her success at the roulette-table: she had won heavily but did not say how much.

'We were both lucky tonight,' she said to me. 'Your sixth transversal paid off on the second roll. That means I owe you 275 francs.'

'But you weren't supposed to try it twice for me. I really owe you twenty-five francs.'

'I've already deducted that from your share of the six hundred I won,' she said firmly, pushing the money at me. 'And now all of you have just time to take me home, have a nightcap there and catch the last bus to Nice.'

Bob fell asleep on the bus and I held Stanley's hand all the way back to Nice. The bus dipped and rose as we hurled onwards in the darkness. The Mediterranean, glimpsed every now and then, was dashed with yellow moonlight. Stanley's rough hand rested in mine like a small antediluvian sea-shell. When I kissed her, just as we lurched around the Quai de Beauté in the old port, I thought she was sleeping and insensible, but the cool ring of her lips was no less beautiful for being unresponsive.

FIFTEEN

Stanley lay *perdue* for the next few days. But I now knew where she was living—in an ugly new building near the Place Magnan. Growing impatient, I called on her.

Her two-room apartment was comfortable but cheerless, with tubular furniture, bare floors, a tiled bathroom and a view of a sunless cemented patio. There was a rudimentary kitchen in the bathroom, with a small gas-stove, a cupboard for dishes and a garbage-can; the wash-basin doubled as the sink. She showed me everything proudly. She was wearing white satin lounging pyjamas cut with the same economy as her duck trousers.

'I can't offer you anything to drink,' she said. 'But would you like a glass of milk and a biscuit?'

The milk, served in jelly-jars, was parboiled, fortified, homogenized and tasted like the dregs of an English rice pudding, and the biscuit was lined with stale fig-paste. I noticed a ukulele on the table beside her.

'Do you play that?' I asked.

'A little. Would you like to hear something?' She picked it up and ran her fingers over the strings. 'Mozart, Ravel, Segovia, or just something simple?'

'Something simple.'

'*Careless Love*, then.'

She handled the little instrument as if it were a guitar, and with corresponding skill. First she played the simple refrain, slowly and clearly, underlining the melody with broad sweeping chords, then rendered the swift little verse in dance rhythm; then repeated the slow refrain with a few grace notes. After that she kept building on both with taste and invention, decorating them with surprising *obbligati*. Her eyes had grown remote, her straw-sandalled foot tapped the chair-cushion. She cuddled the absurd instrument like a baby—and all at once, as if irresistibly compelled, she began to sing in a small husky voice as true as a tuning-fork and with heart-rending pathos:

> *O see, what careless Love has done,*
> *O see, what careless Love has done,*
> *For now my apron strings won't tie—*
> *O see, what careless Love has done!*
>
> *O what will my poor mother say?*
> *O what will my poor mother say?*
> *She'll fold her hands and hold her tongue,*
> *For she had beaus when she was young . . .*

She broke off suddenly. 'It just goes on and on. But the melody is nice, isn't it? It's old English.'

'I didn't know you were a real musician.'

Her mouth drooped. 'I'm not. I'm supposed to be a violinist but I'm no damn good. Don't talk to me about it. What do you do?'

'I don't do anything.'

'You know,' she said sipping her milk and looking at me over the rim of her jelly-jar, 'I think we're going to be real friends.'

The next morning she joined us on the beach outside the Dora Melrose. She was wearing a tan raincoat with a belt, epaulets and *revers*. She and Bob looked each other over carefully: it was clear they were not going to hit it off.

'I'm not intruding, am I?'

'Of course not,' said Graeme. 'Sit down. And take off your coat or you'll be roasted.'

'You should have brought your bathing suit,' I said as I helped him scoop a seat for her among the stones.

'I've got it on underneath.'

We sat and talked for a while. She spoke of New York, and Bob asked her about a number of famous people whom she had never heard of.

'You lived in the Village, I bet,' he said.

'No, I lived in Gramercy Square. With a man called Jackson. Did you ever hear of him—Derr Jackson? He's disgustingly rich.'

'The guy they call Dirty Jackson? You lived with him?'

'He wasn't dirty at all. Just a little odd. He was very nice, he taught me all kinds of things—about books and pictures, I mean.'

'What did he teach you about books?'

'He told me to throw out Edna Ferber and Fanny Hurst. And he lent me Ben Hecht and Cabell and Percy Marks.'

'Jesus.'

'What's wrong with them?' she said. 'They're all pretty good writers, aren't they? Better than Ferber and Hurst, anyway. I liked *Jurgen*, it made me cry: that poor man.'

Bob got up and walked into the ocean.

'Did I say the wrong thing?' she asked.

'He has strong opinions about modern books,' said Graeme. 'He doesn't like any of them. He's a writer.'

'Oh! I never knew. It's just like violinists. You're never supposed to like anybody later than Paganini.'

'How can you like Paganini? Nobody has ever heard him play.'

'That's just it. You go by what Liszt said. The big thing is, he's not in competition, he's dead. You've no idea how jealous musicians are. I had a girl friend who slept with Heifetz once and no one at the conservatory would speak to her for a week.'

'Did you know,' said Graeme after a while, 'Paganini actually died here, right in Nice?'

'We should all go and look for the place this afternoon,' I said. 'It'll be somewhere in the old town. When did he die?'

'On the 27th of May 1840,' said Stanley reverently. 'Of phathisis. Something in his throat.'

'I'll bet the house is still standing,' said Graeme. 'We'll have a swim before lunch first.'

Stanley took off her coat and appeared in a one-piece white bathing suit that emphasized her Maillolesque build.

Bob was coming out of the water as we went in. 'I'm going in to do some work before lunch,' he said shortly.

'Do you think he's still mad?' said Stanley, bobbing up and down in the waves. 'I guess I'll have to read some of his books and tell him how good they are. That'll fix things up.'

I was quite sure it wouldn't.

She met us in a café on the corner of the Place Magnan, wearing a white pleated skirt, a blue sailor's jersey with transversal white stripes and a beret: whatever she wore gave her an outré, carnival appearance.

We asked about Paganini at the tourist bureau. They had never heard of him.

'You say he died here?' said the snuffy little one-armed man behind the desk. It was obvious he regarded the idea as unfavourable to tourism. 'You might look for him in the cemetery.'

'We're really more interested in seeing the house where he died,' said Graeme. 'I heard there was a plaque on it.'

'I doubt it. Paganini,' muttered the old man. 'An Italian. Was he a bandit?'

'No, a violinist.'

'Oh, an *artiste*,' said the old man scornfully. 'My dear sir, we have plaques and statues to the memory of great statesmen and illustrious generals like Marshal Masséna, who was actually *born* in Nice. But I'm afraid we would have no record of any foreign violinist.'

'But he wasn't a foreigner in 1840, when the city was Italian.'

The old man clamped his lips shut in a silent, hideous rage, picked up a newspaper, and waved his stump at us in dismissal.

'We could wander around the old town and try there,' I said. 'It'll be nice and cool.'

We entered the maze of narrow streets and in five minutes were completely lost. Stanley was enthralled.

'This is the nicest part of the whole city,' she said. 'All these little outdoor shops and pushcarts. And the old, old houses, so mysterious! As though they were falling down. I'd like to live here.'

I had often felt the same way about some of the older parts of

Montreal, but I remembered what the houses were like inside—the darkness, dirt, smells and plumbing; here, things would be even worse.

We seemed to be moving constantly into poorer quarters. The streets grew narrower, the houses more broken-down, the washing more ragged, the children dirtier. At last we stopped.

'All I know is, we're lost,' I said. 'You can't even see the sun for direction. How do we get out of here?'

A short thickset man in black came around a corner, singing in a loud, florid baritone. He stopped as soon as he saw us and swept his hat off.

'Gentlemen and lady,' he said. 'We meet again! What a pleasure. You are looking for our little theatre, no doubt. Let me show you the way. We have a matinée that is just beginning. The price is much lower in the afternoon. Only fifty francs for each of you. An excellent movie, *La Bonne à tout faire*, very blue!'

'Thank you, but I'm afraid it's a little early in the day.'

'What we are really looking for,' said Graeme firmly, 'is the house where Paganini died. Is it near here, do you know?'

'Paganini? The immortal Paganini? The great magician? Follow me, gentlemen and lady, it will be a pleasure.'

We fell in beside him and he began singing again at the top of his voice.

'I'll bet he's taking us to the theatre,' I said to Graeme. '"Magician", did you hear?'

'Well, there is a legend he was a magician.'

The man in black, carolling, led us through streets that were still more poverty stricken. We seemed to be constantly going down back lanes and alleys; several times we passed under archways that were almost tunnels; once we went right through the back of a grocery shop and came out on the other side. Suddenly we turned a corner into a blaze of sunlight and our guide swept off his hat and pointed dramatically to a narrow four-storey house of peeling brown plaster with tightly shuttered windows.

'There!' he cried. 'The house of the magician!'

I looked up and saw a weathered stone plaque, the same colour as the wall, with the heavily capitalized name NICCOLO PAGANINI cut into it, surrounded by some writing in ornate smaller script.

'My God,' said Stanley in a hushed voice. 'There it is after all.'

'Gentlemen and lady, our little theatre is right next door, down the passage. I will make you a special price of one hundred francs for the three of you. Agreed?'

'We'll think it over,' said Graeme. 'In any case, we thank you many times for showing us the way here. We are indeed obliged.'

'A pleasure.' He swept his hat low, paused for an instant, then shrugged his shoulders and went off down the street.

We sat on the edge of a stone horse-trough and looked at our find. It was a quite ordinary-looking house, rectangular and without ornament, with a perfumer's shop, a stationer's and a dry-cleaning establishment on the ground floor. I could see no concierge's lodge.

'Shall we try to see the room itself?' said Graeme.

'What does it say on the sign?' Stanley asked.

'"In questa casa",' he said. 'It's all in Italian. Let me see: "In this house towards evening on the 27th of May in the year 1840, died the great Niccolo Paganini, a Genovese. Here his soul rejoined the Muses and was caught up once again in the eternal harmony of things."'

'Oh . . .' said Stanley in a choked voice.

We went into the dry-cleaning shop that spanned the main entrance and asked the *patronne* if we could see the room where the great man had died.

'*Impossibile*,' she said crossly in Italian. 'This is not a public building. Everything is locked up anyway.'

'Isn't there a concierge?' Graeme asked in his rather shaky Italian. 'We would pay something.'

'Mamma Lucia!' she screamed.

An old woman in a black shawl came shuffling from the back of the shop, a hand cupped to her ear.

'These persons wish to see the room of Paganini,' shouted the *patronne*.

'*E morto*,' said the old woman.

'*Ben inteso*. They will pay.'

'*Quanto?*'

'*Cinque francas*,' said Graeme, holding up his fingers.

'*Dieci*,' said the old woman, holding up hers.

'*No, no, e troppo caro. E ladroneccio, signora.*' He turned away.

'Nine francs, *signor*,' she said. 'For the stairs, and my age.'

'Seven francs. No more.'

The old woman suddenly grinned and nodded. 'Seven francs.'

We followed her through the back of the shop and came out into

119

a handsome stairwell that at one time must have connected directly with the street. Panting, a hand pressed to her spine, Mamma Lucia toiled up the shallow steps and paused on the first landing. The whole place was unspeakably dirty and deserted; it looked as if no one had lived there for twenty years. We went on up to the second-floor landing, where the old woman clung to the stair-rail, her hand now pressed to her side. She nodded towards an ornate peeling door. 'One moment and I will open it for you.'

She produced a bunch of keys and began trying them all in turn. At last the lock turned with a screech; she opened the door and gestured silently.

We went in. The room was large, almost pitch dark, covered with dust and absolutely empty.

Mamma Lucia was waiting on the landing outside; she held out her hand and Graeme gave her seven francs. 'Thank you, Madame. You have been very kind.'

'*Niente, signor.*'

We followed her down the stairs and found the woman of the dry-cleaning shop waiting at the bottom and looking up, her hands on her hips.

There was a rapid-fire exchange in Italian: the *patronne* seemed to be accusing Mamma Lucia of fraud. The old woman ran into the shop. The other was still scolding her as we left. The last words I heard were Mamma Lucia's. 'What difference does it make?' she was squeaking. 'It was just the same as the room above! One empty room is as good as another . . .'

'What are they fighting about?' said Stanley.

'I guess the first woman just wants her cut,' I said.

'I'd like to stop at the first bar and have a drink,' she said. 'It's my treat.'

We had three brandies at the counter of a little bar around the corner. It had been a wonderful afternoon.

Soon Stanley was swimming with us every day. Bob became more and more sullen.

'You're not doing any work,' he told me. 'How do you expect to get anywhere if you don't work every day? As for jelly-bottom, she's just a run-of-the-mill parasite. You're wasting your time with her.'

I see now it was more than that: it was a matter of choosing between enjoyment and achievement, between the demands of life and art. The choice is presented several times to everyone at a very early period in his life, and after he has chosen one or the other a few times in succession his course is almost irrevocably determined. Such apparently random and unimportant decisions are much more serious than they appear; for, alas, the direction of one's life does not wait on maturity or wisdom, but is settled in the most offhand manner by emotion, appetite, and caprice. It was Balzac, I think, who said it was vital for a young man to decide very early on his ambition in life, simply because he was bound to attain it. But I did not know this, and telling myself once again that I could always return to the toilsome life of art, I chose once more the primrose path of present enjoyment. The important thing in life was to have a good time.

It is hard to say now whether I regret this reiterated choice wholeheartedly. Considering where it has led me—to the breakdown of my health, the failure of my hopes, the frightening prospect of an early death—I should be more remorseful and repentant than I am, and thus able to give good advice to others. But I can only see, if the choice were presented again, I would be bound to repeat it; and all I can promise myself at the moment is to be a little more careful in exploiting the resources of pleasure in the future—for something tells me I am not going to die, and there is going to be a future after all.

Thus the attractions of literature and authorship yielded to those of Stanley Dahl. The former, in fact, had hardly a chance: my own youth as well as hers, her charm and simplicity, the easiness of our friendship, the sensual feast she spread before me at an age when desire is always clamorous and always insatiable, all carried the day. She also had an allowance of $150 a month from some mysterious source (possibly Dirty Jackson) and seemed ready to share it with Graeme and me.

'Say,' she told us a few days after our Paganini excursion, 'my month in the apartment is up tomorrow and your Madame Gyp has a nice big room free. I think I'll move in—if you and Graeme don't mind.'

We didn't mind at all.

Three days later Bob packed his things and moved out.

'I'm going to Athens,' he said 'to have another look at the Parthenon. You three lovebirds have a good time. I'll be seeing you.'

Sixteen

September on the Riviera was a good month, with just enough rain to start the grass growing again; the shrivelling heat of summer gave way to a gentle warmth, and the ocean was more refreshing than ever. Our relationship with Stanley soon became more complex.

One day Graeme took her on a bus ride to the walled town of St-Paul-de-Vence, a famous tourist attraction; they came back late in the evening, when I was drinking quietly in bed, and I heard them tiptoeing up the stairs to her room. My feelings for the next half-hour were mixed. I wondered if it might not be easier if they were not quite so close by; then I decided it really made no difference. I was relieved when Graeme appeared.

'She wants to join us for a few drinks,' he said.

He had glasses and soda-water ready by the time Stanley came in, carrying her ukulele.

'Could I play you something?' she asked. 'A little Rameau?'

I had never heard Rameau on the ukulele, but the effect was both modest and graceful. It was a country dance, its rhythms underscored by heavy bass strokes. Stanley played it with skill and feeling, leaning back in her chair, her legs crossed, her eyes fixed on the soft night sky beyond the window, humming the melody in her small voice.

'That's a *bourrée*,' she said. 'It's classical, I know, but it's jolly and the way I feel. Could I have another drink?'

It was an idyllic evening. As the level in the brandy bottle sank, the conversation became more uninhibited and Stanley's songs more unrestrained. Our new friend's repertoire included items we had never heard before.

The next two months passed very pleasantly. As we were not impelled by ambition, envy, avarice or pride, none of us did anything at all: we remained sunk in greed, sloth and sensuality—the three most amiable vices in the catalogue, and those which promote so much content and social ease that I could never see what they are doing in it at all, and have often thought they should be replaced by jealousy, exploitation and cruelty, which are much worse sins for everyone involved. I do not think the life we led at the Dora Melrose was in any sense wicked for all its irregularity. It did no harm to anyone—and far from misusing our time, we were really turning it to the best account for our own sakes and the world's as well; for I am persuaded half of man's miseries result from an insufficiency of leisure, gormandise and sexual gratification during the years from seventeen to twenty. This is what makes so many people tyrannical, bitter, foolish, grasping and ill-natured once they have come to years of discretion and understand they have wasted their irreplaceable years in the pursuit of education, security, reputation, or advancement.

I realize that such remarks do not come with much authority from one whose pursuit of pleasure has led him to a hospital bed, but on the other hand I do not think my own want of moderation, and my bad luck, should altogether vitiate these arguments in favour of a youth of wine and roses.

Towards the end of October Madame Gyp told us the Dutchman who owned our suite was coming back. After casting around for new quarters we settled on the Pension Rodolphe Plascassier only half a block away on the corner of the rue de Californie, where we took two rooms, with Graeme and Stanley sharing the larger one.

Like Dora Melrose, Rodolphe Plascassier had been dead for many years, and the *pension* was run by a small beady-eyed Franco-Italian called Amédéo Dongibène. The food here was even better than at the Dora Melrose, for Dongibène had been chef at a number of smart hotels in Paris, Rome and Berlin. He talked familiarly of Jean Negresco and Henri Ritz, with whom he claimed to have worked as a waiter in Vienna; and he had a violent dislike of the English, especially the English nobility.

'Never trust an Englishman,' he said, 'and when he has a title you must be still more on your guard, for the English nobleman is the biggest thief and swindler in the world. People say that Russians of title are unreliable: I have seldom found them so. The French aristocracy are hagglers, but honest in the main; a German baron is a good fellow, and generally pays his bill. An American senator! Ah, there is the perfect gentleman, who tips well. As for an Indian prince, he is a fountain of gold unless he forgets. But most hereditary titles—no. By the way, I notice both you gentlemen are described in your passports as 'Esquire'. Is this a Canadian title, may I ask?'

We were glad to explain this was only a piece of meaningless snobbery on the part of our Department of External Affairs.

Dongibène had many stories to tell of the tricks by which people at his *pension* had tried to escape without paying the bill, and of his own astuteness in circumventing them.

As the weather grew colder we found life becoming rather dull. In spite of Stanley's allowance we found all our money was going on board and lodging. We were obliged to stop drinking brandy and switch to kirsch; we could no longer go to cafés and nightclubs, where the prices had been raised for the winter season; and the totals of Dongibène's illegible bills seemed mysteriously to increase every week. We did our best to meet expenses. Graeme would spend two nights a week rolling dice in Christie's Bar on the rue de France, and for a while I was taken on as a gigolo at the Savoy Grill; but his luck seemed to have left him, and I soon found that piloting old women around the dance floor was both tedious and unprofitable. Stanley alone appeared to be without a worry: when not sleeping or eating, she busied herself composing a sonata for violin, and spent each morning over sheets of music paper, stabbing at them with a pencil, strumming with her fingers and hissing through her teeth.

The winter dragged on, while the heat in our rooms steadily decreased and our spirits worsened. Things seemed to be losing their savour.

'I feel we should get out of here,' said Graeme to me quietly one morning. 'We've had enough of the Riviera anyway. One should never spend more than three months in one place and we've been here six. We're getting hopelessly behind with our bills too.'

'What are we going to do?'

'I'm afraid there's only one thing. We'll have to do a bunk.'

'It doesn't seem quite right. Poor Dongibène, he's always talking of bunks.'

'I know. But he's been padding our bills for the last three months. I've gone over them carefully and we've been overcharged about a hundred dollars since we came. He has a system of interchangeable fives and nines, and units and sevens, a kind of complex service charge that runs from fifteen to twenty per cent, and every third or fourth week seems to have eight days.'

'Have you any kind of plan?'

'Of course. We stage a lover's quarrel over Stanley. I lose, I tell

Dongibène to get your three big trunks out of the cellar, pack all our good stuff, pay my own bill right up, and leave. The same night you and she play at turtledoves, you move into the big room, fill my canvas trunk with old clothes and things for weight, and let him stow it in the cellar because you're staying till May. Then you both pack all the rest of the stuff and slip out at three in the morning. I'll have a taxi waiting around the corner of the Place Magnan. The Genoa-Marseilles express goes through at 3:30.'

'What old clothes were you thinking of leaving?'

'Our winter coats for one thing.'

'My coon coat?'

'It's not worth more than ten dollars. And I'm giving up my grandfather's trunk too.'

'If we've got to have weight, what about the copy of Gertrude Stein's *Making of Americans* Bob gave you?'

'Good idea. It goes in with the coats.'

'When is the day?'

'Why put it off? Tonight.'

Stanley was enchanted with the plan. 'What fun,' she said. 'It's sort of criminal, in a way, except that it's really not. I mean, we're just setting things to rights, like Robin Hood.'

But at night, after Graeme had gone with the trunks, she looked around the big room nervously. 'I'd like to walk in the moonlight,' she said. 'We'll take a romantic farewell of Nice, shall we?'

'Too dangerous. We'd better stay right here.'

'I suppose you're right. But I suddenly hate this room. I feel it's trying to enclose me, possess me. Why?'

'We've already left it. It's not a nice room anyway.'

'Not like the lovely room you had at Madame Gyp's. Funny the way things always seem to get worse.' She looked at me bleakly, then suddenly began to cry. 'No, no,' she said, pushing me away when I tried to comfort her. 'It's no use . . . Life is awful, awful.'

Before we left she had hysterics.

But by the time the train had reached Cannes she had recovered. Opening one of her bags she brought out three enormous ham sandwiches and a bottle of milk.

'I bet neither of you would have thought of this,' she said.

We all ate like wolves.

'Well,' said Stanley after a while, 'here we are. En route, as they say. Where are we going? Paris?'

'Neither Graeme nor I have ever seen Vienna,' I said.

'I have, and once is enough.'

'Our tickets are only good to Marseilles,' said Graeme.

'I'll buy the fares to Paris then. Oh boy, I want to see the Latin Quarter and Montmartre and the Bastille and the Sacré Coeur and everything.'

'You forgot the Eiffel Tower,' I said.

'My God, yes.' In the grey light of the rainy morning her expression suddenly grew rapt. 'The Eiffel Tower!'

SEVENTEEN

Paris revisited was more beautiful than ever. As our taxi took us once again along the sunny high-shouldered streets towards Montparnasse, I seemed to be seeing it through Stanley's eyes as well. We went straight from the station to the Jules-César and took a double room.

'We'll look around for a studio tomorrow,' said Graeme.

Stanley filled the bidet and was soon chirping and splashing around like a bird, while Graeme and I shaved.

It was one of the first warm days of April. The old women were already selling *muguet* from their barrows, and after buying Stanley a bunch we took a table on the Dôme terrace and drank Chambéry-fraise. Everyone we knew stopped to talk, and Stanley, in a tan tailored suit and a lemon-coloured beret, was eyed with amusement and lust. Schooner sat down and was soon joined by Caridad. We said we were looking for a studio or cheap apartment.

'You are in luck,' said Caridad. 'I am going to Amsterdam tomorrow with an industrialist and I will let you have my little place around the corner for a month. Shall we say six hundred francs?'

Schooner rolled his eyes and Graeme protested at the figure.

'Well, since we are friends you can have it for four hundred. Plus the gas, electricity, water, linen, and concierge, naturally. And I hope you will be happy as three pigeons in my little nest. Now, how about lunch? This spring weather makes me so hungry!'

The next day we moved into her apartment on the rue Delambre. The courtyard had a big chestnut tree in the middle, flowering shrubs all around it, and a disused well surmounted by a life-size stone figure of some deity; outside the concierge's lodge was a double cage full of canaries and nightingales, all of them singing like mad.

'How heavenly!' said Stanley, looking around the courtyard as we entered the great doors. 'I didn't know places like this existed.'

'Wait till you see the apartment,' said Graeme. 'It's pretty small.'

It was barely large enough for the three of us, and there was no room for all our luggage. But Stanley ran around the three tiny rooms in ecstasy, poking into drawers and cupboards, bouncing on the big bed and looking out of the window. There was a *bain sabot,* the kind in which one sits instead of reclining—one of those triumphs of French ingenuity, designed to save space, water and physical effort. Stanley climbed into it.

'This is divine,' she said, smiling up at both of us. 'You know, I can hardly believe I'm here, in Paris, in Montparnasse, and in a lovely joint like this. I'm so glad I met you boys. If I'd come to Paris on my own, you know where I'd be?'

'In the Cité Universitaire,' I said, 'in a recommended room.'

'Right. In a goddamn women's hostel, with a lot of stringy school-marms and earnest types with spectacles and cold-sores. Improving myself.'

'We are showing you life,' said Graeme. 'And you are adding charm to ours. Now we'd better go out and lay in a small stock of liquor.'

The following weeks of spring were delightful. We had enough money to eat and drink well; we took Stanley to the Opéra, the Opéra Comique, the Cirque Médrano and the Folies-Bergère. One morning when we were having breakfast at the Dôme, Daphne Berners appeared, elegant but haggard and distrait; she joined us and ordered a Pernod. We had heard that Angela had left her to go to the Marquesas with a surrealist painter.

'You're a painter, Miss Berners?' said Stanley.

'I am indeed.'

'You don't look like a painter. I mean, the only women painters I've ever met had dirty fingernails and were full of a lot of yap about somebody called Turner. I guess they couldn't have been much good.'

'Turner is all very well, of course—but he's no longer a subject of discussion. Any more,' she turned to Graeme, 'than shall we say Tennyson? or Wagner?'

'There's nothing wrong with Tennyson,' said Graeme, 'except his ideas.'

'I cannot *stand* Wagner,' said Stanley. 'All that schmerz. And why does he have to say everything five times? Oh, I hate German music. Bach, Beethoven, Brahms—the three biggest fakes that ever lived.'

'Miss Dahl,' said Daphne in a deep caressing voice, 'you are such a sweet heretic. What kind of music do you like?'

'All the eighteenth-century Italians—Pergolesi, Boccherini, Frescobaldi, Vivaldi, Corelli. And Mozart: he was the best of them all.'

'I'm so glad you have no opinions on painting. I suspect you would like no one but Fragonard, Chardin and Boucher.'

'I've never heard of them. Miss Berners, do you paint from the nude?'

'Of course I do. But please call me Daphne . . . I've been wondering, in fact, if you wouldn't pose for me some day, my dear.'

'When?'

'Why, this afternoon would do very nicely. If you are free.'

'I'm always free.'

When Daphne had left, Stanley looked thoughtful. 'She's awfully nice, isn't she?'

'She's as nice as she's beautiful,' said Graeme.

'I hope we're not in the process of losing our Stanley,' he said that evening as we sat in the little *tabac* drinking Cinzano and waiting for her.

'I suppose we're bound to lose her some time or other. This is almost too good to last. Well, well, here's Morley.'

Morley was bubbling quietly. He told us he had now managed to meet Scott Fitzgerald, Michael Arlen and Helena Rubinstein. Bob had taken him to see Joyce; and his new novel was almost finished. But he was specially pleased to have boxed with Hemingway, and to have either knocked the great man out or given him a nosebleed—it wasn't clear which. He was thrilled by this triumph, though he played it down modestly: in his quiet way he was able to invest the experience with a certain mystical quality. It was clear it was a major event.

'Well,' said Graeme after he had gone, 'I'm glad he pasted Hemingway.'

We agreed it was peculiarly fitting that the master had been bested in the ring by a man smaller and stouter than himself.

'Not that Hemingway hasn't got a few ideas,' said Graeme. 'Underneath all that chest-hair and gush, that adoration of athletes, criminals and plain folks, he has discerned a connection between sexuality and death that is impressive for all its triteness. His heroes seem to equate the fact of love with the experience of death. Anyway, one always follows the other. The formula of the Hemingway hero is that he loves and therefore he dies. As one of his own hardboiled characters would say—he pokes and he croaks.'

'Yes, but the process takes so long. In between, there's all the travelling, drinking, fighting, fishing, laconic fornication, and all those peasants speaking their manufactured dialect. The message gets bogged down. It's a pity he didn't get it all into one short story and then go on to something else or just call it a day.'

'Once you start writing,' said Graeme, 'I suppose it's hard to stop.'

'Neither of us can really tell about that yet. Anyway, I'm glad about Morley.'

'It's a real break for him, bless his heart. Here comes Stanley.'

She sat down and took off her lemon beret.

'How was it?' said Graeme.

'I never got my picture painted at all! You see, she has this marvellous studio, and a gramophone too, with the nicest records. And then she's a very down-to-earth person—really basic and sincere. She's a peach . . . Could I have a champagne cocktail?'

Our month in the rue Delambre was up all too soon and we were as usual faced with the problem of finding a place to live. It was then, in an evil hour, that we moved into a studio in the rue Daguerre, behind the Lion de Belfort. It was cheap and it looked clean; but waking there the first morning we were disagreeably surprised. Stanley's neck and arms were covered with small red spots and so were mine. She looked at herself in the mirror, then at me.

'We've got a disease,' she said. 'God, do you think it's syphilis?'

Graeme drew me outside. 'I don't like to tell Stanley, but it's bedbugs.'

'You're sure?'

'Absolutely. I saw one in the sheets this morning, running for cover. We've got to fumigate the place.'

'Let's move out.'

'We can't afford to. We've paid a whole month in advance.'

'Hasn't Stanley any money?'

'I suppose so, but we can't go on living on her at this rate. No. You take her out for breakfast and then go to the Cluny Museum and show her the chastity belt; she hasn't seen it yet. I'll get some sulphur and have the concierge swab the whole place down.'

Stanley and I went to the Café Buffalo on the place Denfert-Rochereau for breakfast, but she had no appetite; she began talking about syphilis again. To add to the dreariness, it began to rain.

Daphne Berners came in, looking very smart in a long black rain-cape. 'Hullo,' she said, sitting down. She ordered gin fizzes for all of us.

'Do you hear anything from Angela?' I asked.

'Just one card from Nukuheva so far. How's your book coming?'

'Not very well. I'm thinking of stopping writing.'

'Don't be a fool. Bob says you're good. All you need is someone to take you in hand.' She looked so lovely in her felt hat and cape that I had a sudden desire for her. She reached out her hand, the wrist encircled by a silver chain-bracelet, and gripped my arm. 'Someone to make you toe the mark.'

We sat in silence for a few minutes.

'What's wrong, Stanley?' she said.

'I'm not happy in the place I'm in.'

'She thinks she's going downhill,' I said. 'We have to cheer her up.'

'Of course. Come for a stroll with me, Stanley, and tell me your troubles.'

After they had gone I went out and took the first bus that came along. Sitting in the second-class section, I bumped along through a Paris that was grey and sodden with the first rain of summer. The streets seemed unimaginably ugly and desolate, the tall buildings drab and withdrawn. This is an awful city, I thought, and life is terrible in its pointlessness.

The rain stopped and the sun came out. The city was once more all watery silver, unspeakably beautiful—and this only made things worse. I looked out of the window and saw we had reached the end of the line at the Jardin des Plantes. I remembered Samuel Butler had said the cure for all emotional disturbances lay in gazing at the larger mammals—elephants and hippopotami. However, on feeling in my pockets I found I hadn't the price of admission to the gardens so I took the subway back to the Lion de Belfort.

Next day Stanley packed her bags and moved in with Daphne.

EIGHTEEN

It was very sad on the rue Daguerre for a few days. We missed Stanley badly. Moreover, without her money we were soon in financial straits again. Once more we had to eat at *prix fixe* restaurants like Aux Cent Colonnes, where a fee of 28 cents *donnait droit à 1 soupe, 1 entrée, 2 légumes, fromage ou dessert (pain à discretion)*: the enumeration still haunts me, as does the taste of the food. All day long I was hungry. I lowered my eyes when passing the windows of pastry shops, unable to endure the beauty of their displays—the *éclairs, millefeuilles, gâteaux mocha, pavés suisses, barquettes de fraises, madeleines, cake anglais,* and those lovely ones whose name I never knew, shaped like the hull of a sailboat, half the deck plated with chocolate, the other half with mocha, and full of a rich deposit tasting of nuts and nougat. On top of all this the prices of everything in Paris seemed to be rising. We realized we would have to go to work.

For foreigners whose passports were stamped, like ours, with the compulsory declaration to *ne pas prendre aucun emploi salarié*, work was not easy to find. But even our half-hearted efforts bore fruit. Graeme was taken on as a proofreader by the *New York Herald*, thanks to his having met the managing editor at a bar, and I began picking up a little money typing manuscripts for expatriate American writers. His work was monotonous, but mine—beating the pages of some unreadable holograph short story or novel into typescript at 2 francs a page, punctuation included—was depressing: there was not the slightest chance of such work ever being published. I deplored the growing fad for a literary career, even while I was making a bare living from it.

In the United States at this time everyone who could do nothing else had decided to be a writer, for it was clear that writing needed no special training or equipment, like music or painting. After a month my accuracy and good spelling began to pay off: I acquired a reputation. One day I received a call from Gwen Le Gallienne, asking me to type the last three chapters of her stepfather's latest novel under his own supervision.

Richard Le Gallienne! I was filled with awe. I had thought he was dead. I knew of him more by reputation, as the friend of Wilde, Beerbohm and Beardsley, than by anything he had written. I remembered only a few flat, fatigued, ninetyish poems in the decadent manner, a number of essays of almost unbearable whimsy, and the fact that he was vaguely connected, in a purely literary way, with the sea.

I arrived with my typewriter, paper and carbon-paper at his apartment in the rue de Rennes. Gwen and her mother were waiting at the door.

'Mr Le Gallienne is not feeling himself,' said Mrs Le Gallienne, a short, dark, angry-looking woman. 'But there are only about fifty pages of his novel to be typed. He will dictate them to you from the manuscript.'

'I'm afraid I can't type from dictation,' I said. 'Unless he speaks very slowly.'

'Have no fear of that,' she said bitterly.

She showed me into a small, cluttered, dirty room.

'Richard!' she called. 'Come now, here is the young man to type those last three chapters. You know Mr Towne wired he must have them by the next post. It was in the contract.'

The author, who had been hiding behind a screen, came out cautiously. He wore a nautical blue blazer and rumpled white flannel trousers and was quite drunk. I was surprised to see how old, thin, and haggard he was; only his blue eyes held any life, and they were barely able to focus.

'Aha,' he said in a fine light tenor voice. 'There was a ship.'

'Yes,' said Mrs Le Gallienne, as if speaking to an idiot, 'that's the book you're to finish. Now just come and read your manuscript, and this nice young man—he is a Canadian, by the way, and he is a writer too—will type from your dictation.'

Le Gallienne bowed gracefully, clutching at the screen. 'I am happy

132

to have your collaboration, sir. Would you care for a drink? Brandy and soda?'

Mrs Le Gallienne shook her head darkly at me.

'Indeed I would, sir. But not right away.' I set up my typewriter on a table already covered with manuscript in a thin, illegible handwriting.

'I will leave you now, Richard,' she said. 'But remember, Mr Towne must have the three chapters by the next post. Otherwise—' She waved her hand and disappeared.

'Termagant,' said Le Gallienne in a low voice. 'Basilisk, vampire.'

There was a pile of typescript on the table. It ended at Chapter XX. The first sheet of handwritten manuscript seemed to be headed Chapter XXI.

'*There Was a Ship*,' said Le Gallienne in a stagey voice. 'That's the title. A story about the Spanish Main. And a bloody awful story too.'

'How does Chapter XXI go?' I asked, passing him the sheets. 'If you'll read it I'll take it down, sir. But slowly, please—I'm not a touch typist.'

'Good for you. Well, so you're a Canaidjan. I was once in Canada—years and years ago. Lecturing. In a desolate city called To-ron-to. Heavens! You're not from To-ron-to, are you?'

'No, I've never been there.'

'Don't go, my boy. But now, you're quite sure you won't have a drink? Then I'll just have a quick one before we start. Your health, sir.' He pulled a flat nautical-looking bottle from the breast-pocket of his blazer and took a tremendous swig. For a moment his eyes seemed to disappear in his head, then he straightened up, glared at his manuscript and said in a brisk quarter-deck voice: 'Ready? Centre carriage! Capitals Chapter Roman Twenty-one! Double space. New line, no indent. "Odds-fish!" cried the Merry Monarch. "This young fellow warrants our attention. What think you, Barbara?" And he turned to the Countess of Castlemaine . . .'

He read slowly, with ease and expression, giving the text in blocks of ten or twelve words and waiting patiently until I had finished each. I was thinking this was the easiest job I had ever had. We finished Chapter XXI in half an hour.

'Now,' he said, pulling out the case-bottle again, 'a little refreshment. I am afraid we have no tumblers—but what does that signify to a pair of literary men? Come now,' he proffered the bottle, 'as the immortal Sairey Gamp says, "Put your lips to it." No?' He took a long drink, wiped his mouth and sighed. 'You know, I heard Dickens himself publicly recite that whole sublime passage from *Chuzzlewit* when I was just about your age. It was unforgettable.' He suddenly sank his head between his shoulders, put one hand to his breast, rolled his eyes upward, and chanted in a deep hoarse singsong, '"So what I always says to them as has the management of things, be they gents or be they ladies, is: don't ask me whether I won't take none, or whether I will, but leave the bottle on the chimley-piece so I can put my lips to it when I am so dispoged."'

It was a thoroughly professional performance. Listening, I had the sensation of hearing the voice of Charles Dickens, and for a moment felt audibly linked with the splendours of the past. Then he belched, fell into a chair, and waved the bottle at me uncertainly. When I declined, he took another pull himself and seemed to pass out completely, leaning back with his eyes closed and his mouth wide open. But when I began to type the heading of Chapter XXII he got to his feet again, gripped his manuscript and continued dictating.

The next chapter took a good deal longer: he kept losing his place and his speech was thickening badly. After he had skipped three separate paragraphs in succession, destroying the whole sense of the text, I stopped. My copy was becoming badly fouled with blocks of deletions.

'Perhaps you'd better take a rest, sir.'

'Rest? Rest?' he cried. 'Shall I not have all eternity to rest in? No, I'll have another drink.'

'You will not,' said Mrs Le Gallienne in a harsh, sibilant tone, coming in quietly and twitching the bottle out of his hand. 'You may have a cup of tea if you wish. This book must be finished within the hour, in time for the boat-train, or Mr Towne will impose the penalty provided for in the contract. You know what that means, Richard: *it means twenty pounds*. I will make you both a cup of good strong tea and then you can go back to work.' She disappeared.

'Sheridan went through this too, I believe,' said Le Gallienne. 'But he had the advantage of not writing drivel. *My* task is harder.' He sighed deeply. 'My dear young man, let me urge you in the strongest possible terms not to embrace the profession of letters. You see what one comes to in the end . . . Yes, literature is all very well in its way—but only as a *hobby*. It should never be anything but the inspired recreation of a man who has what I have never had—a private ingcum. If I had been so blessed by fortune with a private ingcum, I should have continued to follow my proper bent—poetry.'

Remembering his flat, fatigued, and derivative verse, I thought this was no great loss to English literature, but felt it would do no harm to cheer him up by repeating the best stanza of the only poem of his I could recall, 'The Second Crucifixion':

> '"Poor Lazarus shall wait in vain
>   And Bartimaeus still go blind:
> The healing hands shall ne'er again
>   Be touched by suffering humankind.
> Yet every day my Lord I meet
> In every London lane and street."'

'Good God,' he said, 'you know my work! Marvellous, marvellous. I thought nobody read anything but the poetaster Eliot these days— or that Yankee hooligan Elijah Pound. My dear young sir, I am touched. I even forgive you the misquotation of my own poem. At least you got four lines of it almost right anyway. Come now, a drink.'

He was groping again in the pocket of his blazer when Mrs Le Gallienne appeared with two cups of tea.

In two hours we managed to get through the book. Le Gallienne insisted on writing THE END in a gigantic scrawl on the last page. Mrs Le Gallienne then gathered the typed sheets together, checked the numbered pages with a moistened thumb and put them into a large pre-addressed manila envelope that she sealed with several rapid licks of her tongue and then held firmly to her chest.

'I think you'd better lie down now, Richard,' she said firmly.

'I must offer this young gentleman a drink. He has been so patient.'

'Nonsense. It's time for your rest.' She turned to me with a crafty smile. 'Please send in your bill tomorrow.'

'No need for that,' I said. 'Sixty pages and carbons at two francs each is 120 francs, plus five francs for three spoiled ones. 125 francs please, Mrs Le Gallienne.'

'Later. I must put this in the post at once. Good afternoon.' She disappeared swiftly.

Le Gallienne turned to me with outspread hands. 'I'm afraid all I can offer you is a drink.'

'You haven't got a drink. Mrs Le Gallienne took the bottle. All I want is 125 francs, sir.'

'I haven't a penny in my pocket, I swear. But I have this.' He reached into the opposite breast-pocket of his blazer and produced another flat bottle. 'Come now, a little drink?'

'All right. But you still owe me 125 francs.'

'My wife will pay you tomorrow. Here.' He filled my empty teacup from his bottle and presented it.

'I don't think she will,' I said. 'Well, your health, sir.'

We drank solemnly.

'I hope you don't think,' I said, 'I typed sixty pages for a drink of brandy. Have a heart.'

'I have a heart,' he said. 'I also have a wife. How can we arrange matters?'

'You say you haven't any money?'

'Not a sou.'

'All right then, give me an autographed copy of one of your books.'

'A brilliant idea! What book would you like?'

'*Songs of the Sea.*'

His expression suddenly became guarded. 'That's a collector's item, my dear fellow. And I haven't got a copy here anyway.'

'Yes, you have,' I said, pointing to the bookcase. 'There it is.'

'My very own copy, the only one I have—with all my own corrections! It's worth ten pounds at least. Listen, here's something almost as good. Very rare, too.' He pulled a slim paper-covered pamphlet from the bookcase, opened it, and inscribed it with a frantic flourish. 'This is now worth two pounds anywhere,' he said, pressing it into my hands. 'An edition limited to one hundred copies.'

'It's only a perfume catalogue!'

'You're a hard young man,' he said. 'What about one of my novels there? Take your pick.'

'Give me *The Book Bills of Narcissus* over there and we'll call it quits.'

'But it's worth all of two pounds.'

'Not to a dealer. Just autograph it and if I can get more than a pound for it I'll refund you the difference. Come on, be a sport.'

'Well,' he sighed, '*The Book Bills* it is. How would you like it inscribed?'

'Anything simple and eloquent will do.'

He sat down, opened the fly-leaf and wrote for a few moments. 'There,' he said.

'"To a Young Man of Letters, with gratitude and affection, Richard Le Gallienne, Paris 1929. *The Labourer is worthy of his hire*," I read. 'Why, very nice indeed, sir. I'm sure I can get a pound for this. Thank you very much.'

'Quits?' he said, holding out his hand. 'Paid?'

'Paid and double paid.'

We shook hands.

'Then let's have another drink.' He filled the two teacups again.

I declined with thanks. He accompanied me to the door, weaving from side to side.

'Now remember what I told you about the profession of letters,' he said as we stood on the threshold. 'I beg you to abandon it *at once*, for your own sake. Now, this very afternoon. Tomorrow may be too late. Leave the pursuit of literature to those fortunate individuals who possess a private income.'

I met Graeme at the counter of the Buffalo.

'You're looking tired,' he said.

I showed him Le Gallienne's book. 'I'll go to Galignani's tomorrow and see what they'll give me for it.'

'It should fetch 150 francs,' he said. 'And—well, while you're at it, hadn't you better take Moore's little pamphlet and try to sell it too?'

I nodded sadly. The same idea had already occurred to me.

'After all,' he said, 'it's best not to be sentimental about these things.'

'I suppose not. But I've never been able even to read it properly. I didn't want to cut the leaves.'

'Good. It will fetch more. How was the Old Man of the Sea?'

I told him and mentioned the thrill of almost hearing Dickens reading from *Chuzzlewit*.

'Old fraud,' said Graeme. 'Dickens died in 1870 and he stopped reciting publicly at least five years before then—just about the time Le Gallienne was born.'

Mr Threep of Galignani's, a prognathous old man who wore his necktie enclosed in a wedding-ring, looked me over almost as carefully as he did the two books.

'How did you come by these?' he asked accusingly.

'They are gifts.'

'Would you sign a statement to that effect?'

'Not before we make a price.'

'What are you asking for them?'

'A hundred and fifty francs for the Le Gallienne.'

'Hm-mm.' He picked it up as if it were contaminated. 'This is trash, of course. Shall we say a hundred francs? Only for the superscription, mind you.'

'A hundred and fifty is the limit.'

I had suddenly divined he was really more interested in the pamphlet.

'I'll tell you what we'll do,' he said, suddenly baring his teeth. 'We'll let you have 1,000 francs for the two of them.'

'Eight hundred and fifty francs for a signed and uncut George Moore, in mint condition? You are joking, Mr Threep.'

He gave me a beady stare, but his eyes returned to the immaculate grey wrappers of the pamphlet; he picked it up delicately, examined the inscription again, and looked at the back.

'What are you asking for both these items?'

'2,000 francs.'

He picked up the two books, replaced them calmly in their envelope, and pushed them a few inches towards me. 'I'm afraid we cannot do business,' he said.

I reached for the envelope.

His hands did not relax their hold on it.

'Our final offer,' he said between his teeth, 'is 2,000 francs.'

'Oh, all right.'

He drew the envelope back again. The look of triumph in his eyes was revolting.

I have since learned that an unsigned copy of *Reminiscences of the Impresssionist Painters* sold for two hundred dollars in New York. But that afternoon, coming out on the rue de Rivoli in the sunshine with eighty dollars in my pocket, I was walking on air. The money would keep us in luxury for over a month.

'Do you think Mr Moore knew how much the little pamphlet was worth?' I asked Graeme that night.

'Of course he didn't. We'll have a good dinner tonight and drink his health. I have a feeling he would approve the transaction.'

138

NINETEEN

We now felt much better and for a whole month were happy. Graeme at once left the *New York Herald*, while I stopped typing manuscripts and wrote my first published book, *Contes en Crinoline*. This work was a sequence of historical sketches with a unifying transvestite motif, in which a young man was reincarnated in different varieties of female dress. It was written in French, and all the details of farthingales, plackets, shifts, conical hats and corsets were taken from an illustrated history of costume I had picked up on the quays. The *Contes* were brought out by Elias Gaucher, a fly-by-night publisher on the rue des Saints-Pères, to whom I had been introduced by a surrealist poet. Gaucher specialized in books dealing with shoes, fans and ladies' underlinen, and thought Octave Uzanne the greatest writer in France.

'This is a very amusing manuscript you have turned out,' he told me, while his fingers worried a rubber band, 'although it is inaccurate in places. In the convent episode your hero is wearing closed drawers in the year 1750. They did not exist until almost fifty years later.'

'Are you sure?'

He raised his stubby eyebrows. 'But of course. Penillière says they were not in use until after the public assault on Théroigne de Méricourt in May 1793, and he is the Bible on the subject.'

'I was following Liane de Lauris. I thought she would know.'

He looked at me pityingly. 'My dear young man, Liane de Lauris was the pseudonym of that poor hack Louis Laurens whose only distinction was that he was a friend of Balzac's. His *L'Écrin du rubis* is absolutely unreliable. Moreover, you appear not to have read the work of the greatest *travesti* of all time, Monsieur l'Abbé de Choisy.'

'Indeed I have. I have read *La Comtesse des Barres*, but I regard it as too sacred a text even to steal from.'

His eyes lit up, he snapped the rubber band vivaciously. 'A young man after my heart! Anyone who loves and admires the great Choisy is acceptable on those grounds alone. I will give you 2,000 francs outright for the copyright of your little book of tales. Agreed?'

Eighty dollars, I thought. It was less than I expected; but as usual I was in no position to hold out. 'For cash, yes.'

'Of course. Now, for a pseudonym. Anything you like, provided it has an aristocratic ring.'

'I want the book to appear under my own name.'

'Impossible, sir. You must be a *de*. All my authors adopt the noble particle. Where were you born, if I may ask?'

'In Montreal.'

'Canada!' he exclaimed with delight. 'Well, who would have thought it? I have a Canadian author: my very first. What do you say, then, to Philippe de Montréal? It sounds well, eh? Archaic.'

'Excuse me, it sounds more like a criminal alias. And why Philippe? Can't I even keep my first name?'

'Hmm-mm. Jean de Montréal. Not bad, not bad. But not quite right either: it has not the feudal connotation. Let me see—what street were you born on?'

'St Luke Street.'

'Ah, now we have it. Jean de Saint-Luc! Perfect. *Contes en Crinoline* by Jean de Saint-Luc. That is it! Absolutely! It has the fine medieval ring, and the vowels combine with great sonority. Come now, let us sign the little contract. One copy for you and one for me, eh?'

The contract was six lines of typescript in which I conveyed outright ownership of the book to him, together with all rights of translation, for 2,000 francs, of which I acknowledged receipt by these presents, and five copies of the published book itself.

'Are you paying in cash?' I asked.

'Here is my cheque on the Crédit Lyonnais, boulevard Saint-Germain branch. Just around the corner.'

'In that case, you won't mind my adding the words "by cheque" to my receipt. Only a formality, of course.'

He grinned, snapping the rubber band. 'Certainly. I like to deal with a businessman. "By cheque", naturally.'

We then both signed the contract, which was already witnessed by someone else whose signature was illegible. Jean de Saint-Luc, I thought, this is your passport to a mild erotic fame. This absurd little book— I wonder if it will have an illustrated cover.

When I presented M. Gaucher's cheque at the Crédit Lyonnais next day it was refused for lack of funds.

All the following week I tried to find him but he had disappeared; the little office in the rue des Saints-Pères was locked. I asked the advice of the surrealist poet, who told me to wait. 'He has taken his new mistress to Chartres,' he said. 'She loves religious architecture and may insist on his going still further afield so she can take some rubbings

140

of tombs. But you can generally find him at the Restaurant Petit Saint-Benoît. You must be bold with him since he is a physical craven. Your original mistake was in taking his cheque. There is no use appealing to his mistress, as she is worse than he.'

For the next two nights Graeme and I dined at the Petit Saint-Benoît. It was one of the smallest, cheapest and best restaurants of its kind in Paris. I had never eaten such sweetbreads: sliced very thin, coated with egg-white and breadcrumbs, fried in brown butter and served with a wedge of lemon, they were quite different from the great squishy things that are generally boiled and served in a dull Mornay sauce. Here Graeme and I also met the sculptor Ossip Zadkine, a charming ugly man who wore a wide-brimmed purple fur-felt hat that made him look like a mushroom.

'There are only three great names in sculpture in the western world,' he said. 'Michelangelo, Rodin and myself. We are the only visionaries of plastic form.'

'Will you tell me,' said Graeme, 'whether sculpture is not in danger of succumbing to a bloodless abstractionism—as painting appears to be doing?'

'No danger of that,' he said. 'Sculpture will be saved by its three dimensions. Look at this water carafe.' He picked it up. 'Trite and inexpressive as it is, it cannot be reduced to a system of lines and colours. The logical development of painting is of course towards a square canvas entirely rendered in dull black and entitled anything you like: Hell, Death, The Void, Memory, Madame Untel—whatever the artist's wit or his dealer's venality can suggest. In sculpture, however, we are tied to the object, the thing, and we have also the irrefragable mediums of stone, wood, marble, brass to keep us from such sterility.'

'But Brancusi's *Golden Bird* and his *Fish*,' I said, 'aren't they moving towards a three-dimensional abstraction? The soaring emotion of his bird could be refined and streamlined with very little trouble into the meaningless suavity of a cigar.'

'Exactly. Constantin does not know where he is going. But I do, and I have told him. He will not listen. He is enamoured of the idea of smoothness, which he confuses with simplicity. Now I, on the other hand, find the ultimate plastic expression to be the rendition of strife and tortuosity such as you can find in the contours and crenellations of a baked potato.'

'Then there is no danger of sculpture being reduced to the simplest

141

three-dimensional forms of the sphere and the cube? The exhibition, say, of a cannonball or a child's building block?'

'Not if I have any say in the matter,' he said grimly. 'I am the sworn foe of those geometrical Dutchmen and De Stijl. The real villain, of course, is Father Euclid. We must escape that terrible logic of his if we are to remain human. Art must not be fitted to his bed, or be lopped or stretched for that infernal Greek whose axioms don't even make sense. There are no straight lines anywhere, fortunately: lines only waver, weave, cross and tangle. Geometrical forms are a pernicious nonsense. I object to the full moon, for instance, as a sterile, stupid circle.'

The third time we were at the Petit Saint-Benoît I saw M. Gaucher coming in with a big fair-haired girl. When I went to his table he introduced me with great formality and asked me to sit down and take an aperitif. I excused myself, saying I was with a friend, and after begging his pardon for broaching a matter of business showed him his dishonoured cheque.

'I knew it, I knew it,' he cried, striking his forehead. 'As soon as you left I consulted my bank balance and realized there was not enough to cover that cheque. I offer you a thousand apologies. If you will come to my office tomorrow we will arrange this matter in a twinkling. Shall we say at three o'clock?'

The next day his office was again closed all afternoon. I understood he did not mean to pay anything. It was obvious that direct action was the only course.

After waiting three whole afternoons in a little wine-shop opposite his office, we at last saw him enter. I was already boiling with rage, and Graeme insisted we wait five minutes. 'If the worst comes to worst,' he said, 'we'll take him from both sides.'

We entered his office without knocking. He looked up from his desk and turned pale. 'Gentlemen, gentlemen, please sit down. I have the money here.' He rummaged in a drawer and pulled out his cheque book.

'No more of your cheques,' I said, moving forward. 'I have come for the money you owe me—in cash, as we agreed.'

'My friend,' said Graeme, advancing on the other side, 'has waited long enough. He wants his 2,500 francs.'

'2,500 francs! The price was 2,000.'

'Five hundred francs for collection charges,' said Graeme. We moved behind the desk. 'Come now, sir, you must pay your legal debts.'

The colour came back to M. Gaucher's cheeks. 'This is not a legal debt,' he hissed.

'What about our contract?' I said.

'What contract? Oho, you know as little of business as you do of ladies' underwear, my young Canadian. In France no contract is binding unless it has the government stamps. You are wasting your time.'

'We're not leaving before you pay,' Graeme said, sitting down calmly on the desk. 'Even if we have to stay here all night.'

'Excrements! Gangsters!' M. Gaucher pulled out his wallet and threw its contents on his desk. 'That is all I have. Take it.'

Graeme picked up the pile of small bills. We walked out and up the rue des Saints-Pères to the rue Jacob while I was counting the money.

'We got 1,735 francs anyway,' I said.

'Then we don't have to eat at the Cent Colonnes for a while. And another thing, your book's bound to be printed now. He's got to recover his costs. If we hadn't squeezed this out of him I'll bet he'd have put your manuscript away in a drawer.'

'I never thought of that.'

'I know. If I were you I wouldn't write anything more in French. You see what happens. Get back to your memoirs. And I've been conceiving another book myself. Much better than *The Flying Carpet*. The great Canadian novel. I'm starting in on it tomorrow. It will be a bestseller. I'll be famous and we'll have all the money in the world.'

But the next day he received a telegram saying his father was dying and not expected to live out the summer: it was accompanied by a wired draft for $100 on the Bank of Montreal. 'How can I get home on a hundred dollars?' he said. His hands had been trembling ever since the news. His filial feelings were of a somewhat different order than mine.

'We can get you a steerage passage with the money we've got now,' I said. 'As far as Halifax anyway.'

'No, I've thought of something better. I'll go back as a Distressed Canadian, all the way to Montreal, and leave you the hundred dollars. I'll get into some rags and go to the embassy now.'

'Wear those old flannels with the hole in the knee.'

'Yes, thank God I didn't throw them out. Damn it all, why did I shave yesterday?'

'A good thing you did. You'll look destitute and respectable at the same time. One of the deserving poor. You can even say you're a Bachelor of Arts.'

'Let's get going. Those fellows at the embassy keep leisurely hours.'

We took a taxi to the Avenue Montaigne. I watched Graeme as he went in wearing his tattered trousers; he had even assumed a convincing limp. There were no benches in the avenue and I sat on the curb and studied the ghastly architecture of the big houses. There was a certain forbidding, timorous squatness in the whole street that smelled of wealth, fatigue and ineptitude. A few beautiful melancholy children walked by, escorted by their nannies. The sun was unbearably hot, the plane-trees rustled drily. At last Graeme came out.

'The attaché was very helpful,' he said. 'A nice little man from the sticks somewhere near Ottawa. I'm all fixed up to sail in two weeks. I didn't have to commit perjury. They even gave me five hundred francs out of some kind of I.O.D.E. fund for stranded citizens. You've got to hand it to the Dominion.'

Once again we were rich. But the shadow of parting had robbed the fact of all savour. We took the bus back to Montparnasse and visited all the bars, where everything seemed dead and we found no one we knew. I drank three Pernods without feeling any effect; we had dinner and went home early for the first time since coming back to Paris.

The next two weeks dragged to an end. We were both glad when they were up; it was a relief to say goodbye at the Gare Saint-Lazare. 'Don't get too tired,' he said. 'Try to work on your memoirs. I'll make some money and return in two or three months. D.V.'

'D.V.'

Coming back into the glare of the Place Saint-Lazare I felt immensely alone, and the heat was so stifling I almost fainted. I could not face the prospect of going back alone to the rue Daguerre and wandered around the Right Bank, ending up by walking across the Pont des Arts and up the rue de Seine to the boulevard Saint-Germain. My feet and head both seemed on fire. I remembered hearing that the Brasserie Lipp served the best gin fizz in town and I went inside and ordered one.

The people here were quite different from the Montparnasse types —older, better dressed, with an air of affluence and raffishness. The men were florid, distinguished looking and vaguely rapacious; the women had the air of being kept. But no one looked happy or carefree. I found the atmosphere curiously refreshing and watched a stout iron-grey-haired gentleman with the rosette of the Legion of Honour, who was sitting with a chic, haggard-looking woman, as he guzzled a plateful of langoustines and a bottle of white wine in an ice-bucket. His hands, between cracking the shells, dabbling the bodies in mayonnaise, stuffing them into his mouth, splitting and sucking the claws, wiping his lips, breaking bread, and pouring and drinking wine, were never still—yet the economy of their motion was marvellously organized: there was not a single wasted movement. The performance was underlined by the fact that he never stopped talking to his companion for a moment— and, as far as I could gather, with ease and wit, for she smiled with an amusement that was clearly not assumed.

How wonderful, I thought, to be so distinguished looking, so deft, so self-satisfied, to have such a fine appetite and so smart a mistress; this man is obviously the product of at least three generations of polish, sagacity and indulgence. I watched him as he dished his crayfish and raised his napkin to his lips to smother a slight belch. Already feeling better myself, I was ordering another gin fizz when I saw Daphne Berners coming towards me. Before I had time to rise, she pulled up a chair and sat down.

'What are you doing in this galley?' she said. She was looking sadder and more striking than ever; her thin ash-grey suit was beautifully pressed, her soft white shirt, four-in-hand tie and felt hat gave her an air of elegance that was somehow heightened by the fact that, as usual, she carried no handbag.

'I'm drowning my sorrows. Join me.'

'Gin fizz? I'll have one too.'

'And how is our Stanley?' I said after a few minutes.

'No longer with us, I'm afraid. She was reclaimed.'

'Again? You mean she's gone?'

'Back to New York.'

'Graeme has gone back home too.'

Daphne looked at me impassively for a minute. 'You know,' she said, 'you don't belong in a dull place like this. You're much too young.'

I had the impression she didn't belong there either and wondered why she had come. The men were looking at her with a kind of quizzical salacity, the women with fascination and hatred.

'Let's get out of here,' she said. 'The place is getting on my nerves.'

We left. 'Do you mind my asking what in the world you were doing in that place?' I said as we walked past the Deux Magots.

145

'If you must know, it's where I met Angela. Would you like to go for a walk?'

'I've just walked all the way from the Gare Saint-Lazare.'

'Another mile won't do you any harm. We'll go and look at Notre Dame.'

We walked to the boulevard Saint-Michel, turned down towards the river, and then went along the quais to the rue des Deux-Ponts. Notre Dame looked incredibly beautiful.

We stopped and leaned on the stone embankment. 'You were right,' I said. 'It's a great comfort. I wonder why.'

'Mainly because it's so big, I think. And it's been here so long. It makes us feel small and transitory, and that includes our sorrows. It's not really beautiful at all.'

'The front is nice. I don't like looking at the body of it, where Claude Frollo fell off.'

'Don't be literary. Anyway that horny priest got just what was coming to him. Come on, this isn't the best perspective. We'll go down to the tow-path.'

We went down the stairs to the cobbled walk and sat on the riverside. There was no one there and we were surrounded by the cliffs of honey-coloured stone straddling the grey-green river; the sound of traffic was muffled, and the great twin-towered cathedral seemed to be right on top of us, sailing along like a ship in the fading light. We sat looking at it for a while.

She took my arm. 'Do you know any poetry? Something in French, if possible.'

'Le soir tombait, un soir équivoque d'automne
Ou les belles, pendant rêveuses à nos bras,
Dirent alors des mots si speciaux tout bas
Que depuis ce temps notre coeur tremble et s'étonne.'

'Go on.'

'I don't know any more.'

'Perhaps it's just as well. I'm going to kiss you.'

The softness of her mouth was a revelation. This was without passion or demand, full of affection, sadness, and comfort. I felt her tears pouring around our lips.

'Daphne, Daphne,' I said to myself, wanting this moment to last forever. I felt as if transported out of my own sex and into a region where everything was allowed and where I wanted nothing but this endless salty kiss. I opened my eyes and saw Daphne's enormous grey ones, blind and ecstatic in her pale face, and beyond them the towers of Notre Dame.

'It's getting dark,' she said.

I followed her back up the stairs to the street and into the roar of the evening traffic over the Pont Neuf. We had dinner on the quai des Grands Augustins, hardly exchanging a word as we looked out at the river. Then we walked all the way back to the rue Broca. The studio looked just the same as when I had left it a year before.

'What happened to Stanley?' I asked when Daphne got up to make coffee.

'She went off with a man called Jackson.'

'For God's sake. What did he look like?'

'Tall, thin, guardsman's tie and a panama. The suave type. He seemed to have plenty of money.'

'Stanley was rather strong on money, I'm afraid.'

Twenty

I moved out of the ill-omened studio on the rue Daguerre and Daphne and I lived together happily for almost two weeks, encouraging each other to work.

One evening, however, I came back to the studio and found a note in her square schoolgirlish handwriting: she had gone to meet Angela's boat at Marseilles. 'Leave your traps here as long as you wish,' she had added tactfully.

The next day I went to the Dôme to find somewhere else to live. Paris is not a place where you find an apartment or studio except by nosing around privately; nothing is offered publicly except to the rich and the unwary—and then at high rates. Everything there is done by friendship and favour, and while this is a delightful and primitive way of doing business, there are times when it is frustrating. It is then one discovers the French people are not, as is generally believed, exclusively interested in money, and that their real passion, as an essentially feminine people, is to confer favours, to indulge their egoism and feeling of superiority to the rest of the world by acts of condescension and grace.

On this occasion I could find no condescending or gracious French citizen to solve my problem; it was only early autumn and tourists, laden with dollars, still filled the city. I sat in the Falstaff Bar and meditated on the real cause of the housing situation: there were simply too many people in the world.

After a while I saw I was being watched by a woman wearing a long ragged cloak and sitting alone at the bar. It was some time before I recognized Mrs Quayle in this disguise. I decided she must be slumming, but when she gave me her little secretive smile I thought it safe to bow and join her.

'Oh what can ail thee, man-at-arms?' she whispered. 'Alone and palelee loitering? You have acquired a beautiful tan, as well as a most Birrhonic melancholy since we last met—when was it?'

'Last July 14th.'

'Then let us meet again. In the little café at the corner of the rue Delambre in ten minutes. I shall be in the billiard-room at the back.'

I nodded, breathing in the expensive musky perfume that she still diffused like a crater, and went back to my table. A few minutes later she left without looking in my direction.

She was waiting in the billiard-room, a steaming cup before her, her cloak pulled up to her nose.

'You are alone?' she said.

'Quite alone.'

'What about all your mistresses?'

'Gone, all gone.'

'You haven't even shaved today.'

'Nor the day before.'

'What will you have to drink? You are rather a sot, I seem to remember. I am having a gin with beef broth. Let me offer you one.'

'Could I have a brandy instead?'

'No. Take a sip of this and see if you don't like it.'

'Dry gin, I didn't know they had it in this kind of place.'

'They haven't. I have my flask. Waiter, another bouillon.'

When it arrived she filled the cup to the brim from a leather-covered hunting-flask which she carried on a shoulder-strap under her cloak.

'Madame,' said the waiter crossly, 'this is not allowed.'

'I entreat you,' she said, tucking a fifty-franc note under her saucer. He walked away smiling.

'What a wonderful thing it is to have money,' she said, setting down her cup. 'I have such a lot of it. And I don't imagine you have any at all at the moment. In fact you smell of poverty just now. My senses in these matters are infallible.'

'They are indeed, Mrs Quayle.'

'Call me Honour.'

'Is that really your first name?'

'Certainly.'

'It's lovely. Do you mind my asking why you're dressed in this extraordinary manner?'

'It amuses me, as it did Haroun-al-Raschid.'

'But he always took his vizier and sword-bearer along with him in case of emergency.'

'A puseellanimous Oriental. I'm frightened of nothing.'

'Good for you. Have you had any adventures yet?'

'I am having one now.' Her eyes unhooded for an instant. I remembered the look she had given me at our first meeting—the fixed, mindless stare of a predatory bird. Before I even tried to meet it her blued eyelids dropped again. 'Would you like another cup of gin soup?'

'Very much, thank you, Mrs Quayle.'

'Honour, please.'

When we left the café I was exhilarated with gin. We walked back to the Place Edgar-Quinet, where she flagged a taxi and gave her address in the rue Galilée.

The livingroom of her apartment, which I barely remembered, was large and sombrely furnished, with many photographs framed in silver and leather.

'Let us have just one more cup,' she said.

She brought two cups of cold consommé mixed with gin. She had changed to a knee-length dressing-gown of black suede; her legs and feet were bare. I tried to take her in my arms. 'No,' she said. 'Never kiss me. Go into the bedroom.'

Her bedroom was small and dim. It seemed to be completely done in dark leather—walls, furniture, cushions and curtains—and had the smell of a saddler's shop. The low wide bed was covered with a slippery skin of either kid or calf. Mrs Quayle slipped out of her dressing-gown.

'You must let my man drive you back to Montparnasse,' she said a few hours later. 'The car is ready at any time.'

I said I would rather take the bus. She looked at me with a flicker of genuine affection. 'Really, I do like you tremenjously,' she said. 'And I see you are depressed. I have been very bed-selfish. Try and forgive me. We will see each other again?'

'Whenever you wish.'

We shook hands. I was sure she cared nothing for me and I would never see her again. I stood on the landing outside her door for a few moments, feeling faint with dejection and loneliness. I pressed the elevator button and waited for a while until I noticed the wrought-iron door carried a little porcelain plaque marked FOR ASCENT ONLY. Walking down the stairs I considered the symbolism: so neat, so trite, so literary, so full of premonitions of disaster. I thought of the hero of Daudet's *Sapho*, the young man who carries his fatal mistress up four flights of stairs for their first assignation, arriving at the top completely winded. My own situation, though in one sense reversed, was just the same. I was hopelessly in love.

It's quite simple, I told myself. You'll get over it in a week or so. It won't be too hard; you won't see her again, you'll be looking for a place to live, and you've got financial problems too. On top of that, you've got a book to write. It's just a matter of keeping busy. Try to forget her; she's a selfish, spoiled, perverse woman who would bring you nothing but misery. How in the name of sanity did you fall in love with her anyway?

I wandered down the Champs-Elysées, hardly knowing where I was going. The air was already charged with the first dusty violet colours of evening; automobiles were honking like wild geese; the terraces of the fashionable cafés were filling up with the aperitif crowd of stout men and smart women.

The trouble, I thought, is that my love for her is really pure, the first pure love I've ever felt for a woman—if I exclude a little girl with ringlets whom I loved in kindergarten: why did I love *her*? Perhaps because she used to kick my shins under the table where we used to cut out coloured paper. Why do I love Mrs Quayle? Because she has really done the same thing. But still it doesn't make sense. In the first place, she isn't my type at all. Or isn't that the very reason? Don't I love her because she is incapable of loving me?

I sat down on one of the benches in the Rond-Point des Champs-Elysées. I stayed there for a long time, hearing the traffic going by, trying to gather myself together. Don't lose your head, I kept thinking; all you have to do is not see her again. Try to think how silly and greedy she is.

It was no use. The thought of kissing her was already an obsession; yet I knew that even a kiss would solve nothing. I desired her whole soul, her personality, I wanted her to love me, to tell me I was the only man. I bent over, my head in my hands, rocking from side to side, thinking, So this is love, it's caught up with me at last. I thought I was immune, and I'm not.

It was growing dark when I got up and walked towards the Tuileries. Once in the shade of the gardens themselves I felt protected. I remember passing the bust of Perrault with his circlet of dancing children and then threading the dark alleys of chestnuts and plane-trees. At last I was out in the open, among the statues of Coysevox and Coustou, with the grandiose bulk of the Louvre and the arch of Napoleon in sight.

O soul of Théophile Gautier, I thought, come to my help tonight — you who knew the hopelessness of love and gave yourself to the beauty of forms in good season. O Parnassian gentleman, holding your massive head aloft among the encroaching waves of pimps and arrivistes — you great and honest man, incapable of baseness, you who loved the Tuileries because their symmetry was the shadow of your own devotion to purity, tell me how to overcome my passion for Mrs Quayle!

There was no reply, for Gautier no longer haunts the Tuileries.

I kept on, crossed the river by the Pont du Carrousel and went up the rue des Saints-Pères; then, almost dropping with weariness, I took the bus at Sèvres-Babylone back to the rue Broca. A letter from my father was waiting for me.

'Once again [he wrote] I wish to impress on you my disapproval of your project of a career as a writer, and must now urge in the strongest possible terms the advisability of your returning home. You are of course quite free to remain in Europe if you choose, but in justice to yourself I have decided to discontinue your allowance of $50.00 a month as of

151

this date. This decision has little or no connection with the fact that the Extract from your so-called "Autobiography" in some magazine called *This Quarter* was recently brought to my attention by Colonel Birdlime of the Department of Extramural Affairs, although your remarks about my friend Sir Arthur Currie are in the worst possible taste. Accordingly I enclose my cheque in the amount of One Hundred and Fifty Dollars to cover the cost of your passage to Montreal by the most economical means.'

This seemed to be what the religious writers of the last century had called a *sign*, a leading from above. At one stroke I could now solve all my problems of money, housing and infatuation: I could simply duck them all and get on the boat.

I knew this was the wisest course of action, the properest and most prudent. I could always salve my conscience by telling myself it had been forced on me. The great difficulty was, I did not want to go back home. I also felt, in some obscure way, I ought not to; and on top of this I knew if I ran away from Mrs Quayle I would regret it for the rest of my life. On so many counts, therefore, returning was a simple capitulation, a cowardly withdrawal, an admission of defeat.

The next evening Schooner and I sat at the little *tabac* on the boulevard du Montparnasse and turned the matter over carefully. I said nothing about Mrs Quayle. He advised me to go back. 'In the first place,' he said, 'without any money at all you won't be a free agent. A civilized man must be able to divide his energies between three pursuits—society, art, and sex. This leaves no time for gainful occupation, and such occupation in turn leaves insufficient time for any of the basic activities I have mentioned. In the second place you were, I believe, gently raised—if you will pardon the expression—and you can't live like a bum any more than I can. In fact this is where we are badly handicapped in comparison with so many of our friends who, coming from sturdy mid-European peasant or ghetto stock, find no difficulty in producing their deathless art while living on a slice of bread and an onion. In the third place, you may not have heard of it, but there has been a resounding stock-market crash in New York, London, Paris and Tokyo, and it really looks as if the party is over; anyway, everyone is going home.'

'I feel for me the party is just beginning.'

'At your age it's only natural. But the fact is, you arrived a little late.'

'I came as soon as I could.'

'And very wisely, too. You have brought a fresh vision to bear on a dying epoch. But you can't reanimate it all by yourself, just by looking at it. The expatriate way of life is grinding to a close. The twilight of the gods is drawing in; the international bankers are pulling the portières over the sky, or rather they are rolling down their iron shutters. No more credit, the game is over, the world must go back to work.'

These metaphors were disturbing. But I was unwilling to admit their validity. I was young and in love.

Just then Caridad appeared; she agreed with Schooner. 'It will be sad without you, but it would be more sad to see you around looking hungry.' She fixed me with a swift look. 'I suppose there is no chance of you finding a rich woman to keep you?'

'I don't think so.'

'Would you have dinner with me for a change? I am rich tonight.'

Schooner excused himself, and Caridad and I went to Chez Salto where she plunged gracefully into a mound of spaghetti. Emerging after a while, she looked at me gravely. 'You have a horrible problem which you are hiding,' she said. 'Do not deny it. I know, because I am full of the female intuition of my ancestors, who were gypsies. So I ask myself, "What is a young man's greatest problem?" and I answer "It is love, of course."'

I admitted I was in love.

'And this is the true reason why you don't want to go back home. Of course. I guessed it. Now we are probing the wound. Is your love quite hopeless? Have you no chance of winning her? In such a case you must go back as fast as possible and try to forget her in the great spaces of your homeland. Or perhaps you have won her already?'

'We have been to bed together, yes.'

She attacked the *gâteau maison* with a thoughtful air. 'I see. Is she rich?'

'I don't think I'd better say.'

'I know who she is now. Oh, how sorry I am for you! How could you fall in love with her? She is foolish, affected, neurotic. She sleeps with fifty men every year, this little divorcée from Boston. And she smells like an Asiatic bazaar. How awful, to fall in love with a miserable *mangeuse d'hommes*. You have made a grave mistake. Tell me, how did it happen? What is her attraction? Is it the glamour of her riches?'

'No.'

'Then you were merely ripe for the slaughter. What a pity. Have some more wine.'

'What shall I do?'

'I am not sure. Advice is not much use in these matters. Let us get a little drunk first and then you will come home with me. You are looking exhausted, and in any case you must not be alone in your present mood. You might call on this woman.'

She had read my mind. I had in fact meant to telephone Mrs Quayle.

We sat in the Select for an hour, drinking brandy and talking about love. Apart from displaying a certain prurient curiosity about the physical details of my experience with Mrs Quayle, Caridad was serious and sympathetic.

'But,' she said, 'I do not think there is any hope for you. In love, as Proust has demonstrated in several thousand pages, there is only the lover and the beloved, and the former is always wrong; that little *tapette* knew more about it than Voltaire, Casanova or Stendhal. You should realize it is not this American woman you love—it is her imago, which is in turn only an imaginative projection or radiation of your own other self. You are plagued by your double identity, you wish to adore your passive self, at the same time as you wish to be rejected by it, for reasons which are your own business. Well, you have chosen to burn your incense before this silly little nymphomaniac. You are running headlong to your own destruction—it's a kind of game your fancy is playing. This game can have serious consequences to your health.'

'You make it sound so reasonable. But all I can think of is her mouth, which I feel I must kiss or else go mad.'

'Idiot. Do you think it would end there? You could kiss her all over, it would make no difference. It would be like a bee trying to climb up a window, either to get in or get out.'

We went to the rue Delambre. Her place was just the same as when Graeme and Stanley and I had shared it that spring. The sentimental associations, however, meant nothing to me now. I could think of nothing but Mrs Quayle.

I got into bed and Caridad came to me in the flickering yellow light of the courtyard lamp. Her red hair poured down her back. We embraced long, silently, and without passion. This was the first time in my life I had declined a woman's body. It was lucky I did so, for two days later I found I had acquired a venereal disease.

TWENTY-ONE

The shock was considerable. I had now to contemplate two dreary months of enforced rest, of going without alcohol or coffee, of absolute continence. After some hesitation I confided my situation to Schooner, whose sympathy and encouragement raised my spirits greatly.

'It is nothing serious,' he said. 'Everyone gets it some time or other. Casanova had it, by his own count, fourteen times, though some of them may have been recurrences due to faulty treatment. Here is my own doctor's address; he is young, intelligent, and modest in his charges. His father, by the way, is permanent conductor of the orchestra of the Paris Opera and was a friend of Debussy's. Go and see him right away. Say you don't know where you picked the thing up—it's always safest.'

Schooner had presumed the source of infection was a prostitute, and I did not disabuse him. But I had now to advise Mrs Quayle of her condition—of which, due to the less conspicuous symptoms the malady displays in women, she was obviously quite unaware. Before getting in touch with Schooner's doctor, I telephoned her and broke the news. There was a long moment of silence.

'This is simply fearful,' she said. 'Are you quite sure?'

'I'm going for treatment tomorrow and I really think you should too.'

'I don't dare go to my own medical man for this. He is a nice old man but a Calvinist. Could you not have acquired this wretched thing from someone else?'

'No.'

'You mean you were chaste for several days before our last meeting?'

'For at least two weeks, Mrs Quayle.'

'Honour, please . . . Then it seems I have done you a greevyous wrong. I even think I know the person responsible. A *Hungharian*— yes. But that is neither here nor there. Is your doctor a reliable man?'

'I think so. His father was a friend of Debussy's.' I gave her his address.

'I shall make an appointment with him tomorrow also. If we should meet in his waitingroom it might be advisable if we did not recognize each other.'

Dr Busser lived in a charming small house in a mews off the rue Louis-David in Passy. There was no waitingroom and a parlourmaid

155

showed me into a drawingroom that held a magnificent grand piano. On top of the piano was a large framed photograph of Debussy, with a flowing, fulsome inscription that ran up transversely into the composer's beard, while on the walls were other signed photographs of composers and singers. I was identifying Saint-Saëns, d'Indy, Jean de Reszke and Lucrezia Bori when a plump little old man in a velvet smoking-jacket ran in and seized my hand—then, adjusting a pair of thick pince-nez on a black ribbon, stared, started back, murmured some apologies, and ran out again. A few minutes later a young man in a white coat came in, greeted me with a reserved smile, and took me into the surgery. 'My father,' he exclaimed, 'is as blind as a bat. He thought you were Madame Ponselle.'

My initial treatment was over at last.

'And now for your régime,' said Dr Busser, removing his gloves. 'No alcohol, wine or beer; no strong coffee, tea or spices; no red-blooded meats; nothing fried; no salad dressing; no exercise; never stand when you can sit, and never sit when you can lie down. Eat mostly boiled things. Drink as much mineral water as you can hold. And above all, absolute chastity. If you do as I say, you will be cured in about ten weeks; if you don't, it will take longer and cost you proportionately more. And now,' he fixed me with a piercing look, 'if you will tell me from whom you received this little gift, I would be grateful. If it is a prostitute, give me her address. I don't ask this from curiosity, naturally, but because I am required to report all these cases to the Ministry of Health.'

'This is a difficult question, sir. It was not a prostitute, I assure you, but an American. She may soon be consulting you herself.'

'An American? Then she has already made her appointment. And now, if you will come back in two days we will continue your treatment. By the way, my fees are payable currently. You owe me one hundred francs.'

On my way out I saw a small figure, heavily veiled, seated in a taxi standing at the curb. As I passed, the whiff of musk assured me it was Mrs Quayle. My knees trembled. I was astonished to find I was still in love with her.

Mindful of Dr Busser's instructions, I took a bus back to the rue Broca and lay down. 1 had never felt so depressed; everything seemed to be piling up. I had still to find a place to live, as well as some kind of work—and yet I had to rest . . . After a while I tried to count my blessings. I had a few friends, a good doctor, and almost three hundred dollars; all was not lost. I dressed in my best clothes, brushed my hair and took the Métro back to Montparnasse where I had dinner and then sat in the Falstaff over a small bottle of Vichy. I had decided to feel as tragic as the absurdity of my plight allowed.

In any degrading situation one must refuse to admit the degradation: one is never more ridiculous than one feels. Casanova is the supreme example of a man always rising above his petty misfortunes. He brushed them aside in as lordly a manner as he did the insults of the great men who cut him, of the police chiefs who asked him to leave their cities, of the women who made a fool of him. Or at least that is what he tells us, and this is perhaps one of the few points on which he can be believed. For between the lines of his memoirs we see the pattern of the world's mistrust and rejection of him gradually developing with a certain implacable force. Again and again we suddenly glimpse him not through his own eyes but through those of respectable people— bankers, politicians, diplomats, the police—as a swindler, confidence-man, pimp, card-sharp, bully, a disreputable adventurer with all the swagger and insolence of his kind; and just as often he reasserts himself in an instant, he regains our sympathy and admiration by some flash of insight, some burst of tenderness, some profound aphorism, and we accept him once again on his own terms. We end, in other words, by loving him as much for what he really was as for what he tells us he was, and discover that the two characters complement each other and make an intelligible whole. In this way we grasp the truth that man is not only a living creature but the person of his own creation.

I was consoling myself with these thoughts when Joe the Bum told me I was wanted on the telephone. It was Mrs Quayle; she spoke almost in a whisper. 'It is as you said. I should like to see you.'

'Please, I'm not very good company at the moment.'

'Nor am I. But I thought we might mingle our tears. I am all alone here. Please, you must not be *bitter*. I could not endure that on top of everything.'

My love for her was almost stifling me. I knew she cared nothing for me, she was merely frightened and lonely. 'Where would you like us to meet?'

'Could you not come here?'

'In fifteen minutes.'

'Oh, thank you.'

As I hung up I realized I had made a terrible mistake and was getting still deeper into a hopeless situation. I went back to my Vichy, and for a minute considered not going to the rue Galilée at all. It would be the best way of putting an end to the affair. But even then I knew I could not bear not to see her again, to give her up, to be alone . . .

Today, here in the hospital, I know it was a wrong step. I ought to have stayed on with my loneliness and my Vichy, and spent a night of dejection in the rue Broca. If I had, I mightn't be here now. But I like to think I went because it was my destiny: this spares me a useless remorse.

The little elevator in the rue Galilée delivered me at Mrs Quayle's door, which opened before I had time to ring. She was very pale but her handclasp was firm. 'I am so glad you were able to come. I have been almost out of my mind with despair.'

We sat down in the livingroom.

'My dear,' she said simply, 'I am so sorry.'

'The important thing is to keep the matter quiet,' I said. 'And to keep our spirits up, of course. Everything should be all right in two or three months, Mrs Quayle.'

'Why won't you call me Honour? You never do.'

'Honour.'

She smiled—as if she were smiling through a mist of unshed tears. I had noticed the effect before: it was a trick she had. Then I noticed that she was really crying. My love for her was suddenly overwhelming. She must have seen it, for we both got up at the same time, moved forward and fell into each other's arms like the characters in a Victorian novel.

Even then I knew she had no love for me: we were only partners in misfortune, united by an absurd and sordid accident that was itself the result of promiscuity, boredom and caprice. For her, the embrace must have been both desperate and depressing, a kind of clinging to the only object in sight, towards which she must have even felt a certain resentment engendered by a sense of guilt. But for me, the very act of holding her in my arms was an experience of the wildest ecstasy. She raised her face, drenched with tears, to mine, and I kissed her with my whole heart.

It was not to be the last time. We were to kiss with passion, affection,

158

and comradeship in the coming months, but never with the same rapture. The endless kiss we exchanged that evening in the rue Galilée was emotionally the highest point I was ever to reach with her. From then on everything declined.

TWENTY-TWO

As it turned out, I did not have to find a new place to live in after all. The next day I had a *pneumatique* from Diana Tree asking me to meet her at the apartment of Her Highness the Dayang Muda of Sarawak on the boulevard Beauséjour in Passy.

'This is a cushy, crazy job you can have if you want,' she said as she received me in a large bright drawingroom, furnished in the English style with oversized and overstuffed chintz-covered chairs, broadloom carpeting, a grand piano and a quantity of tasteless and expensive nick-nacks. 'I've been typing out the Dayang Muda's memoirs, which have been superbly ghost-written by Kay Boyle. Now Her Highness is a dear old soul in many ways, but she has two passions which I find rather wearing—a psychopathic craving for publicity and a burning desire for revenge on her husband, who had her interdicted for prodigality and her children made wards of Chancery on the grounds of her moral un-fitness to bring them up.'

'Was he justified?'

'On the first count, definitely: she spends money like water. On the second, I don't think so. I rather think he tricked her through an *agent provocateur*. One thing I know: the Princess is not interested in sex in any known form.'

'You say her memoirs are written?'

'Absolutely. Your job, darling, would simply be to finish typing them out for the printers.'

'But why me?'

'I'll be frank with you. I'm fed to the teeth with the old girl and she needs constant distraction. In fact you'll be expected to live here with her and Mrs Hagreen, her *dame de compagnie*. And she likes to go out on the town now and then, to ghastly smart places like the

159

Maisonette Russe, the Château de Madrid and the Boeuf sur le Toit. You're supposed to squire them there in your nice clothes.'

'Would I have to dance?'

'Definitely not. The Princess never learned how. And she's always in bed by eleven o'clock. The job's a cinch, darling, it was made for you.

'I suppose it doesn't pay much.'

'Only 100 francs a day. But you'll have my lovely room, which looks over the garden, and the food is gorgeous. There's a Chinese chef, by the way. The Princess adores eating. There's no rush about finishing the book. John Lane have been paid off and don't want the manuscript till October. If you don't work too hard you can spin the job out for a month or even two. If you can stand it so long.'

'Why shouldn't I?'

'Because it's just dull. It's eat and sleep all the time. But I thought you might like it for a change. You know, you're looking a bit peaked. A month here would set you up again.'

'This is sweet of you, Di. I think I'll take the job. If she'll have me.'

'She'll love you.'

'Just one thing. What's a Dayang Muda?'

'It's a title the poor benighted natives of Sarawak give to the wives of the Brookes. She liked it so much she decided to use it all the time. Just lately she added the "Highness". But she prefers to be addressed as "Princess". Her legal name, of course, is Mrs Brooke—but don't call her that whatever you do.'

'Di, I think you've saved my life.'

She got up and kissed me. 'You're an angel, and I hope you put on about ten pounds. Just one more thing. I've saved the worst news for the end. The Princess doesn't serve any liquor at all—not even a drop of wine.'

'I daresay I can get used to it.'

'You can always hide a bottle of something in your room.'

'Of course.'

The next month with the Princess was quite pleasant. It was like living in a sanatorium, swaddled in comfort, cut off from life. It was wonderful to sleep again on a spring-filled mattress spread with percale sheets, to enjoy the taste of early morning tea served in bed and the sheer volume of an English breakfast of grapefruit, scrambled eggs, grilled sheep's kidneys, milky coffee and pre-buttered toast and marmalade. I soon got used to eating luncheons as big as dinners, and dinners of lobster Newburgh and roast beef and saddle of mutton and creamed vegetables and savouries on toast and desserts like blancmange and open tarts and apple puddings and trifle. The Princess was delighted to find me such a good trencher-mate. Her great jaws crunched away on second helpings of everything.

She was a big woman, originally blonde, six feet tall and weighing over 200 pounds, with a face at once wise, sad, petulant, surprised and infantile. She ruminated all day long on the two subjects closest to her heart: newspaper publicity and getting even with her husband.

At this time the English and American newspapers were full of the case of the beautiful Mrs Nixon Nirdlinger, who had shot her elderly millionaire husband in a hotel-room in Nice and was later acquitted by a gallant French jury on the grounds that he had been trying to ravish her. The Princess was consumed by envy. 'Sickening, isn't it?' she would exclaim, throwing down the newspaper. 'The publicity that woman gets!'

Her greatest pleasure was in having me read from her own memoirs, in which Kay Boyle had managed, with consummate skill, to make everybody ridiculous except the putative authoress, who was an incredible mixture of saintliness and naïveté. The passages in which Mr Brooke was represented as a fool, a snob, a coward, a lout, a tightwad and a nitwit filled her with joy.

'That's him to a T,' she would murmur; or, 'Just wait till he reads this'; or, 'Ah, won't that put him in a wax!'—while her faded periwinkle-blue eyes would light up and her great mouth assume the lines of a croquet hoop.

In the next few weeks I grew to feel rather sorry for Mr Brooke. His family, it turned out, had practically brow-beaten him into marrying this spoiled giantess; for the Princess was the only child and sole heir of Sir Walter Palmer, of Huntley and Palmer's biscuits, and the Brookes, for all their honours and closeness to royalty, seemed never to have quite enough money or always to want a great deal more. The only member of the family with any ability was her brother-in-law, the current Rajah, of whom the Princess was frankly terrified; for his wife, the Ranee, she entertained feelings of the purest and most venomous hatred.

As I read these memoirs, letters, documents, and gossip of the fabled

161

Edwardian era, what struck me most about these wealthy people was the sheer misery in which their lives were passed. Between hating, hurting, cheating and overreaching each other, licking the boots of dukes, trying to wangle invitations to royal garden-parties and devising new ways of exploiting their tenants and overworking their servants, they had apparently never passed a carefree hour; all their pleasures were so tainted by shame and fear, all their loves and ambitions were so stultified and debased, and their very existence rendered so stupid by the absurd conditions and taboos under which it was passed, that it was no wonder the women had taken refuge in pet animals and scatological toys and the men in the process of getting joylessly drunk.

The Princess, however, had risen slightly above this, thanks to her consuming hatred of her husband and his family. In fact she had no time for anything else. For her everything was plain: she had been robbed. Again and again, rehearsing her grievances against Mr Brooke and the act of perfidy by which he and his brother, the Rajah, had managed to save almost half her fortune and settle it on her children, she would end by saying through gritted teeth, 'But it was my money— *my* money!'

Her spending had indeed been prodigious. She had bought a yacht, which she used twice and kept fully manned and staffed at Cowes for about two years; she had bought six racehorses, and when they turned out to be crocks and cripples she still kept them; she had bought a 1,000-acre farm in Wales and filled it with thousands of sheep that all died and were replaced by fresh purchases every year. It was only when she began making a moving-picture that the Brookes took action. The movie, a strictly amateur project with a story centred on the Staffordshire ceramic industry, was called *Potter's Clay* and was to star Ellen Terry at an enormous salary. Taking one look at the Princess's commitment to this undertaking, the Brookes had her interdicted for prodigality; they halted the filming of *Potter's Clay*, they paid off Ellen Terry, they sold the yacht, the racehorses, the farm and the last consignment of sheep. The Princess was wild with fury, bewilderment and grief. She had never sold anything in her life.

What she did with the remains of her fortune—which yielded her an allowance of almost $2,000 a month—was a mystery. A great deal must have gone on rent, servants, food, flowers, taxis, nightclubs, and as much again on various schemes of personal publicity and a succession of expensive alterations of things she already had: she was always having her jewels reset, her furniture re-covered, her clothes enlarged, her hats retrimmed, her furs re-cut—for she never bought anything new. Yet there should have been something over and there was not. There were never more than a few hundred francs in the house, and after a week I gave up expecting any pay: she simply did not have it. No one, in fact, received any regular salary except the Chinese chef. The housemaids left every week, cursing. Mrs Hagreen, a desiccated woman who belonged in one of Thackeray's novels, confided to me that she was owed 50,000 francs.

'But I trust the Princess absolutely,' she said, rattling her false teeth 'She has had reverses, but as soon as her meemoirs are published she will recoup and we shall all be paid to the uttermost farthing. Mark my words.'

I was under no such illusion. The memoirs were almost unreadable. All Kay Boyle's skill had been unable to make the Princess's absurd life interesting.

But I had no real need for money. I was content to gorge on the wonderful food, lie around the apartment, read the Princess her memoirs, and type about two pages a day. I even grew to enjoy the style of furnishings in the rooms, with their all-engulfing deeply-sprung sofas, their profusion of tabourets and family photographs, and the life-size reproduction of her late Aberdeen terrier cast in hollow bronze from a plaster-cast of its corpse, which lay in a life-like attitude on the hearth-rug. My cure was also coming on well, and Dr Busser complimented me on my observance of his regime.

'I had imagined you as a dissipated young man,' he said, 'and I find you a paragon.'

'Your lady patient is progressing?'

'Very well also. She has asked after you.'

Around this time the Princess decided to join the Church of Rome. She had discovered it could be done in about a month and thought it would be a fine prelude to her campaign of insult and outrage against the Brookes—who were of course Anglican—which was to culminate in the publication of her memoirs.

The details of her conversion were soon arranged with the concurrence of Monsignor McDarby of St Joseph's Cathedral on the avenue Hoche. This jolly old potato-faced Irish prelate, no more venal than any other churchman, was delighted to give the Princess the necessary religious instruction; the financial arrangements were of course secret, unformulated, and in the end unsatisfactory to everyone.

The Princess gave a great deal of thought to choosing a godparent. As she herself was over sixty, the choice was limited; moreover, the person had to be famous enough to assure a photograph in the newspapers, since the Princess would not rate one by herself.

'I have it,' she announced to me at luncheon one day. 'I'll get Madame Alphonse Daudet. Her boy Lucien tried to marry me in 1890, but Daddy thought Brooke was the better match. If he'd only known!'

'Madame Daudet? I had no idea she was still alive.'

'Of course she is. She's only eighty-five and as sound as a nut.' Her jaws crunched away on buttered toast and asparagus for a minute. 'The beauty of it is, she's madly devout and can't wriggle out of it. McDarby tells me it's a sin to refuse to sponsor a convert.'

As soon as the chocolate blancmange was finished she drafted a note to Madame Daudet that I put into French. It was a graceful and informal request, but it ended by saying that the Princess's aide-de-camp would wait on Madame Daudet at a certain hour the following week with the formal invitation, endorsed by Monsignor McDarby, and would be happy to receive the gracious interim reply.

'Your aide-de-camp?'

'That's you, my boy,' she chuckled. 'You're being promoted. And while we're at it, I know you won't mind taking some kind of smart French name for the occasion.'

'Not at all. In fact, I've got a rather nice pen-name. Jean de Saint-Luc.'

'Tremendous! "My aide-de-camp, Monsieur Jean de Saint Luc".'

She then copied out the note on a large sheet of her best crested and coroneted writing-paper. 'Take this around to her place right away in a nice-looking taxi and keep it waiting in the courtyard.'

'I'll get the little limousine at the corner stand. It won't cost more than thirty francs.'

'Hmm-mm. I suppose you haven't got thirty francs yourself.' I shook my head. 'Oh well, here's twenty francs; it's all I have in hand. Off with you now.'

The next day she brandished the reply triumphantly at me. Madame Daudet was honoured, was prepared to accept, and was expecting the formal invitation at the stated hour.

Things then moved swiftly. The engraved invitations were ordered and inscribed in haste. The Princess took enormous pleasure in writing little personal notes on them and signing her new Catholic name of Veronica (she had been originally christened Gladys).

'And here's the first one to go off,' she said. 'The whole show hinges on it, so you're to take it personally to Madame Daudet this time. Here's my card. I've written your new name on it. Give the card to the butler, but be sure you hand the invitation itself to her. And wait for her written reply. Don't let her put you off, mind.' Her great jaws clamped shut. 'Nail her!'

'Shall I take the limousine taxi?'

'Yes. Here's another twenty francs.'

Riding to the Saint-Germain quarter I was in a fever at the prospect of meeting the great lady. It would be like meeting a ghost out of the Third Empire. I kept telling myself I was going to speak to the brilliant and beautiful Julie Allard, the collaborator of her famous husband, the woman who had perhaps even composed the insufferably righteous dedication of his *Sapho*, the correspondent of Flaubert himself. I was going to lay my hand on the living pulse of French literature. Good God, I thought, she has probably spoken to Gautier! I looked at the streets and houses flashing by with a sensation of unreality, for an instant seeing them filled with horses, carriages and top hats.

I left the little limousine in the courtyard again and went up the wide shallow turning stairway. The door was opened by a lean, angry-looking gentleman in a tight-fitting frock-coat and a strangling stiff white collar; his hair, eyebrows and moustache were dyed jet black. I recognized Lucien Daudet from the old photographs of him in the Princess's album. Biting his lips, he took the card I presented and asked me to enter.

'My mother will be happy to see you in a few minutes,' he said between his teeth. 'Pray sit down.'

The hall where he left me was square, dark and damp, with waxed red tiles on the floor and heavy provincial armoires and chairs against the walls; there was also a faint but unmistakable smell of sewage in the air. After a while Lucien came back and asked me to follow him. We went along a dark passage; he tapped at a door, waited an instant, and opened it.

Madame Daudet was seated on a kind of throne at the far end of the large dim room. She was dressed entirely in flowing black cerements and wore a little lacy mob-cap on a mass of dead-looking yellowish white hair; her features were still beautiful, but her face was completely covered with mauve face-powder.

'Maman,' said Lucien with a stiff gesture, 'I have the honour to present to you Monsieur de Saint-Luc, on behalf of the Princess of Saràwak.'

Madame Daudet gave me a long piercing angry look, then inclined her head slowly. She seemed to embody all the most appalling virtues of France. Was this what the pretty little Irène of *Sapho* had turned into, that child 'with the light-brown hair and the laughing mouth'?

'*Enchantée, monsieur*,' she said in an icy voice that seemed to come from her boots.

I remained silent for a few moments, waiting for her to go on. Then I produced the engraved invitation from my breast-pocket and held it in my hand. 'Allow me, madame,' I said, trying to roll my r's fashionably, the way they do at embassies, 'to offer you this testimony of the respectful homage of Madame la Princesse. I am instructed to await the honour of your reply.'

She made a fearful grimace and held out her hand. I presented the big envelope. As she took it I understood from her expression that she was indeed, as the Princess had said, unable to evade this religious obligation.

'Thank you, monsieur,' she said in the same sepulchral voice. 'Lucien, offer Monsieur de Saint-Luc some sherry, if you please.'

He raised his dyed eyebrows at me, I bowed, and he pulled a tasselled cord. Madame Daudet ripped the envelope open, adjusted a lorgnette, and studied the card while an old man-servant in a badly made-up white tie tottered in carrying a pewter tray with two tiny glasses. I realized the whole interview had been stage-managed and began to feel a little better.

'Pray sit down, sir,' Lucien said stiffly, drawing me to a window, 'while my mother is reading your communication.' Then raising his glass slightly, 'Your health, sir.'

'And yours, sir.'

He cleared his throat and seemed to be trying to think of something more to say. I gave him no help, for by now I was so ashamed of my part in the whole travesty that I had, by a natural reaction, become incensed against both mother and son. I had not until this moment grasped the extent of the affront being put on them. On the boulevard Beauséjour the project had seemed trivial, unimportant, even amusing;

166

here it appeared as what it really was, a brash vulgar stroke. I was glad I was not figuring in it under my own name.

'Lucien, my writing-board, if you please.'

He sprang forward and arranged in front of her an ingenious contrivance, rather like a small card-table, with a blotter and stationery. She jabbed a long steel pen into the inkwell and began scratching away with great force and speed. Lucien stood before her, his hands clasped behind his back, looking at the ceiling. I watched humbly from beside the window. It was like a historical painting of the signing of some treaty or warrant of execution. Everything this dreadful old woman did was instinct with a kind of ferocious grandeur.

She blotted the sheet, and without looking at it again folded and pushed it into an envelope; then, leaning back, she waved her hand in a gesture of resignation. Lucien picked up the envelope and handed it to me. I bowed, making a faint sound of gratification. Madame Daudet sat up, bent deeply and gracefully from the waist, and gave me a freezing smile. As I left she sank back again, with the original expression of outrage on her mauve face.

The Princess's conversion was quiet and almost perfunctory. The cathedral was nearly empty. Madame Daudet occupied the place of honour and gave her responses in French. The ceremony itself took less than five minutes, and Monsignor's final allocution was a model of brevity and restraint. He touched on the beauty of conversion, and neatly separated converts into two classes with respect to their support of the church, describing them as either pillars or buttresses: the Princess, he said, was a buttress. Mrs Hagreen wept silently, as if it were a wedding, and clung to my arm. For reasons of economy there was no music.

We all then went to the boulevard Beauséjour for a splendid luncheon. The Chinese chef had surpassed himself, with a salad of hearts of artichoke, fillet of sole in brown paper, a *tournedos bouquetière* and a chocolate soufflé. During the whole meal, though she ate with discrimination and appetite, Madame Daudet did not utter a word to anyone but her son. Monsignor McDarby carried the whole conversation. The Princess herself was grim and preoccupied—matters had apparently gone much too quietly for her. But when we had risen from table her face became bright and purposeful. This was the moment for the newspapermen and photographers.

They arrived on time, and I passed out the press releases we had prepared. The photographers then invaded the livingroom and set up their apparatus.

'*Zut alors,*' Madame Daudet said hoarsely to her son. '*Cela, c'est trop! C'est inouï.*'

But Lucien seemed suddenly fascinated by the idea of having his picture taken for the newspapers and showed surprising energy in arranging chairs for the group.

'Maman,' he said, 'you will sit here, between our dear Veronica and Monsignor, will you not?'

She waved a hand in assent.

The Princess was speechless with rage: she had naturally planned to be in the centre of the picture. But Madame Daudet, moving with surprising speed, had already taken the middle chair and McDarby had adroitly moved into the one beside her. It was a moment when I felt an overmastering pity for the Princess: she had been outmanoeuvred once again. Meanwhile Lucien had assumed a rigid stance just beside his mother, leaving the Princess at the far end of the group. I moved behind McDarby, leaving Mrs Hagreen to take the other central standing position behind Madame Daudet. The camera-shutters clicked several times and the party broke up.

The pictures appeared in the newspapers next day. The Princess surveyed them with clamped jaws.

TWENTY-THREE

'My dear Saint-Luc,' Mrs Quayle wrote me at the Princess's next day, 'I did not know where you were, and I have missed you enormously — in more ways than one. Will you not telephone me some day if the pressure of your duties as aide-de-camp to royalty should permit?'

Since our last evening in the rue Galilée we had held no communication. The style of this note now brought her sharply before me: it was like smelling her perfume, hearing the very tone of her precise mocking voice. Forgetting all my resolutions I telephoned her. Once again I heard her thrilling whisper in my ear: 'My dear, I have missed you.'

'So have I.'

'How are you, may I ask?'

'I am almost well.'

'Did you know, I am saving myself for you . . . I can say no more—
now. *Au revoir*. Until then, I am embracing your image.'

'Until then I am kissing yours. Honour.'

As I hung up I was once more filled with love and adoration. I
had no thought for anything but the mouth, the odour, the body of
Mrs Quayle. However short the time, it would be all too long before
I saw her. I did not think I could hold out for another month.

But it was not to be so long. I was soon restored to the world
of poverty and action. A few days later the princess announced that
Lord Alfred Douglas was coming to stay with her. 'He'll only be here
a week or two. He's been wanting to visit Paris ever since he got out
of jail. You shan't mind letting him have your room, shall you?'

'Of course not. By the way, I sent the final draft of the book to
John Lane yesterday, with an index. They already had glossy prints of
all the illustrations.'

'You're sure? The snap of Meredith in the wheel-chair? The one
of Ruskin wearing the fur mitts Daddy gave him?'

'Yes. And the ones of Kubelik pitching hay and Oscar Wilde making
a comic face. There's really nothing left for me to do.'

'But you're not leaving! You mustn't. You've been such a help. And
Bosie will want to see you; he's always so interested in young men
he can talk about his poetry to.'

I did not like moving into the little maid's room off the kitchen,
but I was not going to miss Lord Alfred—the incarnation of the nineties,
a man of whom I knew nothing beyond the legend of his youthful
beauty, indiscretion, perfidy and general waspishness. I had read his
poetry, which was beneath serious criticism, but had never taken any
interest in the dreary scandal of his relations with Oscar Wilde, which
seemed hopelessly involved in exhibitionism and falsehood.

I was not prepared for his overmastering charm. He was much
smaller than I had thought, and the delicate curved nose of the early
portraits had developed into a monstrous beak; but he had an irresistible
warmth that saved him from insignificance, an inner glow that was
simply due to his fondness for people in general. Never was there a
more sociable man, a man with better manners or more exquisite grace
of movement, speech and behaviour. His one desire seemed to be to

please—and this ability was so innate, and brought by practice to such a degree of effortless perfection, that it had given him a second nature distinct from his own, a character into which he threw himself with delight. He enjoyed playing the part of Lord Alfred Douglas so much that one was carried away. After a half-hour in his company one was still impressed by the skill and force of the portrayal; and even then, when he tired, there was another mask beneath it that was still more charming and impenetrable.

It was surprising to find that he considered himself, with bland and unshakeable assurance, the greatest living English poet. How he had come to this conclusion was his own secret. It had probably been forced on him by an imperious inner command, an absolute refusal to accept the fact that, like Enoch Soames, he was the echo of an echo. He was determined to be first in his field; his grand passion, like the Princess's, was for the limelight: he too had been overshadowed and squelched by his father at several crucial periods in his childhood and had spent the rest of his life seeking the public eye. It was however clear that the only important thing that ever happened to him was his friendship with Oscar Wilde, and he had been trading on it ever since. All that could have saved him from utter nonentity was some fund of genuine physical desire; but this (as I soon discovered) he did not have. And his own personal attractions, which had originally driven him into a sterile narcissism, had in the end compelled him to spend the past thirty years in a tedious re-hashing of the only occasion when the world had paid him any attention. But what else could he do? Like any other ineffectual, he was always a passive agent. He wanted to take everything and give nothing—not so much from selfishness as because he needed so much and could offer nothing but the beauty and title that he had always used so adroitly. He was not untrustworthy, merely weak; not stupid, merely hollow. I had never met a man so lacking in human dignity.

Soon after this Dr Busser told me I was cured. I had now, however, no money at all, and having decided to leave the boulevard Beauséjour, which was beginning to bore me as much as it had Diana Tree, I thought I would try to collect at least half my promised salary. The result was much as I had expected.

'Three mille!' cried the Princess. 'I haven't got it. Anyway, I don't want you to leave.'

'But I've no money, not even for cigarettes.'

She clamped her jaws shut. 'Stay on for another two weeks,' she said at last, 'and I'll give you a mille.'

'But you were going to pay me a hundred francs a day two months ago.'

'I know. But d'you realize what my expenses are? My food bill is appalling, simply appalling. Between Bosie and you and Mrs Hagreen I'm being eaten out of house and home! And Wang must have his money every week—every week, mind you—or else he threatens to leave. He did actually leave for a day, did you know? Yes, I had to send Mrs Hagreen round to him with his money before he'd come back. And the company or whatever it is that owns this flat, they won't take no for an answer either. They want the rent paid every month or else I'll be hoofed. The kind of people I'm surrounded with! It's just pay, pay, pay from one week's end to another. I tell you frankly I'm overdrawn at my banker's. Yes, they're kicking up a row too. I can show you their last letter. Three mille!'

I saw it was hopeless. I toyed with the idea of stealing an autographed copy of Meredith's *Lord Ormont and his Aminta* and selling it to Mr Threep, but thought better of it. I was not going to lose my moral character altogether.

'Then I'll just have to go unpaid. I'm leaving this evening, Princess.'

'Don't be ridiculous. Where'll you go? You haven't any money.'

'I've enough for a week's rent.'

'See here, I'll give you half a mille to stay.'

'Right now?'

'The day after tomorrow.'

'No, I think I'd better go now.'

'You're a most ungrateful boy. I thought you cared for me.'

'I'm sorry, Princess. It's been lovely living here, you'll never know what it's meant to me—but I can't live without any money at all. I'll have to go out and make some.'

'Where?'

I had a moment of inspiration. 'I thought I'd go to Madame Daudet and help her with her memoirs.'

'*Her* memoirs! *Hers*! That brazen old woman! Is she writing her memoirs too?'

'I'm sure she is,' I said, inventing as I went on. 'She knew a lot of famous people. She has letters from Flaubert, Victor Hugo, King Edward VII . . .'

'I won't have you going to her.' She looked ready to weep.

'I'm going to try.' I went into the maid's room, packed my two suitcases and carried them out into the hall. She came up with a man's sealskin wallet and put it into my hands.

'Here's a little present for you. There's half a mille in it. Now go back and unpack your things.'

'Why, thank you, Princess.'

I took my suitcases and unpacked them again. Examining the wallet, I discovered it had Mr Brooke's name stamped on it in gold and held only 400 francs. By then it was time for dinner and Bosie had arrived back from the races at Longchamps. We had a very good dinner of saddle of mutton with green peas, hearts of artichokes with hollandaise sauce and roly-poly filled with black-currant jam. After sitting in the drawingroom while Bosie played a little easy Chopin, we went to bed at nine o'clock as usual. By ten I decided the coast was clear, and having packed again I slipped out of the apartment, took a taxi to the Jules-César and paid for the cheapest room they had for a week. This left almost 300 francs, enough to keep me, with rigid economy, for a week.

Montparnasse looked as gay and crowded as ever but I could see no one I knew. I had been looking forward to a drink for over two months and stood by the counter of the Dôme and drank three small neat brandies; they had no effect at all. I began to feel sad and oppressed and for a few moments seriously considered going back to Montreal. After a while I heard Serge Kirilenko, an off-white Russian photographer of doubtful repute, speaking to me over a veal sandwich into which he was tearing with his large pointed teeth. 'How is it going? You look sad.'

'I am sad.'

'Money?'

'Among other things.'

'Do you want to make some money?'

'How much?'

His handsome Mongolian eyes closed under their white eyelids. 'A thousand francs. For nothing.'

'Is it legal?'

'What do you take me for? This is a small proposition. You know, I am a photographer, *portraitiste*. I make artistic pictures, eh? I have taken you twice already in the Coupole, you remember, for nothing. Good pictures, eh?'

I agreed they had been very good pictures. He then made his small proposition. I was to pose for a series of twenty pornographic pictures; he would pay 1,000 francs outright. I would not be involved in marketing the product.

Forty dollars: it seemed fair enough. As far as I knew, posing for such photographs was not a criminal offence—or if it was, the law had not been enforced for the last ten years. However, my experience with Richard Le Gallienne, Monsieur Gaucher and the Princess had made me wary. 'Would you pay in advance?'

The eyes closed again. 'Yes. Come to my studio in the rue Guy-Robert tomorrow afternoon.' He handed me his card. 'We can finish the job in two hours.'

'Just one thing. I want to wear a mask.'

'Hm-mmm. A very small one, then. Your expression will be important.'

The next day I bathed, shaved, brushed my hair carefully and went to the rue Guy-Robert. It was a golden October day, the plane-trees had turned a pale yellow, and I was feeling very cheerful: 1,000 francs would set me up for a whole month. I told myself I might even be able to finish another chapter of my book. At the Princess's I had been unable to write a line. The atmosphere of the boulevard Beauséjour had been stupefying.

Kirilenko's studio was on the fifth floor of a run-down building. It was large, light, and extremely dirty.

'Let me present Monsieur Jules, our principal,' he said. I shook hands with an expensively dressed man whose bullet-shaped head and hair-line moustache diffused an air of crime. 'And here are Cécile and Carmen. Are they not charming girls?'

They were indeed. Young, fresh, beautiful and debonair, they were of quite another race than the blowsy barrel-shaped women who generally figure in pornographic art. I eyed them with an approval that they seemed to return. We were all surprised; they had probably expected someone like the Rajah.

Kirilenko, who in the meantime had locked and double-bolted the door, trained his big old-fashioned standing camera on a low settee covered with a leopard-skin and backed by an oversized cheval-glass and a tapestried screen representing nymphs and satyrs. The effect was not inartistic.

'On the scene, my friends,' he said jovially.

The girls stripped in a businesslike way and I followed suit. I was unpleasantly aware of the cold scrutiny of Monsieur Jules. Kirilenko quickly arranged the first pose which, while simple, showed both taste and imagination. When we were all disposed he switched on two strips of lights: as soon as he ducked under the black cloth of his camera I pulled on the little silk mask I had bought that morning in the rue de la Gaîté.

'What's this?' snarled Monsieur Jules. 'This is not in the bargain, young man!'

'Indeed it is. And please do not call me "young man".'

'Jules,' said Kirilenko, putting his head out from under the cloth, 'I beg you to keep quiet. I know my business. Monsieur's disguise will be highly piquant. It adds salt to the dish, don't you see?'

'*Merde*,' said Monsieur Jules. 'It looks too amateur.'

Kirilenko threw up his hands. 'My friend, go and sit down over there, I implore you. Monsieur has an artistic temperament and this is only making it worse.'

Our principal shrugged his padded shoulders and spat blank. 'I leave it to you. But show me the first plate.'

'You will love it, I promise you.'

Kirilenko winked at us, and then going to the girls he patted them gently. 'You have plenty of time, my children. Relax, be easy. Monsieur, look at these girls for a minute. And you, Carmen, encourage him a little.' In less than a minute everything was as it should be. 'Perfect! Exquisite!' he murmured, adjusting one of Cécile's legs. 'Can you hold that, sir?'

'Certainly.'

He switched on the top lights and dived back under the black cloth. 'All smile, please . . . the soft, sensual smile. Ah . . . Right. Splendid.' The shutter clicked. 'Break.'

The girls relaxed and sat up. Kirilenko cut the lights, removed the plate and covered it.

'Jules, I will develop this one now. Come into the darkroom. You are about to witness my art.'

While they were in the little closet at the end of the room the girls and I smoked and chatted. 'Who is Monsieur Jules?' I asked.

'He is a big man in Montmartre, my dear,' said Carmen. 'He is in everything. Do you know how much he is going to make out of our pretty pictures? Why, he will clear fifty thousand at least. I have that on authority. How much is he paying you?'

'1,000 francs.'

'The same as for *both* of us. Is it not shameful? We are being used.'

'But of course,' said Cécile, flicking the ash of her cigarette on the already littered floor. 'He is able to. He controls the distribution. And he takes the risk. He is not a bad fellow when you know him.'

'No, not bad,' said Carmen. 'He is devoted to his mother, they say. Hush!'

Kirilenko and our principal came out of the darkroom. The latter was smiling with one corner of his mouth.

'Didn't I tell you?' Kirilenko was saying. 'Not bad, not bad. Go ahead and take the rest.'

This, I felt, was the time to make my strike. 'Monsieur, I will ask you for my money now,' I said, getting up from the settee. 'As agreed between M. Kirilenko and myself last night.'

'In good time.'

'At once.'

He scowled. 'I never pay until a job is done.'

'Then you can have your one picture for nothing. I am leaving.' I walked across the room and picked up my clothes. Kirilenko ran after me, waving his arms. The girls, seeing their money vanishing also, set up a cry. At last Jules produced a gargantuan wad of bills, peeled off a thousand-franc note and thrust it at me.

The work was finished in less than two hours. Kirilenko had com posed all the pictures beforehand and had only to consult his schedule.

A few days later he showed me the series of pictures, all printed in the handy postcard size. They were very fine of their kind, and I bought a set for 100 francs, which he told me was one-fifth of their retail price. I was glad to have them as souvenirs. Also, by a curious imaginative projection I was even able to summon up a feeling of pleasurable envy for this masked young man who was enjoying himself with such carefree abandon.

Kirilenko was delighted with these examples of his art. He already wanted to do a movie in the same genre. 'The difficulty will be to secure girls who really can act. By the way, would you be interested in taking the juvenile lead? I have my little scenario all made.'

As I doubted my abilities in this line, I refused. Moreover, I thought

I was getting a little too deep in petty crime. I could not forget I was a foreigner without an identity card.

TWENTY-FOUR

For the next two weeks I lived quietly and worked on my book. I also wrote three poems in which I began feeling my way towards genuine communication. They were tight and formal exercises on the subject of death and were greatly influenced by the Elizabethan Samuel Daniel, whose work I had just discovered and whose handling of vowels had opened up to me new possibilities in the use of sound. I soon became lost in the exploration of poetic techniques, working at least six hours a day and only leaving my room to eat at a soup-kitchen near the Montparnasse railway station. There I met a wholesome young waitress with whom I slept from time to time in her tiny bedroom on the sixth floor of the passage de l'Enfer. Her courage, cheerfulness and simple passion were infinitely touching, but the affair ended by giving me such a vision of the sadness of her life and the misery of her future that I stopped seeing her. The vie de Bohême was not for me. I had always despised the Rodolphes of this world and did not mean to become one merely to overcome my dangerous and consuming desire for Mrs Quayle.

In the meantime winter was coming on and my money was giving out. The number of Americans in Paris was dropping as steadily as the stock-exchange averages and I saw fewer familiar faces in the quarter. I began to wonder how I was going to last till spring; for never had I less wanted to return home. I felt I was on the brink of writing passable poetry and must continue living in the atmosphere of this city or else I would cease to write altogether.

The problem was how to live in Paris at all. It soon became acute. By November 1st I had not paid my hotel bill for three weeks, having counted on at least a month's grace. But I had not properly grasped the principles of Parisian hotelkeeping and one morning found that my baggage had been seized and my room rented to someone else.

'I trust you will not be inconvenienced,' the proprietor of the Jules-César said with a smile. 'But better you than I. It is a question of priority of interests. You owe me six hundred francs. Shall we say it is payable in three days?'

I had no idea where to find such a sum. When I turned it into dollars it seemed trifling: only $24.00. But when I turned it back into francs it assumed its proper proportions. It was too small a sum to be frightening but too large to borrow. I decided to forget about it for this one afternoon. I had still fifteen francs, the remains of Monsieur Jules' honorarium.

In any case it was too beautiful a day to worry. That year's autumn seemed to have turned back into summer. The air was warm and fragrant with the smell of the chestnut trees, the sky over Montparnasse a tender windless blue, and I decided to take a walk down by the river and to the Île Saint-Louis where I had not been for many months.

This island had always evoked my special love. It was so remote, quiet and run-down—this little lozenge of land swimming along behind the imposing Île de la Cité. The pitted stone of the quays, the paintless, light-coloured uneven buildings that hugged its curves so closely, the absence of traffic—all this gave it a strangely reticent and provincial air. I arrived by the rue de l'Archevêque and crossed by the little Pont Saint-Louis, went around the Quai Bourbon and through the heart of the island by the rue des Deux-Ponts, coming back to the sun-drenched Quai d'Orléans. There, sitting on the parapet of the quay near the corner of the rue Le Grattier, I gave myself up to daydreams. I chose the house where I meant to settle down one day—a small Louis xv hôtel, only four storeys high, with a miniature cour d'honneur. The stone was pale grey, yellowed with age; the windows were high, indicating high ceilings inside; there were dozens of chimney-pots on the roof, bespeaking at least four fireplaces on each floor; and there was an ornate iron-railed balcony serving three rooms on the third floor. In those three rooms I would live, I decided. They commanded a fine view of the river, the ivied wall of the square de l'Archevêque, and the back of Notre Dame— so much finer than the front—and would have all the afternoon sun; on fine days I would have breakfast on the balcony, dressed in a Balzacian dressing-gown; all night I would be able to see the lights on the river . . .

This was my dream of life in Paris in November 1929, with the sun on the yellow buildings and the bronze-green river flowing by, the muted roar of the traffic in the distance and the spire of Notre Dame rising into the smoky blue sky. How far away it seems now, in this granite hospital where all I can see from my narrow bed is a strip of soot-covered Montreal snow and an oblique glimpse of the new Maternity Wing.

Evening was falling when I left the Quai d'Orléans, crossed the Pont de la Tournelle and went along the Quai de Montebello to Saint-Michel. I felt the city had swallowed me and I now made part of it. It was an experience of possession by something so stately and vivid that I walked along in a dream of absolute subservience to stone and river and sky. After a while I realized I was hungry and bought a half-baguette of bread, a small sausage and a bottle of ordinaire in the rue Saint-André-des-Arts. Sitting on the embankment at the tip of the Vert Galant, at the very prow of la Cité, I supped while watching the lights come on along the banks and in the moored barges. Everything down here was quiet. The sounds of the city passed overhead and, like Sir Bedivere, all I could hear was the water lapping on the shore.

It was the velvet hour, the hour of meditation, when one dares try to crack the two ultimate riddles of man: Why are we here and how do we really know we *are* here? These two questions, which lie at the root of the mystery of all being, had not been answered by my favourite philosopher Bishop Berkeley. He had unaccountably bypassed them both. As a conscientious Christian he had of course not seen fit to examine the first in a critical way, much less to give his private answer, which might have been interesting; as for the second, he had quite shirked the task of refuting that miserable Descartes, treating the question much as Schopenhauer had done when he said solipsism was an impregnable castle that a good general had better leave untaken and press on to further conquests—a simile that was both weak and evasive. Both philosophers, in declining to answer these questions, were obviously at the mercy of their temperaments; their minds were similarly fixed on the corner-stones of their system—the Deity and the Will. This, I told myself, was where I had the advantage of them.

The question of why we were here gave me no trouble. I had always suspected that all life and indeed the whole universe of phenomena existed only as a kind of mistake, an accident, an interruption of nothingness: this made sense. The second question, that of consciousness, was more difficult; but I had already made some progress towards its elucidation as a result of my Bastille Day meditations outside the row of toilets in the rue Broca, and now determined to do some hard thinking on the subject during the coming winter.

My thoughts then took another turn. Suppose I should never really solve either of these problems? Might it not be better? If I did solve them, might it not be to possess what Péguy called man's *liberté à l'état absolu*, or *le secret de Dieu sur l'homme*? What would come after such knowledge? Simply, Péguy had warned, the consciousness of damnation. Just what he meant by this impressive word was uncertain, but his horror of the condition was eloquently conveyed. That night on the Vert Galant I envisaged it as a plateau of absolute boredom, indifference, *acedia*. If this was the price of such knowledge, I was certainly not going to pay it: *nolo nescire* would be the safest motto. On the other hand, I did not altogether trust Péguy, perhaps because of the high stiff collar and pretentious moustache of his portrait. At last I decided that if I was to be damned to eternal boredom I would have to take the chance. Even if it were true, there was always Paris and poetry, for my own lifetime at any rate. It suddenly struck me that the modern philosophers had not taken sufficient account of man's apprehension of beauty.

The Vert Galant was now in pitch darkness and the air was cooler. I had still to find a room to sleep in. But I could not yet bear to leave the lights of the river. I felt I had not yet been fully possessed by the city, or rather that the possession might be further extended and deepened. The idea then came to me to spend the night there, by the river. This was a project I had always entertained and its realization now seemed indicated; it would also leave me enough money for both breakfast and dinner next day. But the breeze was growing cold, and packing up the remains of my bread, sausage and wine I went to look for a more sheltered spot under the Pont Neuf. I found a fine place well up under the first arch, where the fine clean dust would make a comfortable bed. I burrowed in, uncorked my wine, and leaning on one elbow began drinking peacefully.

I could now see both up and down the river. The cross-town traffic still went by, but without shaking the massive stone arch over my head; the sound was as soothing as rain on a roof. I tried to remember who had first built the Pont Neuf: Henri III or IV? Anyway it had taken almost twenty years to finish. And still, with its ten or twelve laborious arches, it was the loveliest bridge in Paris, much better than Napoleon's

Austerlitz and Iéna bridges, and still better than the Invalides, Alma and Solferino ones, which, as the guidebooks said, 'are all handsome structures, adorned with military and naval trophies commemorative of events and victories connected with the Second Empire . . .' I was falling asleep when a hoarse, tearful voice cried in my ear:

'Monsieur, this is my place!'

A bulky, bearded man entirely in rags, with a canvas wallet slung over his shoulder and carrying a camp-stool, was staring down at me; behind him was a shapeless old woman lugging an enormous paper shopping bag.

'You have taken my place,' he repeated in a heavy Béarnais accent. 'This is mine, by right.'

'By what right?'

His bearded mouth fell open; he began to sputter. 'Gaby,' he turned to the old woman, 'this is our place, isn't it?'

'Yes, yes, our place,' she mumbled.

'There's room for all of us,' I said.

'But I like my privacy. Besides, you are new. You're not even Parisian. Is he, Gaby? He doesn't speak right.'

'No, not a man of Paris.'

'You're not of Paris either, monsieur,' I said.

'I, not of Paris! I am the man of the Pont Neuf.'

'So am I, for tonight. Don't bother me, I'm going to sleep.'

'Henri, Henri,' muttered the old woman, pulling him by the sleeve.

They moved a few dozen yards away. He put down his campstool, while she dug a bottle of wine from her shopping bag. After a while I looked over at them. They were lying not quite motionless, their arms around each other . . .

Waking at dawn, the first thing I saw was the twin towers of Notre Dame. They seemed almost on top of me, squarely outlined against the sun that was rising over the Quai des Orfèvres. The air was chilly with the first hint of winter, but it was another beautiful day. There were seagulls swooping over the pale-green river, and smoke from the cookstoves on the barges was rising in the air. The city was stirring into life, and Paris,

en se frottant les yeux,
Empoignait ses outils, vieillard laborieux.

I got up and went down on the tow-path, standing over the water and looking right across to Saint-Germain-l'Auxerrois. The Pont Neuf still strode on its solid arches to the Cité, as it had for three hundred years and would keep on doing while civilization and consciousness lasted. I looked at the Seine and the island in a kind of rapture. This morning I felt for the first time fully implicated in the Paris of Villon, Nerval and Baudelaire, in an existence that would have been meaningless without the city. As I went back I saw that the two *clochards* were still sleeping in their dusty burrow, wound together in their rags. It was still the kindly autumn . . .

That night it suddenly turned bitterly cold and an icy rain began to fall. I was sitting over a bouillon in the little *tabac*, in the comparative warmth of the back room and the perennial café smell of spilt beer, sawdust and wet mops, when Serge Kirilenko came in. He was looking unusually prosperous in a fur-collared overcoat and an astrakhan cap; he sat down and offered me a gold-tipped cigarette.

'You don't look well, my friend. You are losing weight. How goes the life of literature?'

'Very well. I am beginning to comprehend my genius.'

'Good, good. I also am a lover of poetry. I like everything gentle and beautiful. In the meantime I wonder if you would be interested in a little proposition that could be profitable to both of us?'

'Some more posing?'

He clasped his white hands under his chin and appeared to meditate deeply. 'In the spring, perhaps. You have lost too much weight, I fear. What I had in mind was something different. Have you ever heard of Madame Godenot? No? A very practical woman who runs an exclusive establishment on the rue Blanche. She caters to women of a certain age—very fine clientèle in the Étoile and Parc Monceau districts. Idle women, widows, spinsters.'

'How touching.'

'You are facetious. But I am serious. These ladies are, to speak plainly, starved for love. And you seem starved for common nourishment. Have you not thought of a possible combination of these needs?'

'Not until now.'

He smiled. 'Excellent. We understand each other. Now to business. Madame Godenot will introduce you to these ladies as a healthy, clean, affectionate and reliable young Canadian. I personally am vouching for you. She operates on a high percentage, of course, and receives all the proceeds. May I give her your address? She has seen the postcards we made and she is impressed. I hope you will not disappoint us.'

'May I ask the tariff?'

'It varies. But let us say, roughly, 1000 francs a séance. Half for you, and half for Madame.'

'Nothing for you?'

He laughed. 'A trifle, a mere trifle. Then shall I put you on her little list? You will find the employment rather tedious, perhaps, but more rewarding than poetry.'

Looking at him I was struck by this curious restatement of the theme of Mephisto and Faust, of Vautrin and Rubempré, here reduced to its crassest terms—but no less powerful, no less irresistible. Homeless, cold, and hungry, I made the classic response. 'You might as well.'

His face did not change. 'Would you like a small advance?'

'1,000 francs will do.'

Without a flicker he passed me the two large pink bills, got up, settled his astrakhan cap over his ear with a tap of the finger, and took his leave. The next day I received an unsigned *pneumatique* in a spidery commercial hand telling me to telephone a Montmartre number and give the name 'Soulage'. A man's rough throaty voice answered when I phoned. 'Who is calling?'

'Soulage.'

'Solange? Who in hell is she?'

'Not Solange. Soulage.'

'One moment.'

I waited for almost five minutes. Just as I was ready to hang up, a woman's gravelly voice hit my ear like a mallet. To my astonishment its owner spoke in English, with a mid-western American accent. 'Who is that?'

'Soulage.'

'Oh-ho! Soulage, is it? Well, well. My dear, come to number 65 rue Blanche tonight. I want to see you first.'

'Am I addressing Madame Godenot?'

'And how. Ten o'clock.' She hung up with a crash.

After a hearty dinner at Chez Salto I took the Métro to the Place Blanche station and found the address. The house was less sinister in appearance than I had expected and a pink light glowed above the door.

My ring was answered by a coal-black Negro in a dinner-jacket, who stood squarely in the doorway and looked me up and down with a mixture of suspicion and geniality.

'I want to see Madame Godenot,' I said. 'I have an appointment.'

'How are you called, sir?' His accent was strongly American.

'Soulage.'

His face split in a flashing watermelon grin. 'You the Canadian boy, huh?' he said in English. 'Come right in. The old lady see you right off. Step this way.'

I followed him along a dark passage and climbed a steep flight of heavily carpeted stairs. The house seemed to be filled with badly fitting doors rimmed with faint yellow light, but everything was strangely quiet. The Negro trod before me with a silent pantherish gait. A strong scent of sandalwood filled the air and I heard a muffled gramophone playing somewhere. If this was a house of assignation, I thought, it was living up to everything I had read of such places in nineteenth-century fiction: the atmosphere was pure Maupassant. I could not match it up with the breezy, brassy voice of Madame Godenot.

'Forgetting my manners,' said the Negro, stopping outside a heavy baize-covered door. 'Tom Cork is my name. Glad to know you.'

'So am I. A pleasure.' We shook hands. I had already taken a liking to him, for although built like a heavyweight boxer he had none of the air of a strong-arm man. He knocked and showed me into a small brightly lit room furnished like an office. Behind the desk sat a woman with a face like a bulldog. She was wearing a purple cocktail dress and a red pompadour and her fingers and wrists were covered with jewellery; her eyes were small, blue, and shrewd. There was a square bottle of Johnnie Walker Black Label at her elbow but no glass.

'Hello,' she said. 'You're right on time. O.K., Tom, bugger off.' He flashed his grin and disappeared.

'Smoke?' said Madame Godenot, pushing a mauve package of Salâm-mbos towards me after taking one herself.

'Please.'

'Drink?'

'Not now, thanks.'

'You don't drink, or just pretending?'

'Of course I drink. Brandy, if you've any.'

'In the box over there. Help yourself.'

I opened the cabinet and poured a small Courvoisier.

'Cheers.' She made a pretence of drinking from the bottle on the desk. I saw she was still studying me carefully. 'Well, are we doing business?'

'I trust so, Madame Godenot.'

'Call me Lolotte. O.K., now we talk money. Your price is a thousand francs a whole night. Four hundred an hour.'

'And in between that?'

'There's nothing in between, kid. I've only two kinds of clients. Travesties are extra and you rent your own costume from the house. You get paid by me, understand: half of everything. For shows, you get a quarter. Right?'

'Right.'

'You're on call from four o'clock till midnight, either by *petit bleu* or telephone. Give me the names of three bars where I can get you. O.K. You'll be making 2000 a week without even trying.'

As it turned out I made over 3000 francs in the first week, mostly from a hysterical elderly Spanish-American woman who was not un-attractive and had the further merit of not wishing to talk.

During the following month I discovered several curious things about woman as a sexual predator. Unlike man, she does not seek sex on a sudden impulse, at any time of the night or day; on the contrary she makes an appointment for it as she would with her manicurist or hairdresser. Moreover, she is much more coldblooded and condescending than man. I never met a woman at Madame Godenot's who showed the least tenderness or humour in the course of our relations: without exception they were entirely selfish in their love-making. When a client caressed me it was not from a desire to give pleasure but with a sense of ownership. When I caressed her there was the same cold, selfish, remote look on her face: these were attentions she could enjoy by herself without the feeling that her lover enjoyed the mixture of familiarity, depreciation, and contempt with which so many men treat the bodies of women and to which she had doubtless become accustomed. For her it was the triumph of egotism, a kind of effortless masturbation. God knows what she was thinking. In the little plush-curtained room with its great bed, its mirrors, its gramophone (it was remarkable how many of the women required music) and its rosy lights I felt I was assisting at the rebirth of mysterious, unnameable dreams, the deferred reveries of children and virgins. I was a leading character, hero or villain, of the interior novel my partner had been writing for many years in—

as a romantic prose-writer would put it—the privacy of her soul. I found my experiences in the rue Blanche far from pleasant. The attitude of these greedy women would soon have destroyed me altogether if I had been obliged to continue for long in their service. Worst of all, I found I was no longer able to write my poetry.

Fortunately Bob McAlmon returned to Paris in December.

TWENTY-FIVE

'How did you get into these shenanigans?' Bob wanted to know. 'Couldn't you find any work? I heard you were typing.'

'The American writers all went home.'

'What about Morley?'

'Loretto does all his typing. Anyway they've gone back to Toronto.'

'Did you see the story he wrote about you and Graeme and Stanley in *This Quarter*?'

'"Now That April's Here"? Not very good, was it? Rather nasty—and it's full of holes.'

Bob was once more magnificently in funds and had sublet a large furnished apartment in the rue d'Assas. I was glad to join him there and said goodbye to Madame Godenot and Tom Cork the next day.

'Sorry to see you go, kid,' she said. 'You made a real hit with the clients.'

'I hope so. You still owe me 500 francs.'

'Like hell I do. What for?'

'That last show.'

'I don't remember a thing. Tom, is that right?'

'Come on, Lolotte, have a heart.'

'Listen to him. He goes into keeping and he wants money. Which of the old ladies is it? You're the one should be giving me a cut.'

'Let's forget it. Give my love to everyone. It's been nice knowing you.'

'Now don't go away like that. Here's 100 francs. And let me give you a call some time. Don't be proud, you never know when you'll need a pal.'

'Right,' said Tom. 'Part with a smile, I always say.'

Life in the rue d'Assas was wonderful. I liked best the steam heat. It seemed years since I had been properly warm in winter and able to soak myself for hours in a big bathtub. I also resumed the modern cultural thread by reading all the publications and manuscripts of Bob's Contact Press—Williams' *Spring and All*, Mary Butts' *Ashe of Rings*, Marsden Hartley's *The Eater of Darkness*, and Ken Sato's *The Yellow Jap Dogs*. Faced with all this original work, I suspended my critical faculties altogether and enjoyed everything. I read these books the way I had once read Spenser to the music of Bach, opening my mind to all the resources of sound, rhythm and syntax, without judgement, embracing the effect of nuance, drowning myself in a feast of images and vowels, in a kind of sensuous verbal fog. I also began to eat heartily and was glad to see my legs filling out again. But with the removal of my worries and plenty of leisure, I was once again pursued by my thoughts and recollections of Mrs Quayle. I dreamed of her night and day.

'What do you really think of Bill Williams' poetry?' Bob asked. 'Sometimes I think it's a lot of tripe. But he's such a nice guy.'

'I don't like that flat Japanese style.'

'I know. You like Keats and that kind of crap. Anything drenched in beauty. But Bill has got one hell of a technique. He can get a picture or a point across in five lines.'

'But it's always the same picture and the same point. Little negative things.'

'He hits the spot every time.'

'Like a fly-swatter.'

'You don't go for imagism.'

'It's too easy, naïve, sentimental, infantile. But perhaps poetry needs to get back to two-dimensional things—the wheelbarrow and the chickens. Just as long as it doesn't stop there—with the image as an absolute. Even if it does, it's better than the poetry of social comment.'

'Balls to that. Anger, despair and history are the only materials of poetry. Ideas don't belong. Who the hell cares what a poet thinks? His job is just to yell.'

Bob was writing a new long poem in which he was yelling louder than ever. It was a love poem full of frustration, agony, desire and scurrility and was almost impressive; the obscenity of the language was also striking. As usual he had a good title, 'No for an Answer'; but he kept padding the poem by his favourite device of inserting prose extracts from catalogues and encyclopaedias, the lines being chopped up and set as verse.

'It gives variety,' he said. 'Lets the reader breathe and look around a bit. Don't tell me those parts are dull. Hell, they're *supposed* to be dull! And I can't be bothered to write them myself. Why should I? You can't improve on nature, kid.'

This idea of literary collage sounded well enough, but in practice the effect was unsatisfactory. I found the extracts tasteless, distracting and ineffective. When I told him so he was delighted.

'Just what I want,' he said. 'This poem is going to be like life— lousy in spots. Where it's bad, it's really crap. It's going to be the worst poem ever written, see? I'm dedicating it to you.'

One day he suggested we go and see James Joyce. 'He's all alone and there's some kind of eye operation coming up, so the old Irish tenor's not feeling his oats. He said to bring along anyone I wanted. But don't talk about his work, we'll just get a little stinko together. Now's the time, when Nora's not there.'

He shaved carefully, put on a dark grey suit that didn't fit him at all, a white shirt, and a rather frayed four-in-hand tie.

As we rode along in the taxi he warned me again not to question Joyce about anything he had written. 'And whatever you do, don't ask him what he's going to call his *Work in Progress*. He has a bee in his bonnet that he'll never finish it if he tells anyone what it's called.'

'I can't make head or tail of it anyway.'

'Good, tell him that if you get a chance. He'll like it.'

'What do you think of it yourself?'

'If he thinks it's good, it's good enough for me.'

This, for Bob, was extraordinary. I had heard him dismiss Milton, Spenser, Donne, Wordsworth, Thackeray, Conrad, and Meredith (he had read only a few pages of each, but enough, as he said, to get their quality)—as well as any living author one could name—and this un-questioning acceptance of Joyce was surprising. I did not share his en-thusiasm. I knew the *Portrait* and *Ulysses* almost by heart, and thought them the greatest English prose works of the century; but I saw faults in each, and I had a feeling that his *Work in Progress*, the first two chapters of which I had read in *transition*, was moving in the same direction Flaubert had taken in *Bouvard et Pécuchet* and the *Dictionnaire des idées reçues*—into a fragmented chaos. This was perhaps the only

187

avenue to these virtuosos of the particular, who had so mastered their medium they had nowhere else to go but onward into a deliberately disformed universe of words and impressions. After all, what else could they do? I remembered Flaubert's execrable verses and thought of Joyce's own *Pomes Penyeach* in their little apple-green cover—so melodiously weak, so drowned in Celtic twilight, so spineless and sentimental, that you wondered why he had published them. Both were poets who had missed their vocation and only tampered with ideas. After their fiftieth year all that remained of either of these two great artists were tears, petulance, laughter, and a superb technique. But as the taxi went along the rue de Grenelle I was as excited as if I were going to see Flaubert himself.

On the landing of Joyce's apartment Bob twitched his necktie nervously before rapping at the door. A maid in a soiled apron showed us into a dimly lit room, and a low voice called from beside a glowing fireplace, 'Is it you, McAlmon? Come in.' A slender, elegant, curved figure rose and weaved towards us. 'Ah, it's good to see you. And this is the young fellow you've brought, is it? You're most welcome, sir.'

While he and Bob discussed mutual friends I breathed the homely smell of onions and furniture-polish. In the dim light I could see on the walls a number of what Bob had told me were the family portraits, and I made out the picture of Joyce's father over the mantelpiece—a ponderous figure who didn't look like Simon Dedalus at all; it was impossible to visualize this dignified old gentleman singing catches on a summer afternoon in the Ormond Hotel in Dublin.

'I've some good wine there,' said Joyce. 'McAlmon, it's right to your hand.'

The room was so dark, Bob said, he could see nothing, and he asked if he could turn up the lights.

When he did so I had my first sight of Joyce. He was almost as distinguished looking as in his posed portraits; but the thin twisted mouth was now little more than a slit, the bibulous nose was pitted with holes like a piece of red-coloured cork, and the little goatee looked affected and out of place; his eyes were almost invisible behind thick glasses. Of the sarcastic bounderish air of the snapshots there was not a trace: he was reserved, charming, gracious, and his voice was music. He had a good figure for clothes and very narrow feet, but he was wearing a very badly cut suit.

The chilled wine was a coarse Niersteiner—light, dry and aromatic. Joyce sipped it with gormandise.

'I'm getting on well with the *oeuvre grandissime*,' he said. 'You'll be seeing another piece of it in Mr Jolas's little magazine soon. Tell me now, McAlmon, do you still like it?'

Bob jerked himself around in his chair. 'It's great, sir, simply great. It has a wonderful flowing quality, the quality of Molly Bloom's thoughts, only it's got more variety. I think you're breaking up the language damn well. In a few years nobody'll be able to write a book in English any more, the words will be out of date.'

Joyce shrugged deprecatingly. 'Oh no.'

'Rats, I don't pretend to understand it yet. This young fellow here doesn't either.'

Joyce turned to me courteously, his eyebrows raised.

I was seized with panic and stammered something about finding it more like the monologue in the tavern scene in *Ulysses* than Molly Bloom. 'It's like listening to a lot of people in a pub, all speaking at the same time—but I'm not sure what they're talking about.'

'This is a great compliment,' he said, smiling. 'So you liked the scene in the tavern?'

Thinking he was referring to the scene in Barney Kiernan's in *Ulysses*, I told him this was my favourite section of the book and that I had privately given the name of Begob to the nameless speaker; then, unable to control my curiosity, I asked, 'Was he M'Intosh?'

He looked at me quickly and I realized I had made a mistake: he had been referring to a chapter in his *Work in Progress*.

'No,' he said shortly, 'he is not M'Intosh. Begob—it's as good a name for him as any—was not at the funeral, of course.'

The first bottle of wine was emptied and Joyce became more animated. He spoke of puns, saying they were the highest form of humour and that Spoonerisms ran them a close second. In the Middle Ages, gatherings of learned men were great festivals of puns, anagrams, leonine verses and so forth.

'It doesn't sound like much to laugh at,' said Bob.

'Oh but it was, McAlmon. It was the great recreation of the schoolmen in those days. For politics and religion were dangerous subjects, and sports had not been invented, and as they were all in holy orders of some kind or other they could not very well talk smut.'

'Rats. Those old schoolmasters were always talking and writing about sex.'

'No, no, the schoolmaster was then in a very low rank in life—he was the pedant, the male nursery-governess, the minder.'

'The profession of schoolmaster should be abolished,' said Bob, emptying his glass.

Joyce was sipping his wine thoughtfully. When he licked his lips he licked only the upper one, very daintily, like a cat. 'Yes, I think that the schoolmaster, like the policeman, is an unnecessary evil.'

'A kind of leech,' said Bob.

'Perhaps. But I see him,' said Joyce with a slightly intoxicated pseudo-earnestness, 'as doing more harm to himself, d'ye see, than to his pupils. The young people can always look after themselves, we know that. It is the poor teacher himself who should be protected against his terrible propensity to be among children all his life. It's he is the cazhalty, he's refused to grow up. Did you ever know a schoolmaster,' he turned to me, 'who was not a great big boy?'

'No, sir.'

'And that's the dominie's cross,' he said with mock sadness, 'to be a cipher out of his classroom. Like Gulliver, he's either in Lilliput or Brobdingnag. But he's willed it, nobody forced the thing on him.'

'My sister Victoria teaches school in Los Angeles,' said Bob. 'She loves her job. But she's a woman.'

'And a very fine job it is for a woman,' said Joyce. 'Like being a nurse or a nun—but these are not callings for a man, as you can see from the poor type of creature who becomes a male nurse or a monk.'

'You put them in the same boat? Monks and male nurses. You're right. Men in skirts. Does that go for priests too?'

Joyce gave a twisted grin. 'For some, I think. But there's the power, too. Now how did we get to be talking about religion, boys? McAlmon, you're always drawing me out.'

'Haven't you got any whisky?'

Inside the next hour they both became pleasantly drunk and so did I—though more by listening than by drinking. I remember little of the talk, except that Joyce ended by tearing the English novelist Richardson to pieces. 'A spider,' he said, 'a remorseless, cruel, miserable spider is what he is. For there's something wrong with that *Clarissa*, and I do not mean the plot but the very subject. These two people, she and Lovelace, are daft on an epic scale, with their struggle to the death over a maidenhead, their clash of wills that rises to some very sinister heights indeed—but they are not alive. Nothing in all these thousands and thousands of pages is alive except the miserable intelligence that keeps the fight going. Oh, it's a cold, relentless, Anglo-Saxon intelligence that devises all these scenes of cruelty and prurience: now it's taunting, and now it's vindictive, but it's always bent on tormenting someone and by heaven it reaches some surprising peaks of gloating. I really think the man was a little mad.'

I was struck by this original view of Richardson, whom I had never liked. 'You say he's an Anglo-Saxon, sir,' I said, 'but surely his book has always been more popular in France.'

'Yes,' he said. 'The French have always loved the persecuted maiden too. They are forever crucifying some poor woman or other, from Diderot to Sade to Flaubert right down to Mr Proust, who kills his old grandmother in such a way as will hardly bear reading. Flaubert, great as he is, is the worst of them all at this woman-racking. Have you, sir, ever turned a cold eye on the death of Emma Bovary?'

I agreed it was rather graphic.

'Yes, but have you stopped to inquire into any good reason why it should be so?' He cocked a blind eye at both of us. 'I have always wondered why did the poor creature choose arsenic, of all the drugs she could have had? As a doctor's wife and a woman of some reading she'd surely know its effects. Why, a few ounces of laudanum would have done her business, and she could have bought the stuff anywhere. But no, it had to be arsenic or there'd have been no retching or convulsions, no fine edifying anti-Christian agony to make our hair stand on end. Oh, it's a bad and a weak ending for Emma, it does not make sense, and I wonder no one has noticed this foolish matter of the arsenic before.'

As we went home I told Bob I had never thought of Joyce as an original critic.

'Oh, the old Irish tenor's got sides to him that don't show in his writing,' he said. 'Too bad he's gone off the deep end with language.'

Now that Bob had plenty of money again he began to give parties that often lasted for two or three days.

'We're having all the Blackbirds tonight,' he told me one afternoon.

'Let's get in a few cases of Scotch. And some *siphon* too—for the gals and the sissies. Order a few buckets of cracked ice.'

'What about gin and brandy?'

'Too much trouble. If these coloured pukes don't like scotch they can skedaddle. Have you seen their show? I bet it's lousy. They're all being so goddamned *black*.'

'How do you know if you haven't seen it?'

'I don't have to see it. Dinges are always in blackface, they can't help it. Just as we're always in hoods and bedsheets to them. What the hell, people think we can all get together and be chummy on the basis of humanity or art or some kind of tripe. Like hell we can. You can't even talk to a coon or a chink like a human being, so why pretend you can? A lord can't talk to a miner, can he? Let's face it, kid, Communism is the only thing, the breakdown of class and colour barriers. Take everyone's money away, then jumble them all up and let them screw each other for twenty years, that's the answer to the race problem. In the meantime let's be ourselves, let's not go round kissing black asses or letting them kiss ours.'

The party got off to a slow start. Fortunately Florence Mills left early, taking her dignity with her, and Jazzy Lips Johnson and Snaky Hips Tucker began to be themselves. After midnight the crowd increased steadily; no one left and the apartment was soon jammed. I remember the cherubic jowls of Picabia, the swollen forehead of Allen Tate, the prognathous jaw of Cummings, Nancy Cunard's elegant painted mask, the calm monastic skull of Marcel Duchamp. In a corner Cyril Connolly was quietly entertaining a small group with a parodic imitation of a German describing the charms of the Parisian prostitute. '*Kokott . . .*' he was murmuring, making expressive movements with his hands, '*unbeschreiblich pikant—exotisch . . .*' By the mantelpiece Foujita, with his sad monkey-face, was holding court with his usual entourage of beautiful women. Soaring effortlessly above the noise was the husky parrotlike scream of Kiki, now very fat but as beautiful as ever: she was displaying her thighs and bragging, as usual, that she was the only woman in Paris who had never had any pubic hair. In the kitchen, where I went to open the bottles, Ford Madox Ford was towering like an elephant, talking almost inaudibly about Thomas Hardy.

'The greatest English novelist of the last fifty years,' he was wheezing to Narwhal. 'After my old friend Conrad, of course.'

'I can't altogether go along with your verdict,' said Narwhal in his soothing nasal voice. 'I've read books by both those authors and they struck me as too sad. I don't like an unhappy ending to a book. I'm not saying I like a happy ending either. I'm led to wonder if a book should end at all.'

'You may have stated a great truth,' whispered Ford, brushing his great moustache. 'But it's not really practicable to keep a book going indefinitely.'

'I suppose it would set a problem,' said Narwhal, settling his spectacles on his nose. 'I'm not a literary ahtist, but I suggest there might be some merit in a book that was either left unfinished or ended, say, by repeating the sense of its beginning I mean a kind of discontinuous or possibly circular, rather than a linear, structure.'

'It would be a *tour de force*, of course.'

'Then I'm against it. Cancel all I said.'

'It would also, I think, be a bore. Not that I'm wholly against boredom in literature. It has its place—Arnold Bennett and Compton Mackenzie have shown us that.'

'I'm glad to hear you say so.'

'But they're not great bores, my dear fellow. Now Dickens, for instance, among his other supreme accomplishments, can be tedious on a really grand scale. He has created at least two of the supreme bores in English literature, Mr Peggotty and Stephen Blackpool. Like everything of Dickens, their stature is epic, mythological. Beside them Jean Valjean and Lambert Strether are quite insignificant.'

The heat and noise began to give me a headache. I went into my bedroom and lay down; for a minute I didn't see a haggard, white-faced, smartly dressed young man sitting quietly in a corner, his well-brushed head in his hands.

'Tired?' he said, looking up. 'Oh, sorry, you're the co-host. Don't mind me, please.'

'I'm not tired. Just had a little too much to drink for the moment.'

'Take a sniff of this,' he said, producing a small gilt flask. 'It's only ether.'

The effect was extraordinary. My headache vanished as if by magic, and all at once I felt gay and lighthearted. 'Where can I get this stuff?'

He stoppered the flask and put it away. 'You're a little young to get the habit. By the way, you're the chap who wrote that autobiographical bit in *This Quarter*, aren't you? Tell me, where can I buy a dozen copies?'

I started to give him Ethel Moorhead's address, but he stopped me and pulled out a cheque book. 'I'll buy them now and you can send them to me. Right?'

'But this cheque is for 1000 francs! Too much.'

'Ordering, postage, handling, your own trouble,' he said, waving his hand. 'Think no more of it. I write verse myself. I'm thinking of starting a magazine.'

'Why don't you take on *This Quarter*? Titus must be almost finished with it now.'

'No, I want to start from scratch. I've got a publishing house too. I'd like to see your book. How long is it?'

'I don't know. I'm still writing it.'

A handsome hard-faced woman put her head in at the door. 'Jimmy, come on out now.'

'So long,' said Jimmy, getting up and leaving.

I washed my face and went back to the party. 'Who is he?' I asked Bob, indicating the man with the ether.

'It's a young moneybags who's trying to move in on culture. His name is Carter. He calls himself the Man in the Moon.'

'He just gave me a cheque for a thousand francs.'

'The son of a gun! Tell him to double it. What's it for?'

'A dozen copies of *This Quarter*.'

'Let me see it. Now look at that, for Christ's sake.'

The signature was flanked by a childish scribble representing a crescent with a blind eye and a hook nose.

'He's a megalomaniac,' said Bob.

'I thought he was rather nice.'

'He's nuts. Who's the old bat with the dinge over there?' He pointed to Madame Godenot and Tom Cork, whom I had asked to the party by telephone. 'She looks like the keeper of a cathouse.'

'She is. Let me introduce you.

'I can do it myself. Why be formal?'

He went off jauntily. At that moment I saw Mrs Quayle and my heart turned over. She was looking more beautiful than ever in a short jacket of black monkey-fur, a little hat and a half-veil through which her enormous eyes were glittering. She was standing by the door talking to a large man who had his arm around her shoulders and whose back was to me; as he turned I saw the long ginger moustache.

'What a lot of abominable people, Honour,' he was saying. 'Do let's go. This is just scruff.'

'How do you do, Mrs Quayle,' I said. 'I don't think I have met your friend. May I have the pleasure?'

'Why,' he said, 'it's you again.'

'Dearest,' said Mrs Quayle to me, 'let me introduce Hector MacSween.'

We bowed, showing our teeth, but did not shake hands. I had never felt such a violent dislike for any living man; the feeling seemed to be returned.

'Mrs Quayle,' I said, 'let me get you something to drink.'

'Some gin, please. And a little ginger-ale. And ice.'

'I'm afraid there's only Scotch. Won't you change your mind?'

'Certainly. Scotch and water with ice will be lovely. Hector, a little of the same?'

'Yes. No ice. Hold on, what kind of whisky is it?'

'Dewar's.'

'Very well. But no ice, mind.'

I brought their drinks. My brain was in a turmoil of love and jealousy. MacSween's hand was once more curved around Mrs Quayle with playful protectiveness. I stood looking at her for a few moments and then moved away. The party was quite spoiled for me. I looked for Jimmy Carter, thinking how much I would have liked another sniff of his ether, but he had disappeared. Madame Godenot came up and kissed me on the cheek.

'Congratulations,' she said. 'A swell layout you've got here. Nice drapes, nice carpeting, everything. Lot of smart people too. Nice going.'

'Thanks, Lolotte. How are things at number 65?'

'So-so. Up and down. Ha, ha! You know how it is.'

'We-all sure miss you,' said Tom Cork. 'Hope you come back some day.'

The Blackbirds were now taking over the party with their songs and dances. Snaky Hips was whirling like a dervish, circled by shining black faces; people were rocking and clapping their hands; Kiki had at last taken her clothes off. In little knots people were arguing intensely, even acrimoniously, over art. The party was obviously a success. Then I saw in a corner MacSween brushing Mrs Quayle's neck with his ridiculous moustache, and her eyes closing in apparent bliss. The sight pierced me and all at once I was gripped with an emotion so devastating that I felt I was being drawn into an abyss. I suddenly understood how deeply I was involved, and that nothing mattered to me any more: ambition, friendship, literature, my whole mental and physical being were of no importance. Everything had been absorbed by my passion for that absurd woman in the corner.

I had already had too much to drink and felt the cold sweat of nausea breaking out between my shoulder blades. I went into my bedroom, opened the windows to the little balcony and stepped out into the cold air. I was staring into the frosty night sky over Paris when I heard my name called behind me; then Mrs Quayle's arm was around my neck. Her eyes were almost invisible behind the little veil.

'Let me tell you how much, how very much I love you,' she said.

Five minutes later Bob and Mr MacSween came in.

Next morning in the rue Galilée I had the worst hangover of my life, a black eye, and terrible memories—of a quarrel with Bob and our parting, of a fist-fight with Hector MacSween, provoked by Mrs Quayle, in which I was finally knocked down at least twice, and of a long, inept and unsuccessful attempt to make love to Mrs Quayle in the early hours of the morning.

It was in her nature, I think, insensibly to court and even encourage emotional outbursts in others: more than most women, she throve on 'scenes'. That morning, however, I saw myself as mover rather than instrument of the passions of the night before and blamed myself for everything. The months of shameful illness, hopeless passion, boredom, poverty, prostitution, and dependence had made me behave, for about five minutes, as I had never done in my life. I was appalled by a new aspect of my nature—my hitherto unsuspected capacity for violence . . . Waking alone in an unfamiliar bed, with dim light coming through the heavy leather curtains, I seemed for a whole minute to descend into a dizzy blackness, a gulf of such unbearable remorse and shame that I suffered an actual loss of identity before managing to swing my legs to the floor and sit up. A full tumbler of gin and a bottle of aspirin were on my bedside table. I was overcome with gratitude. What a wonderful mistress I had! In fifteen minutes I was restored. I went and knocked at her closed door.

'No, no,' she cried from inside. 'My door is locked, I am making my toilet.'

'I cannot wait. I am on fire with love.'

'I am invisible. Take some gin. I will ring.'

A few minutes later I heard the silvery tinkle of a small handbell.

This signal, which I was to hear so often and with such rapture in the months to come, summoned me to a vision of beauty and warmth. Entering her bedroom, I was engulfed by the colour of rose and the odour of leather and musk. My mistress, looking very small in her enormous bed, held out her bare arms in welcome. I sprang to their embrace like a deer . . .

TWENTY-SIX

Here in this awful hospital I can still savour the sweetness of our transports on that morning two years ago. This is saying a good deal, for two years is a long time in my life these days—with its dreary round of boredom, pain, fear, and sobriety. It is only the remembrance of such moments that sheds any brightness over the interminable days and nights I am now going through. I keep asking myself whether I will ever live such moments again: that is, if I am going to live at all—for I am sure if I do I will find a way to enter once more the enchanted circle of such a love as I enjoyed in the rue Galilée—an experience too beautiful to be offered only once in a lifetime. After all, I am only twenty-two. There must be still a good deal of life in me; and though my back is badly disfigured by rib-section and I feel one shoulder is already two inches higher than the other, the rest of me is pretty much the same. My spirit, above all, is as sprightly as ever. This is to say, I suppose I have learned nothing and forgotten nothing and will return to habits of dissipation with the same appetite—but on the other hand I have promised myself to do so with a little more caution, and to fall in love with a little less abandon the next time, if possible.

There are some natural philosophers and wiseacres who affirm that what a man has done he will do again, but I do not think they are right: he will follow the same pattern, perhaps, but not so recklessly. This is shown in the memoirs of all the great sensualists like Pepys and Rousseau, and of all the great scoundrels like Casanova and Frank Harris. It is a pity that more memoirs like theirs are not written. These are the best we know of the life of individual man; from them alone we discern the probable pattern of our own lives, to what extent it

197

must conform to our given nature, what penalties and rewards are entailed by our wilful departures from it, and whether any effort to change that pattern is either possible or worth while. Everything a man writes about himself is instructive. Young as I am, I have read widely and lived freely and am convinced that the best rule of conduct is impulse, not reason. Of course if I die from my operation next week, I will have been proved wrong; on the other hand, if I live it will prove nothing. But then nothing can be proved about a man until he is dead.

I admit I am worried about this operation. *Timor mortis conturbat me*. Dr Archibald assures me there is an even chance of my surviving; the administrative head of the hospital has also advised me, very tactfully, to make my will.

Fortunately I have nothing to leave but my clothes, books, and manuscripts—none of them of any value. But the impulse to leave things tidy behind me, which is after all the whole duty of man when faced with death, has made me draw up a will properly witnessed, in which I have left everything, including the six scribblers in which this book is written, to Graeme. He was touched to hear it.

'I haven't read the last three-quarters of your book, of course,' he said, 'but it should be quite amusing. As for the clothes, they wouldn't fit me without extensive alterations, and the truth is they're rather ragged by now. There won't be any succession duties anyway.'

'I don't seem to be able to leave you anything.'

'You leave me the remembrance of a number of years we spent together. With a few highlights like the way we left Montreal in three taxis, spring in the rue Broca, the walk in Luxembourg, and the moonlight bunk from Dongibène's.'

'You're forgetting Stanley.'

'She wasn't really important,' he said.

'I've been thinking, I should have come back to Canada with you as another distressed Canadian.'

'But you wouldn't. You were in love with Paris. You thought it was the Great Good Place. Well, it's not. You were in love with a dream.'

I see he was right. It was a dream of excellence and beauty, one that does not exist anywhere in real life. Montparnasse and its people came very close to it. But no city or society in the world, even the Paris of those days, can realize the elusive dream I had. Though the plum-blue light of Montparnasse evenings and the sun-washed clarity of its noon seem in retrospect an idyllic setting, and I shall never know again such freedom, lightheartedness and comradeship, they were not enough. Now I may be in the position of having to leave this insufficient world. It's not a pleasant thought—and so I revert to Mrs Quayle's bed.

It was henceforth to be the arena of our love, the scene, in the words of Victor Hugo, of our sublime combats; if I had known the toll they took of my strength and health, I might have made them less sublime. Here I should like to warn all young men against nymphomaniac women: these lovely succubi are still as dangerous as they were thought to be by the medieval clergy, their smiles will lure you to perdition, their loins will fit you for the bone-house within half a year. Drink to excess, stay up all night, walk around hungry, write poetry, smoke, take drugs, indulge in all the varieties of youthful despair, but do not squander your vital forces in the arms of a woman.

This was something I did not know in the winter of 1929. There was no one to tell me, for from the moment I began living with Mrs Quayle I saw none of my friends and companions: my life was passed in the scented prison of the womb-like apartment in the rue Galilée. Whenever my mistress and I went out it was to the stuffy restaurants and theatres of the Étoile quarter. I never saw Montparnasse again.

It was a life much like the one I had led on the boulevard Beauséjour, with the addition of unlimited alcohol and endless dalliance. I felt at times like Tannhäuser in the Venusberg, except that I had no desire to return to the upper world: I had no Elisabeth to woo or knell me back to the light of common sense, and the allegory of the dead olive staff never occurred to me.

Even Mrs Quayle's jealousy was something I accepted without protest. Every glance I turned on a woman in a public place provoked a show of pique; and every attempt I made to write was greeted with derision. 'You will never be a poet, my dear,' she would say.

This verdict was irritating, but by dint of repetition it assumed for me the sad colour of truth. I no longer even looked at the wad of scribbled pages I had carried around with me; in fact it was a blessed relief at last to seal them all up in a large brown envelope and bury them at the bottom of my trunk, along with my literary ambitions. I told myself that my desire to write had never been more than a kind of itch, a disease I had caught at McGill University, a symptom of juvenile revolt. I came to believe I was lacking in any seriousness or sense of dedication and had written merely out of vanity. Literature had been for me simply an instrument of self-assertion, an excuse for leaving home, a pretext for idleness. I had really nothing to say.

Now, of course, it is different. I keep on writing this book for the best reason in the world: to recapture a little of the brightness of those days when I had health and spirits; for that brightness even seems to gild these long dreary days. As I write, I escape this ugly applegreen room, I forget the ache of my sawn ribs and my fear of death, and every day when I finish my quota of pages I have a sense of accomplishment, of not having wasted what little time I may still have to live. Moreover, Dr Archibald approves my industry. 'What chapter are you on now?' he asks, or, 'I can tell you have done a good day's work yesterday, your colour is improved.' The nurses also marvel and twitter at the pile of scribblers that is growing beneath my bedside table. I am indeed sailing along like a clipper. I'm only worried that I won't finish this book before my operation, for there are still two chapters to write.

I would be furious if anyone were to destroy my scribblers. My feeling for them is quite unlike what I had for the papers I stowed in my trunk in the rue Galilée—those abortive poems, plays and stories had hung around my neck like millstones. One day I found they were gone.

'I looked them all over,' Mrs Quayle said, 'and burnt them. They were quite unworthy of you, my lovely child.'

I was more disturbed by her highhandedness than by any sense of loss.

'Anyway,' she went on, 'I have been thinking you might like to travel with me to a warmer climate and would like to clear out your old effects, as I always do myself from time to time. This Paris winter is lasting much too long.'

'Where are we going?'

'To the land of sunshine and dancing. Spain.'

Postscript

My manuscript ended at this point. The operation was suddenly set forward a week, and there was no time to start on Chapter 27, much less to write the final one. I can reconstruct the bare events themselves only from a very distant memory.

Mrs Quayle and I travelled in luxury to Barcelona and then went to a house she owned in Majorca. There, after a happy month together, she became infatuated with a married Englishman who possessed an imposing physique and two children. When he sent his family home and moved in with us I was completely destroyed by jealousy and despair. My suffering was indescribable: I was not meant for a *ménage à trois* of this kind. Soon after this, Mrs Quayle withdrew her affections from me altogether and I began to spit blood. A month later, at her urgent request, I returned alone to Paris and entered the American Hospital at Neuilly, then run by the celebrated Dr Gross.

Tuberculosis was already far advanced and a pneumothorax was done. The still more celebrated Dr Sergent was called in. He shook his head; but on finding I was a native of Montreal he assured me my best chance lay in putting myself in the hands of Dr Edward Archibald, the surgeon who had lost fewer patients by thoracoplasty than anyone else. In the spring I was strong enough to be sent back to Montreal.

NOTES ON THE TEXT

2   *Colonel Birdlime*. Identified by Glassco in a note as Colonel Wilfrid Bovey.

3   *Hôtel Jules-César*. Now the Hôtel Unic on the rue du Montparnasse.

4   *Here, as Eliot's girl says*. T.S. ELIOT, *The Waste Land*, I. 'The Burial of the Dead', line 17.

        Apollo's upward rising fire. From 'Endymion', lines 96-7, by the English poet John Keats (1795-1821).

6   *Vanity Fair*. A popular New York weekly magazine (1868-1936) devoted to political, social, and literary subjects; it was revived in an entirely different format in 1983. Its title has its origin in John Bunyan's *Pilgrim's Progress* (1678, 1684): a fair in the town of Vanity.

8   *Captain Korniowski*. Joseph CONRAD's family name was Korzeniowski.

        'Conan's Fig'. Unknown, although Glassco included it as one of his works in 'John Glassco: List of Publications in Book Form', initialled and dated February 27, 1964, which he supplied to Michael Gnarowski for use in a special issue of *YES 15* (September 1966) in which Glassco was featured. He describes *Conan's Fig* as a pamphlet and gives *transition* and 1928 as the publisher and year of publication. He notes that he does not have a copy.

9   *There was no telephone*. George MOORE refused to have a phone. Important messages were relayed to a nearby pharmacy.

        Café de la Nouvelle-Athènes. Mentioned in Moore's *Confessions of a Young Man*, Chapter VII. Moore writes: 'I did not go to either Oxford or Cambridge, but I went to the Nouvelle Athènes . . . a *café* on the Place Pigalle.'

        '*We have come across the ocean to pay our respects to Mr Moore*.' There is a question whether this meeting ever took place, since Glassco and Taylor would have arrived in London on 21 or 22 February 1928, and Moore was in a nursing home at 7 Portland Place from 14 February to 21 April.

10   *mal de mer*. Sea-sickness.

        vieux jeu. Old-fashioned.

        that little shop in the rue Dupuytren. Sylvia BEACH's Shakespeare and Company at its first address. In her memoir Beach describes the incident differently— at the bookshop on the rue de l'Odéon. In April-May 1928 Joyce was recovering from a serious eye operation and said he did not want to meet anyone. When MOORE entered the shop, Joyce was at the back, and Beach—mistakenly, as she later realized—did not introduce them: Joyce said afterwards he would have liked to meet him. Some time later Moore wrote a friendly letter to Beach asking if the man with an eyepatch had been Joyce. The two Irish writers did meet in London in August 1929.

11   *By the time you're eighty-seven.* MOORE was actually seventy-six.

12   *a graduate of an institution of learning.* Graeme TAYLOR is not listed in the *Directory of Graduates, 1890-1965* of McGill University.

14   *The Dial* (1880-1929). Beginning as a literary journal in Chicago, it moved to New York in 1918 and became the most distinguished American literary monthly until it ceased publication in 1929.

      transition. See PEOPLE I: JOLAS.

15   *Emma Goldman.* She had not just left Russia—she left in 1921. See PEOPLE I: GOLDMAN. This repeats a similar statement by Robert McALMON in his *Being Geniuses Together.*

16-17 *we went to the party at the house of . . . Rupert Castle.* In an annotation Glassco gives Castle's real name as Rupert Fordham. In McALMON's *Being Geniuses Together* (pages 256-7) he describes a similar party, which Robert DESNOS also attended— though it was given by Raymond DUNCAN.

18   *maquillage.* Make-up.

19   *chuchotte.* Probably someone who is a secret paramour, as the verb *chuchoter* means 'to whisper'.

21   *boulets.* Coal *briquettes*, presumably deposited *in* the stove.

      Echo and Narcissus. An opera by the German composer Christoph Willibald Gluck (1714-87), *Echo et Narcisse* was first performed in Paris in 1779.

      Pagan Love Song. A popular song that was current, it was composed and written in 1929 by Herb Brown and Arthur Freed respectively; it was sung by Ramon Navarro in the film *The Pagan* (1929) and by Howard Keel in *The Pagan Love Song* (1950).

22   *Offenbach.* The German-French composer Jacques Offenbach (1819-80) wrote many tuneful operettas and an opera, *Tales of Hoffmann.*

      the nasal breathy voice of Rudy Vallee. Rudy Vallee (1901-86) was the first 'crooner', becoming popular with his own band in 1927 and singing through a megaphone until microphones were used. Through radio and films his popularity continued for some three decades.

      the silver snarling trumpets of Purcell. Made organist of Westminster Abbey in 1679, Henry Purcell (1659-95) is perhaps the greatest English composer.

      he was selling ewe's milk from the udder. The flock must have been sheep, not goats. There is a similar scene in HEMINGWAY's *A Moveable Feast.*

      the Lion de Belfort. A heroic monument at the Place Denfert-Rochereau commemorating the heroism of the citizens of Belfort during the siege of that city in the Franco-Prussian war of 1870-1.

23   *Ducasse.* Isidore Ducasse (1846-70), under the pen-name Comte de Lautréamont, wrote hallucinatory prose that was a precursor of Surrealism.

'What'll we call it?'. Two of the suggested titles are Shakespearian: 'The Ides of March' (*Julius Caesar*) and 'The Great Bed of Ware' (*Twelfth Night*).

'I'll do a portrait of you for it.' Adolf DEHN's portrait of Glassco is reproduced as Plate V.

24   *we absolutely refused to enter the Louvre.* This affectation of Glassco and TAYLOR was presumably well known because Morley CALLAGHAN attributes it to Charles Milford (Taylor) and Johnny Hill (Glassco) in his story 'Now That April's Here'.

Les Fleurs du mal. The volume of poetry by Charles BAUDELAIRE.

Jimmie Charters. See PEOPLE I.

25   *'Deaf Mute'.* This two-page story by Graeme TAYLOR did appear in *transition*, No. 13, Summer 1928.

McGill Fortnightly Review. See PEOPLE II: SCOTT.

James Joyce's 'Work in Progress'. See PEOPLE I: JOYCE.

Charlie Chaplin's natural right. See PEOPLE II: CHAPLIN.

26   *pirating of 'Ulysses' by Samuel Roth.* In 1921 an American, Samuel Roth, wrote to James JOYCE expressing his admiration for the extract from *Ulysses* that he'd read. But in July 1927, in his literary review *Two Worlds Monthly*, he published without permission the first three episodes. Joyce instigated a lawsuit and an International Protest that was signed by many famous writers. Roth continued to publish the work up to the end of 'Oxen in the Sun', when he suspended publication.

Raymond Knister, Arthur Smith, Frank Scott, and Leo Kennedy. The names of these Canadian writers, mentioned by TAYLOR, were chosen by Glassco gratuitously. It is not likely that Glassco knew KNISTER, who would die prematurely in 1932, and the other three may have been known slightly as the group that was involved with the *McGill Fortnightly Review* (1925-7). KENNEDY moved to the United States in the 1930s. SMITH and SCOTT did not become Glassco's close friends until the 1960s, when they introduced him to his publisher Oxford University Press Canada and acted as referees for several Canada Council grants that Glassco received.

For other names on this page see PEOPLE II and PEOPLE I: JOLAS, JOYCE.

27   *Georges Pol.* Marcel NOLL, according to Glassco. See also below.

Circoncision du Coeur. Glassco's annotation gives the author as Georges Mignet. However . . . on 17 October 1979 he received a letter from Mme R.P. Minet, who wrote that a booklet of poems entitled *Circoncision du Coeur* by her husband, Pierre Minet, then aged 19, had been published by Edward TITUS in 1928—and that Minet had a poem, translated by Eugene JOLAS, in *transition* 7 (October 1927), and another poem, 'Overture' (in reality not a poem but a prose meditation), translated by Titus, in *This Quarter* ([Jan./]Feb./Mar. 1930). She asked who Georges Pol was. Did Glassco know Pierre Minet? She said that she and her husband met and married after the Second World War and that he died of cancer in 1975. Would Glassco have the kindness to reply? There is no record that he ever did.

28   *I found Narwhal much more sympathetic.* The description that follows of MAN RAY is inaccurate: the horn-rimmed glasses and neat bang are associated with FOUJITA.

29   *Al Capone.* The notorious Chicago gangster (1899-1947) was not 'nailed' for income-tax evasion until 1931, so this reference is incorrect.

      Freivögeln. There is no such German word, but the intended meaning is 'free, carnal-minded spirits'.

30   'To a Skylark' by Percy Bysshe Shelley (1792-1822) and 'Pied Beauty' by Gerard Manley Hopkins (1844-89) are among their best-known poems.

      Other names on this page are identified in PEOPLE II.

32   *dancings.* Dance-halls.

      'Merde!' Shit!

      'Why?' she said, repeating Dr Johnson's mot. The major English literary figure in the second half of the eighteenth century, Samuel Johnson (1709-84) was a brilliant conversationalist, as James Boswell's *Life* of him reveals. The uncivil 'Why?' riposte does not sound like him and has not been found.

33   *bourreau des coeurs.* Don Juan, ladykiller.

34   *the page proofs of a book.* This was *The Ladies Almanack* by Djuna BARNES (Willa Torrance), which was published in 1928 in a small edition by Robert McALMON. The author was identified as A Lady of Fashion. One of several examples of lesbian writing that circulated in the expatriate community of Paris, it was intended by Barnes as a 'slight satiric wigging' of the lesbian coterie assembled around Natalie Barney. It can also be read as a critique of patriarchy and a celebration of women turning to one another in pleasure and joy.

36   *the brightly lit Bobino Theatre.* A popular variety theatre of the time, the Théatre Bobino on the rue de la Gaité still thrives. It was where KIKI was crowned 'Queen of Montparnasse'.

37   *the Sphinx.* A famous and quite sumptuous brothel that opened in 1931—three years after the events Glassco is recounting—and was the object of much comment in the press because of its unusual and lavish appointments, and its reputedly powerful and highly placed clientele. Located at 31 boulevard Edgar-Quinet, it was built specially for its purposes as a three-storey building of which the first floor served as an elaborate reception area with an ornate bar decorated with Egyptian statuary, while the second floor consisted of rooms for clients and their chosen companions; the third floor housed the private living quarters of the owner. Widely advertised, it was so well known that, so the story has it, when Hitler made his lightning visit to an occupied Paris in June 1940, and after he had seen sights that included the Opéra, Les Invalides, the Panthéon, and the Arc de Triomphe, as well as the great cafés, he asked to be shown the Sphinx—before proceeding to the Louvre! The Sphinx no longer survives. It has been replaced by a hideous multi-storeyed apartment building of the most banal design.

      travesti. Transvestite, a man disguised as a woman.

40   *the Three Graces*. A statue of the three naked daughters of Jupiter embracing by the Italian Neo-classical sculptor Antonio Canova (1757-1822). It is in the Victoria and Albert Museum, London.

Lady Duff Twysden. The model for Lady Brett Ashley in HEMINGWAY's *The Sun Also Rises*, she had lived in the studio on the rue Broca, with her younger boyfriend, which explains why Glassco found paintings by her there. Glassco's saying she had 'later figured' in the novel should have been expressed simply as 'figured', since *The Sun Also Rises* was published in 1926.

42   *I was in the Canadian army*. There is no evidence that McALMON was ever in the Canadian Army; he was in the American Air Force briefly in 1918.

43   *canard pressé*. Pressed duck.

'. . . *up to your old tricks again?*' A reference to McALMON's homosexuality, which he was careful to mask—HEMINGWAY loathed homosexuals. However, the time of this meeting is questionable, since Hemingway left Paris in March 1928, and was in Florida in April/May.

'*And how is North America McAlmon . . .?*' Hemingway's retort alludes to McAlmon's 'North America: Unfinished Poem', which was published in *This Quarter*, No. 4, Spring 1929, and then as *North America: Continent of Conjecture* in an edition of 310 copies under the imprint of Contact Editions.

44   *rue de Lappe*. This street was known for its brothels and the wide and wild range of 'amusements' available there. Brassaï, the famous photographer of Paris who frequented the places mentioned by Glassco in the company of the likes of Henry Miller, described it as '. . . a sordid street near Les Halles, [which] became the favorite street for pimps, but it was there that the ladies of easy virtue and their young hoods began to congregate. . . . And one after the other, in red lights the color of blood, the signs of a dozen popular dance halls went up, giving an air of tragedy to this ill-famed street.' Today its short span, between the rue de la Roquette and the rue Charonne, in its narrow and run-down state, is a host to seedy bars and equally shabby restaurants with a South American flavour offering *fajitas*, *tapas*, and the like. A tiny bit of its *passé louche* lingers in a couple of bars with names like 'Some Girls' and 'Pick Me Up', the latter suggesting exactly what it says, but also harking back to the 1920s when Paris drank a popular cocktail called 'Pick Me Up' (which, so the story goes, originated at the Café Certa, an early surrealist hangout of André BRETON and Louis Aragon).

the Bastille. The Place de la Bastille—the Bastille, a fortress and prison, having been demolished some 200 years ago.

46   '*Perhaps he is too Protestant, a Jansenist.*' Jansenism was a controversial movement in the Roman Catholic Church (HARDY was not a Catholic) that originated with the Dutch-born theologian Cornelius Jansen (1585-1638) and stressed moral rigour, original sin, an extreme form of predestination, and discouraged frequent communion. Its opponents branded Jansenists as 'Calvinists', but the movement was unsympathetic to Protestantism.

Egdon Heath. This is the gloomy and symbolic scene of *The Return of the Native* by Thomas HARDY.

mousseux. Sparkling wine.

dinge. An insulting epithet for a black person.

Bricktop's. See PEOPLE I: BRICKTOP.

47   *vasistdas.* Peep-hole (What is that?).

48   *I recognized Beatrice Lillie.* This scene at BRICKTOP's, which included Beatrice LILLIE, is a striking re-creation of an event of mid-July 1923 described by McALMON in his own *Being Geniuses Together,* where he also describes a St Patrick's Day dinner at the Trianon when bibulous guests started to sing and he 'broke loose on my "Chinese Opera"'.

    War and Peace? The great novel by Leo Tolstoy (1828- 1910). In Glassco's 'From a Commonplace Book' (*The Tamarack Review* 58, 1971), he included it among 'The World's Ten Worst Novels', calling it—as Graeme TAYLOR does here—'a movie by DE MILLE'.

    Berlin or Porter. Irving Berlin (1888-1989) and Cole Porter (1893-1964) were perhaps the two greatest popular songwriters and composers of this century.

49   *like Alice Faye singing.* Alice Faye (b. 1915), a blonde singing actress in films of the late 1930s and 1940s, introduced many popular songs with her pleasing low voice. (The mention of her name in a 1928 context is inappropriate.)

    Chloë. A popular song written and composed in 1927 by Gus Kahn and Neil Morat respectively.

50   *we saw a two-man bicycle patrol.* Morley CALLAGHAN had described a similar experience in his *That Summer in Paris* (page 147).

    eever. Graeme TAYLOR is trying to say that McALMON is drunk: *ivre* = drunk.

53   *platt. Platt deutsch* = Low German, but the common language in Luxembourg is a Germanic dialect called *mosel-fränkisch*; the official languages are French and German.

    Fournisseur de la Cour Supplier to the Court (of Luxembourg).

54   *en brosse.* Crew-cut or brush-cut hair.

    chaise percée. Chair with a hinged cover over an opening and concealing a chamber-pot.

55   *we were not involved in the late dreadful war.* The Grand Duchy of Luxembourg was invaded by the German army on 2 August 1914 and was occupied until the end of the war.

56   *our national poet Lenz.* See the second-last paragraph of PEOPLE I: McALMON.

57   *La sorcière glauque.* The blue-green sorceress—absinthe.

58   *he mentioned having already written nine books.* Between 1921 and 1926 McALMON published seven books, plus one in 1929, the year after the trip to Luxembourg, and three more in the ensuing years, culminating in his *Being Geniuses Together* (1938).

60   *This Quarter.* See PEOPLE I: MOORHEAD.

I knew by now that he had published . . . Marsden HARTLEY's publication was not a novel but *Twenty-five Poems* (1923) and McALMON had not published 'all his own work': three of his seven books that were published up to 1928 appeared under the imprints of The Egoist Press and the Three Mountains Press. See also PEOPLE I: McALMON.

61   *Le nègre, dont brille les dents.* These stanzas are from 'Batterie', a poem in Jean COCTEAU's *Poésies 1920.*

62   *Marvell's poem.* The poem by the English poet Andrew Marvell (1621-78) is 'The Nymph complaining for the death of her Faun', lines 90-1, beginning correctly: 'Had it lived long, it would have been . . .'

Saxo Grammaticus. He was a thirteenth-century Danish historian whose partly mythological Latin history of the Danes, *Gesta Danorum*, contains the *Hamlet* story.

63   *the great American novelist Fenimore.* James Fenimore Cooper (1789-1851), the author of *The Last of the Mohicans* (1826) and *The Deerslayer* (1841), both classics in the romanticized nineteenth-century depiction of Indian life and warfare on the American frontier.

the Paris apache. A tough, or a pimp.

65   *'Dr Breakey Opposes Union'.* A story by TAYLOR that was published in *This Quarter*, vol. II, no. 2, Oct./Nov./Dec. 1929. 'Union' refers to the union of the Canadian Presbyterian, Methodist, and Congregationalist churches in 1924-5.

Being Geniuses Together. The suggestion that McALMON was in the throes of finishing *Being Geniuses Together* in Luxembourg some time in the early summer of 1928, or that Glassco read it six months later, is both absurd and untrue. McAlmon, who began to write *Being Geniuses Together* some time in 1932-3, completed it in January 1934; he finally found a publisher for it in London, where it appeared in 1938. According to Glassco's comment in his annotated proof of the *Memoirs*, only the title of the work alluded to here was used for the published book.

66   *'It reminds me of Thoreau'.* Henry David Thoreau (1817-62) was an influential American writer and thinker who advocated, among other things, individualism, self-sufficiency, and reflection, and built a cabin on Walden Pond, near Concord, Massachusetts. He lived there for two years, producing his classic work *Walden* (1854).

two of his published books. McALMON's *A Companion Volume* (1923), a collection of eleven stories, and *Village: As It Happened Through a Fifteen Year Period* (1924), a group of sketches about the repressive effects of one American village on its youth.

I would have liked to admire them but it was impossible. What follows in this paragraph is a grotesque and ungenerous attempt at an appraisal of McALMON's writing that flies in the face of contemporary critical opinion. In avant-garde literary periodicals McAlmon appeared in the company of Ezra POUND, James

JOYCE, Ernest HEMINGWAY, and his story 'Potato Picking' appeared in Edward J. O'Brien's *The Best Short Stories of 1929*. As for his being a 'genuine illiterate' etc., he was not only a friend of Joyce but the associate and publisher of William Carlos WILLIAMS, Ford Madox FORD, Gertrude STEIN, Hemingway, Pound, Emanuel CARNEVALI, H.D. (Hilda Doolittle), and Djuna BARNES. See the last paragraph of PEOPLE I: McALMON for Glassco's mature feelings about him.

67   *he was working on two great panoramic novels.* This whole paragraph is a careless fiction because neither work was a novel, and 'The Portrait of a Generation', a long poem in two parts, had been published in 1926. The other work, a prose narrative, was published as 'Politics of Existence: 2 Extracts from' in *This Quarter*, No. 4, Spring 1929—the same issue that contained the 'Extracts' by Glassco and Graeme TAYLOR respectively.

68   *the Douanier Rousseau.* See PEOPLE II: ROUSSEAU.

small baby carriage. Glassco says that it was actually a bicycle that appeared repeatedly in Hilaire HILER's (Schooner's) paintings—though this note may have simply been the result of his seeing, in a painting by Hiler called 'Theory' reproduced in a 1928 issue of *transition*, prominence given to a bicycle in this pseudo-surrealist composition of different objects.

69   *Lombroso.* An Italian physician and criminologist, Cesare Lombroso (1835-1909) pioneered in the study of social deviance, writing a three-volume work, *L'uomo delinquente* (1896-7), that was translated in part as *Criminal Man* (1911).

Bébé Cadum. An advertisement for Cadum soap (Savon Cadum) featured the photograph of a baby.

72   *Jeanne du Barry.* Madame du Barry (1743-91) was a mistress of King Louis XV of France. (*'Je l'ai traité en simple putain':* I treated him like a simple whore.) She was guillotined during the French Revolution.

73   *Her fourth or fifth novel had just appeared.* This was one of Glassco's attempts to make Diana Tree different from Kay BOYLE, whose first book, *Short Stories*, was published in 1929 by Harry and Caresse CROSBY's Black Sun Press.

one of Goethe's young men. Early in his career as a great German poet, playwright, and thinker, Johann Wolfgang von Goethe (1749-1832) wrote the famous *Sorrows of Young Werther* (1774, revised 1786), a romantic epistolary novel.

74   *'His name is Callaghan . . .'* Literary licence is at work here: Morley and Loretto CALLAGHAN arrived in Paris in late April 1929. Callaghan's first story in *The New Yorker* appeared in the issue of 24 November 1928.

Strange Fugitive. In scribbler #3 Glassco first gave the correct title of Callaghan's novel, *Strange Fugitive*, then crossed it out and substituted *Irregular Runaway*. In the final typescript it appeared under yet another title, *The Imitation Sun*. His editor, William Toye, persuaded him to give the real title and absent-mindedly wrote into the typescript *Strange Interlude*, which appeared in the First Edition.

The New Yorker. The sophisticated weekly magazine has been published since 1925.

'*Fitzgerald says he's good . . .*' This, and some other details in the following passage about Callaghan, are obviously drawn from Callaghan's *That Summer in Paris* (1963).

75   '*I've never read your stuff.*' Highly improbable, since CALLAGHAN had two stories in *This Quarter*, 2 and 3, in which McALMON's work also appeared.

76   *poules*. Prostitutes.

     Guide Rose. An annual publication listing brothels and other amusing 'houses', in Paris and the provinces, with advertisements relating to the 'industry' and an appendix on legal information.

     Chez Suzy. A small brothel on the rue Grégoire-de-Tours that had stained-glass windows, giving it the air of a chapel: its discreet arrangements made clients feel secure. The building survives as part of a school for the fine arts.

78   *another requisition on his father-in-law*. In fact, after McALMON's divorce from Winnifred Ellerman in 1927, he received an unusually generous settlement from his former father-in-law, Sir John Ellerman.

     down the Boulevard Raspail. Actually down the boulevard du Montparnasse and up the boulevard Raspail to get to the rue de Fleurus.

79   *Braques, Matisses, Picassos, and Picabias*. Gertrude STEIN, guided by her brother Leo, befriended, and collected paintings by, many avant-garde artists of her time, including Georges Braque (1882-1963), Henri Matisse (1869- 1954), Pablo Picasso (1881-1973), and Francis PICABIA (1879- 1953).

     '*I have been reading the works of Jane Austen*'. The English novelist Jane Austen (1775-1817) wrote six novels—published between 1811 and 1818—whose brilliant satirical comedy, subtle treatment of human nature, and perfection of style earned her the accolade of the greatest woman novelist. The characters mentioned on the next page are in *Sense and Sensibility* (Marianne and Elinor Dashwood, John Willoughby), *Pride and Prejudice* (Lydia Bennett runs off with George Wickham, a militia officer), *Emma* (Emma Woodhouse), and *Persuasion* (Anne Elliott and Captain Wentworth).

80   *Prince Lucifer*. In Book I of the great epic poem *Paradise Lost* by John Milton (1608-74)—about the Fall of Man through disobedience—Lucifer becomes Satan after his fall.

     See also PEOPLE II: LAWRENCE.

81   *a chromo*. A chromolithograph—a coloured picture produced by lithography.

82   *Hotel New York*. This hotel, on the rue de Vaugirard, was recommended to the CALLAGHANs by Robert McALMON, who was staying there when they arrived in Paris. In his memoir Callaghan calls it the Paris-New York.

     '*they certainly make time.*' They certainly make sexual advances.

     the superlative technique and polish of his own stories. This insincere comment about Callaghan's writing was perhaps grounded in a combination of admiration, jealousy, and some derision on Glassco's part.

Montmartre. This hill on the Right Bank—originating as a district for artists and poets—had become transformed, by the time of Glassco's arrival, into a place of cabarets, fleshpots, and seedy nightclubs catering to tourists.

82-3 *Le Palermo . . . Joe Zelli.* The American Joe Zelli ran Au Zelli's, not Le Palermo; both nightclubs were on the rue Fontaine (not the rue Blanche) in Montmartre on the Right Bank. But it was Au Zelli's that was on the corner of the rue Fontaine and the rue Douai and had photographs of topless bar girls in the window and a prominent electric sign.

84 *the King Eddy.* The King Edward Hotel on King Street East, Toronto, which is still in use.

'Miss Knight'. This story by McALMON (the title character is a male homosexual), which was admired by James JOYCE, was included in McAlmon's collection *Distinguished Air (Grim Fairy Tales)*, published in Paris in 1925 in a limited edition of 115 copies by his friend William Bird under the imprint of Three Mountains Press. William Carlos WILLIAMS said that this volume, which draws on the dissipation and drug-laced wantonness of life in Berlin in the early 1920s, was McAlmon's best writing and stood out as a 'brilliant piece of work', though 'all but unpublishable' because of the subject matter.

85 *Cowperwood books.* Frank Cowperwood is the central character in Theodore DREISER's *The Financier* (1912), *The Titan* (1914), and *The Stoic* (1947).

a man only ten years older than myself. CALLAGHAN was six years older than Glassco.

86 *The Exile.* Four issues of this literary periodical, edited by Ezra POUND, were published in 1927-8. It was intended to assail the sensibilities of philistine America and trumpet the virtues of art in exile, publishing work by HEMINGWAY, McALMON, and others. The third issue, Spring 1928, included YEATS's poem 'Sailing to Byzantium' and CALLAGHAN's story 'Ancient Lineage'.

pneumatique. A special-delivery letter in Paris, originating in a system for sending messages through pneumatic tubes by compressed air.

88 *Empress Eugénie hats.* Spanish born (1826-1920), Eugénie was empress of France from 1853 to 1870 as consort of Napoleon III and, having great beauty and charm, became an arbiter of world fashion.

89 *Esse est percipi.* Bishop BERKELEY's belief that there is no existence of matter independent of perception: the 'support' of ideas or sensations is percipient mind.

A phrase of Schopenhauer occurred to me. See PEOPLE II: SCHOPENHAUER.

90 *like Léon Dupuis in 'Madame Bovary'.* Riding with Emma Bovary in a carriage in Rouen, her lover Léon calls out: 'Keep going!' and 'No, straight on!' See PEOPLE II: FLAUBERT.

91 *Eisenstein's 'Ivan the Terrible'.* Released in two parts (1944 and 1958), this was one of the great films of the Russian director Sergei Eisenstein (1898-1948).

Cortot. The Swiss-born French pianist Alfred Cortot (1877-1962).

Salle Pleyel. A concert hall in Paris.

Chopin Études. The *Études* of Frédéric Chopin (1810-49) are of course not 'soft, romantic slush' as Diana Tree claimed.

For all other names on this page, see PEOPLE II.

94   *Keatsian.* Calling to mind the many epiphanies of beauty and joy in the poetry of John Keats.

95   *down the Avenue Victor-Hugo.* It runs parallel to the Promenade des Anglais in Nice, which follows the curvature of the Baie des Anges (Glassco's Bay of Angels), so that driving down the Victor Hugo would not have taken them to the sea.

97   *Promiscuous Boy.* In May 1929 McAlmon informed Sylvia BEACH that he had completed a short novel called *My Susceptible Friend, Adrian.* See PEOPLE I: McALMON.

99   *Mary Reynolds.* Marcel DUCHAMP had a long and happy relationship with Mary Reynolds, an American war widow he met in 1926, until her death in 1950.

       So is Aleister Crowley. An English author (1875-1947) of books on magic and the occult who also celebrated Black Magic rites.

100   *chasseur.* Bellboy.

101   *Frank Harris's place.* Glassco has stated that it was Graeme TAYLOR, not he, who visited HARRIS, whose residence was not 'a small ugly house'. The Villa Edouard VII is a luxurious seven-storey apartment building with a beautiful wrought-iron gate dating from the 1920s.

       I thought he was better than Rousseau. Glassco was thinking of the *Confessions* (12 volumes, 1781-8) of the Swiss-born French philosopher and political theorist Jean- Jacques Rousseau (1712-78).

103   *old L. and Ls.* Copies of Frank HARRIS's *My Life and Loves.*

105   *Dr Caligari.* A German Expressionist silent film, *Das Cabinett dies Dr Caligari* (1919), directed by Fritz Lang (1890-1976).

106   *'Song of India' or 'Dardanella'.* Two saccharine tunes, the first based on an aria in Rimsky-Korsakoff's opera *Sadko* and popularized in 1937 by Tommy Dorsey's band (making it anomalous in this reference), and the second written and composed in 1919 by Fred Fisher and Felix Bernard and Johnny S. Black

       The Gipsy Baron. An operetta by Johann Strauss II (1825-99).

108   *even better than Dufy.* The French painter Raoul Dufy (1877-1953) is particularly known for his gaily coloured and witty watercolours of scenes in the Mediterranean area of southern France.

109   *Poetry.* Often called *Poetry* (Chicago), it is an influential and enduring literary magazine that was founded in Chicago by Harriet Monroe in 1912.

111   *Miss Pankhurst.* The first English suffragist, Mrs Emeline Pankhurst (1857-1928) founded in 1903 the Women's Social and Political Union dedicated to votes for women. In 1906 her eldest daughter Christabel, at a meeting, confronted Winston Churchill—the newly appointed President of the Board of Trade and member

of Cabinet; he was fighting for his seat in Parliament and was sympathetic to her cause, while declining to stand up for it publicly—and created (in Churchill's words) a 'painful sccne' of protest. He lost his seat in that election—but women's voting rights (for those of thirty or over) were won in 1918.

113   *Bock.* A strong, dark German beer.

114   *perdue.* Hidden away.

115   *Ravel, Segovia.* The French composer Maurice Ravel (1875-1937) and the Spanish guitarist Andrés Segovia (1893-1987).

Careless Love. A blues song composed and written by W.C. Handy in 1921.

116   *what Liszt said.* When the young Hungarian piano virtuoso and composer Franz Liszt (1811-86) heard PAGANINI play in Paris in April 1832, he wrote to a pupil: 'René, what a man, what a violin, what an artist! Heavens! what sufferings, what misery, what tortures in those four strings!'

'Something in his throat'. Paganini died of consumption of the larynx.

117   *Marshal Masséna.* André Masséna (1758-1817) served in the French army under Napoleon.

118   *La Bonne à tout faire. A Maid of All Talents.*

119   *e troppo caro. E ladroneccio* . . . It's too expensive. It's theft . . .

122   *a little Rameau?* The great French composer Jean-Philippe Rameau (1683-1764).

123   *Amédéo Dongibène.* Glassco has given his real name as Alberto Poggi.

126   *muguet.* Lily of the valley.

127   *bain sabot.* Hip-bath.

Marquesas. Islands in the South Pacific Ocean.

128   The many names recklessly mentioned on this page are those of:

J.M.W. Turner (1775-1851), the foremost, and most innovative, English landscape painter of his time.

Alfred, Lord Tennyson (1809-92). The great poet of the Victorian age, who was made Poet Laureate in 1850, was the favourite target well into this century of young poets for whom the Victorian sensibility and standards were anathema.

Richard Wagner (1813-83). In his many music dramas (including *Tannhäuser, Lohengrin, Tristan and Isolde,* and *Parsifal*), for which he also wrote the librettos, he employed the *leitmotif,* a recurring theme for each appearance of a given character or emotion. *Schmerz* means pain, or emotional anguish.

Bach, Beethoven, Brahms. Stanley here dismisses three giants of music: Johann Sebastian Bach (1685-1750), Ludwig van Beethoven (1770-1827), and Johannes Brahms (1833-97).

the eighteenth-century Italians. Giovanni Battista Pergolesi (1710-36), Luigi Boccherini (1743-1805), Girolamo Frescobaldi (1583-1643), Antonio Vivaldi (1678-

1741), and Arcangelo Corelli (1653-1713) were not all of the eighteenth century.

Wolfgang Amadeus Mozart (1756-91) was Austrian, not Italian, but he was influenced by Italian opera, and most of his operas are sung in Italian.

Fragonard, Chardin, and Boucher. The Rococo painter of lighthearted romantic scenes, Jean-Honoré Fragonard (1732- 1806), was a pupil, briefly, of Jean-Baptiste Chardin (1699- 1779), who painted memorable still-lifes and images of everyday life, and of François Boucher (1703-70), also a Rococo painter of charming scenes that include wittily indelicate treatments of mythological subjects.

130 *Cluny Museum*. The Musée de Cluny, housed in fifteenth-century abbey buildings in Montparnasse, displays among its medieval art and artifacts the six tapestries known as *The Lady and the Unicorn* and two 'girdles of chastity'.

139 *Contes en crinoline*. There is no evidence that this was ever published, or even that there was such a book, other than Glassco's including it as one of his works in 'John Glassco: List of Publications in Book Form'—initialled and dated February 27, 1964—which he supplied to Michael Gnarowski for use in a special issue of *YES 15* (September 1966) in which Glassco was featured. The list states that it was published in French in Paris by Gaucher in 1930 and that an anonymous German translation, *Märchen in Krinoline*, was published in Leipzig in 1931. Glassco noted that he did not have a copy.

a surrealist poet. Robert DESNOS.

Octave Uzanne. A French writer (1852-1931) who wrote books on clothes and fashion, and a fanciful and arch history of the fan, published in English in 1884.

Penillière. Unknown.

assault on Théroigne de Méricourt. This was the name by which Anne Josèphe Termagne (1762-1817) was known. Called an 'Amazon of liberty', she was a moderate (a Girondist) during the First Republic of the French Revolution. In May 1793 she was publicly whipped by another woman, a fierce revolutionary, who was finally restrained.

Liane de Lauris. Unknown.

Monsieur l'Abbé de Choisy. François-Timoléon, abbé de Choisy (1644-1724), though a priest, loved to masquerade as a woman; his most interesting book is *Mémoires pour servir à l'histoire de Louis XIV* (1727).

140 *St Luke Street*. Glassco was actually born on Simpson Street.

141 *Michelangelo, Rodin*. See PEOPLE II: ZADKINE.

Madame Untel. Madame So and So.

142 *De Stijl*. A name ('The Style') given to a group of Dutch artists, formed in 1917, and to a journal they published, that advocated austere, abstract clarity based on equilibrium and harmony. It had its greatest influence in architecture and the applied arts (notably at the Bauhaus in Germany).

Father Euclid. A Greek mathematician, Euclid (*fl.* 300 BC) taught in Alexandria and wrote a 13-volume work, *Elements* (of geometry), whose treatment of plane geometry became the basis for all introductory works on the subject.

144   *D.V.* God willing (*Deo volente*).

146   The poem extract is from 'Les Fêtes Galantes', the third and last stanza of 'Les Ingénues', by Paul Verlaine (1844-96). The fourth line should read: *Que notre âme depuis ce temps tremble et s'étonne.*

149   *Haroun-al-Raschid.* Harun ar-Rashid (763-809) was the powerful caliph of Baghdad who appears in many tales of the *Arabian Nights*, along with his vizier Jaffar and his executioner Mesrour.

150   *Daudet's Sapho.* Published in 1884, *Sapho*, a novel about two lovers whose relationship was continually broken off, was by Alphonse Daudet (1840-97), the father of Lucien DAUDET.

151   *bust of Perrault.* The French writer and critic Charles Perrault (1628-1703) is chiefly remembered for *Les Contes de ma Mère l'Oye* (1697). Translated as *Mother Goose Tales* in 1729, they included 'The Sleeping Beauty', 'Little Red Riding-Hood', and 'Cinderella'.

Coysevox and Coustou. Antoine Coysevox (1640-1720) was a French sculptor who enjoyed the patronage of Louis XIV. His nephew Nicolas Coustou (1658-1733) was also a noted sculptor who studied with him.

O soul of Théophile Gautier. This French poet (1811-72) is associated with the Parnassian school of French poetry that advocated detachment and precision, and objectivity, in opposition to the emotionalism of the Romantic movement.

154   *Tapette.* Fairy, homosexual.

156   *He thought you were Madame Ponselle.* The legendary American opera star Rosa Ponselle (1897-1981) sang often at Covent Garden in London, and at the Metropolitan Opera in New York from 1918 to 1937.

157   *a small bottle of Vichy.* Vichy water.

159   *superbly ghostwritten by Kay Boyle.* Kay BOYLE was indeed the ghostwriter of these memoirs.

160   John Lane (1854-1925) was co-founder in 1887 of the London publishing firm called John Lane, The Bodley Head.

170   *Enoch Soames.* The title character in a fantasy by Max BEERBOHM, included in his collection of stories *Seven Men* (1919). A writer, Soames has several meetings with the narrator but is described at the end of the story as 'an authentic, guaranteed, proven ghost'.

172   *Serge Kirilenko.* He was identified by Glassco as Prince Ivon Nikolenko. Several photographs of Glassco in the National Archives of Canada, dating from 1928 and 1929, bear the stamp of the Niko Lenko Photo Studio of Paris/Nice. A note in the scribbler #1 manuscript draft of the *Memoirs* suggests that it was indeed for him that Glassco posed for pornographic photographs.

176   *Samuel Daniel* (1563-1619). He was an English poet and dramatist who was known for the grace of his verse and the purity of his diction: as a younger contemporary poet (William Browne) said, he was 'well-languaged'.

178   *Vert Galant*. This point of land on the Île de la Cité, as a scene for reflection and escape from the bustle of the city, echoes a similar episode in HEMINGWAY's *A Moveable Feast*, where he compares it to 'the sharp bow of a ship'.

     Sir Bedivere. In Alfred Tennyson's poem 'Morte d'Arthur' (1842), when asked by King Arthur if he had flung Arthur's sword Excalibur into the lake as he had requested, Sir Bedivere, unable to do so, answered simply: 'I heard the ripple washing in the reeds/And the wild water lapping on the crag.'

179   *acedia*. Listlessness.

     nolo nescire. I do not wish to know.

180   The two lines of poetry are from Charles BAUDELAIRE's poem 'Le Crépuscule du matin': '[gloomy Paris,] the hard working old man, was rubbing his eyes and picking up his tools.'

181   *the Paris of Villon, Nerval and Baudelaire*. François Villon (1431-?), who led a turbulent life in and out of Paris, is now considered to be the finest poet of the late Middle Ages. Gérard de Nerval (1808-55), born in Paris, was a prolific writer who first achieved fame as a poet for his sonnet sequence *Les Chimères* (1854). See also PEOPLE II: BAUDELAIRE.

     clochards. Tramps.

     Madame Godenot. In an annotation Glassco identifies her as 'Martha Arlington, brothel-mistress'.

182   *Mephisto and Faust, of Vautrin and Rubempré*. Georg Faust (1488-1541), a wandering necromancer in Germany, became legendary and the subject of dramas by Marlowe and Goethe, and of an opera by Gounod, that focus on Faust's conflict with the tempter from Hell, Mephistophales (Mephisto). Vautrin is the master criminal in several novels of Honoré Balzac's *Comédie Humaine* (17 vols, 1842-8). Lucien de Rubempré is the hero of one of these novels, *Illusions perdues*, in which the evil Vautrin, in disguise, promises him wealth and success.

183   *pure Maupassant*. Guy de Maupassant (1850-93), a writer of naturalistic fiction, wrote novels and many short stories that were marked by their sombre and detached descriptions of everyday life; his stories often end with an ironic twist.

184   *petit bleu*. Telegram.

186   *reading all the publications and manuscripts of Bob's Contact Press*. The books of Robert McALMON's Contact Publishing Company bore the imprint of Contact Editions. *The Eater of Darkness* (1926) was by Robert Coates, not Marsden HARTLEY, and the book by Ken SATO was *Quaint Stories of the Samurais* by Saikaku Ibara, which he translated.

187   *'Work in Progress'*. See PEOPLE I: JOYCE.

     'Bouvard et Pécuchet'. See PEOPLE II: FLAUBERT.

'Dictionnaire des idées reçues'. See PEOPLE II: FLAUBERT.

For other authors' names on this page, see PEOPLE II.

188   *Simon Dedalus*. The father of Stephen Dedalus, the hero of James JOYCE's autobiographical novel *A Portrait of the Artist as a Young Man* (1916).

190   *Like Gulliver*. In *Gulliver's Travels* (1726), the satirical novel by Jonathan Swift (1667-1745), Lemuel Gulliver, a ship's physician, travels to Lilliput, whose inhabitants are six inches tall, and to Brobdingnag, a land of giants.

190-1   *Richardson . . . Clarissa . . . Lovelace*. See PEOPLE II: RICHARDSON.

191   *Diderot*. Denis Diderot (1713-84) was a great French thinker, encyclopedist, novelist, satirist, dramatist, and art critic. The reference is to his novel *La Religeuse* (*The Nun*, 1796) about the misfortunes of Suzanne Simonin. Badly treated by her family, she is forced into entering a convent, where she is brutally treated by the Mother Superior (who dies in a delirious state of religious mania), escapes, flees to Paris, and dies as the result of a fall.

Sade. See PEOPLE II.

Flaubert . . . the death of Emma Bovary. See PEOPLE II: FLAUBERT.

Mr Proust. Marcel PROUST's *The Guermantes Way* (in *Remembrance of Things Past*) describes how the narrator M's beloved grandmother suffers a prolonged, bedridden end to her life (after a slight stroke, she was diagnosed as having uraemia) that includes temporary blindness and deafness, and a seizure, before her final death agony.

Blackbirds. An unidentified group of black musicians. A series of famous *Blackbirds* revues, featuring black artists, began in London in September 1926—when Florence MILLS was one of the stars—and continued off and on, in London and New York, until 1936.

192   *unbeschreiblich pikant—exotisch*. Indescribably appetizing—exotic.

193   *Mr Peggotty* A character in Charles DICKENS's *David Copperfield* (1849-50).

Stephen Blackpool. A character in Dickens's *Hard Times* (1854).

Jean Valjean. The hero of Victor HUGO's *Les Misérables* (1862).

Lambert Strether. A character in Henry JAMES's *The Ambassadors* (1903).

194   *the Man in the Moon*. According to Glassco's annotation, Harry CROSBY (called Jimmy Carter here) referred to himself as The Rising Sun.

a crescent with a blind eye and a hook nose. Crosby's signature was actually a few lines representing a half-sun, with rays emanating, on a horizon.

198   *Timor mortis conturbas me*. Fear of death dismays me. The Latin was used as a refrain in 'Lament for the Makaris', a poem by the Scottish poet William Dunbar (1456?-1513).

199   *Tannhäuser in the Venusberg*. Popular ballads about this legendary 13th-century German figure relate how he entered Venusberg and enjoyed the pleasures of

the goddess Venus. His story is the basis of Richard Wagner's opera. It is also the story of Aubrey BEARDSLEY's work *Under the Hill*, which Glassco completed and published in 1959 with the Olympia Press.

PEOPLE I

Barnes, Djuna (1892-1982). The occasionally heterosexual poet, playwright, short-story writer, and novelist from New York (she was Laurence VAIL's mistress when he lived in Greenwich Village in 1919-21) appears as Willa Torrance in the *Memoirs*. She had a stormy lesbian relationship with Thelma WOOD (Emily Pine in the *Memoirs*); they lived together in Paris from 1922 to 1931. Among Barnes' numerous books are *Ladies Almanack Written & Illustrated by a Lady of Fashion* (1928), a satirical look at the self-adoring circle of Natalie Clifford Barney (1876-1972), a wealthy American and lesbian *grande dame* of the expatriate community who had lived in Paris since the turn of the century. It is the page-proofs of this work that were being passed around in the dark corner of the Falstaff (page 54). Barnes' fame rests on two unusual and ground-breaking novels, *Ryder* (1928) and *Nightwood* (1936). In these she created the character of Dr Matthew O'Connor, an extraordinary figure of eloquence and outrage who was based on the legendary denizen of Paris, Daniel Mahoney, and who appears in Glassco's account as Dr Maloney (page 20). Opinions vary greatly about this man, although Glassco's suggestive portrayal probably comes closest to the truth. Mahoney appears to have been a witty quack with a seedy reputation as an abortionist that combined with his homosexual posturing and generally disreputable behaviour. In scribbler #1 Glassco calls him 'the most-quoted homosexual in Paris' and in Robert McALMON's short story 'Miss Knight' he appears as a coarse 'queen'.

Beach, Sylvia (1887-1962). The celebrated American founder, in 1919, of the English-language Paris bookshop and lending library Shakespeare and Company on the rue Dupuytren, she moved it in 1921 nearby, to 12 rue de l'Odéon, across the street from her friend Adrienne Monnier's La Maison des Amis des Livres. Shakespeare and Company was visited and patronized by all the leading English-speaking writers resident in, or visiting, Paris, and by some French writers as well—André Gide was a loyal supporter. Robert McALMON, whom Beach liked, often brought writers there. Ernest HEMINGWAY went there as soon as he arrived in Paris in 1921. James JOYCE used it as his mailing address. Under the imprint of Shakespeare and Company, Beach published in 1922 the first edition of Joyce's *Ulysses*, withstanding the horrific printing costs when Joyce increased the length of the book by one-third with his additions in galley proof; and in 1927 she published his *Pomes Penyeach*.

Berners, Daphne. See Gwen LE GALLIENNE

Boyle, Kay (1902-92). One of the most colourful figures in modern American literature, Kay Boyle had a very long life in which she was an innovative and distinguished short-story writer (*Fifty Stories* [1980]), a novelist (*Plagued by the Nightingale* [1931], *Gentlemen, I Address You Privately* [1933], among other novels), poet (*Collected Poems* [1962]), staff correspondent in Europe for *The New Yorker* in 1946, teacher at San Francisco State College, and political activist (in her seventh decade she was a supporter of the Black Panthers, and was imprisoned twice for blocking the induction center at Oakland in opposition to the Vietnam War). A great beauty, she had many lovers (including Ernest Walsh [see Ethel MOORHEAD] and, briefly, John Glassco, whom she seduced—and she was in love with Robert McALMON, who could not reciprocate); three husbands, including Laurence VAIL, the ex-husband of Peggy GUGGENHEIM; six children, and seventeen grandchildren. (Of her children, only her son Ian, and not her four living daughters, attended her funeral and memorial services.)

She had been living in France, and briefly in England, for five years when she arrived in Paris for a prolonged stay in March 1928 and was able to find a job as ghostwriter for Gladys BROOKE, the Dayang Muda of Sarawak, who wanted to have her memoirs published. Kay Boyle is Diana Tree in the *Memoirs of Montparnasse*, whom Glassco meets at the first literary party he attends in Paris, an affair hosted by Eugene and Maria JOLAS. She was the only witness to the Paris years with whom he kept in touch. When she read portions of the *Memoirs* that Glassco sent her in 1968, she wrote him that she wanted her conversation and personality to be portrayed accurately. Feeling unable to do this, Glassco attempted to disguise her identity by naming her Diana Tree, a 'famous British novelist', but endowed the character with some of the juicy circumstances of Boyle's real life. He refers to her editorial work on the magazine *Hemisphere*, and to a 'baby boy who was one of its visible fruits'. The truth was that Boyle had attached herself to the *ménage* of Ethel Moorhead and Ernest Walsh, who were publishing their own literary journal, *This Quarter*, at Grasse in the south of France. Boyle became pregnant by Walsh, the great love of her life. The result was a baby girl, Sharon (called Bobby).

Twice Kay Boyle re-entered Glassco's life fortuitously, when he needed 'rescuing'. In Chapter 22 of the *Memoirs* he is about to look for a new place to live, and is staggering emotionally from the knowledge that he has contracted a venereal disease (from Mrs QUAYLE). Enter Diana Tree, with an offer of accommodation and a job typing (and, as happened, assisting her with) the memoirs of the Dayang Muda. Four decades later, in the summer of 1967, Glassco received a letter from Kay Boyle informing him that she was revising McAlmon's memoir, *Being Geniuses Together*. This news prompted him to revisit the rejected manuscript of his *Memoirs*, and to start preparing it, once more, for publication.

Breton, André (1896-1966). The French poet and novelist was the leader of the Surrealist movement, founded in 1924, and its theorist. The last of his manifestos was published in English as *What Is Surrealism?* (1936). Glassco is advised to read his newly published semi-autobiographical novel *Nadja* (1928) on page 17.

Bricktop (1894-1984) was a 'coloured girl' born in West Virginia of parents who named her Ada Beatrice Queen Victoria Louise Virginia Smith, as she discloses in her memoirs; she was known as Ada Smith and was born with red hair. In her teens she became a saloon singer and dancer and worked in Chicago, Los Angeles, San Francisco, and New York, becoming known as Bricktop, or Brick or Bricky to her friends. In 1924 she went to Paris to sing in, and then manage, a small nightclub called Le Grand Duc at 52 rue Pigalle. About 1927 she opened her own nightclub called Bricktop's. Kay BOYLE and Robert McALMON were *habitués*. She was very popular with celebrities of the time—including the Prince of Wales and Wallis Simpson; Cole and Linda Porter were friends. Cole Porter wrote 'Miss Otis Regrets' for her. She left Paris in 1939 with the onset of war and went on to have clubs in Mexico City, in Paris again after the war, and in Rome.

Brooke, Gladys Palmer (1884-1957), the Dayang Muda of Sarawak. Born into the wealthy family that founded Huntley and Palmer biscuits—her grandfather began the firm—Gladys Palmer married Bertram Brooke, the Tuan Muda of Sarawak, son of the second Rajah of Sarawak, a British Crown colony in the island of Borneo. It had been ruled by the Brooke family, which had been given hereditary rights, since James Brooke was made Rajah in 1841. In 1917 Sir Vyner Brooke became Rajah—the third and last of the white Rajahs of Sarawak—and his brother Bertram reigned alternatively in his absence, though Gladys, his wife, made only one visit to the colony because they became estranged (after having four children). Living, in 1928 and after, in a luxurious Paris apartment as the Dayang Muda (Princess) of Sarawak, Gladys Brooke met Kay BOYLE first in 1926 in the south of France when Boyle's lover, Ernest Walsh, was editing *This Quarter*. In 1928 Boyle was hired by the Princess to ghostwrite her memoirs. This was a difficult task, because the Princess had a poor memory, and Boyle thought she was dull and had a commonplace mind. 'It was therefore necessary to invent the story as one went along, and she herself was entranced as it unfolded' (*Being Geniuses Together*). It is a measure of Kay Boyle's skill as a writer that the mainly trivial incidents in the memoir, *Relations and Complications* (1929), are narrated in a flat, restrained style (unlike Boyle's own) appropriate to an unimaginative woman born to privilege in the Victorian age; but, though it has only two dates—and despite what Glassco says—the book is not without interest. Many famous names crop up, including Gladys Brooke's friends: the celebrated violinist Jan KUBELIK, the famous actress Ellen TERRY and dancer Isadora Duncan, and her brother Raymond DUNCAN. George MEREDITH was her godfather; 'Uncle' Oscar WILDE was a family friend and she played with his two sons as a child. We are told in her memoirs that Gladys Palmer's great love, when she was young, was Lucien DAUDET, only a year older, who visited her family in England; when he asked her parents for her hand in marriage, he was rejected because they didn't want their daughter to marry a foreigner. (He reappeared in her life in 1928 and she attended the afternoon salon of his mother, Madame Alphonse Daudet.) She refers briefly to being received into the Roman Catholic Church, without including any of the details provided—perhaps somewhat fictionally—by Glassco. Though Kay Boyle says that she 'reconstructed for her [the Princess] what had perhaps never taken place', so many incidents are described that only the Princess could have witnessed, or known about, that it is hard to discern where Boyle is inventing or simply embellishing. But towards the end of the book various pronouncements on modern writers, a laudatory description of Ernest Walsh, and the statement that *This Quarter* was 'undoubtedly the greatest Quarterly of Arts ever printed', announce very clearly that Kay Boyle is having her say.

Callaghan, Morley (1903-90). In 1923, when Callaghan was a cub reporter on the Toronto *Daily Star* during a summer vacation from university, he met Ernest HEMINGWAY, who was also working for the paper. Hemingway encouraged Callaghan in his ambitions as a writer and took some of his stories to Paris. Callaghan's first published story, 'A Girl With Ambition', appeared in *This Quarter* in 1926. Hemingway's editor at Scribner's in New York accepted Callaghan's novel *Strange Fugitive* (1928), and his story collection *A Native Argosy*, which was published in 1929, the year Callaghan went to Paris for the summer, with his wife Loretto, where he saw much of Hemingway and Scott FITZGERALD—and Glassco. (The Callaghans and Robert McALMON had dinner with James and Nora JOYCE, who invited them back to their apartment in the square de Robiac for drinks.) The current editor of *This Quarter*, Edward Titus (see Ethel MOORHEAD), suggested that McAlmon and Callaghan both write stories centred on their respective impressions of

John Glassco and Graeme TAYLOR, who had made themselves well known for their eccentric and arrogant behaviour. McAlmon did not comply, but Callaghan's story 'Now That April's Here' was published in *This Quarter* in the issue of October/ December 1929. For many years Glassco nourished a grudge because of Callaghan's portrayal of them in his story as 'snickering' and having ambiguous sexuality— which, in turn, coloured his portrayal of Callaghan in the *Memoirs*.

Caridad. The woman whom Glassco called Caridad de Plumas, and who (like McAlmon) showed Glassco and Taylor about Montparnasse, may have been modelled on Caridad de Laberdesque, who was part Spanish or Cuban, and who made a precarious living as a dancer and/or lady of no visible means of support, but who nevertheless managed to land the odd part in films. She was the mistress of the expatriate painter Georges Malkine, who in the mid-1920s was connected with the Surrealists. Malkine and Robert DESNOS (whom Caridad introduced Glassco to) had become friends and were both users of opium, even though the Surrealists disapproved of any 'excesses', such as drug use.

Carter, Jimmy. See Harry CROSBY.

Castle, Rupert. An annotation by Glassco gives his real name as Rupert Fordham.

Charters, Jimmie (1897-?). Born in Wales and brought up in Liverpool, he was a popular bartender in Paris who charmed everyone with his manners, his tact, and his cherubic 'Liverpool smile'. He arrived there in 1921, and worked in various hotel bars before bartending at Le Trou dans le Mur (the Hole in the Wall) on the Right Bank. He then transferred his skills to the Left Bank, and his Montparnasse clients followed him as he moved from the Dingo, to the College Inn, the Parnasse, the Trois et As, the Falstaff, and other cafés. (He had his own bar for a while, Le Bec de Gaz (gas jet), but his partner defrauded him.) He was often barman at parties given by Peggy GUGGENHEIM and her husband Laurence VAIL. In 1934 he published his memoirs, called *This Must Be the Place* (see page 255), with an Introduction by Ernest HEMINGWAY. The following paragraph appeared on pages 115-16: 'Two more writers who were great friends were Buffy Glassco and Graham [*sic*] Taylor, both Canadians and fine chaps. They would sit at one end of the bar . . . discussing serious subjects that I did not understand and being superior to most of the others at the bar.'

Crosby, Harry (1898-1929). Making a brief appearance in the *Memoirs* as Jimmy Carter (pages 193-4), he was a nephew of the American financier John Pierpont Morgan and worked for the Morgan Bank in Paris beginning in 1922. He and his wife Caresse were well known in the Anglo-American community in Paris, living at a succession of elegant addresses and leading hedonistic lives—though they also founded the Black Sun Press, which published Harry's diary, *Shadow of the Sun* (1928), and Kay BOYLE's first book, *Short Stories* (1929), as well as authors who were much better known at the time. In New York in December 1929, after shooting his mistress, he shot himself; the *Chicago Tribune* wrote that he had 'lived more fully than any man of his generation.'

Dahl, Stanley (Sibley Dreis of Winnipeg). See Graeme TAYLOR

Daudet, Lucien (1883-?). The younger son of the famous French novelist Alphonse Daudet, and the author of a biography of his father, he was a friend of Marcel PROUST, twelve years older, who met him when he was in his middle teens (and may have had an affair with him then). According to the memoirs of Gladys Palmer BROOKE, he was in England as a young man and visited her family. They fell in love, and when he asked her parents for her hand in marriage, they rejected him (because he was a foreigner). He reappeared in her life in 1928 when she was living in Paris as the Dayang Muda of Sarawak. We are told in her memoirs that she visited his mother, Madame Alphonse Daudet. Their role in the ceremony of the Dayang Muda's conversion to Roman Catholicism, as described by Glassco so amusingly in the *Memoirs*, may very well be an elaborate invention.

Dayang Muda (Princess) of Sarawak. See Gladys Palmer BROOKE.

Dehn, Adolf. A minor artist, he did a drawing of Glassco that was reproduced as the frontispiece of the original publication of the *Memoirs* and is included in this edition (Plate v).

Desnos, Robert (1900-45). Journalist, poet, and novelist, he was a prominent member of the Surrealist movement in Paris in the 1920s. He was a visionary and often fell into trances in which he would speak in a distant voice (and was photographed by his friend MAN RAY in this state). Desnos was closely connected and, typically, feuded with other avant-garde and experimental writers, notably the confirmed Dadaist, Tristan TZARA , Jean COCTEAU, the early Dadaist and experimenter with automatic writing Philippe SOUPAULT, and with André BRETON, co-founder of the Surrealist movement—in whose semi-autobiographical novel *Nadja* (1928), which Glassco was advised to read, Desnos supposedly figures. (He is the 'surrealist poet' mentioned on page 139.) Involved in the Resistance during the Second World War, Desnos was arrested and dispatched to the concentration camp in Terezin, in occupied Czechoslovakia, where he died of malnutrition and typhoid fever a few days after the liberation. The pitiful remains of this man—described by Eugene JOLAS as 'an iconoclast of the imagination' and 'one of the hopes of French literature'—were returned and, as Kay BOYLE tells it, 'the great and the humble of Paris kneeled in the street outside St-Germain-des-Prés (kneeling in homage even on the terrace of the Deux Magots) the day of your funeral, of the burying of the handful of bones that were left, in 1945, of all you were' (*Being Geniuses Together*).

Douglas, Lord Alfred (1870-1945). His relationship with the famous dramatist, wit, and novelist Oscar WILDE, whom he met when he was 21 (Wilde called him Bosie), angered Douglas's father, the Marquis of Queensbury, and provoked him to make a statement about Wilde that caused the writer to bring action for libel. This resulted in Wilde's being convicted of homosexuality and imprisoned for two years with hard labour. While in prison, Wilde wrote a letter of confession and reminiscence, *De Profundis* (1905), addressed to Douglas. A minor poet, Douglas wrote two defensive books about his relationship with Wilde, and in 1924 he himself was imprisoned for a libel against Winston Churchill. Glassco confessed to a sexual interlude with Douglas when both were staying with the Dayang Muda of Sarawak (Gladys Palmer BROOKE).

Duncan, Raymond (*c.* 1875-?). He arrived in Paris in 1900 with his sister—the innovative, and for many years internationally popular, dancer Isadora Duncan. A sometime teacher, lecturer on ancient Greece, and actor (one performance of Sophocles's *Electra* in Paris in 1912), he became a guru to a colony of like-minded people who professed Spartan living, a rigid vegetarian diet, and an array of back-to-nature beliefs. He was also a merchant, maintaining two successful shops that sold togas, sandals, and fabrics, one on the Boulevard St-Germain on the Left Bank of the Seine, the other on the rue du Faubourg St-Honoré on the Right Bank. He dressed in a long cloak over a tunic, his bare feet were in sandals, and his long hair was often braided and coiled in a crown-shape on his head (though his hair was sometimes flowing, as Glassco describes it). After Kay BOYLE finished working on Gladys Palmer BROOKE's memoirs, she agreed to work in one or other of Duncan's shops, putting her daughter Sharon in the care of the colony. When, six months later, Boyle decided to break her connection with Duncan, Sharon had to be virtually kidnapped from the Duncan establishment (with the help of Robert McALMON).

Ford, Ford Madox (1873-1939) began his influential literary career as a collaborator with Joseph CONRAD on two novels— *The Inheritors* (1901) and *Romance* (1903)— and went on to publish some 80 books, including his important novel *The Good Soldier* (1915), and the four-part novel that appeared under the overall title *Parade's End* (1924-8). In the 1920s he lived for several periods in Paris (in 1928 on the rue Notre-Dame-des-Champs). He founded the literary periodical *The Transatlantic Review* there, with Ernest HEMINGWAY as his editorial assistant. The first issue appeared in January 1924 and the last exactly a year later, in January 1925.

Foujita, Tsuguharu (or **Leonard**) (1886-1968). A Japanese Expressionistic painter and graphic artist, he settled in Paris in 1913, leaving it only for a world tour in 1929 and a move to Tokyo during the Second World War. Wearing his hair in bangs— and round horn-rimmed glasses, a small moustache, and earrings—he was a well-known figure in Montparnasse.

Goldman, Emma (1869-1940). The Russian-born American anarchist was deported to the USSR in 1919—with her comrade, Alexander Berkman, who had been imprisoned for 14 years for attempting to murder the American industrialist Henry Clay Frick—for opposing the draft. Disillusioned with the Bolshevik government, they left Russia in 1921. For a few years Emma Goldman lived in England, where she married a Welshman she hardly knew, and never lived with, and acquired a new name, Mrs E.G. Colton, and a British passport. She then moved to Paris, where she was often seen, subdued and bitter, sitting in the cafés of Montparnasse. Peggy GUGGENHEIM (Sally Marr in the *Memoirs*) was impressed with her at first, and in the summer of 1928 she and Frank HARRIS and his wife bought her a villa in St Tropez (Guggenheim supported her), where she wrote her two-volume memoirs, *Living My Life* (1931). She died in Toronto.

Guggenheim, Peggy (1898-1979). A member of one of the wealthiest families in the United States, she left New York for Paris in 1920. In 1922 she married a flamboyant figure in Montparnasse, Laurence VAIL. (They are Sally and Terence Marr in the *Memoirs*.) It was a tempestuous marriage, though they had two children, but she made friends of many of the cultural figures in Paris; they divorced in 1930. Peggy Guggenheim then pursued an active love life that included a brief marriage to the painter Max ERNST. After the Second World War she became a noted collector of modern art, housing her paintings in her palazzo on the Grand Canal in Venice, which is now a public museum.

Harris, Frank (1856-1931). This Anglo-Irish editor and writer—who spent his youth in the United States—edited the famous London journal *Saturday Review* (1894-

8), which published, among others, Bernard SHAW (as a drama critic), H.G. Wells, and Max BEERBOHM—to all of whom Harris was well known. (Harris was also a friend of Oscar WILDE.) Shortly before the meeting described in the *Memoirs*, Harris had published the final volume of *My Life and Loves* (4 vols, 1922-7), a purportedly autobiographical work that created a sensation for its sexually explicit passages couched in a boastful style. Now seen to be completely unreliable, it offers interesting insights into the Victorian literary scene in London.

Hemingway, Ernest (1899-1961). The famous American writer, and winner of a Nobel Prize for literature in 1954, spent much of the 1920s in Paris. He and his first wife Hadley Richardson went there shortly after their marriage in 1921—when he was European correspondent for the Toronto *Daily Star* and later the *Star Weekly*; they left Paris for Toronto in 1923 so that their first child would be born in North America, and returned in 1924. After his divorce from Hadley in 1927 he married Pauline Pfeiffer, and they lived at 6 rue Férou until January 1930, when they left France for Key West, Florida. In this period Hemingway published the story collection *In Our Time* (1925) and the novels *The Sun Also Rises* (1926) and *A Farewell to Arms* (1929).

Hiler, Hilaire. Called Sidney Schooner in the *Memoirs*, he was an American painter and musician who, in 1923 (succeeding an ex-jockey called Miller), became manager of the Café Caméléon on the Boulevard du Montparnasse at the corner of the rue Campagne-Première, turning it into a very popular night club called The Jockey. Hiler covered the exterior with his paintings of Mexicans, cowboys, and Indians, and the interior with posters. The whole artistic community of Montparnasse supported it, and it also attracted American expatriates, as well as French patrons. Hiler played jazz piano, and KIKI became a fixture, hoarsely singing her bawdy songs. The studio she lived in with MAN RAY was nearby on the rue Campagne-Première.

Jolas, Eugene (1894-1952). Born in the United States, he grew up in Europe and was trilingual—he spoke German, French, and English. He returned to America when he was 15, but in the early 1920s he was a rewrite man and then city editor for the Paris edition of the *Chicago Tribune*; in 1924 he began a column called 'Rambles Through Literary Paris', which lasted for a year. He gave up his newspaper job in 1926 and, with his wife Maria, began a literary journal, *transition*, which was subtitled *An International Journal for Creative Experiment*; Elliot PAUL was associate editor for a year. The first issue appeared in April 1927 and the journal lasted until 1938, publishing Gertrude STEIN, Ernest HEMINGWAY, William Carlos WILLIAMS, Hart Crane, Elliot Paul, Kay BOYLE, among others, and James JOYCE's *Work in Progress* in thirteen issues between 1927 and 1929. In the summer of 1938 Joyce challenged his friends to guess the title of his *Work in Progress* and Jolas eventually did, winning the prize of 1000 francs, which Joyce delivered to him in a bag filled with 10-franc coins. *Finnegans Wake* was published the next year. Shortly before the first issue of *transition* appeared, the Jolases left Paris for a rented house in the country at Colombey-les-Deux-Églises (where the journal was printed); after the Second World War it was purchased by Charles de Gaulle.

Joyce, James (1882-1941). The famous Irish writer and his family lived in Paris from 1920 to 1939 at numerous addresses. On his arrival there he had already published the short-story collection *Dubliners* (1914) and his autobiographical novel *A Portrait* *of the Artist as a Young Man* (1916). His great novel *Ulysses* was published in 1922 by Sylvia BEACH under the imprint of her Shakespeare and Company. In November 1927, at a tea party in his apartment, he read the 'Anna Livia Plurabelle' section from his *Work in Progress* to a large group of friends that included Robert McALMON, Ernest HEMINGWAY, Sylvia Beach, and Padraic and Mary Colum. At the end of the reading he asked Mary Colum what she thought of it, and she replied: 'Joyce, I think it is outside literature.' He said nothing. But later he told her husband to tell her that 'it may be outside literature now, but its future is inside literature.' (Richard Ellmann, *James Joyce*, page 635.) *Finnegans Wake* was published in 1939. Its playful obscurantism, its puns and dabbling in childish wordplay, its sly wisdom and antic manner conveyed the revolution of language that had been so cleverly but randomly introduced by the Surrealists.

In the folder containing Glassco's scribbler #1 in the National Archives there are many scraps of paper bearing notes, including one, devoted to Joyce, that records a number of impressions that are in the *Memoirs*, plus the following: 'Bob tells me afterwards that Joyce liked me and said I spoke very good English. "I gather people speak very well in Montreal."' Also: 'He's a fine pedantic boy. Bring him again some time.'

Kiki (1901-53), whose real name was Alice Prin, was born in Burgundy. Unconventionally attractive, she was a truly remarkable woman whose essential existence was that of a *demimondaine*, but whose claim to our attention is based on her central presence in Montparnasse in the 1920s. She created an aura for herself through striking make-up and costume, and above all by her high spirits—she was always smiling—and her risqué stories. In a husky voice (Glassco's description—Kay BOYLE called it coarse), she sang bawdy songs in cafés and was a fixture at Hilaire HILER's The Jockey when it opened in 1923. She appeared in eight films and was the model for an extraordinary number of painters and sculptors, and for many photographs by MAN RAY (Narwhal in the *Memoirs*), whose mistress she had become in 1922. (During her six years with him, she referred to herself as Kiki Man Ray.) Man Ray found in Kiki the perfect model to work with systematically in an exploration of moods revealing the personality through photographs—many of them posed in the nude. She was not, however, a passive individual satisfied to be the object of the attention of artists and men. She was an interesting painter in her own right, with a naïve style, but good enough to warrant a solo exhibition in 1927—which, the press reported, 'brought out the habitués of the Quarter *en masse*'. Called 'the most successful *vernissage* of the year', it was all but sold out. Robert DESNOS wrote the preface for the catalogue.

In 1929—the year Kiki was elected Queen of Montparnasse—her memoir, *Kiki: Souvenirs*, was published. The launching *cum* book-signing took place at the Falstaff, followed by a drinking party at the bar of the Coupole. An English translation by Samuel Putnam (published by Edward TITUS and his Black Manikin Press), with an introduction by Ernest HEMINGWAY, followed the next year. When Bennett Cerf, editor-in-chief of Random House, attempted to import 300 copies into the United States, the US Customs blocked the book's entry.

In a letter of 3 March 1970 to William Toye—who had sent him photocopies of two pages on Kiki late in life from *Paris Sketchbook* (1950; rev. 1957) by the artist Ronald Searle and Kaye Webb—Glassco wrote:

Thank you so much for the Kiki piece—though it, and the Searle drawing, were a bit of a shock. She must have been over 50 by that time (1953) . . . Yet I suppose even this total wreck might have been foreseen 25 years earlier: Kiki was always a *sauvagesse* who didn't care what happened to her.

It is terrible, to *us*, to compare her as she was in [Amedeo] Modigliani's and [Moïse] KISLING's paintings and in Man Ray's photographs, with what she became in the '50s. But I don't think it bothered her at all. She always did just what she wanted. All she ever craved was fun, liquor and *attention*: she knew how fleeting all physical beauty is, above all her own. She used to say, 'Modi and Kiki (her pet name for Kisling, whence her own, via "Madame Kiki") have done me: what more can a tart want than that? I look at their pretty pictures and I think *That's me, you know*. (Then the beautiful up-from-under look and the husky laugh) It's nice, eh?' She was very proud of her 'likenesses'. She cared nothing for money.

Man Ray, who lived with her for almost four [actually six] years, knew her better than anyone else. The last time I saw him and Juliet in Paris in 1958 he told Elma and me, in the rue Férou, that towards the end she was absolutely uncontrollable, irreclaimable, devoted to self-humiliation, laughing at the wreck of her face and figure, 'making a kind of sacred fool of herself'.

Le Gallienne, Gwen. A talented painter and sculptor and local character in Montparnasse, the stepdaughter of Richard LE GALLIENNE, she is Daphne Berners in the *Memoirs*. Though she was the sometime object of the lesbian interest of Djuna BARNES (Willa Torrance), she was involved with Yvette Ledoux (Angela Martin), a Canadian nurse who stayed in Paris after the First World War. Le Gallienne and Yvette Ledoux travelled to Tahiti with the surrealist painters Émile Savitry and Georges Malkine in January 1929. Yvette Ledoux and Malkine became lovers on the trip (see the bottom of page 127), and in 1931 they were married.

Le Gallienne, Richard (1866-1947). Born in Liverpool, he became a poet and one of the *fin-de-siècle* aesthetes who joined the Rhymers Club, which met for a few years after 1891 in Fleet Street and included William Butler YEATS, Ernest Dowson, and Arthur SYMONS among its members. Le Gallienne wrote a novel, *The Quest for the Golden Girl* (1896), and continued to publish books after settling in the United States in 1903. But in the 1920s he moved to Paris, where he was a journalist. When Glassco met him he was living at 60 rue de Vaugirard. The painter Gwen LE GALLIENNE (Daphne Berners in the *Memoirs*) was his stepdaughter by a previous marriage of his third wife Irma. The American actress Eva Le Gallienne was his daughter by his second wife Julie. Among Le Gallienne's books was *From a Paris Garret* (1936), a fond portrayal of bohemian life in the city that was a compilation of his weekly columns for the *New York Sun*.

Lillie, Beatrice (1894-1989). The internationally popular entertainer, who was born and educated in Toronto, was a friend of the composer and lyricist Cole Porter, who probably told her about BRICKTOP's.

McAlmon, Robert (1896-1956)—whose favourite expletive was 'Rats!'—is the major literary connection on whose presence Glassco's *Memoirs* pivots. A handsome homosexual American expatriate (with a 'long Barrymore nose') who had moved to London and then to Paris from New York in 1921, he had entered into a marriage of convenience with Annie Winifred Ellerman, the daughter of the English shipping magnate Sir John Ellerman. She was a poet, novelist, and pioneer film critic who wrote under the name of Bryher, and was the lover of the American poet H.D. (Hilda Doolittle). A knowledgeable, rowdy, and prominent member of the 'Quarterite' community in Paris, McAlmon received a handsome settlement when the marriage broke up, thus provoking Ernest HEMINGWAY's snide 'Robber McAlimony' epithet. But he was talented, and his contribution to the advancement of modernist writing has never been fully recognized or appreciated. A prolific if not a particularly disciplined writer, he helped the cause of modern letters both by his generosity towards hard-up writers (some of whom treated him abominably) and, more lastingly, as publisher of Contact Editions, whose books were almost all printed by Maurice Darantière of Dijon, the much-tried printer of JOYCE's *Ulysses* in 1922. He was also an associate of, and a bit of a financial angel for, William (Bill) Bird, the printer/publisher of Three Mountains Press. The Contact Publishing Company produced books by McAlmon himself and by Bryher, along with Hemingway's *Three Stories and Ten Poems* (1923), *Spring and All* (1923) by William Carlos WILLIAMS, Gertrude STEIN's monumental *The Making of Americans* (1925), and, among other experimental writings, *The Ladies Almanack* (1928) by Djuna BARNES. Hemingway's *in our time* (1924)—a slender booklet that was followed by the American publication of 15 stories, *In Our Time*, in 1925—and Ezra POUND's *A Draft of XVI Cantos* (1925) both carried the imprint of Three Mountains Press.

In *Memoirs of Montparnasse* McAlmon is shown as someone who befriends Glassco and his friend Graeme TAYLOR shortly after their arrival in Paris, and introduces them to the Quarter. Notorious for his hard-living ways, he takes Glassco and Taylor with him not only on his rounds in Montparnasse and Montmartre but also on trips out of town. He was attracted, in Morley CALLAGHAN's words, to the 'two bright little devils, Buffy and Graeme. . . . Two slender boys in their early twenties . . .' Glassco, in a section of his manuscript that was expunged from the published text of the *Memoirs*, records evidence of an overt sexual act that was visited upon him by McAlmon; and in his 'Autobiographical Sketch' he states that he had a homosexual relationship with McAlmon. It is very likely that, because of the homosexual overtones of the friendship between McAlmon and Glassco, McAlmon—who never admitted his homosexuality publicly— left the two Canadian 'boys' out of his memoir *Being Geniuses Together*, which was published in London in 1938. The antipathy between McAlmon and Hemingway, as well as Glassco's dislike of Hemingway, was probably due to Hemingway's openly expressed contempt for homosexuals. In the *Memoirs* we note Hemingway's taunting McAlmon about being up to his old tricks when he meets him in the company of Glassco and Taylor. And it was obviously a mixture of personal antipathy, coupled with what was probably McAlmon's jealousy at Hemingway's rising star, that resulted in physical violence between them on the sidewalk in front of the Falstaff bar—with McAlmon, the smaller man, coming away much the worse for it.

The wildness and the sexual carryings-on notwithstanding, McAlmon was a serious and committed writer who had been publishing in magazines since 1919 and books since 1921, and whose short stories and articles on Stein and Joyce appeared in the most prestigious periodicals such as *transition* and Ezra Pound's *The Exile*, as well as in *The Best Short Stories of 1929* and *The New American Caravan: A Yearbook of American Literature* (1929). All of this happened in the period 1927-9, when McAlmon was closely associated with Glassco and Taylor, and when he surely provided an example that was not always that of a typical Quarterite given over to drink and dissipation. It was in May 1929 that McAlmon informed Sylvia BEACH that he had completed a short novel that he intended to incorporate into a reprint edition of his collection *Distinguished Air* (1925). Significantly, he writes: 'The Novel' "My Susceptible Friend, Adrian" is, I think, the best thing I've ever done, but it is SHOCKING in what it says and knows, though by no means a fairy story. Only the life of any of several of the boys about Paris, composite, with other characterizations and episodes therein' (Hugh Ford, *Published in Paris*, page 82). Here we have 'the boys' again, and it is worth mentioning that Glassco had considered calling his memoirs 'The Susceptible Boy'.

With McAlmon, Glassco and Taylor travelled to Luxembourg (pages 52-9), where they were invited to participate in a cultural festival. Glassco's description of the event is a spoof on long-winded and declamatory occasions that cultural celebrations frequently become. The surreal *opéra bouffe* quality of the proceedings is emphasized by the focus on celebrations for the centenary of the birth of Luxembourg's national poet, an individual named Lenz—'a great poet' of whom the Luxembourgeois are prepared to concede, 'Perhaps you have not heard of . . .'. There are, in fact, two possible candidates for this celebration, although Glassco seems to have confused names and dates. Michel Lentz (1820-1893) was a writer of romantic poems, while Michel Rodange (1827-1876), whose centenary it might very well have been (although internal dating suggests that Glassco, McAlmon and Taylor were in Luxembourg in May 1928), was the author of *Épopée nationale des Luxembourgeois* (*National Epic of Luxemburgers*).

In a letter of 28 June 1968 to Kay BOYLE, after saying that he could not read most of McAlmon's writings, Glassco wrote: 'But it was a tremendous experience knowing him. He was always so alive and refreshing. And I was very fond of him—even when he became intolerably insulting: somehow, one excused him everything . . . .'

McKay, Claude (1889-1948). Jack Relief in the *Memoirs*, he was a Jamaica-born American poet, novelist, and short-story writer who was a prominent black writer of his period, publishing his fourth collection of verse, *Harlem Shadows*, in 1922. Racial prejudice in the United States led him to leave the country in 1919 for England, Russia, Spain, and France. His novel *Home to Harlem* was published in New York in 1928, and he was living in Paris in 1929 when Glassco met him (they had a brief sexual relationship). He returned to the United States in 1934.

MacSween, Hector. Unidentified.

Maloney, Dr (Daniel Mahoney). See Djuna BARNES.

Man Ray (1890-1976). Narwhal in the *Memoirs*, he was born Emmanuel Radnitsky, in Philadelphia, of Russian Jewish parents. He was called Manny, but he changed his name to Man Ray (always to be listed with the Ms) when he was a young and precocious avant-garde painter in New York. When the painter Marcel DUCHAMP arrived there in 1915 (the two remained friends for the rest of Duchamp's life), he, Man Ray, and the painter Francis PICABIA formed a Dada movement in New York, at the same time as Tristan TZARA was forming a similar group in Zurich. A multi-talented man—painter, collagist, photographer, sculptor, printmaker, and film-maker—Man Ray moved to Paris in July 1921, where his skills as a photographer took precedence, and he became known to most of the cultural figures of the time (some became his friends) for his skill as one of the great portrait photographers. (He also earned a living as a noted fashion photographer.) His friend Sylvia BEACH, who sent James JOYCE to him to be photographed early in 1922, later had displays of his portraits in Shakespeare and Company. He was asked to photograph Marcel PROUST on his deathbed on 20 November 1922, two days after he died, by Dr Robert Proust, the writer's brother. The people he photographed who are mentioned in the *Memoirs* included not only Joyce, but Kay BOYLE, Robert DESNOS, Peggy GUGGENHEIM, Ernest HEMINGWAY, KIKI (his mistress for six years), Gertrude STEIN, and Tristan TZARA. He spent the war years in Hollywood and returned in 1951 to Paris, where he worked for the rest of his long life.

Marr, Sally. See Peggy GUGGENHEIM.

Marr, Terence. See Laurence VAIL.

Martin, Angela (Yvette Ledoux). See Gwen LE GALLIENNE

Mills, Florence (1895-1927). An American singer and dancer, she appeared in five all-black reviews in New York and London between 1921 and 1926. Glassco could not have seen Mills in a Paris performance in 1929 because she had died in New York in 1927. However, she had appeared in London in a *Blackbirds* revue in 1926, when he might very well have seen her.

Moore, George (1852-1933). An Anglo-Irish man-of-letters, he waged a literary war against prudery and censorship in his many publications. Among his novels are *Esther Waters* (1894) and *The Brook Kerith* (1916), a religious pseudo-epic. His autobiographical *Confessions of a Young Man* (1888) made a great impression on Glassco, who aspired to model his own memoirs on Moore's style and method.

Moorhead, Ethel (*c.* 1884-1939). A woman of means who wore a *pince-nez* (eyeglasses with a nose-clip) and dressed in plaids, she was a Scottish painter—she had studied painting with Whistler in Paris—and had been a suffragist in England. She was living in the Claridge Hotel in Paris in 1922 when she met the tubercular American ex-serviceman and poet Ernest Walsh (1895-1926) in the bar. (He had just moved to Paris.) She quickly adopted him as her friend and responded eagerly to his desire to start a literary magazine by financing, and sharing in the administration of, *This Quarter*, which—before Walsh died in October 1926—published Ernest HEMINGWAY (he oversaw the production of the first issue in Paris), Kay BOYLE, Ezra POUND, Djuna BARNES, and Morley CALLAGHAN, *et al*. Walsh and Kay Boyle met early in 1926 when, at his invitation, she went to Grasse in the south of France, where he and Moorhead were living and where succeeding issues of *This Quarter* were published. He and Boyle then began their affair. Moorhead, furious, left for Monte Carlo. It is unlikely that she and Walsh ever had a sexual relationship. In the memoirs of Gladys Palmer BROOKE, the Dayang Muda of Sarawak, we read that she lent Moorhead the sexually explicit *My Life and Loves* by Frank HARRIS, whom the Dayang Muda knew. 'Half an hour later, when I came into the room, she looked at me severely in the eyes and asked me if I possessed a dictionary, or, if I could tell her what the word "orgasm" meant.' This reads like a barbed anecdote by Kay Boyle, the ghostwriter of the memoirs. However, both Moorhead and Boyle were at Walsh's bedside when he died; and Moorhead saw Boyle through the birth of her baby by Walsh—though Moorhead never faced the fact that he was the father. The mutually antagonistic Moorhead and Boyle soon parted company. Moorhead attempted, unsuccessfully, to continue the publication of *This Quarter*. The last issue under her editorship, Spring 1929, contained Glassco's 'Extract from an Autobiography' and Graeme TAYLOR's 'Extract I' and Extract II'. She handed *This Quarter* over to Edward W. Titus, husband of Helena Rubenstein of cosmetics fame and fortune and owner of the Black Manikin Bookshop on the rue Delambre, around the corner from the Dôme. Titus ran the bookstore as well as the Black Manikin Press, whose publications included Pierre Minet's *Circoncision du coeur*, KIKI's *Memoirs*, and Morley CALLAGHAN's *No Man's Meat* (1931), a novella. Under his cautious editorship, however, *This Quarter* ceased publication in 1932.

Narwhal. See MAN RAY.

Noll, Marcel. He was director of the Galérie Surréaliste. Poems and a prose piece by him appeared in *transition*, and he was also instrumental in providing photographs of surrealist art from his gallery for reproduction in that magazine.

Pine, Emily. See Thelma WOOD

Pol, Georges. See Marcel NOLL.

Quattrone, Hugo. He was identified by Glassco as Hugo Scatena.

Quayle, Mrs. Identified in fugitive notations as Margaret (also Marguerite) Whitney, she may have been the Peggy Lippe for whose address Glassco anxiously asked McAlmon some fifteen years after the events described in the *Memoirs*. In a file of Glassco's unpublished verse, there is a poem of three stanzas that is first dated Westmount, March 20—a notation that is then superseded by another note that reads 'Revised (Montreal) 1933'—that was originally entitled *Ukyo's Song*, Ukyo being the homosexual page-boy lover in one of Ken SATO's *Quaint Stories of the Samurais*. It was later rededicated, in a pencilled note, 'For Marguerite Whitney'. The first stanza reads as follows:

> *I loved you early, lost you soon:*
> *With promise that I never knew*
> *You passed like a spring afternoon,*
> *Woke me to dream and follow you.*

Referring to his various sexual affairs in the conclusion of his brief 'Autobiographical Sketch' of June 1961 (quoted in the Introduction), Glassco mentions 'Mrs Wm. Whitney'; and, later, 'Mrs Marguerite Lippe-Rosskam', with whom he experienced his first 'real love' and a trip to Spain, 'where Marguerite took another lover', and he suffered. The second person connects very well with 'Mrs Quayle'. But in March 1969, when William Toye was working with Glassco as his editor and asked him about Mrs Quayle, he identified her as Marguerite Whitney, a member by marriage of the wealthy American family. Glassco showed him a 'society' photograph of her (Plate XI), taken when she visited Montreal—and saw Glassco. One can therefore surely assume that both Marguerites contributed to the portrayal of Mrs Quayle.

Relief, Jack. See Claude McKAY.

Schooner, Sidney. See Hilaire HILER.

Stearns, Harold (1891-1943). In his *America and the Young Intellectual* (1921) he expressed his contempt for 'the people who dominate our present civilization'. A symposium he then edited, *Civilization in the United States: An Inquiry by Thirty*

Americans (1922), enlarged on this sentiment, attacking the falsity, hypocrisy, and repression of American society; it signalled the departure for Europe of many Americans in search of a more spiritual, less materialistic life—or, in more mundane terms, of a life of pleasure aided by the weak French franc. As soon as Stearns delivered the manuscript of this book to his publisher he left America, arriving in Paris in August 1921. He was interested in horses and wrote a popular racing column, 'Peter Pickem', for the Paris edition of the *Chicago Tribune* from 1925 until 1929, the year he returned to the United States. His later books were *The Street I Know* (1935) and another symposium, *America: A Re-Appraisal* (1937). He was the model for Harvey Stone in HEMINGWAY's *The Sun Also Rises*.

Stein, Gertrude (1874-1946). The American writer of unconventional prose—she ignored normal punctuation and syntax, using words for their sound and associations rather than mainly for their meaning, creating a version of stream-of-consciousness—moved to Paris in 1903 and lived there, with her friend Alice B. Toklas (1877-1967), for the rest of her life. (Stein's best-known and most readable book is her own memoir, of which she made Toklas the ostensible author: *The Autobiography of Alice B. Toklas*, 1933.) Her brother Leo, a dilettantish art scholar but a gifted and prescient collector, had established himself in a studio at 27 rue de Fleurus in 1903, where Gertrude Stein joined him in the fall of that year. Alice B. Toklas joined them in 1909. Leo Stein moved away in April 1914, while Gertrude and Alice stayed on until 1938. Receiving on Saturday evenings, they turned it into a famous salon and art gallery that attracted writers and most of the avant-garde painters of the day. It became a place of pilgrimage, a fact that Glassco, when he visited them there, knowingly or unknowingly disdained. Maria JOLAS said of Stein that she would 'tolerate no relationship that did not bring with it adulation.'

Stein, Leo. See Gertrude STEIN.

Taylor, Graeme (1907-57). He is an important, if indistinct, figure who remains unrealized and obscure to the present day. His role in Glassco's account is that of a companionable Montreal friend to whom Glassco is attached in a real, but not clearly defined, relationship. He is one of three personages (the other two are Robert McALMON and Mrs QUAYLE) whose role is clearly major both in terms of the story that Glassco tells and also as a considerable influence that will continue to play a role in Glassco's life long after the Paris years—indeed, until Taylor died. Little is known of Taylor other than what Glassco chose to record, along with a few photographs preserved in Glassco's family archives. In Plates II and III we see him with McAlmon and Glassco in Nice, and again with Glassco and Sibley Dreis (the Stanley Dahl of the *Memoirs*) on the Promenade there. He is thin, narrow-cheeked and with a high brow. There is not much humour in the eyes; the mouth is generous. He is very much one of a trio. He is not only the George in Glassco's 'Extract from an Autobiography', which appeared in *This Quarter* in Issue No. 4, Spring 1929, but is himself the author, in the same issue, of a piece in two parts entitled 'Extract I' and 'Extract II' set in Baie d'Urfé near Montreal, to the writing of which Glassco refers in the *Memoirs*. He is identified in the 'Notes on Authors' as 'a Canadian, 23 years old, and a graduate of McGill University, Montreal.' The association with McGill is mentioned in the *Memoirs*, although the McGill roster of graduates does not list a Graeme Taylor.

In his 'Autobiographical Sketch', dated June 9, 1961, writing of his time at McGill, Glassco says: 'More importantly, I met Graeme Taylor, with whom I was to spend the next 30 years in a close friendship.' And, in another fragment entitled 'For Continuation of Autobiographical Note', Glassco goes on to say: 'Together with Graeme Taylor I rented an enormous house in Baie d'Urfé (20358 Lakeshore Road) on the shore of Lake St. Louis outside Montreal, & gave myself up to the pleasures of the country (as it was then) . . . .'

Kay BOYLE added a paragraph by McAlmon about Taylor and Glassco to one of the McAlmon sections of her edition of his *Being Geniuses Together* (1968), prompted by Glassco's minding being excluded from McAlmon's original text. The reference to 'two Canadian boys from Montreal' echoes Morley CALLAGHAN's calling them 'two bright boys from Montreal' in his *That Summer in Paris* (1963). (In her own sections of the book, Boyle makes numerous references to Glassco, sometimes linked with Taylor.) Callaghan's portrayal of Glassco and Taylor in Paris as being trivial—constantly 'snickering'—and of ambiguous sexuality in his story 'Now That April's Here', published in vol. II, No. 2 of *This Quarter*, Oct./Nov./Dec. 1929, offended Glassco for many years. Interestingly, in this same issue was a story by Taylor called 'Dr Breakey Opposes Union'. Another story by Taylor, 'Deaf Mute', had appeared in *transition* the previous year.

Titus, Edward. See Ethel MOORHEAD.

Toklas, Alice B. See Gertrude STEIN.

Torrance, Willa. See Djuna BARNES.

Tree, Diana. See Kay BOYLE

Tzara, Tristan (1896-1963). Poet, playwright, and man of letters, he was born Samuel Rosenstock in Romania. In 1915—while still in his teens, and writing—he changed his name. In that year he moved to Zurich, where in 1916 he was one of the instigators of the anarchic Dada movement, which celebrated the irrational in artistic creation—the illogical, the absurd, and chance—in reaction to the First World War. In 1920 Tzara moved to Paris, at the urging of André BRETON, but did not join his Surrealist movement until 1924 (he left it in 1935). A member of the Resistance during the Second World War, he pursued an active literary career thereafter.

Vail, Laurence (1891-1968). The son of a French father and a German mother, he was born in New Jersey (he was an American citizen) but raised in France. A painter, he was a well-known figure in Montparnasse in the 1920s—witty, handsome, attractive to women, though sometimes violent and jealous and given to street brawls. In 1922 he married Peggy GUGGENHEIM. (They are Terence and Sally Marr in the *Memoirs*.) It was a stormy marriage, though they had two children. Before their divorce in 1930 both had embarked on affairs, he with Kay BOYLE, whom he married in 1932. (Peggy Guggenheim was a guest at the wedding!) They had three daughters, but were divorced in 1943 after Kay Boyle's affection had turned elsewhere. When Jimmie CHARTERS was thinking of writing his memoirs, he solicited advice from Vail, who replied with a long letter, reminiscing about Montparnasse in its heyday, which Charters included at the end of *This Must Be the Place*.

Walsh, Ernest. See Kay BOYLE and Ethel MOORHEAD.

Wood, Thelma—sculptor and silverpoint artist from Missouri (an American sculptor named Emily Pine in the *Memoirs*)—was the beautiful woman whom Glassco snatched from a group of middle-aged women in the Falstaff bar, to whom he was introduced by Diana Tree. Thelma Wood, as Emily Pine—whom Glassco seduced with such disappointing results—was the major attachment, during the Paris years, of Djuna BARNES, who appears as Willa Torrance in the *Memoirs*. They lived together from 1922 to 1931.

Emily Pine/Thelma Wood, whom Glassco called a torturer of hearts, was a difficult and sexually tempestuous personality. She took the mannish identity of Simon in her relationship with Barnes, and appears as Robin Vote in Barnes' *Nightwood*. She is the 'T.W.' to whom Barnes dedicated her first novel *Ryder* (1928).

PEOPLE II
WRITERS AND OTHERS MENTIONED IN PASSING

Apollinaire, Guillaume (1880-1918). Born in Rome out of wedlock to Angelica de Kostrowitzky, and gallicized by virtue of his mother's longtime residence in Monaco, he became an important avant-garde critic and French poet who experimented with punctuation and typography. He was a friend of Picasso and Braque, whose ground-breaking work in Cubism he helped to promote with his pioneer study *Les Peintres cubistes* (1913).

Aragon, Louis (1897-1982). The French poet and novelist was one of the founders of Surrealism.

Arlen, Michael (1895-1956). Born in Bulgaria (his original name was Dikran Kuyumjian) and educated in England, he wrote novels about fashionable life in London, notably *The Green Hat* (1924).

Arp, Jean (1887-1966). The French painter was associated with Dada and Surrealism before he turned to sculpture in the 1930s and produced many famous works.

Baudelaire, Charles (1821-67). An important critic, he was also one of the great French poets, whose very name suggests decadence to some people (his life was replete with excesses of various kinds and ended in sordidness). His seminal volume of poetry, *Les Fleurs du mal* (1857), is a masterpiece in which beauty is found in the corrupt, the perverse, the morbid. Its publication led to trouble with the law for Baudelaire, and a fine. But his obsessions, and his extraordinary symbolist language, which is both evocative and musical, had a major influence on the development of modern French poetry.

Beardsley, Aubrey (1872-98). Notorious in the 1890s for his erotic black-and-white drawings and book illustrations, he also wrote and illustrated a romance about Tannhäuser and Venus that was unfinished at his death. *Under the Hill*, 'now completed by John Glassco', was published by The Olympia Press, Paris, in 1959.

Beerbohm, Sir Max (1872-1956). A notable English writer and caricaturist. His novel (*Zuleika Dobson*, 1911), stories (*Seven Men*, 1919), parodies, and theatre criticism—as well as his caricatures of leading writers and artists before and after the turn of the century—were all marked by their elegance and wit.

Bennett, Arnold (1867-1931). One of the leading figures of English literature after the turn of the century and until his death, Bennett wrote many naturalistic novels, of which *The Old Wives' Tale* (1908) is considered a classic. Among Bennett's comic novels are *Buried Alive* (1908) and *The Card* (1911). For Glassco, Bennett represented boredom in literature (along with Compton MACKENZIE): see page 193.

Berkeley, George (1685-1753). An Irish-born philosopher, and Bishop of Cloyne from 1734, he was an influential thinker, associated with the school of idealism, whose philosophical writings were praised for their clarity and literary distinction.

Bori, Lucrezia (1887-1960). A Spanish-born opera singer, she was a leading singer in Paris and Rome before she embarked on a long career as a star of the Metropolitan Opera in New York.

Bowles, Paul (b.1910). An American composer and the author of novels (including *The Sheltering Sky*, 1949), short stories, and poems, he has lived for many years in Morocco.

Brancusi, Constantin (1876-1957). Born in Romania and living most of his life in Paris, he was one of the great modern sculptors and had an important influence on other artists. His works reduced natural forms, often human, to ultimate simplicity.

Buckland, Francis T. (1826-80). An English naturalist, he wrote *Curiosities of Natural History* (1857), among other books.

Bulwer-Lytton, Edward George Earle Lytton (1st Baron Lytton, 1803-1873). Though a Member of Parliament for fifteen years, and Colonial Secretary in 1858-9, he financed his extravagant personal life by writing a very large number of popular novels, the best known today being *The Last Days of Pompeii* (1834).

Butler, Samuel (1835-1902). The great English satirist is remembered today mainly for his brilliant Utopian novel *Erewhon* (1872)—the title is an anagram of 'Nowhere'—which satirized English attitudes, and his semi-autobiographical novel *The Way of All Flesh*, which was published posthumously in 1903.

Butts, Mary (1893-1937). An English writer, she was admired by Ford Madox FORD, who published her in *The Translatlantic Review*. In the mid-twenties she lived in Paris, where she was considered a fascinating woman. She was the author of ten books, including three short-story collections and three novels.

Cabell, James Branch (1879-1958). An American writer, he wrote many novels in the 1920s (and before and after). He is remembered for a long series of witty romances set in a mythical kingdom, of which *Jurgen* (1919) is noted for having been attacked as obscene.

Carman, Bliss (1861-1929). Born and educated in Fredericton, New Brunswick, and briefly at Harvard University, he achieved a wide reputation for over fifty volumes of poetry, many of them romantic landscape poems—one of the best of them 'Low Tide on Grand Pré'—notable for their word music, haunting atmosphere, and soulful expressions of grief or rapture, which often subside into monotony and vagueness. On page 27 Glassco calls him the Canadian Swinburne—after the English poet Algernon Swinburne (1837-1909), who combined a pagan spirit and musical effects in his poetry.

Carnevali, Emanuel (1898-*c*.1942). As a very young Italian writer he immigrated in 1914 to the United States, where he washed dishes in New York while learning to speak, and write in, English (as described by William Carlos WILLIAMS in his *Autobiography*). He was briefly on the staff of *Poetry Magazine*, Chicago, before he contracted encephalitis and was sent back to Bazzano, Italy, in 1922. He was visited there by Robert McALMON—who published his collection of stories, *A Hurried Man*, in 1926—and Ernest WALSH. Kay BOYLE had already discovered his writing and corresponded with him, visiting him in Bazzano—ill though he was—in 1933.

She compiled fragments of his writings as his *Autobiography*, which was not published until 1967. In acknowledging the copy Boyle sent him, Glassco (in a letter of 21 December 1967) called it 'marvellous': 'I prefer his prose to his poetry: it has the colour and the ideas. But his poetry is splendid: lyric at its best.'

Casanova, Giacomo (1725-98). An Italian adventurer who led a colourful life throughout Europe, he wrote in French his famous *Mémoires* (12 vols, 1826-38), which combine sexual escapades and other scandals with a portrait of the age that is of great historical interest. Glassco, in a letter, called him 'the greatest writer of Memoirs the world has ever seen', and refers to him, along with Laurence STERNE, on page 53 when the eighteenth-century Europe he discovered in Luxembourg reminded him of their writings.

Chaplin, Charlie (1889-1977). The celebrated comedian was at the height of his worldwide fame as the director and star of a long series of silent films when he became involved in a notorious divorce from his teen-aged wife Lita Grey, which Glassco alludes to on page 25. The actual events that Glassco neatly and wickedly folded into his story—which took place about a year earlier—concerned proceedings that took place in a California courtroom in which Chaplin's nineteen-year old wife (and the mother of their two children), whom he had married when she was sixteen, sought a divorce. This action captured the headlines in the international press, which was variously amused, titillated, and scandalized by the revelations and allegations made by the very young Mrs Chaplin against her much older movie-star husband. In the carefully inventoried list of Chaplin's transgressions against his young wife, the divorce complaint, filed with the court on 10 January 1927, claimed that '. . . throughout the entire married life of said parties and at times too numerous for the plaintiff to more particularly specify, defendant has solicited, urged and demanded the plaintiff submit to, perform and commit such acts and things for the gratification of defendant's said abnormal, unnatural, perverted and degenerate sexual desires, as to be too revolting, indecent and immoral to set forth in detail in this complaint.' The avant-garde Paris magazine *transition*, having no such qualms, took up the quarrel in explicit fashion on Chaplin's behalf, publishing an eleven-page manifesto entitled 'Hands Off Love' in its September 1927 issue, authored by writers and artists given to the Surrealist cause. They expressed their enlightened indignation at what they felt was a mean-spirited and *petite bourgeoise* complaint of Mrs Chaplin, whom they mocked by saying: 'But to restrict ourselves to the very episodic scruples of the *virtuous* and *inexperienced* Mrs Chaplin, it is comic to find that by her the practice of fellatio is considered: *abnormal, against nature, perverted, degenerate* and *indecent*.' ('But all married people do this,' Chaplin replied.')

They urged the court to quash these charges brought by a wife who had '. . . thus shown to have *inhumanly* refused herself to such a general, pure and defendable practice.' There were thirty-one distinguished signatories of this manifesto—all male.

Chirico, Giorgio de (1888-1978). The Greek-born Italian painter worked in both Italy and Paris. He was known for his strange, disturbing, powerful works that in the 1920s made him seem to be a precursor of Surrealism.

Choquette, Robert (b. 1905) was a poet whose early collections *À travers les vents* (1925) and *Metropolitan Museum* (1931) attracted much attention; he was also a novelist in the grand style, somewhat reminiscent of Victor HUGO, a script writer for radio and television, and a Canadian diplomat, serving as ambassador to France and several South American countries. On page 27 he is called the Canadian Hugo.

Claudel, Paul (1868-1955). He was a prolific and renowned French poet and dramatist (as well as a diplomat) whose writings were informed by his mystical Catholicism.

Cocteau, Jean (1889-1963). Poet, painter, novelist, film-maker, playwright, performer, and a collaborator with leading French composers, he was at the very centre of the avant-garde in Paris for forty-five years. Cocteau is remembered particularly for having made some classic films, including the surrealistic *Le Sang d'un poète* in 1930 and *La Belle et la bête* in 1946. All his works were infused with surrealistic fantasy. The paradox he coined, 'I am a lie that always tells the truth', fortuitously relates to Glassco's *modus operandi* in writing *Memoirs of Montparnasse*. A homosexual, Cocteau became addicted to opium when his friend Raymond Radiguet died in 1923. Glassco has said that he had a brief sexual liason with Cocteau.

Congreve, William (1670-1729). A Restoration playwright, one of the great English literary figures of his age, he was a master of comedy whose plays include two classics: *Love for Love* (1695) and *The Way of the World* (1700).

Connolly, Cyril (1903-74). The English writer and editor was a journalist, living in Paris, for the London weekly *The New Statesman* in the 1920s. His best-known literary accomplishments lay ahead of him, including his novel *The Rock Pool* (1936); *Enemies of Promise* (1938), critical essays; and the co-founding, in 1939, and editorship, of the English literary magazine *Horizon*.

Conrad, Joseph (1857-1924). Polish-born, he went to sea on a British merchant ship in 1878, when he began to learn English; he became a British subject in 1886, adopting a British name. After he left the sea in 1894 to settle in England, he became one of the great British novelists, the author of *An Outcast of the Islands* (1896), *The Nigger of the Narcissus* (1897), *Lord Jim* (1900), *Typhoon* (1902), *Heart of Darkness* (a long short story, 1902), *Nostromo* (1904), and *The Secret Agent* (1907), among other novels.

Craig, Archibald. This was the pen-name of a minor English poet, Cedric Harris, who was a cousin of Gladys Palmer BROOKE, with whom he lived for a while in Paris. He became a friend of Kay BOYLE, for whom he was 'the fairy who is all kinds of comfort', and with whom Boyle planned to publish an avant-garde literary periodical to be called *Living Poetry*, which was duly advertised in *transition* in the summer of 1928 for publication in September. It did not appear.

Cummings, E.E. (1894-1962). The American poet spent several periods in Paris in the early 1920s, and from 1928 to 1930 part of each winter there. He published his autobiographical novel, *The Enormous Room*, in 1922, and three collections of poetry—in 1923, 1925, and 1926 respectively—that were marked by experiments in language, grammar, punctuation, and typography. In the 1930s he abandoned the use of capital letters in his poetry.

Cunard, Nancy (1896-1965). Descended from Samuel Cunard, founder of the Cunard line, and therefore wealthy, she epitomized the daring free woman for the expatriates in Paris in the 1920s. William Carlos WILLIAMS said of her: 'I never saw her drunk; I can imagine she was never quite sober.' But she also wrote poetry and collected modern art. A close friend of George MOORE, and very friendly with Robert McALMON and Kay BOYLE, she was also the model for leading characters in several novels, including Michael Arlen's *The Green Hat* (1924) and Aldous Huxley's *Point Counter Point* (1928); was painted by Oskar Kokoschka, among others; and inspired a famous sculpture by Constantin BRANCUSI, *Jeune Fille sophistiqué*. In 1928 her interests changed when she acquired a printing press and began to publish, successfully, fine books under the imprint of the Hours Press. She was known for helping to breach colour barriers by her interest in the work of black writers, her collection of African bracelets, and by flaunting her relationships with black men.

Currie, Sir Arthur (1875-1933). The first Canadian-born commander of the Canadian Corps in the First World War, and one of the most respected commanders in the British forces, he was principal of McGill University from 1920 until his death.

Dahlberg, Edward (1900-77). An American novelist and critic, he spent the late 1920s in Europe and knew Ethel MOORHEAD and Kay BOYLE; his first novel, *Bottom Dogs*, was published in England in 1929.

Danton, Georges-Jacques (1795-95). A lawyer and brilliant orator, he was a leader in the French Revolution and in the overthrow of the monarchy. Though he acquired great powers in the republic, he was eventually overthrown (partly because he wanted to relax the Reign of Terror) and guillotined. His name is associated, on page 15, with 'Rosa'—Rosa LUXEMBURG, the Polish-born German revolutionary.

Debussy, Claude (1862-1918). The French composer's many works, and their influence on other composers, place him among the most important composers of the twentieth century.

DeMille, Cecil B. (1881-1959). The Hollywood silent- and sound-film director was best known for epic biblical films such as *The Ten Commandments* (1956).

De Reszke, Jean (1850-1925). One of the great tenors of all time, he was born in Poland and had a long career singing opera in Paris, London, and at the Metropolitan Opera in New York. He later taught in Paris, and then Nice.

Desbordes-Valmore, Marceline (1786-1859). An actress, she was also a poet who was highly regarded by the famous critic Sainte-Beuve (1804-69), who edited a collection of her poems, and the poet Paul Verlaine (1844-96).

Descartes, René (1596-1650). The French philosopher and mathematician attempted to reconstruct philosophy on the basis of some self-evident intuitions, such as *Cogito ergo sum*, I think therefore I am. His published discourses and meditations earned him the reputation of being the founder of modern philosophy. His approach to philosophy is called Cartesian.

Dickens, Charles (1812-70). The highly prolific English writer was unequalled among great novelists in capturing the popular imagination while also earning critical esteem. Many of his novels—including *Oliver Twist* (1837-9), *Martin Chuzzlewit* (1843-4), *David Copperfield* (1849-50), *A Tale of Two Cities* (1859), and *Great Expectations* (1860-1)—have a large readership even today.

D'Indy, Vincent (1851-1931). French composer and teacher of music.

Donne, John (1572-1631). Ordained a priest of the Church of England in 1615, he became Dean of St Paul's Cathedral, London, six years later, and one of the great preachers—as well as the greatest poet—of his age. His love poems, elegies, meditations, religious sonnets—and their powerful metaphysical imagery—place him among the finest poets in the language. It was not until two years after he died that his poetry was published.

Dos Passos, John (1896-1870) was a prolific American novelist who described American life from a left-wing perspective, beginning with *Three Soldiers* (1921) and *Manhattan Transfer* (1925).

Douanier Rousseau. See Henri ROUSSEAU.

Dreiser, Theodore (1871-1945) was a memorable exponent of American naturalism in his many novels, which at their best—as in *Sister Carrie* (1900) and *An American Tragedy* (1925)—are very powerful, although ungainly in style.

Drieu La Rochelle, Pierre-Eugène (1893-1945). A well-known French novelist and essayist between the two world wars, he was pro-fascist in his views. After the execution by firing squad of his collaborationist associates, he committed suicide.

Duchamp, Marcel (1887-1968). This French artist, called the most charming man in Paris, lived there most of his life, but achieved a *succès de scandale* in 1913 for his painting *Nude Descending a Staircase* when it was exhibited in New York, where he and Francis PICABIA founded the New York Dada movement and where he met MAN RAY and began a lifelong friendship. With his 'ready-mades', for which he selected at random one or more mass-produced objects and presented the result as a work of art, he had an enormous influence on the perception of art and beauty.

Eliot, T.S. (1888-1965). The American-born English poet, critic, and dramatist was one of the most influential figures in modern English literature, beginning in the 1920s. He won the Nobel Prize for literature in 1948.

Éluard, Paul (1895-1952). One of the finest modern French poets, noted for his love poems, he was a leading Surrealist.

Ernst, Max (1891-1976). A German-born French artist, he was one of the major figures of Surrealism. He worked in the United States from 1941 to 1948 and was married briefly to Peggy GUGGENHEIM.

Fargue, Léon-Paul (1876-1947). An esteemed Parisian poet, he was associated with several literary movements, including Symbolism and Cubism.

Ferber, Edna (1887-1968). An American writer of popular fiction and plays. Among her bestselling novels, many of which were filmed, were *So Big* (1924, Pulitzer Prize) and *Show Boat* (1926).

Firbank, Ronald (1886-1926). A homosexual dandy and aesthete, he wrote novels (including *Valmouth*, 1919) whose innovative language, images, and dialogue did much to liberate the novel from nineteenth-century conventions and influenced many later novelists.

Fitzgerald, Scott (1896-1940). The American novelist and short-story writer—considered the spokesman for the Jazz Age—made several prolonged visits to Paris with his wife Zelda, latterly in 1928, 1929, and 1931. (Morley CALLAGHAN became a friend when he met him there in 1929.) Among his novels are *This Side of Paradise* (1920), *The Great Gatsby* (1925), *Tender is the Night* (1934), and *The Last Tycoon* (1941), which was unfinished. Notable among his short-story collections are *Tales of the Jazz Age* (1922) and *All the Sad Young Men* (1926).

Flanner, Janet (1892-1978). An American journalist and novelist, she moved to Paris in 1922, and from 1925 until 1975 she wrote an occasional 'Letter from Paris' for *The New Yorker* over the name Genêt. Among her several books was *Paris Was Yesterday: 1925-1939* (1972), containing mostly passages from her *New Yorker* writings on people and events.

Flaubert, Gustave (1820-80). Working very slowly, revising and revising—his commitment was to absolute objectivity and *le mot juste*—the great French novelist wrote one acknowledged masterpiece, *Madame Bovary* (1857, first serialized in the *Revue de Paris* in 1856), about the sad life of a romantically minded provincial woman, yoked to a boring husband and frustrated in her love affair, who eventually kills herself by taking arsenic powder. Flaubert laboured on *Bouvard et Pécuchet*, a satire on human stupidity, for over ten years; it was unfinished when he died and published the next year. A second volume was to be a *Dictionnaire des idées reçues* (*Dictionary of Received Ideas*), containing his collection of trite remarks that he had been compiling in a scrapbook for most of his life. Some of them were printed as an appendix to *Bouvard*; the *Dictionnaire* was also published separately (1951) and translated.

Forster, E.M. (1879-1970). Five of his novels—beginning with *Where Angels Fear to Tread* (1905) and ending with *A Passage to India* (1924)—placed him among the leading English novelists of the twentieth century.

Frost, Robert (1874-1963). One of the most popular American poets whose collections, *A Boy's Will* (1913) and *North of Boston* (1914), laced with a strong New England flavour, helped to make his reputation. He wrote flinty narrative poems about country ways and short, sharp pieces of disturbing folk wisdom delivered in a deceptively calm and colloquial drawl.

Gissing, George (1857-1903). English novelist, critic, and essayist. The best known of his many novels is *New Grub Street* (1891), a grim portrait of the London literary world of his time.

Hardy, Thomas (1840-1928). An important English poet and short-story writer, he was one of the great Victorian novelists, with many powerful and classic novels to his name that portray characters struggling against the forces of nature, their own impulses, and vicissitudes caused by chance. Among his novels are *The Return of the Native* (1878), *Tess of the d'Urbervilles* (1891), and *Jude the Obscure* (1895).

Hartley, Marsden (1877-1943). A leading American painter of his time, he often visited Paris, always staying at the Hôtel de l'Odéon (now Michelet-Odéon), near Sylvia BEACH's Shakespeare and Company. Robert McALMON published his *Twenty-five Poems* in 1923.

Hecht, Ben (1894-1964). An American novelist, playwright, and screenwriter, he wrote numerous novels (now forgotten) in the 1920s, and a famous play, *The Front Page* (1928), with Charles MacArthur.

Henty, G.A. (1832-1902). Having a background as a soldier, he wrote numerous novels that had little success until, in the 1860s, he began to write the first of some 35 boys' novels with a strong military/historical content.

Honegger, Arthur (1892-1955). He was a member of a group of innovative French composers called *Les Six*, which was formed in 1920.

Hugo, Victor (1802-85). French poet and novelist. His most famous novels in English translation are *The Hunchback of Notre Dame* (1831) and *Les Misérables* (1862).

Hurst, Fannie (1889-1968). A popular American writer of romantic and sentimental novels—including *Back Street* (1931) and *Imitation of Life (1933)*—and stories, many of which were adapted for films.

Huxley, Aldous (1894-1963). An English novelist and essayist, he was afflicted by near-blindness for much of his life. Among his best-remembered novels are *Point Counter Point* (1928), a satirical portrait of London intellectuals and the English upper class in the 1920s, and the futuristic *Brave New World* (1932), which satirizes the problems created by scientific progress, and warns of the moral anarchy in a scientifically controlled world of a conditioned and subordinate humanity.

James, Henry (1843-1916). The American-born writer, who lived most of his life in England, was a great critic and essayist, but above all a master of fiction in both the novel and short-story form. His novels—whose subtle examinations of character and complex style, and occasionally their length, produce barriers for some readers—include *Daisy Miller* (1879), *The Portrait of a Lady* (1881), *The Turn of the Screw* (a novella, 1898), *The Wings of the Dove* (1902), and *The Golden Bowl* (1904), which is considered to be his masterpiece.

Jefferies, Richard (1848-87). He was a writer and naturalist who wrote many books, including *The Gamekeeper at Home: Sketches of Natural History and Rural Life* (1878) and *The Story of My Heart* (1883), an autobiographical discourse that explains his great attachment to nature.

Kennedy, Leo (b. 1907). While a student at the University of Montreal he was asked to join the *McGill Fortnightly Review* by its editors, Frank SCOTT and A.J.M. SMITH. A modernist poet, his first and only collection, *The Shrouding*, was published in 1933.

Kisling, Moïse (1891-1953). The Polish-born painter moved to Paris in 1910, when he was nineteen, and joined the French Foreign Legion during the First World War. He lived off and on in Montparnasse and was known for his elegant draughtsmanship and his portraits and female nudes, including a stunning one of KIKI, which seems to confirm Kiki's claim that she did not have pubic hair—although some paintings and photographs of her suggest otherwise.

Klee, Paul (1879-1940). The Swiss-born painter was one of the most gifted and influential artists of modern times.

Knister, Raymond (1899-1932). Born in southwestern Ontario, he attended briefly the University of Toronto and Iowa State University, and worked on his father's farm from 1920 to 1923 while pursuing his vocation as a writer. His poem sequence 'A Row of Horse Stalls' and his stories 'Elaine' and 'The Fate of Mrs. Lucier' appeared in *This Quarter* in 1925. He wrote two novels: *White Narcissus* (1929) and the award-winning *My Star Predominant*, which was published posthumously in 1934. Knister's imagist and prose poems place him among the first modern Canadian poets.

Kreisler, Fritz (1875-1962). The Austrian-American violinist, and composer of many popular violin pieces, was one of the greatest violinists, perhaps the most popular, of his time.

Kubelik, Jan (1880-1940). A Czech-born violin virtuoso and composer, he was the father of the conductor Rafael Kubelik and a friend of the Dayang Muda of Sarawak (Gladys Palmer BROOKE).

Labisse. Unknown.

Lampman, Archibald (1861-99). Born in a small town in Ontario, he spent all his working years as a clerk in the Post Office Department in Ottawa while pursuing his vocation as a writer. He is probably the most distinguished of the Confederation Poets—Canadian poets (including Bliss CARMAN) who were born in the 1860s—mainly for his intense, musical, and pictorially vivid landscape poems, such as 'April', 'Heat', 'In November', and 'Winter Uplands'. *The Poems of Archibald Lampman* was published in 1900. On page 27 Glassco calls him the Canadian Keats.

Lawrence, D.H. (1885-1930). Novelist, short-story writer, and poet, he is one of the great figures in modern English literature, who was centrally involved in the struggle against censorship. His signal essay, 'Pornography and Obscenity', appeared in the July/September 1929 issue of *This Quarter*, following hard on the heels of his best-known novel *Lady Chatterley's Lover*, which had been privately printed in Florence in 1928 and caused a scandal and debate in literary circles. His early novels about strong women and their ways of relating to men in their lives— *Sons and Lovers* (1913), *The Rainbow* (1915), and *Women in Love* (1920)—and his later ones about the dominant male (e.g. *The Plumed Serpent*, 1926) perhaps lie behind Glassco's *outré* comparison of him (on page 80) with Jane Austen, as a result of Narwhal's (MAN RAY's) eccentrically seeing 'the dark life-principle of action and virility' in Austen's work, and 'the life force of female letting go'.

Luxemburg, Rosa (1871-1919). A Polish-born German revolutionary writer and orator, she co-founded the Marxist Spartacus Party in 1916 and was murdered while in the custody of soldiers who had arrested her following the Spartacist uprising in Berlin in 1919. She is the 'Rosa' mentioned on page 15 (with DANTON).

Mackenzie, (Sir) Compton (1883-1972). An intelligence officer and a prolific English author, he wrote a two-volume autobiographical novel, *Sinister Street* (1913, 1914), that gained him fame, and probably attracted the attention of Glassco (who pronounces him dull on page 193). His later novel *Whisky Galore* (1947), a comic treatment of the emergence of Scottish nationalism, was the basis for a successful film.

Mallarmé, Stéphane (1842-98). A leading Symbolist poet in France, he believed that poetry should approach the abstraction of music, and that words should have an evocative significance beyond their usual meaning—with the result that many of his poems are obscure. His *L'Après-midi d'une faune* (The Afternoon of a Faun) inspired Claude DEBUSSY to write his famous *Prélude*.

Marks, Percy (1891-1956). American novelist and professor of English. Beginning with *The Plastic Age* (1924), about the Jazz Age in an American college, he wrote many novels in the 1920s and after, which are now little read.

Mauriac, François (1885-1970). Writing novels grounded in his profound (though non-conformist) Catholicism, he created characters torn by temptation, sin, and redemption. He won the Nobel Prize for literature in 1952.

Meredith, George (1828-1909). An English poet and critic, Meredith was also one of the great Victorian novelists. (He was the godfather of Gladys BROOKE.) His novels, written over 36 years, include *The Ordeal of Richard Feverel* (1859), *The Egoist* (1879), and *Diana of the Crossways* (1885).

Miró, Joan (1893-1983). A Spanish painter and graphic artist who lived much of his life in Paris, he was a prominent Surrealist.

Molière (1622-73). The famous French playwright, whose real name was Jean-Baptiste Poquelin, wrote 30 brilliant comedies exposing the frailties of human nature, many of which are still performed in English translation. These include *Tartuffe* (1664), *The Misanthrope* (1666), *The Doctor in Spite of Himself* (1666), *The Miser* (1668), *The Would-Be Gentleman* (1670), and *The Imaginary Invalid* (1673).

Morin, Paul (1889-1963). Born in Montreal and called to the bar at the age of 20, he devoted much of his life to teaching literature and translating, though in 1911 and 1922 he published two remarkable collections of poems in French whose sensual imagery and themes were quite new to ultra-Catholic Quebec. On page 27 he is called the Canadian Gautier (after the French poet Théophile Gautier, 1811-72).

Nelligan, Émile (1879-1941). The French-Canadian poet had written all his sad, nostalgic, lyric poems by the time he was 20 when, mentally disturbed, he was confined to an institution. On page 27 he is called the Canadian Verlaine, after the French poet Paul Verlaine (1844-1896), one of several French writers who influenced young Nelligan.

Oppenheim, E. Phillips (1866-1946). A prolific English author of thrillers, dealing particularly with espionage and international diplomacy.

Ouida. A childish pronunciation of 'Louise', Ouida was the pen-name of Marie Louise de la Ramée (1839-1908), an English-born author who wrote 45 popular novels. Though criticized for being extravagant and inaccurate in details, she was also appreciated for writing strong and energetic stories. Among her novels were *Under Two Flags* (1867) and *A Dog of Flanders* (1872).

Paganini, Niccolò (1782-1840). This Italian musician was both a supreme virtuoso on the violin and a distinguished composer. The aftermath of his death in Nice from consumption of the larnyx was undignified and macabre. Because Paganini had reportedly led a dissolute life and, on his deathbed, had refused the ministrations of a priest, he was deemed unfit for burial in consecrated ground. Initially, so that people could pay tribute—which they did in great numbers—his body was displayed in the house of the Count de Cessole, where Paganini had spent his last days. After many unsuccessful appeals to church authorities that went as high as the

Pope himself, the remains were eventually transported to his native Italy and placed in a mausoleum at the family villa at Gaione—to be interred, later, in the cemetery near Parma.

Pascin, Jules (1885-1930). An American painter, born Julius Pincas in Bulgaria and naturalized in 1914, he was on the Paris scene as early as 1905 without attaching himself to any artistic movement. Recognized for the powerful sensuality with which he depicted his models, and famous for his riotous behaviour and happy-go-lucky manner in Parisian bohemian circles, he eventually took his own life.

Paul, Elliot (1891-1958). The American-born *littérateur* was literary editor, and then city editor, of the Paris edition of the *Chicago Tribune*, succeeding Eugene JOLAS. In 1923 he moved into a two-room top-floor apartment in the Hôtel du Caveau de la Terreur on the rue de la Huchette, which he portrayed in great detail in *The Last Time I Saw Paris* (1942); he lived there for eighteen years. He was listed first as co-editor and then as contributing editor (until 1929) of Jolas's literary journal *transition*.

Peacock, Thomas Love (1785-1866). This English writer produced both satire and criticism in his novels, caricaturing contemporary figures. His most famous novel is *Nightmare Abbey*. (1818), which mocks the gloom-ridden writings of some of his contemporaries, including Coleridge, Byron, and Shelley.

Péguy, Charles (1873-1914). A French essayist and poet, he wrote numerous books of polemical prose—at first anti-clerical, he was later a fervent Catholic—and collections of poems.

Pepys, Samuel (1633-1703). His uninhibited *Diary*, written in a kind of shorthand, was deciphered and first published in part in 1825, in ten volumes in 1893-9, and in eleven volumes in 1970-83.

Péret, Benjamin (1899-1959). A French author of several Surrealist works.

Picabia, Francis (1879-1953). A French artist of Cuban extraction, he was one of the founders of the Dada movement in Zurich, in New York (where he was associated with Marcel DUCHAMP), and in Paris. He moved to Provence in 1925.

Pound, Ezra (1885-1972). One of the giants of modern English literature—a poet, editor, and critic who was highly influential (and controversial) in all these roles— he was a man of strong convictions, great generosity of spirit, and crackpot inclinations in politics who was imprisoned and confined to a psychiatric hospital after the Second World War for his fascist sympathies. The first issue of *This Quarter* was dedicated to him 'for his creative work, his editorship of several magazines, his helpful friendship for young and unknown artists . . . .' (Ethel MOORHEAD withdrew this dedication in a later issue; she calls him 'Poond' on page 109.) He lived a great part of his life in Rapallo, Italy. Pound's major work, the *Cantos*, a powerful if rambling sequence of meditative and polemical poems, began to appear in 1917.

Proust, Marcel (1871-1922). He was the author of the rich and complex seven-part novel *À la recherche du temps perdu* (1913-27), about Parisian society, that has time and memory as its theme and relies on image and evocation, and a concealed emotional life, to convey a sense of the meaning and mystery of existence. The seven volumes were published in English under the title *Remembrance of Things Past* (1922-31); a recent translation bears the more correct title *In Search of Lost Time*.

Ransom, John Crowe (1888-1974). American poet and critic.

Ribemont-Dessaignes, Georges (1884-1974). He was a Dadaist whose manifestos, poems, articles, and projects (1915-30) were collected and published around the time of his death.

Richardson, Samuel (1689-1761). His novel *Pamela; or Virtue Rewarded* (2 vols, 1740-1) is generally considered to be the first modern English novel. It was followed by *Clarissa; or The History of a Young Lady* (8 vols, 1747-9)—the longest novel in the English language. Both are epistolary novels. The letters in *Clarissa* recount her cruel treatment by Robert Lovelace, who becomes obsessed with seducing her and eventually drugs and rapes her, whereupon she dies of grief and shame.

Rimbaud, Arthur (1854-91). A French poet of genius—a precursor of the Symbolists—he wrote his important and influential poems over only two years, until he was 19. He explored the subconscious and used language for its evocative value in arousing sensations, disregarding the usual syntactical relationships of words. He said: 'I write about silences, nights, I record the inexpressible.' Among his works are the autobiographical prose-poem *Une Saison en enfer* (1873) and *Les Illuminations* (1886).

Rochester, John Wilmot, second earl of (1647-80). A courtier in the reign of Charles II, he was also known as a poet whose writing was notable for its wit, its emotional complexity, and occasionally for its uninhibited treatment of sex. He influenced some leading poets of his time and later.

Rothenstein, Sir William (1872-1945). A British painter who, from about 1898, specialized in portraits. He was also an official artist in both world wars.

Rousseau, Henri (1844-1910). A French naïve painter, he was known for his detailed, colourful, childlike paintings that project images of extraordinary power and inventiveness. He was nicknamed Le Douanier Rousseau because he worked in the Paris Customs Office for 22 years before he retired to paint.

Ruskin, John (1819-1900). The most influential of the many books of this English art critic included *The Seven Lamps of Architecture* (1849) and *The Stones of Venice* (3 vols, 1851-3)—in which Ruskin's scholarship and observations led him to enunciate moralistic principles about beauty and art, and to advocate social reforms in education and labour, while expressing a strongly critical view of wealth and the exclusive pursuit of profit.

Sade, marquis de (1740-1814). The French novelist and pornographer—whose writings were banned in France as recently as 1957—led a life of debauchery and sodomy and other sexual perversions for which he was condemned to death in 1772. Sade spent 27 years in various prisons, including the notorious Bastille. In 1801 he was confined for his licentious books in Charenton, a mental hospital near Paris, until his death. His enormous output of novels, short stories, and plays—most of them written in prison, where he tried 'to reach the limits of the human sexual imagination', in the words of Camille Paglia—influenced BAUDELAIRE, and his writings have now been given a reputable place in French literature for their style and their pyschological significance. His works include *Les 120 Journées de Sodome* (1784), *Justine* (1791), and *Les Crimes de l'amour* (1800).

Saint-Saëns, Camille (1835-1921). French composer of symphonies, piano concertos, and operas (including *Samson et Dalila*).

Sato, Ken. He was a Japanese expatriate writer who lived in Montparnasse in the 1920s and was known to Robert McALMON, who published his translation of the work of Saikaku Ibara as *Quaint Tales of the Samurais* in Paris in 1929, ostensibly as a private imprint because of the explicit homosexual nature of the stories. McAlmon reports that Sato had studied at Columbia University and that the manuscript of *Quaint Tales* had come to him through the good offices of Havelock Ellis at the same time as the novel that Sato had written about the life of the Japanese in America, which he called 'The Yellow Jap Dogs'. Glassco maintained an ongoing interest over the years in *Quaint Tales*, querying McAlmon in February 1941 and June 1947 about the fate and whereabouts of Ken Sato. In 1970 Glassco arranged for the publication of this work with a California publisher under the title *Temple of Pederasty*, attributing it to one Ihara Saikaku and providing it with an introduction.

Schopenhauer, Arthur (1788-1860). A pessimistic German philosopher, he reduced the forces of nature and the drives of people to the will to live, which produces frustration and pain that can be reduced only by the intellect and the renunciation of desire. The quotation on page 89 is from *The World as Will and Idea* (1819).

Schwitters, Kurt (1887-1948). A German artist who became associated with the Dada movement, he was also a poet whose several books made him a forerunner of concrete poetry.

Scott, F.R. (1899-1985). Frank Scott was a founder in 1925, with A.J.M. SMITH, of the *McGill Fortnightly Review*, which published innovative writings that were a precursor of the avant-garde publications that the members of the Montreal Group of poets would produce. Scott's long life encompassed careers as a law teacher at McGill, as an authority on constitutional law—he was dean of the McGill Law School in 1961-4—and as an influential figure in the development of the socialist movement in Canada. But literature, particularly Canadian literature, held a central place in his life, and with his several volumes of poems he was one of the important Canadian poets of his time. He was a friend of John Glassco.

Shaw, George Bernard (1856-1950). The great Irish-born music and drama critic, and author of over 50 plays—some of which (e.g. *Pygmalion* and *Saint Joan*) are almost always being performed somewhere—won the Nobel Prize for literature in 1925.

Sheridan, Richard Brinsley (1751-1816). The Irish-born English playwright is remembered particularly for two classic satirical comedies, *The Rivals* and *The School for Scandal*, which are performed to this day.

Smith, A.J.M. (1902-80). Born and educated in Montreal, he founded with Frank SCOTT the *McGill Fortnightly Review* in 1925, and was its guiding spirit, introducing modernist poetry to his colleagues. A masterly craftsman as a poet—alone among the Canadian modernists, he employed a wide range of styles and infused a cosmopolitan strain into his work—he also wrote two of the most memorable Canadian landscape poems: 'The Lonely Land' and 'The Creek'. Respected also as a teacher and as an influential anthologist of Canadian literature, he was a friend of John Glassco, who says on page 27 that Smith 'is sometimes hailed as the Canadian YEATS'.

Soupault, Philippe (b. 1897). The French poet, novelist, and critic was one of the founders of Surrealism. His novel *Les derniers nuits de Paris* was published in 1928.

Spenser, Edmund (1552?-99). The first important English poet after Geoffrey Chaucer (near whom he is buried in Westminster Abbey), he wrote *The Shepheardes Calender* (1579), twelve eclogues, one for each month of the year; and *The Faerie Queene* (Books I-III, 1590, Books IV-VI, 1596), an epic poem that is a religious/political allegory of the times.

Stendhal was the pen name of Henri Beyle (1788-1842), one of France's greatest writers, whose most famous novel is *Le Rouge et le noir* (1830).

Sterne, Laurence (1713-68). He was an English clergyman and novelist whose *A Sentimental Journey Through France and Italy* (1768) was based on his two visits to the Continent in 1762-4 and 1765. Glassco was probably alluding to this book in his reference to Sterne on page 53.

Sternheim, Carl (1878-1942). A German dramatist—and novelist and short-story writer—he was known mainly for his plays that satirized the corrupt manners and morals of bourgeois society.

Stravinsky, Igor (1882-1971). The Russian-born French and American composer was a seminal figure in twentieth-century music.

Symons, Arthur (1865-1945). As a poet (his poems celebrated decadence, and the theatre and street life of London) he belonged to the Rhymers' Club in London, with William Butler YEATS, Richard LE GALLIENNE, and others. He also translated the poems of the French Symbolists, and wrote an important introductory critical work, *The Symbolist Movement in Literature* (1899).

Tanguy, Yves (1900-55). A French painter who joined the Surrealists in 1925, he became an American citizen after 1939.

Tate, Allen (1899-1979). The American poet and influential critic lived in Paris in 1929—with his wife, the novelist and short-story writer Caroline Gordon—in an apartment in the rue de Vaugirard lent to them rent-free by Ford Madox FORD.

Terry, Ellen (1847-1928). A legendary English actress, she was a family friend of the parents of the Princess (Dayang Muda) of Sarawak (Gladys Palmer BROOKE), who called her Nell and continued the friendship. After the First World War the Princess financed a film for the actress, as Glassco describes on page 162.

Thackeray, William Makepiece (1811-63). One of the great nineteenth-century English novelists, he wrote satirical, moralistic novels and short stories about upper- and middle-class English life. His classic novel is *Vanity Fair* (1848), whose famous central character is the coolly unprincipled and selfish Becky Sharp. Thackeray's many other novels include *The Memoirs of Barry Lyndon* (1844) and *The History of Henry Esmond* (1852).

Turgenev, Ivan (1818-83). A great Russian dramatist (*A Month in the Country*, 1850) and novelist (*Fathers and Sons*, 1862).

Utrillo, Maurice (1883-1955). The illegitimate son of another French painter, Suzanne Valadon, he was encouraged by his mother to become a painter and became renowned for his Paris street scenes, particularly those centred on Montmartre, achieving the height of his powers between 1908 and 1916; his success led him to repeat himself thereafter.

Varèse, Edgard (1888-1965). The French-born composer (he became an American citizen in 1926) was a musical innovator who employed extreme registers of instruments to produce dissonant effects.

Vitrac, Roger (1899-1952). A French poet (his collected poems were published in 1964) and dramatist (his plays were published in four volumes in 1946 [I], 1948 [II], and 1964 [III] and [IV]).

Vogel, Joseph. An American writer of poetry and prose who had appeared in *New Masses*, he described himself as 'a railroad laborer and mule feeder'.

Voltaire was the pen name of François-Marie Arouet (1694-1778). Through his writings as a satirist, novelist, historian, poet, dramatist, polemicist, moralist, and critic, he was a leading figure in the French Enlightenment. His influence as a thinker lasted long after his lifetime.

Waterton, Charles (1782-1865). An English naturalist, he lived in British Guiana from 1804 to 1812. He published his *Wanderings* in 1825 and later a series of essays on natural history in 1838, 1844, and 1857.

West, Dame Rebecca (1892-1983). This English writer was known for her interesting novels—published between 1918 and 1966—and her vigorous, sometimes acerbic, journalism.

White, Gilbert (1720-93) was an English clergyman, a curate of Selborne, who wrote a classic work on his observations of wild life, and the picturesque in nature, in his *Natural History and Antiquities of Selborne* (1789).

Wilde, Oscar (1854-1900). The famous novelist (*The Picture of Dorian Gray*, 1891), dramatist (*Lady Windermere's Fan*, 1892, *The Importance of Being Earnest*, 1895, among other plays), and wit had a homosexual affair with Lord Alfred DOUGLAS that led to his imprisonment (1895-7). He was a friend of the parents of Gladys Palmer BROOKE, who played with his two sons when she was a child.

Williams, William Carlos (1883-1963). One of the great American poets (he was also a medical doctor), whose importance was not recognized until the 1950s, Williams visited Paris in 1924 and 1927, and among his friends there were Robert McALMON, Sylvia BEACH, Kay BOYLE, Peggy GUGGENHEIM, Laurence VAIL, and Djuna BARNES.

Woolf, Virginia (1882-1941). One of the great innovative English novelists of this century, she was also a distinguished essayist and letter writer: virtually all her writings are available in recent publications.

Wordsworth, William (1770-1850). The great nature poet and leader of English Romanticism in poetry, who changed poetic diction when he espoused 'a selection of language really used by men', wrote a number of great poems after 1798 (see Glassco's comment on page 59), the year of the publication of *Lyrical Ballads*, which contained poems by him and Samuel Taylor Coleridge.

Wycherley, William (1640?-1716). His two best-known Restoration comedies are *The Country Wife* (1675), a witty and bawdy satire of marriage conventions and sexual morality, and *The Plain-Dealer* (1677).

Yeats, William Butler (1865-1939). Irish-born, and one of the great poets of the twentieth century, he was awarded a Nobel Prize for literature in 1923. He is called Willie Yeats by Ford Madox FORD on page 30.

Zadkine, Ossip (1890-1967). A Russian-born sculptor, the creator of powerful expressionistic works, he had his studio in Paris in the 1920s and 1930s, returning there from New York after the war. On page 141 he is described as boastfully associating himself with the legendary Italian sculptor (and painter and poet) Michelangelo Buanarroti (1475-1564) and the great French sculptor Auguste Rodin (1840-1917).

Ziegfeld, Florenz (1867-1932). His fame as a producer of costly and beautiful Broadway musicals—which included the first production of *Show Boat* in 1927, and its revival in 1932 starring Paul Robeson—began in 1896 and lasted until his death and after.

Zola, Émile (1840-1902). He was a leading exponent in French fiction of naturalism in a grand cycle of twenty novels called collectively *Les Rougon-Macquart* (1871-93), of which *Nana* (1880) is perhaps the most famous. Zola is also remembered for his courageous espousal of the cause of the falsely accused Captain Dreyfus, a victim of anti-Semitism in the French army.

PLACES

Many members of the expatriate community in Montparnasse were layabouts and led lives in striking contrast to the industry and professional dedication of writers like JOYCE, HEMINGWAY, and STEIN. The latter roundly despised the easy-going and non-productive ways of most Quarterites. Those people who were serious at being, or trying to become, writers, and those who were not, formed two distinct groups that were openly and publicly at odds. The easy-going contingent were called 'tawdry bums' by the columnist Alex Small in the *Paris Tribune* of April 1929. He summarized their style and their *raison d'être* in the following words: 'One could dress as one pleased and one could get as drunk as one pleased, and one did not have to account to the neighbours for one's private life . To add to the gayety, and to the unreality of the atmosphere, no one in the crowd [of Montparnassians] I am describing ever worked. . . . The fantoches who gave Montparnasse its reputation, though they some-times vaguely hinted that soon they were going to get down to work, knew that they were fooling no one, not even themselves.'

Glassco, and his friend Graeme TAYLOR, fitted into this portrait of denizens of the Quarter, of which Robert McALMON—if only by virtue of his industry on the type-writer, which was always clattering in his room—was a not entirely typical member.

Other than the well-known bars and a few restaurants, Glassco's references to specific locations are, at best, occasional and not always reliable. **No. 147 rue Broca** is the most precisely identified private location in the *Memoirs*. Fortunately, it is one that has survived the many changes that have overtaken the Quarter in the intervening years. The section of the rue Broca (page 21) where #147 is located was renamed the rue Léon-Maurice-Nordmann in 1944. No. 147 is on a long street that ends in a *cul-de-sac*, consisting of one- and two-storey artists' studios that stand in a relatively modern neighbourhood of handsome, bourgeois six- and seven-storey apartment build-ings dating from the 1930s. The entrance to the laneway is a metal gate very much as Glassco describes it (minus the ornamental iron arch in plate XVI), and there is still visible on one wall an advertisement for a grocer that must date from the 1920s The studios are in various states of upkeep, and here and there one sees bits and pieces of unfinished sculpture and abandoned statuary lying about—much like the sight that greeted Glassco when he escorted Daphne Berners (Gwen LE GALLIENNE) and Angela MARTIN (Yvette Ledoux) for their night of lyrical love-making *à trois*. The actual studio in which they cavorted (I was told by a longtime resident of the street) was lost to a fire. The convent that abuts on this bohemian preserve is a girls' school of the Re-ligieuses Fidèles Compagnes de Jésus—identified by Glassco, likely in error, as Ursulines, perhaps because of the street's ancient name of the rue de l'Ourcine and its association with the ancient artisans of Lourcine who set up here and were exempt from certain taxes. In general, Glassco tends to be casual in his urban geography, as he was con-veniently flexible in the dating of some events. Thus we are told that Emily Pine parked her mufflerless Bugatti 'somewhere near the Sphinx', which we are then told was an 'imposing Egyptianesque building which housed that extremely high-priced brothel.' But the Sphinx did not come into existence until 24 April 1931, almost three years after the episode recounted by Glassco. There are other examples where Glassco strays. The rue de la Glacière, which he describes as a 'narrow white winding street', is, in fact, straight and quite wide. Similarly, the 'rue de l'Archevêque' and the 'rue Le Grattier' are, to name them correctly, the quai de l'Archevêché and the rue le Regrattier.

The famous bars and cafés of the 1920s have suffered with the passage of time. Some have disappeared completely, others have been changed into newly named establishments with, of course, the to-be-expected alterations that new ownership usually makes. Glassco reports on this sadly in a letter to Kay BOYLE in August 1967. 'The city is a beautiful shell,' he wrote. 'The Coupole is a chic bedlam, the Dingo a Japanese restaurant, the Select hip.—The Jockey has been redecorated; the garden of the Closerie des Lilas is a parking space.'

Near the great intersection of the Boulevard Raspail and the Boulevard du Montparnasse—the actual focal point of Montparnasse—are four famous cafés: the Dôme, Rotonde, Select, and Coupole. Although busier with traffic, the district has remained essentially true to the past. One can still visit these cafés (now greatly expanded), most of which started out as modest, usually working-class, bars that catered to a local clientele. After the First World War and the growing influx of foreigners into the Montparnasse quarter, a gradual transformation of the bars and cafés began to take place. In the 1938 edition of his *Being Geniuses Together*, McAlmon reported that 'the various cafés around Montparnasse had been or were being enlarged and become bourgeois, . . . Moreover a new generation was flooding Paris, and a change of custom and habits is quick in the post-war age.' 'Flooding' is the right word, since contemporary records suggest that anywhere from thirty to fifty thousand Americans flocked to Paris at the time, and a goodly number of them became fixtures in Montparnasse.

The desire to cater to the American presence became evident in the advertising, which stressed the 'Bar Américain' motif, but the American influence was most spectacularly seen in the night-life of the city. Many black American musicians and entertainers made their way to Paris, where they found greater freedom to perform and circulate, and were enthusiastically received by the French. As McAlmon puts it about one such *artiste*: 'When the then seventeen-year-old Josephine Baker wriggled on to the stage, cockily exotic, the French audience went wild.' He might have added that the stunningly statuesque Baker was topless and wore only a string of bananas for demureness' sake! Parisians responded eagerly to the new and suggestive music by black musicians, whether it was jazz, or other forms that were being improvised, developed, and performed. Robert DESNOS wrote an article about West Indian music, helping to popularize it, and about the Bal Nègre, which rapidly became very chic. Thus the popularity of a bar like BRICKTOP's, to which Glassco and McAlmon repaired. Though it was in Montmartre—on the Right Bank, distant from Montparnasse—it was eagerly frequented by both locals and visitors, many of them celebrities.

The Jockey—at the corner of the rue Campagne-Première on the Boulevard du Montparnasse—was another American-style bar that, with the Falstaff, serious pub-crawlers made part of their itinerary. It was the creation of Hilaire HILER, the Sidney Schooner of the *Memoirs*, and was the first nightclub that he decorated (he also decorated the Jungle, and the College Inn, with French street scenes, cabarets and views of seaports). The Jockey had a fresco of an American Indian on horseback with a tomahawk on its front, while the other external walls of its pie-shaped building were adorned with cowboy figures, serape-clad Mexicans, blanket-wrapped Indians, and the skull of a Texas longhorn. The Jockey had a reputation as an amusing and sociable rendezvous where, in McAlmon's words, 'dramas and fights did occur, but generally comedy and good will prevailed.' Hiler played jazz piano, and KIKI was a fixture. The building no longer exists.

The Falstaff—at 42 rue du Montparnasse—which survives with its original décor of wood-panelled walls, dark-green velvet banquettes, heavy wood bar, and tile floor with its small-patterned design—was a cosier and more comfortable establishment. For McAlmon and his friends it was 'our rendezvous. It was comfortable and tastefully decorated and the Dutch barman, Jack, refused to serve various people, and that was nice. He could not stand just the ones most of us could not stand.' It is now a restaurant/brasserie (the Restaurant Falstaff) with a large variety of beers on tap.

The **Dingo** was not as fortunate. It started life in 1924 as Le Dingo, at 10 rue Delambre, and announced itself to the passerby as 'Dingo American Bar and Restaurant'. It was originally a workingman's bar and took its name from *le dingo*, slang for a crazy person. It was later owned by Louis and Yopi Wilson, an American-Dutch couple. A popular drinking establishment, it was immortalized by its famous barman, Jimmie CHARTERS, a former Liverpool boxer whose memoir, *This Must Be the Place* (1934), was named for an anecdote in the book in which Charters saw a Rolls Royce draw up in front of the Dingo, depositing two fashionable women who peered through the front window uncertainly, just as his friend Flossie Martin proceeded to walk in, muttering 'You bitch!' 'Come on, Helen,' one woman said to the other. 'This must be the place.' After his visit in 1960 Glassco reported that the Dingo had become a Japanese restaurant. It is still a restaurant, but called the Auberge de Venise.

The two premier *cafés-térrasses* establishments of the period, though, were the Dôme, and—a block west across the Boulevard du Montparnasse—the Select, with the Rotonde and the Coupole running close seconds.

The **Café du Dôme**, at the southwest corner of the Montparnasse-Raspail intersection—also known as Le Dôme—was a favourite haunt of expatriate artists and writers, as well as their models and girl-friends, and was founded in 1898. In *A Moveable Feast* (1964), Hemingway declared it to be a more reputable hangout than the other neighbourhood bars because its clientele was made up of serious and working artists rather than *poseurs* and layabouts (though in the 1920s he had written an article about it for the Toronto *Star Weekly*, describing the Americans who went there: 'They are nearly all loafers expending the energy an artist puts into his creative work in talking about what they're going to do . . .'). The Dôme came in for its fair share of criticism as a 'second home' for the seriously underemployed. Al Laney, the jaundiced newspaperman, saw the Dôme in a different light. He wrote:

> This group   centred around the intersection of the boulevards Montparnasse and Raspail . . . was composed almost entirely of semi-permanent exiles, male and female, who invariably spelled art with a capital A. Their meeting place, almost their home, was the Dôme, a café which . . . [was] by all odds the most interesting place in all Paris. . . .
>
> Hundreds of Americans lived as close to it as they could, and if they could not find places in the quarter they came every day to the Dôme anyhow. . . . They would leave the terrace at dinnertime only to rush back to find seats for the evening and especially for the early morning hours.

The **Select**—at 99 boulevard du Montparnasse—opened in 1925 and catered essentially to the same crowd, although it had its own distinctive feature in Madame Select, who presided over the cash with fingerless gloves, and over a house specialty, Welsh rarebit (it is still a specialty). Both are mentioned by Glassco. The Select was the first café/bar in Montparnasse to stay open all night, an innovation soon copied by the competition in the neighbourhood. It attracted various writers—including Hemingway, Callaghan, and McAlmon—but was not particularly favoured by other artists, who suspected Madame Select, the presiding wife of the owner, of being too close to the police, whom she was inclined to call at the slightest hint of a disturbance. It was at the Select that the American poet Hart Crane got embroiled in an argument with a waiter and hit a policeman who had been hurriedly summoned by Madame. Crane was brutally treated by the police and spent a long week 'as a guest of the City of Paris', with his case not helped at all when various of his well-meaning but boozy friends tried to form a barricade across the rue Vavin to prevent his being carried off to prison.

La Coupole, just down the Boulevard du Montparnasse from the Dôme, opened on 27 December 1927, not long before Glassco arrived in Paris, at number 102. It advertised itself as a 'Bar Americain'. With its cavernous interior, 15-foot-high ceilings and pillars decorated by Montparnasse artists, its restaurant and *dancing* and its famous bar, it quickly became the hang-out for denizens of the quarter. It is still a 'Bar Americain' with 'Dancing', occupying the ground floor of what has been remodelled to look decidedly like a six-storey modern office building. At the end of her edition of *Being Geniuses Together*, Kay Boyle writes of visiting it in August 1929, when Paris was deserted. She sat on a high stool and talked with Gaston, the barman and part-owner: '. . . without his handsome presence, his quiet generosity to artists, his beguiling smile, and his white-lipped fury for any kind of violence, the Coupole would have been a quite undistinguished place.' Gaston suddenly remembered a pencilled note Robert McAlmon had left there for her when he was about to leave Paris, telling her where she could pick up his 'fairly new' Remington portable typewriter.

Café de la Rotonde—at 105 Boulevard du Montparnasse, directly across from the Dôme—was founded in 1911. Hemingway hated it, saying (in his article for the Toronto *Star Weekly*) that it attracted the 'scum of Greenwich, New York', and then tourists from across the ocean—the 'scummiest scum'. Nevertheless, the Rotonde was popular.

The **Closeries des Lilas**, at 171 Boulevard du Montparnasse—one of Ernest Hemingway's favourite cafés—was the scene on 17 February 1922 of an inflammatory 'Congress' of a large gathering of modernist artists and intellectuals that included the composer Erik Satie; the artists Fernand Léger, Constantin BRANCUSI, Henri Matisse, and Jean COCTEAU; and the writer Andre BRÉTON—a friend of the Dadaist Tristan TZARA, who did not attend. Breton was charged, fallaciously, with disrupting the modernist movement by antagonizing the Dadaists. He therefore broke away from the Dadaists, and his other modernist friends, and founded the Surrealist movement.

Lipp's, or the Brasserie Lipp, was (and still is) across the Boulevard Saint-Germain from the Café de Flore and the Deux Magots. It had the advantage of serving late-night meals—Hemingway praised its food.

The Gypsy Bar, which Glassco visited on the boulevard Edgar-Quinet with Daphne Berners and Angela Martin (pages 20-1), is different from Gypsy's Bar on the rue Cujas, which McAlmon and Joyce liked as a late-night hangout in 1921. Both are now gone.

It used to be said about one of the painters in Montparnasse that, although he appeared to be well informed about world events, no one had ever caught him reading a newspaper. The same observation may be made of the people who inhabit Glassco's *Memoirs*. They seemed to be cocooned against the outside world, and Glassco's own narrative is almost totally devoid of references to the times. If the young generation had come to Paris in search of freedom and pleasure, or some sort of spiritual enlightenment, it was clearly determined not to allow the world, as inhabited by their families, to interfere with their own restricted universe defined by little magazines, eccentric art, personal relationships, and *outré* behaviour. Immersed in all this, as described by Glassco, readers have to remind themselves that his sojourn in Paris was more or less bracketed by Charles Lindbergh's solo transatlantic flight in May of 1927—which had all of Paris, where he landed, in an absolute tizzy and talking about it for months afterwards— and the great stock-market crash of October 1929, which precipitated the Depression and sent many of the remittance expatriates reeling home.

BIBLIOGRAPHY

Baedeker, Karl. *Paris and Its Environs with Routes from London to Paris: Handbook for Travellers*. Leipzig: Karl Baedeker, Publisher, 1924.

Bald, Wambly. *Of the Left Bank 1929-1933*. Edited by Benjamin Franklin V. Athens, Ohio/London: Ohio University Press, 1987.

Baldwin, Neil. *Man Ray: American Artist*. New York: Da Capo Press Inc., 1988; the Da Capo paperback, 1991.

Baum, Timothy. *Man Ray's Paris Portraits: 1921-1939*. Washington, D.C.: Middendorf Gallery, 1989.

Beach, Sylvia. *Shakespeare and Company*, New York: Harcourt Brace, 1956.

Benjamin, Walter. *Illuminations*. New York: Harcourt Brace, 1968.

Benstock, Shari. *Women of the Left Bank: Paris 1900-1940*, Austin: University of Texas Press, 1986.

Berger, Pierre. *Robert Desnos*, Paris: Seghers, 1970.

Boudard, Alphonse et Romi. *L'Âge d'or des maisons closes*. Albin Michel, 1990.

Brassaï. *The Secret Paris of the 30's*. Translated by Richard Miller. London: Thames & Hudson, 1976.

Breton, André. *What is Surrealism? Selected Writings*. Edited and introduced by Franklin Rosemont, London: Pluto Press, 1978.

Bricktop (Ada Smith, with James Haskins). *Bricktop*, New York: Atheneum, 1983.

Brome, Vincent. *Frank Harris: The Life and Loves of a Scoundrel*. New York/London: Thomas Yoseloff, 1959.

Brooke, Gladys Palmer. *Relations and Complications: Being the Recollections of H.H. the Dayung Muda of Sarawak*, London: John Lane-Bodley Head, 1929.

Brown, Russell. 'Callaghan, Glassco, and the Canadian Lost Generation' in *Essays on Canadian Writing*, Nos. 51-52, Winter 1993-4, pp. 83-112.

Callaghan, Morley. 'Now That April's Here' in *This Quarter*, Vol. II, No. 2, Oct./Nov./ Dec. 1929.

Callaghan, Morley. *That Summer in Paris: Memories of Tangled Friendships with Hemingway, Fitzgerald, and Some Others*. Toronto: Macmillan, 1963.

Canadian Poetry, No. 13, Fall/Winter 1983, an issue devoted to John Glassco, containing important articles by Thomas E. Tausky ('Memoirs of Montparnasse: "A Reflection of Myself"') and Stephen Scobie ('The Mirror on the Brothel Wall: John Glassco, *Memoirs of Montparnasse*').

Carpenter, Humphrey. *Geniuses Together: American Writers in Paris in the 1920s*, London/Sydney: Unwin Hyman, 1987.

Charters, Jimmie 'the Barman'. *This Must Be the Place: Memoirs of Montparnasse* (as told to Morrill Cody), with an Introduction by Ernest Hemingway. London: Herbert Joseph; Second Edition edited with a Preface by Hugh Ford, New York: Collier Books, Macmillan, 1989.

Cowley, Malcolm. *Exile's Return: A Literary Odyssey of the 1920s*. New York: The Viking Press, Compass Books Edition, 1956.

Crespelle, Jean-Paul. *La Vie quotidienne à Montparnasse à la Grande Époque 1905-1930*. Paris: Hachette, 1976.

Crowley, Aleister. *The Confessions of Aleister Crowley: An Autohagiography*. Edited by John Symonds and Kenneth Grant. London: Penguin/Arkana, 1979.

Dudek, Louis. 'Literary Fistfight in Paris' in *Compass: A Jesuit Journal*, March/April 1992, pp. 12-13.

Ellmann, *James Joyce*. New York: Oxford University Press, 1959. New and Revised Edition, 1983.

Field, Andrew. *Djuna: The Formidable Miss Barnes*. Austin: University of Texas Press, 1985.

Fitch, Noel Riley. *Sylvia Beach and the Lost Generation: A History of Literary Paris in the Twenties and Thirties*. New York/London: Norton, 1983.

Flanner, Janet. *Paris Was Yesterday: 1925-1939*. Edited by Irving Drutman. New York: Viking, 1972.

Ford, Hugh. *Four Lives in Paris*. With a Foreword by Glenway Wescott. San Francisco: North Point Press, 1987.

_____. *The Left Bank Revisited: Selections from the Paris Tribune 1917-1934*, edited with an introduction by Hugh Ford. Foreword by Matthew Josephson. University Park/London: Pennsylvania State University Press, 1972.

_____. *Published in Paris: A Literary Chronicle of Paris in the 1920s and 1930s*. With a Foreword by Janet Flanner. New York: Collier Books/Macmillan Publishing Co., 1975.

Gautrand, Jean-Claude. *Photographers' Paris*. Paris: Bookking International, 1989.

Gnarowski, Michael. 'Notes Towards a Sometime and Probable History of John Glassco' in *Reflections. Autobiography and Canadian Literature*. Edited and with an Introduction by K.P. Stich. Ottawa: University of Ottawa Press, 1988.

_____. Interviews with John Glassco, tape-recorded June-August 1964 at Jamaica Farm, Foster, Quebec.

Hamnett, Nina. *Laughing Torso: Reminiscences*. London: Constable, 1932.

Hanscombe, Gillian & Virginia L. Smyers. *Writing for Their Lives: The Modernist Women 1910-1940*. Boston: Northeastern University Press, 1987.

Hansen, Arlen J. *Expatriate Paris: A Cultural and Literary Guide to Paris of the 1920s*, New York: Arcade Publishing (Little, Brown), 1990.

Hemingway, Ernest. *A Moveable Feast*, New York: Scribner, 1971.

Hoffman, Frederick J. *The Twenties: American Writing in the Postwar Decade*. New York: Collier Books, 1962.

Huddleston, Sisley. *Back to Montparnasse*. London/Bombay/Sidney: Harrap, 1931.

Klüver, Billy and Julie Martin. *Kiki's Paris: Artists and Lovers 1900-1930*. New York: Abrams, 1989.

Knoll, Robert E., editor. *McAlmon and the Lost Generation: A Self-Portrait*. Lincoln/London: University of Nebraska Press, 1962.

Knoll, Robert E. *Robert McAlmon: Expatriate Publisher and Writer*. Lincoln: University of Nebraska Press, 1959.

Kokotailo, Philip. *John Glassco's Richer World: Memoirs of Montparnasse*. Toronto: ECW Press, 1988.

Laney, Al. *Paris Herald: The Incredible Newspaper*. New York/London: Appleton-Century, 1947.

Lapierre, Dominique et Larry Collins. *Paris brûle-t-il? (25 août 1944): Histoire de la libération de Paris*. Paris: Laffont, 1964.

Leibowitz, Herbert. *Fabricating Lives: Explorations in American Autobiography*. New York: Knopf, 1989.

Lejeune, Philippe. *On Autobiography*. Edited and with a foreword by Paul John Eakin. Translated by Katherine Leary. Minneapolis: University of Minnesota Press, 1989.

Levisse-Touzé, Christine. *Paris libéré, Paris retrouvé*. Paris: Découvertes Gallimard, 1994.

Littlewood, Ian. *Paris: A Literary Companion*. London: John Murray, 1987.

McAlmon, Robert. *Being Geniuses Together: An Autobiography*. London: Secker & Warburg, 1938.

―――――. *Being Geniuses Together 1920-1930*. Revised and with supplementary chapters by Kay Boyle. New York: Doubleday, 1968.

―――――. *North America: Continent of Conjecture*. Drawings by Raymond Obermayer. Afterword by Edward Dorn. [California ?]: Dark Child Press, 1983.

―――――. 'The Politics of Existence: 2 Extracts From:' in *This Quarter*, No. 4, Spring 1929, pp. 17-32.

―――――. 'Unfinished Poem' in *This Quarter*, No. 4, Spring 1919, pp. 149-179.

Mellen, Joan. *Kay Boyle: Author of Herself*, New York: Farrar, Straus & Giroux, 1994.

Mellow, James R. *Charmed Circle: Gertrude Stein & Company*. New York: Avon Books, 1975.

Milner, John. *The Studios of Paris the Capital of Art in the Late Nineteenth Century*. New Haven/London: Yale University Press, 1988.

Morton, Brian N. *Americans in Paris*, New York: Morrow, 1986.

Penrose, Roland. *Man Ray*. London: Thames and Hudson, 1975.

Putnam, Samuel. *Paris Was Our Mistress: Memoirs of a Lost and Found Generation*. New York: Viking, 1947; London: Plantin Publishers, 1987.

Sers, Philipp. [], *Man Ray: Photographe*. Introduction par Jean-Hubert Martin. Paris: Philippe Sers, 1985.

Smoller, Sanford J. *Adrift Among Geniuses: Robert McAlmon Writer and Publisher of the Twenties*. University Park/London: Pennsylvania State University Press, 1975.

Stearns, Harold. *The Confessions of a Harvard Man & The Street I Know Revisited*. Edited & Introduced by Hugh Ford with a Preface by Kay Boyle. Sutton West/ Santa Barbara: Paget Press, 1984.

Stein, Gertrude. *Autobiography of Alice B. Toklas*. Harmondsworth, Middlesex: Penguin Modern Classics, 1977.

―――――. *Paris France*. New York: Liveright, 1970.

―――――. *Selected Writings of Gertrude Stein*. Edited, with an Introduction and Notes, by Carl Van Vechten, and with an essay on Gertrude Stein by F.W. Dupee. New York: Vintage Books, 1972.

Sutherland, Fraser. *John Glassco: An Essay and Bibliography*, Downsview, Ont.: ECW Press, 1984.

Toklas, Alice B. *What is Remembered*. San Francisco: North Point Press, 1985.

Weld, Jacqueline Bograd. *Peggy: The Wayward Guggenheim*, New York: Dutton, 1986.

Weld, John. *Young Man in Paris*. Illustrations by Jeremy Blatchley. Chicago: Academy Chicago Publishers, 1985.

Wickes, George. *American in Paris*. New Foreword by Virgil Thomson. New York: Da Capo Paperback, [1980?]

Williams, William Carlos. *The Autobiography*, New York: New Directions, 1967.

Wiser, William. *The Crazy Years: Paris in the Twenties*, London: Thames and Hudson, 1983.